Other Books In This Series

AMAZING CANADIAN SPECULATIVE FICTION

TESSERACTS ELEVEN

EDITED BY
CORY DOCTOROW
AND HOLLY PHILLIPS

EDGE SCIENCE FICTION AND FANTASY PUBLISHING
AN IMPRINT OF HADES PUBLICATIONS, INC.
CALGARY

EDGE

Edge Science Fiction and Fantasy Publishing
An Imprint of Hades Publications Inc.
P.O. Box 1714, Calgary, Alberta, T2P 2L7, Canada

In house editing by Justyn Perry
Interior design by Brian Hades
Cover Illustration by Jeff Johnson
ISBN-10: 1-894063-03-1   ISBN-13: 978-1-894063-03-6

EDGE Science Fiction and Fantasy Publishing and Hades Publications, Inc.
acknowledges the ongoing support of the Canada Council for the Arts and the
Alberta Foundation for the Arts for our publishing programme.

The Alberta Foundation for the Arts
COMMITTED TO THE DEVELOPMENT OF CULTURE AND THE ARTS
Alberta COMMUNITY DEVELOPMENT
Canada Council   Conseil des Arts
for the Arts   du Canada

Library and Archives Canada Cataloguing in Publication

Tesseracts eleven: amazing Canadian speculative fiction / Cory
Doctorow and Holly Phillips, editors.

ISBN-10: 1-894063-03-1   ISBN-13: 978-1-894063-03-6

1. Science fiction, Canadian (English) 2. Fantastic fiction, Canadian
(English) 3. Canadian fiction (English)--21st century. 4. Short
stories, Canadian (English) I. Doctorow, Cory II. Phillips, Holly

PS

FIRST EDITION
(p-20070918)
Printed in Canada
www.edgewebsite.com

Contents

AMAZING CANADIAN SPECULATIVE FICTION

TESSERACTS ELEVEN

Introduction
Cory Doctorow

Does the world need "Canadian" science fiction? When I lived in Canada — as I did until I was 29 — the answer to this question was entirely self-evident. Of *course* the world needed Canadian science fiction. Our Canadian-ness (nearly always defined in ways that we were no like Americans), was so much more Canadian than the Americans' Canadianness or even the Brits' Canadianness, who else would supply it if we didn't?

Last summer, I was co-Guest of Honor at ConJure, the Australian national sf convention, held that year in Brisbane. I attended the launch of a new collection of Australian science fiction, and had a little conversation with my co-GoH, Bruce Sterling. Sterling, a Texan raised in India, now residing in Belgrade, seemed a little skeptical about the whole business.

Sterling, in his curmudgeonly way, opined that no one outside of Australia was crying out for more Australian science fiction. No one, apart from an Australian, felt any lack of Australianness in their sf diet.

I had to admit he had a point.

✢┽•┼•┼•┾

And yet. I grew up on the Tesseracts anthologies. I was 14 when Judy Merril's first edition of this series shipped, in 1985. I remember reading it, curled into myself on a TTC bus, heading home on a cold winter night, nothing visible outside the windows except the lightsPaolo of snowed-in houses streaking past as we shushed through the awful, grey snow.

In that volume, I found stories that were not quite like anything I ever read before. Of course, I'd read "Canadian" authors all my life — I was already a Spider Robinson fan, I'd always liked AE Van Vogt, and I had really enjoyed Phillis Gotleib's Sunburst. But I'd never read a collection of works whose unifying theme was that they were written by Canadians.

It was a heady experience. It's not that Canadians write quiet, introspective stories while Americans write stories about kicking ass. It's not even that Canadian stories are particularly incisive on the subject of what it means to be Canadian.

But there's one thing that Canadian stories get right more than American stories — and it's the same thing that defines Aussie sf (Aussies being a sort of antipodean Canadian with a higher propensity for skin cancer): we're good at looking at figuring out what makes other cultures tick.

※·┼·※·┼·※

I bought that Australian sf anthology. Bruce was right: I didn't really care about "Australian sf" as a category distinct from "good sf." But it looked like a good book (and I was the Guest of Honor) (for the record: it was a good book).

What I discovered, in that Aussie book, was the same thing that had caught me about that first volume of Tesseracts: these authors wrote science fiction with a keen appreciation of what it was like to be eclipsed by something bigger than themselves.

Some of the funniest Americans in the world are Canadians. We're good at making 'em laugh — because we know more about them than they do, themselves. We pass among them, unnoticed and invisible, eavesdropping on their TV, books, conversation. We're like the class nerd — at the edge of the other social groups, keenly attuned to their social outcomes. The beta never knows when an alpha will lose a dominance struggle and take it out on the beta. Best to watch very closely then, so you can get out of the way when the moment comes.

This is a robust position from which to write science fiction.

➤⊢•⊢•⊢•⊢◄

After all, science fiction is ultimately about the present day, what William Gibson calls "speculative presentism." Reading sf tells you more about the social response to technology in the author's own present day than it tells you about the future. For all the airy pronouncements about futurism, about worldbuilding, about future histories, science fiction can never do more than look keenly into the present moment and describe the parts of it that most of the world hasn't noticed yet.

Gibson also said, "The future is here, it's just not evenly distributed." Some of us live and breathe wikis. We also inhabit a world populated by stone-agers who still rent rotary-dial phones from the state monopoly telco. In an era of exponential technological change, our social worlds fragment based on technological brain-plasticity. When you hit the wall on adapting to technological change and get off the upgrade curve, you strand yourself — temporarily, if not forever — on an island distant from those strivers who continue to chase Moore's Law into infinity.

We are a collection of technological nations. The Distributed Republic of Blogistan. The Islets of SMS-thumb. The Duchy of Just Wordprocessing and a Bit of Google, Thanks.

And that's where that Canadianness comes to bear again. This fragmented, post-national world of striated, isolated technology tribes needs keen observers to find the common threads, to see what's happening from moment to moment.

These stories, collected from our peers from across the country, from transplants and native-born, have more to say about the present of Canada than they do about the future.

In Which Joe and Laurie Save Rock N' Roll

Madeline Ashby

March 26, 2031

In high school, I had this boyfriend named Joe. Things were serious. He had a drawer in my bureau where he kept socks, deodorant, a toothbrush, and condoms. He woke me for school every morning by rapping at my ground-floor window, then letting himself in through it. My parents, S-level Microsoft people who took advantage of their company-paid gym memberships, were already gone by seven a.m. Through a cunning blend of sexual bribery and promises of food, he got me out of bed and dressed and in his car. Then we were off for school. We met in the tenth grade. Our mornings proceeded this way for almost three academic years, until his eighteenth birthday.

✦•❙••❙••❙•✦

March 27, 2001

"Laurie," Joe said. I felt him part my hair and pepper the back of my neck with little kisses. "*Laur*ieee..." He gave me a little nip on the ear. "Time to get up now..."

"Fuck off," I said into the pillows.

"Is that any way to speak to a man after his birthday?"

"Your birthday is the reason I'm so goddamn sore this morning, you asshole."

More little kisses. "I seem to remember you enjoying yourself..."

He had me there. "Yes, but this morning I think walking might pose a problem."

Joe had pressed himself so close that I felt his skin dimpling against my neck in what was surely a smug smirk. "If you're a good girl and get out of bed, I'll kiss it better."

Still naked, I rolled over. "Promise?"

He grinned.

⇥⬥⇤⬥⇥⬥⇤

In the car, Joe directed my attention to a shoebox. "Thanks for that."

I flipped up the lid. There, on a nest of brown tissue paper, was a white sequined glove. "It looks like Michael Jackson's."

Joe beamed. "You should know. You gave it to me." Joe had posted an absurd birthday wish list online. On it were things like alien autopsy footage — on 35 mm film — and "George Lucas' dignity, preferably on a silver platter beside his testicles." Somewhere near the bottom of the list was a request for Michael Jackson's glove.

I frowned. "No I didn't."

He stiffened. "You didn't?"

"I make minimum wage, remember? Even if it is real, things like that wind up in the collections of geeky millionaires, not in the hands of mere mortals like us."

Joe turned to me. His sloppy dark bangs flipped as he did so. "But..." He rustled through the box, and retrieved a slip of paper. "Read this."

> Joe,
> *This fits you better than me.*
> *Happy birthday,*
> *Michael Jackson*

"There was no name or return address. I thought you were just being cute." He eyed me up and down. "You'd better be careful. I have a secret admirer."

"I'm jealous. Really."

He frowned. "Do you need Starbuck's, or will the bitchiness go away on its own?"

"I'm not bitchy. I'm freaked out, because we have a fucking stalker."

I cranked the seat back so that I stared at the ceiling of Joe's car. It was a positively ancient Oldsmobile 98 Series that still smelled like the cigarettes its previous owner had smoked. I couldn't explain my lashing out. The soreness and hunger probably had something to do with it. Joe had made good on his promise, but it meant going without breakfast.

"Did I really hurt you?" He could practically read my mind sometimes.

"Not like that," I said. "Not like the first time or any-thing."

He sighed and rolled his eyes heavenward. "Thank God."

"Yeah." I stretched, and winced. "A hot bath should take care of it."

✦✦✦✦✦

We arrived at school. Joe parked the car in our usual spot. "I can take you home before work," he said.

"Okay." I ventured a sideways look. "Still love me?"

"Of course I do. What's that for?"

"I mean when I'm being a bitch for no real reason."

He rolled his eyes. "I didn't mean that. I was only teas-ing. Don't take me so seriously." His morning grin returned. "Besides, if you're bitchy because I wore you out, that's no reason for me to complain."

My stomach gurgled. "I'll feel better after I eat some-thing."

Joe checked his watch, then scanned the parking lot. "I think you've got time for a quick nosh, if you're feeling exhibitionist."

I slammed the door. "Pervert."

"I'm not a pervert, I'm an opportunist. There's a dif-ference." He nodded at the school. "Once more unto the breach, dear friend?"

"Once more," I said.

→•I•I•I•←

I didn't see Joe until lunch. That was unusual. We made it a point to run into each other. So when I scanned the commons for him at lunch, I was a little nonplussed not to find him. Then he came up behind me with a tap on the shoulder. "Have you got your backpack?" he asked.

"Yes," I said, nodding at its place on the floor. "Why?"

"Come on," he said, picking up my bag and heading for the nearest exit.

"Joe, what's going on?"

"Outside," he said.

"Did someone key the car?"

"The car's fine." He pushed open the exit doors for the small, hidden parking lot behind the school auditorium. He wore the sequined glove. "I've got something to show you." He handed me my pack, then adjusted his own. Going nose-to-nose with the wall, he knelt down. With the index finger of his gloved right hand, he began drawing something.

"You know how in those old Looney Tunes cartoons, if you drew a door on a rock face, it would just... happen?"

Where Joe's finger traced the brick, a trail of blue light appeared. It wavered unsteadily like iridescent slug slime. "Um, yes," I said. Joe was obviously drawing a door. He reached high and traced the topmost edge of the frame.

"What day did Kurt Cobain die?"

"There's conflicting reports," I said. The light grew brighter. Joe drew a knob. "The people who think he was murdered—"

"What day, Laurie?"

"April 5, 1994."

In block letters, Joe wrote "APRIL 4, 1994, SEATTLE." He turned to me. "We'll arrive a day early."

I licked my lips. My throat had gone terribly dry. "What is that?"

He held up one gloved finger. "It may in fact be the world's first real magic marker."

"The light, Joe! What the fuck is going on with that light?"

The door blazed with light. "I'm not sure. But I know it's safe." He smiled. "I've been playing with it all morning."

"*What?*"

He nodded sheepishly and looked at the glove. Its sequins glittered in the noontime light. "I sort of spent the morning at Woodstock."

Without a word, I slapped him as hard as I could. He reeled, reaching for his jaw. "What the fuck was that for?" Genuine anger radiated from his eyes, and a tiny part of me winced at my over-reaction. "That really hurt, Laurie."

"I could have lost you!" My voice shook, and I realized my entire body was doing the same. I balled fists to stop the tremor in my hands. "How could you just run off like that? What if you couldn't come back?"

"Hey..." His voice was quiet. He stepped forward, and hugged me. He rocked from side to side. "Give me some credit. I experimented a little first."

"Oh yeah? How?"

"I bounced a ball in. It bounced back."

"And that ball is still okay?"

"I've got it right here." He produced a softball with the words "gym property — do not remove" on it. Tentatively, I pressed it with one finger. It felt solid and normal.

"Why Woodstock?"

"It only goes to rock dates. Well, rock and pop." He sounded wistful.

"How do you know?"

"I tried April 4, 1968." I watched his face. He paled under the smattering of freckles across his nose. "Then I tried November 22, 1963. No dice."

I frowned. "You tried to stop Kennedy and Dr. King from being killed."

"Who wouldn't?"

I stared at the door. It shimmered, as though preening. "How did you figure out that something would open in the first place? Did it just occur to you?"

He shook his head. "I was wearing the glove in class. Everyone got a kick out of it. So I was just writing stuff on the desk, just to watch the glove sparkle. I was trying to figure something out, so I did some math on the desk. I ended up writing the date my parents met."

Something clicked. "And your parents met at a Bowie show, right?"

Joe nodded. "Yeah. I went to that show." Again, he looked at the door. "The numbers just lit up, right there on the desk. So I skipped second period and did some playing around."

I followed his gaze to the door. "Did you see your parents?"

He shook his head. "I had nothing to say to them."

"You could have prevailed upon them about the evils of infidelity."

He shrugged, and looked away. "Maybe. But I got distracted. Bowie's pretty damn good live." He tugged me toward the door. "I'm not sure how long the door's going to last. We should go."

"But..."

"Laurie, we have a chance to stop something really bad."

"Yeah, and possibly wreck the future!"

Slowly, Joe shook his head. "No. I've already thought of that. We're supposed to do this."

I stepped away. "How do you know?"

"Because if this weren't an important date in rock history, I wouldn't have been able to come back to it," he said. "But this day is important, because you and I are going to change some things."

"You don't know that we're the important part! Somewhere across the world, a really special band could be forming!"

Joe looked at me as though I'd clearly lost my senses. "Laurie, today we're capable of jumping through time. I think that ranks above the formation of the next super-group." He looked at the door. "Now come with me."

"Why?"

"Because convincing a strung-out heroin addict not to put a shotgun in his mouth isn't going to be easy, and I'll need your help!" He grabbed my hand and pulled.

"No! We shouldn't do this! It's wrong!"

"It's wrong to stop a man from shooting himself?"

"It's his life, and even if he makes mistakes with it, they're his own!"

Joe enlaced our fingers. "What if those conspiracy theorists are right? What if he was murdered? Shouldn't we stop that?"

Again I looked at the door. It beckoned temptingly, glittering like a spangled dress under a spotlight. "Maybe, if we went back just to be sure..."

"That's the spirit." He started for the door.

→·I·•·I·•·I·←

APRIL 4, 1994
SEATTLE

We emerged in parkland during what was definitely Seattle in April. Joe squinted into the rain, and pointed. "That's the house." He started walking.

"Shouldn't we plan something?"

"What, like pretend we're selling Amway and ambush the guy?"

In fact, that was exactly what I was about to suggest, and I felt very embarrassed about it just then. "Something like that," I said.

"I figure we'll just tell him we're from the future. If we're lucky, he'll be just high enough to believe us."

I stopped. Joe's shoes squelched in the mud for a moment before he stopped to glance back at me. Rain pattered on the leaves of cherry trees surrounding us. "You have a pretty low opinion of the man you're trying to save," I said.

"To tell you the truth, I have a pretty low opinion of his music, too. But the guy left behind a kid, and that's not right."

"His kid still has her mother."

"Correction: his kid still has Courtney Love. There's a difference." And with that, he marched toward the house.

Several tries with the doorbell and frequent knocking roused no reply at the house. A chill settled over me that had nothing to do with the rain. "You don't think he's already done it, do you?"

"Done what?" a voice behind us asked.

Slowly, we turned around. There he was. Nothing had prepared me for it. In 1994, Joe and I were eleven. We had never seen this man perform live — the closest we'd ever gotten to him were post-mortem re-hashings of his recorded interviews, the sort played by the local radio station on his birthday. And yet there he was, wearing torn sneakers and an olive-drab jacket, his dirty blond hair stringy with rain. He had three days of grizzle on his face. The skin around his eyes was pinched tight, like he was trying hard not to scream at something. In short, he looked pained and sad — but alive.

"Kurt," I said.

"I want you off my property," he said. "You people can't do this."

Joe put up his hands. "We're not fans. Well, we are, but that's not why we're here. I mean, it is sort of, but not really." He looked at me. "The thing is, my girlfriend can really sing, and I want you to—"

"I can't sing," I said, stepping forward. "I'm a terrible singer. But I do have something to tell you." Forcing myself to look at his eyes, I said: "I know what you're thinking of doing."

His mouth opened to say something, but nothing came. He licked his lips. There was a split down the center of the lower lip. As his tongue swept over it, fresh blood welled up. I took a deep breath. I tried not to think about how he would be dead tomorrow, if I screwed up. "I want you to know that you will — would — be missed." I thought of his face immortalized on a hundred different t-shirts and posters. "I know it all seems bad, but..." I thought of what Joe had said earlier. "You want to see your daughter grow up, don't you?"

Kurt's eyes took on a lethal edge. "You stay the hell away from my kid."

Joe's feet shifted. "Courtney's going to get worse — she'll be in and out of rehab while your kid learns to ride a bike from her fucking nanny!"

"Shut up!" Kurt lurched awkwardly for Joe, who ducked and jumped down into some rhododendrons.

"It's going to happen," Joe said.

Kurt trembled, staring down at Joe. With an audible swallow, he straightened and looked at me. "I want you to go. Leave me alone."

To my surprise and shame, I felt tears coming. He was going to blow his brains out, and I couldn't stop it. "You don't get it!" I said. "You don't have to do this! Lots of people love you, and—"

"*Leave me alone!*"

He screamed so loud that I jumped and lost my footing. I stumbled backward and gripped a brick pillar for support. "Okay." But he was already fishing for his keys. I watched him look nervously at us, then work the key in the lock. Then he was gone.

Joe pushed through the bushes. He brushed leaves and pink petals from his shoulders. "Come on," he said. "We're going back." He tugged my elbow.

"I fucked it up," I said, feeling the tears really start.

"You don't know that," Joe said. "Maybe it worked. We won't know until we go back."

→·I··I··I·←

MARCH 27, 2001

The lunch crowd had thinned significantly. Everyone was running off to class. "Did that just happen?" I asked.

Joe stopped a kid with long hair and a t-shirt with Kurt's face on it. "Hey. Is he still on tour?" He pointed at the shirt.

"He's dead, you dick," the kid said, and continued on his way.

I sat down heavily in a hard plastic chair. "I told you," I said. "I fucked it up."

Joe shook his head. "He didn't say how it happened. Maybe it was something else. Maybe we stopped him from shooting himself, but something else got him later."

I wiped my eyes. "No. He shot himself." I looked at the sequined glove. Its fingers flopped loosely from Joe's pocket like rabbit ears from a top-hat. "We have to get rid of that thing."

Joe shook his head. "Maybe we were wrong to interfere with a suicide. That's someone's personal choice. But it can't be wrong to get in the way of an accident, or a murder."

I sniffled. "So, what, you want to go back and stop Buddy Holly and Ritchie Valens from getting on that plane? We'll lose that Weezer song."

"Yeah, that's a real fucking tragic loss, Laurie."

"Don't talk to me like that! I'm just trying to think about what we're changing, here!" I stared at Joe. "Maybe we're not supposed to change anything."

"Oh yeah? Then why'd I get this glove?"

"I don't know! Maybe..." I looked around at the big, empty hallways leading from classrooms to the commons. "Maybe we're just supposed to go back and experience it, so that we can document it later, or something."

Joe took out the glove, and waved it. Its sequins glittered under the fluorescent rods above. "I refuse to believe that this thing wound up on my doorstep for the purposes of historical verification!"

"Fine!" I said. "You figure it out. But figure it out on your own. I have to get to class."

"Class?" Joe asked. I picked up my bag and shrugged it on. "*Class?*"

"You heard me." I started for the stairs, then turned around. "Just be careful, okay?"

Joe smiled, walked over, and kissed me. "Will do," he said.

→•I••I••I•←

FOURTH PERIOD

Just as my Spanish class settled down to filling out worksheets on the preterite tense, I noticed the girl sitting beside me attempt to surreptitiously change the CD in her player. It was Weezer's blue album. She held the CD case in the other hand. When she flipped it over, I saw the track listing. "Buddy Holly" had vanished. In its place was one called "Patsy Cline."

Joe had gone back again. He had saved Buddy Holly, Ritchie Valens, and the Big Bopper. When class ended, he was waiting for me outside.

"You did it! How?"

"I phoned in a bomb threat. Did you know there was a horrible fucking blizzard that night? It's why their plane crashed originally. I wish I'd had a better coat." He dug in his pocket for the glove, and pulled me into an alcove. "I've got our next mission."

I frowned. "Now what do you want to change?"

But Joe was already drawing. In the center of the blazing door, he wrote "DECEMBER 8, 1980, NEW YORK CITY." He wiggled his fingers inside the glove. He looked at the floor, then at my face. When he spoke, it sounded rehearsed. "I want to stop a murder. It's going to be dangerous, and you don't have to come if you don't want. But it'll be easier with two people."

Something about his hopeful face convinced me. "Okay."

Joe smiled. "Good." He took my hand, and off we went.

⇥⊹⊹⊹⇤

DECEMBER 8, 1980
NEW YORK CITY

Instantly, I regretted not having a scarf. Night had fallen on New York. Across the street stood a stretch of trees strung with Christmas lights. I plunged my hands in my pockets. "Is that Central Park?"

"Yeah," Joe said. "We're on Central Park West." He pointed. "See that guy? Smoked lenses and a green scarf?"

"Yeah."

"Well, he's got a gun full of hollow-points. See those two?" He pointed at a Japanese woman and a white man wearing glasses. My mouth formed an O. "John Lennon needs our help, Laurie."

"Oh, my God."

"Yeah, I know. Try not to think about how huge this is. Here's the plan: you go and ask them for autographs. Try to prattle. Meanwhile, I'm going to beat the shit out of that guy. We'll meet back here." He nodded at the man with the scarf, who I now recognized as Mark David Chapman.

"He's bigger than you are," I said. "Shouldn't we take him together?"

"Honey," Joe said. He hiked up his jacket. Inside his baggy jeans, I saw something cylindrical and metallic with the words "Louisville Slugger" on it. "Don't I always come prepared?"

"You stole a bat from the gym?"

"Sure did." He pulled it up a little out of his jeans. He looked across the street, then back at me. "Kiss me."

I did so. "Try to hurt his hand so he can't shoot."

Joe smiled. "Good thinking." He turned his collar up, looked both ways, and dashed across the street. He disappeared into the park.

I fixed my gaze on John Lennon and Yoko Ono. They walked close together, heads bent. And even as I smiled at the sight of them, I felt myself start running. I dodged New Yorkers and skipped over a steaming sewer grate. "Mr. Lennon!"

He turned to face me, and it felt like being cut off at the knees. Suddenly, I understood my mother's Beatlemania in a completely new way. She had once confessed a high school crush on John Lennon, and I had thought it silly. But in the flesh, John Lennon was the epitome of all her sighing, nostalgic descriptions. My lungs went tight, and it had nothing to do with the cold air. I stood panting in front of him.

"Yes?"

"I..." He smiled. This probably happened to him all the time. I blushed and felt stupid for it. Here I was star-struck when I should have been thinking about how to save his life. "I'd really like your autograph." I looked at Yoko Ono. "I mean both of your autographs."

Lennon paused. He seemed to be expecting something. I gave my biggest smile. He looked at me carefully. "What would you like us to sign?" he asked.

I slapped my forehead, and felt stupid for that too. "I'm sorry!" I said. "I guess I'm just... overwhelmed." I took off my backpack, and began digging for something they could sign. "Um..." I had several textbooks and binders, but nothing that was really appropriate. It just didn't make sense to ask John Lennon and Yoko Ono to sign my Spanish homework. My hand closed over something soft and papery — my novel for English class. I withdrew it, and remembered with a sickening sense of irony that it was *The Catcher in the Rye* — the very novel my study guide said police found Lennon's killer carrying after the shooting.

"Could you sign this for me, please?"

Lennon smiled. "Do you have a pen in there?"

"Oh, yeah, of course!" I dug further in the bag, and produced a pen.

Lennon took it, and flipped the book open to the title page. "This book says it's the property of a high school in Washington State," he said. He pointed to an ink stamp.

"I bought it used," I said.

Nodding, Lennon uncapped the pen and quickly signed his name. As he handed it to Yoko, he frowned and said: "My God, that boy is beating that man!" He pointed. There was Joe, the aluminum bat in his hands reflecting the thin glow of traffic lights. He hefted the bat and swung straight for Chapman's face. At point-blank range, he destroyed Chapman's glasses and his nose. Chapman went down to his knees and Joe swung for his stomach. The older man bent double, and Joe cracked him one across the shoulders.

"We should call the police," Yoko said.

"That's a good idea," I said.

Lennon shouted above the traffic: "Hey! You there! Stop it! We're calling the police!"

Joe stopped. He gave Lennon a strange look. Then he stomped on what must have been Chapman's fingers. I saw him bend and pick something up before running away. Sirens wailed up the street, and I saw the first flashes of blue and red light. I took off running.

As I hopped around a taxi, Joe reached out and grabbed me. He pulled me into an alley. The door glimmered before us. "Lennon looked like he wanted to help," I said.

"I took the gun and threw it in a trashcan," Joe said. "Don't worry."

→·[·•·]·•·]·←

MARCH 27, 2001
FIFTH PERIOD

My biology class was dull and boring, and I was grateful. I arrived late. First the class tracked the progress of DNA through electrophoresis gels. My hands shook when I tried drawing the results in my lab book. Then it was off to the library. Rather than finding books, I pulled out my study guide. It made no mention of Lennon's killing. I covered my mouth, blinking back tears. Our plan had worked. We saved him.

"Laurie," Joe's voice said. I felt his hand on my shoulder.

Shifting in my chair, I suppressed a scream upon seeing Joe's face. It was Joe, but not Joe — he was taller, leaner, and his head was shaved. His clothes were too small. He knelt. "Don't be scared." He held my hands. His felt rough and callused. "I don't have much time, Laurie," he said.

"What's going on?"

From one pocket, he withdrew a single key. I recognized it as belonging to the Oldsmobile 98. "They took everything else. I want you to—"

"*Who* took everything else?"

He reached for my face. "You know I love you, right?"

I nodded. "I know. I love you, too." I held his hand against my face. It was cold. "What's going on?"

"I managed to get out for a little while."

"Out of *where?*"

"Keep your voice down." His thumb drifted over my lips. "You left a book with John and Yoko." Joe gave a half-smile, half-grimace. "It was a fortieth-anniversary copy from 1991."

I blinked. My stomach hit my toes. "Oh, my God."

"That's when they first noticed something was wrong," Joe said, "and began tracking us."

"Who?"

"The bad guys," Joe said. "Like the RIAA, but worse. They really hate music. They're made of sound. Music hurts them. It's like when our cells go cancerous. Their whole civilization was brought down by a Lennon-inspired song-meme that left the rest of them wandering. They nabbed me on my next trip. I'm in their time now." He squeezed my other hand. "They took the glove, Laurie. But I stole it back." He reached into his shirt and pulled the glove free, leaving it on the table.

I sniffed. "Do you want me to stop you? I can find the real you — the other you, I mean, and I can stop him from leaving."

Joe shook his head. "I've already left," he said. "I left right after the fifth period bell rang. I got cocky. I thought I could go save Janis Joplin. That's when they got me."

I frowned. "But then why are you here? Aren't you going to stay? Don't you want me to help you?"

Joe shook his head. "You can't. And I can't stay, either. They'll come looking for me before long. But since I won't be coming back, I wanted to tell you... well, everything." He pressed the key into my palm. "There's something for you in the glove compartment. I was going to wait until graduation, but..." He shrugged.

Something nagged me. "Can't you just go back and stop yourself?"

"They thought of that. They've sealed off those paths. I can't go anywhere I've already been." He tilted his head. "You're the only one I wanted to see anyway. You're all I've thought about for five years. Well, you, and how to get out, that is."

"Five *years?*" I reached out and touched his shaven head. "Didn't those thoughts get boring?"

"Well, hiding certain indulgences from their monitoring devices is sort of a pain." He winked.

He was still my filthy-minded boyfriend despite five years in whatever awful place he'd been. I couldn't help hugging him. "I love you," I said.

"I love you, too." He pulled away. "It's funny. I've been rehearsing this for a long time, and I'm still really nervous. How can I be nervous about kissing my own girlfriend?"

I hugged him tighter. "Other parts of you are doing just fine."

"There's a lesson in that," he said, and gave me my five-years-late parting kiss.

‹‹•I•I•I•›

SIXTH PERIOD

Naturally, I could not concentrate through American Government. Instead, I skipped and stayed inside the library. Reality had yet to hit. I should have been crying my eyes out. Joe was gone. He wasn't coming back. He would be the face on someone's milk carton for a while. Then he would fade away. No one but me would know what really happened. I rubbed the key to his car and wondered what was in the glove compartment. I really hoped it wasn't what I imagined — because if so, I was really going to lose it.

Only righteous indignation propped me up. I started thinking in Aretha Franklin tones, and wondered what the hell right Joe had to leave me out of the game. He'd let someone else break us up. Moreover, he'd been absurdly vague in his explanation. Worse yet, I'd let him get away with it. I'd been too dazzled, too saddened, and too horny.

"You stupid bastard, you're not getting away with this," I said, and fetched the nearest volume of music history.

An hour later, I had my destination. Any self-respecting tyrant who hated Lennon's music would want to kill it in its cradle. The trick to discovering the beginnings of rock n' roll was not in listening to a bunch of music theorists, or even looking up back issues of Rolling Stone. It wasn't in drug-fueled autobiographies or liner notes. The only reasonable place for Joe's captors to hide was the place most shrouded in myth.

Slipping on the glove, I felt a heady rush of temptation despite the way the fabric wilted from my too-short fingers. I suddenly understood Joe's speedy conquering of time. His desire to leave his mark on every important date was completely natural. History spread out like a puddle begging to be splashed in. Grinning, I drew a door.

✦✧✦✧✦

OCTOBER 31, 1930
HAZLEHURST, MISSISSIPPI
THE CROSSROADS

"It's the Devil's music," said a woman's voice.

I stood under a big yellow moon on a dirt road. The air held Halloween crispness. Wind blew, and with it came the distant wail of a freight train. To my left, a field of pumpkins lay picked clean. Only the deformed and rotten plants remained.

"You don't really want to play the Devil's music, do you?"

At the crossroads up ahead stood a group of people wearing their Sunday best. The men had hats, and the women wore white gloves. None of their skirts ended above the ankle. Most of them were black, but I saw a handful of white faces. Someone had left a camping lantern on the road. Standing closest to it were two men, one black and one white. In the black man's hands was a guitar.

"Why don't you go on home, and learn a useful trade?"

The man holding the guitar ignored them. He stroked the neck of his guitar. The white man, wearing a straw hat and a suit the color of good stationery, said: "You don't really want to listen to them, do you? Those people can't even sing."

I was close enough now to see the black man frown. He looked back at the assembled group. "They look like the kind that sings in church."

"Then ask them what their favorite hymn is," the white man said. I recognized Joe's voice. He was much older now. Silver glinted at his temples. His easy smile made deep creases in his face. He wore very dark glasses.

The group seemed at a loss. They shifted on their feet. For a moment they seemed translucent, like they weren't quite there. "We don't have a favorite," one of the men said. "They're all God's songs."

"Ask them to sing some of the old songs," Joe said, "the ones about getting free." The edge of hate in his voice told me all I needed to know: these were his prison wardens.

They looked uncomfortable. They moved again and it was more like a communal shiver, like a breeze through tall grass. "We know how important those songs are," a tiny woman said. "We understand what they mean to you."

I said: "Ask them to sing "In the Pines." Go ahead and ask them, Mr. Johnson."

Joe spun in the direction of my voice. He stood with one hand raised, as though having discovered a long-forgotten toy in the chilly basement of his childhood home. His mouth opened, closed, and opened again. "Why, hello, Laurie. Long time no see."

"Hi," I said. The crowd began whispering. It sounded like wind through dry leaves.

Joe turned, and pointed. "Laurie, this is Robert Johnson. Laurie's here to show you what your music can do, Mr. Johnson. Laurie doesn't think she can sing very well. In fact, she doesn't sing unless she thinks no one else can hear her." Joe dropped his hands to my shoulders. "But I'll tell you what; you should really hear her when she's cooking."

Johnson smiled. "Is that so?"

I smiled back. "That's so, Mr. Johnson. And it just so happens that I can sing a song that you know how to play. Unlike that pack of know-nothing cowards over there, I know "In the Pines." I just know it under a different name."

Joe squeezed my shoulders. "You do?"

I swallowed. I hated singing in front of others. I knew my voice was no good. But we were talking about Joe's freedom. "Could you give me a few chords, please?"

"Mr. Johnson, don't do that!" one of the others said. She pointed her white glove at us. Moonlight shone straight through it.

"Quit giving me orders!" Johnson said over his shoulder. "If you can't sing along, then just shut up!" He grinned, and started strumming.

"Go ahead, Laurie," Joe said. "It's been thirty years. I've really missed it."

So I opened my voice, and sang: *"My girl, my girl, don't lie to me..."*

The crowd gibbered and squawked like a murder of crows. They screeched and moaned. As I realized that they were trying to cover my voice, I felt the anger I'd been holding back. These people had taken Joe and hurt him. They had no right. A wave of possessiveness assailed me, and my voice surged. Joe was mine, and they couldn't have him. Johnson's guitar seemed strangely loud and resonant for such a simple instrument, but its strength carried me upward. I belted out the song.

One by one, the bawling horde disappeared. They shrank smaller and smaller before finally popping out of existence. So I sang louder. They squealed and screamed and threw themselves on the ground. They kicked their transparent legs and flailed like sizzling bacon before imploding for good. The last one went out with a high hiss. When the song ended, my throat was ragged. But they had gone.

"That's the last of them, Mr. Johnson," Joe said. "They won't be bothering you again."

Johnson looked at the empty road where the hecklers had once stood. "You really are the Devil," he said. His glance hit Joe, then the dirt. "I suppose you want my soul."

"Just write a song about this, Mr. Johnson. That's soul enough for me."

Joe waited until Johnson had vanished into the dark night before speaking. We were alone under the moon, and we sat on the grass overlooking an empty field. "That man's going to invent rock n' roll."

I hugged my knees. "I figured as much."

Joe pinched his nose. "I should have guessed you'd show up. How long did it take for you to find us?"

"About an hour, with the Internet's help," I said. "They wanted him dead, right? Who were they, Bible-thumping aliens?"

Joe took off his glasses. His eyes were gone. Empty sockets stared at me. "Yes, and you just killed the last of them."

I reached for his face. "Joe..."

"Punishment," he said, answering my unspoken question. "They got pretty mad, the last time I escaped."

"You mean in fifth period?"

He smiled ruefully. "Yeah. Fifth period." He looped an arm over my shoulders. My head fell against him.

"Explain it to me again."

"Lennon was the key. With him dead, we wouldn't have the song that destroyed them. With him safely dead, they could pick off all the other threatening talents. But then they noticed me — us — dicking around with his timeline." He squeezed my hand. "At least we know we were right to save him."

I almost laughed. "Talking to him was so embarrassing... I blushed really bad."

"He was forty years old when you talked to him! You were — are — eighteen!"

"You're like forty-eight, and I still..." Joe's eyeless stare stopped me.

"Really?"

"Really," I said.

He smiled, and folded me closer. "Well, that's something." He rested his chin on my head. "Still have the glove?" I nodded. "That's good. When you get back, destroy it."

I sat up. "Hey. I can still use it. I can go back, and stop you from trying to save Janis in fifth period. I can stop this whole thing."

Joe shook his head. "You can't. All my travel dates are sealed off."

"Then I can go back and stop you from receiving the glove!"

Again, he shook his head. "We'll all die. Well, not us — the song that kills them all hasn't been written yet, but it will be. But the point is that without that glove, we can't avoid disaster. We need it."

"So... what, then? I have to help you somehow."

"You have. You sang. You killed the last of them, and now Robert Johnson goes on to play guitar to his heart's content. We as a race keep our music, John Lennon lives, and we fight another day." He stretched out and rested on his elbows. "I've had decades to think this out, Laurie." He found his glasses and slid them on.

"So now what happens?"

"Do you have the key to my car?" I did. He withdrew something like a cigarette case. Opening it, he pressed the key inside. When he returned it, it felt much heavier. "What happens is that you go home. I've just calibrated this key to your settings. Keep it on you, and it should return you to your departure point."

"And I just leave you here?"

"Yes."

"Why can't you come back with me?"

"Going back to a time where DNA testing and finger-prints can identify me is a bad idea. It would cause all kinds of trouble for both of us." He reached for my hand and squeezed. "Besides, it would be difficult..."

"So? Stay with me! It doesn't matter to me that you're older!"

Joe paused. "Laurie, I've seen the future. Yours is great."

"What happens?"

"Oh you know. The usual. You fall in love with someone else — someone who *isn't* forty-eight, and has a decent pair of eyes."

"Is he cute?"

"Not as cute as me." He smiled at his own joke. "It's about time for you to use your key."

I looked at it there in my palm. "I don't want to."

"I know you don't. But you'll thank me later." He stood up. I followed. He hesitated before asking: "May I use your surname here?"

More than anything else so far, this choked me up and made talking difficult. "Yes..."

"Thanks." He reached down, and held his face in my hands. When he kissed me his lips were tinder-dry.

"What's in the glove compartment?"

He smiled. "Oddly enough, a key fob." He picked up my hand, and adjusted the key in it. "Just unlock the door," he said, twisting my fingers.

›•‡•‡•‡•‹

March 26, 2031

It was in fact a key fob. I sat in Joe's car for an hour with the blue Tiffany's box, wondering if he'd lied. Instead he simply downplayed the truth. Engraved on one side was: "How about living together?"

Today would have been Joe's birthday. On this day every year, I take out the glove and examine it. I'm forty-eight, and I've had thirty years to think over a problem that's bothered me since I opened that Tiffany's box. Namely: *Where did this thing come from?*

Now I think I finally have my answer. So after some research, I've found my destination. On March 24, 2001, I'll mail Joe his much-belated birthday gift. I have only to write the note: *This fits you better than me.*

I hope he enjoyed Woodstock.

Swamp Witch and the Tea-Drinking Man

David Nickle

Swamp witch rode her dragonfly into town Saturday night, meaning to see old Albert Farmer one more time. Albert ran the local smoke and book, drove a gleaming red sports car from Italy, and smiled a smile to run an iceberg wet. Many suspected he might be the Devil's kin and swamp witch allowed as that may have been so; yet whether he be Devil or Saint, swamp witch knew Albert Farmer to be the kindest man in the whole of Okehole County. Hadn't he let her beat him at checkers that time? Didn't he smile just right? Oh yes, swamp witch figured she'd like to keep old Albert Farmer awhile and see him this night.

That in the end she would succeed at one and fail at the other was a matter of no small upset to swamp witch; for among the burdens they carry, swamp witches are cursed with foresight, and this one could see endings clearer than anything else. Not that it ever did her much good; swamp witch could no more look long at an ending than she'd spare the blazing sun more than a glance.

As for the end of this night, she glanced on it not even an instant. For romance was nothing but scut work if you knew already the beginning, the end and all the points between. The smile on her lips was genuine, as she steered past the bullfrogs, through the rushes and high over the swamp road toward the glow of the town.

By the time she was on the town's outskirts, walking on her own two feet with the tiny reins of her dragonfly pinched between thumb and forefinger, the swamp witch had a harder time keeping her mood high. Her feet were on the ground, her senses chained and she could not ignore the wailing of a woman beset.

It came from the house which sat nearest the swamp — the Farley house — and the wailing was the work of Linda Farley, the eldest daughter who swamp witch knew was having man trouble of her own.

She had mixed feelings about Linda Farley, but for all those feelings, swamp witch could not just walk by and she knew it. There was that thing she had done with her checkers winnings. It had made things right and made things wrong, and in the end made swamp witch responsible.

"One night in a week," swamp witch grumbled as she stepped around the swing-set and onto the back stoop. "Just Saturday. That's all I asked for."

→·[··]··]··

Linda Farley was a girl of twenty-one. Thick-armed and legged, but still beautiful by the standards of the town, she had been ill-treated by no less than three of its sons: lanky Jack Irving; foul-mouthed Harry Oates; Tommy Balchy, the beautiful Reverend's son, who wrangled corner snakes for his Papa and bragged to everyone that he'd seen Jesus in a rattler's spittle. Swamp witch was sure it would be one of those three causing the commotion. But when she came in, touched poor Linda's shoulder where it slumped on the kitchen table, and followed her pointing finger to the sitting room, she saw it was none of those fellows.

Sitting on her Papa's easy chair was a man swamp witch had never seen before. Wearing a lemon-colored suit with a vest black as night rain, he was skinny as sticks and looked just past the middle of his life. He held a teacup and saucer in his hands, and looked up at swamp witch with the sadness of the ages in his eye.

"Stay put," said swamp witch to her dragonfly, letting go of its reins. The dragonfly flew up and perched on an arm of the Farleys' flea market chandelier. "Who is this one?"

The man licked thin lips.

"He came this afternoon," said Linda, sitting up and sniffling. "Came from outside. He says awful things." She held her head in her hands. "Oh woe!"

"*Awful* things." Swamp witch stepped over to the tea-drinking man. "Outside. What's his name?"

The tea-drinking man and raised his cup to his mouth. He shook his head.

"He-he won't say."

Swamp witch nodded slowly. "You won't say," she said to the tea-drinking man and he shrugged. Swamp witch scowled. People who knew enough to keep their names secret were trouble in swamp witch's experience.

The tea-drinking man set his beverage down on the arm of the chair and began to speak.

"What if you'd left 'em?" he said. "Left 'em to themselves?"

Swamp witch glared. The tea-drinker paid her no mind, just continued:

"Why, think what they'd have done! Made up with the Russians! The Chinese! Built rockets and climbed with them to the top of the sky, and sat there a moment in spinning wheels with sandwiches floating in front of their noses and their dreams all filled up. Sat there and thought, about what they'd done, what they might do, and looked far away. Then got off their duffs and built bigger rockets, and flew 'em to the moon, and to Mars. Where'd they be?"

The tea-drinking man was breathing hard now. He looked at her like a crazy man, eyes wet. "What if they'd been left on their own?"

And then he went silent and watched.

The swamp witch took a breath, felt it hitch in her chest. Then she let it out again, in a low cough.

"You're infectious," she said.

"What?" said Linda from behind him.

"Infectious. The dream sickness," she said. "You look at the past and start to think maybe that could be better than now. You can't move it's so bad — can't even think."

The tea-drinking man shrugged. "I been around, madame."

"*Around*," said swamp witch. "Surely not around here. This place is mine. There's no sickness, no dreaming sadness. These folks are happy as they are. So I'll say it: You're quarantined from this town." She glanced back at Linda, who looked back at her miserably, awash in inconsolable regret.

"That's how it is."

Swamp witch glared once more at the tea-drinking man.

The tea-drinking man smiled sadly.

"I am—"

"—sorry," finished swamp witch. "I know."

And then swamp witch raised up her arms, cast a wink up to her dragonfly, and set a hex upon the tea-drinking man. "*Begone*," she said.

He stood up. Set his saucer and cup down. Looked a little sadder, if that were possible.

"I was just leaving."

And with that, he stepped out the door, through the yard, over the road and into the mist of the swampland.

"Stay away from my hutch, mind you," swamp witch hollered after his diminishing shade. "I mean it!" and she thought she saw him shrug a bit before the wisps of mist engulfed him and took him, poor dream-sick man that he was, away from the town that swamp witch loved so.

⋙⋆⫶⋆⫶⋆⋘

Swamp witch left shortly after that, and she didn't feel bad about it either. If she'd been a better person, maybe she'd have sat with the girl until she'd calmed down. Maybe cast another little hex to help her through it. But swamp witch couldn't help thinking that one of the things poor old Linda was regretting was her own complicity in the bunch that'd driven swamp witch from her home those years ago and into the mud of the Okehole Wetlands for good.

Let her stew a bit, an unkind part of swamp witch thought as she left the girl alone in her kitchen.

And even if swamp witch wasn't feeling mean, she felt she had an excuse: after having spent a moment with the tea-drinking man, swamp witch couldn't be sure what regret was real and what was just symptomatic. So she called down dragonfly to her shoulder and headed off to town. That's what Saturday was for, after all.

✢✢✢✢✢

It was very bad, worse than she'd thought. This tea-drinking man hadn't, as swamp witch first assumed, just started his visit to town setting in Linda's Papa's easy chair. That was probably his last stop on the way through, spreading his dreaming sickness all over the town. Wandering here or there, giving a little sneeze or a cough as he passed by a fellow fixing his garage door or another loading groceries into his truck, or worst of all, a woman by herself, smoking a cigarette and staring at a cloud overhead wondering where the years had gone. He would leave behind him a wake of furrowed brows and teary eyes and fresh fault-lines in healed-up hearts.

And those were the ones he'd passed. The others — the ones he spent a moment with, said hello to or spoke of this or that—

—there would only be one word for those:

Inconsolable.

Swamp witch was set to figuring now that the tea-drinking man wasn't just a carrier of the bug, like she'd first thought. He was guilty as sin. He was a caster.

And swamp witch was starting to think that he might not be alone. He might not, he might not...

She closed her eyes and took a breath.

When she opened her eyes, swamp witch headed across the downtown with more care. Her dragonfly hid in the curl of her hair and she kept underneath awnings and away from street lamps, and as she did, dragonfly asked her questions with the buzz of its wings.

— What does tomorrow bring? he asked.

Swamp witch opened her mouth to speak it: *Sorrow*. But she did not. She simply stopped.

— And the day after? wondered dragonfly.

— Who knows? whispered swamp witch. But she did know, and she stopped, in the crook of two sidewalk cracks. All she could see was her boy, whose name would be Horace, lying with the gossamar yellow of new beard on his face and his eyes glazed and silvered in the sheen of death. Her girl Ellen, old and bent, rattling in a hospital bed. These were not tomorrow — nor the day after either. But they were bad days ahead — days she'd rather not have happen.

— Dream sickness gotcha, said dragonfly. Only you regret what comes, not what's been.

— You are wise, said swamp witch, her voice shaking. She tried to think of a hex to drive it off, but the ones she knew were all for others.

— Think backwards then, dragonfly suggested. Think of the time you were born.

Swamp witch tried but it was like trying to turn a boat in a fast-moving river. Always she was bent back to forward.

"Need help?"

Swamp witch looked up. There, standing in the middle of the road, his hands behind his back, was the yellow-jacketed tea-drinking man. He had a half-way grin on him that salesmen got when they wondered if maybe you were going to buy that car today all on your own, or maybe needed a little help. He unfolded his hands and started strolling up the way to see her.

"You were banished," said swamp witch. "I said *begone!*"

"I went," said the tea-drinking man. "Oh yes. I *begonned* all right. Right through the swamp. Steered clear of your home there, too. Like you demanded."

"Then why—?"

"Why'm I here?" He stepped up onto the curb. He shook his head. "Let me ask *you* a question."

Swamp witch tried to move — to do something about this. She didn't want him to ask her a question particularly: didn't think it would go anywhere good.

"Just hypothetical," he said.

Shut up, thought swamp witch, but her lips wouldn't move, plastered shut as they were by contemporaneous regret.

"Oh what," he said, "if the town were left on its own?"

"You asked me that earlier."

"Well think about it then. What if you'd just left it. Left it to have a name and a place in the world. Left the folks to see the consequences of their activities. Vulnerable you say and maybe so. But better that than this amber bauble of a home you've crafted, hidden away from the world of witches and kept for yourself. Selfish, wicked swamp witch."

"What—"

The tea-drinking man leaned close. He breathed a fog of lament her way.

"I didn't care for it," he said. "Tossin' me out like that."

Swamp witch swallowed hard. "I don't," she said, "feel bad about any of that."

He smiled. "No?"

Swamp witch stood. "No." She stepped over the crack. Away from the tea-drinking man. "No regrets."

As she walked away, she heard him snicker, a sound like the shuffling of a dirty old poker deck.

"None," she said.

Swamp witch lied, though. To hide it, she meandered across the parking lot of the five and dime, tears streaming down from her eyes, feeling like her middle'd been removed with the awful regret of it all but hiding it in the hunch of her shoulders.

It was low cowardice. For what business had it been of hers, to take the town and curl it in the protection of her arms like she was its goddamned mother and not its shunned daughter?

She took a few more steps, over to the little berm at the parking lot's edge. Then she walked no more — falling into the sweet grass and sucking its green, fresh smell.

"You lie," said tea-drinking man.

She looked up. He was standing over her now, his grin wider than ever she'd thought it could be, on one so stoked with regret.

"You are beset with it," he said.

And then he spread his fingers, which crept wider than swamp witch thought they could — and down they came around her, like a cage of twig and sapling.

"Begone," she said, but the tea-drinking man shook his head. He didn't have to say: *Only works if you mean it, that hex. And then, it only works the once.*

And with that, he had her. Swamp witch fell into a pit inside her — one with holes in the side of it, that looked ahead and back with the same misery. She shut her eyes and did what the sad do best: fell into a deep and honeyed sleep, where past and future mixed.

⁂

She awoke a time later, in a bad way for a couple of reasons.

First, she was in church: Reverend Balchy's church, which was not a good place for her or anyone.

And second, dragonfly was gone.

In the church this was a bad thing. For swamp witch knew that Reverend Balchy had against her advice gone in with the snake dancers' way, turning many in his Baptist congregation from their religion, and welcoming in their place whole families of the Okehole corner rattlers that the Reverend used. Sitting up on the pew, swamp witch feared for dragonfly, for there was nothing that a corner rattler liked better than the crunch of a dragonfly's wing.

Swamp witch called out softly, looking up to the water-stained drop-ceiling with its flickery fluorescent tubes, the dried, cut rushes at the blacked-out windows, the twist of serpent-spine that was nailed up on along the One Cross' middle-piece.

She poked her toe at the floor, and snatched it back again as the arrow-tip head of a corner rattler slashed out from the pew's shadow. Swamp witch wouldn't give it a second chance. She gathered her feet beneath her and stood on the seat-bench, so she could better see.

"*Dragonfly!*" she hissed.

There was no answer, but for the soft *chuk-a-chuk* samba of snake tail.

That, and an irregular thump-thump — like a hammer on plywood — coming from the hallway behind the dias.

Swamp witch squinted.

"Annabel?" she called.

"Yes'm."

From around the top corner of the doorframe, Annabel Balchy's little face peered at her.

"You come on out," said swamp witch.

Annabel frowned. "You ain't going to transform me into nothing Satanic, are you?"

"When have I ever done that?"

"Papa says—"

"Papas say a lot of things," said swamp witch. "Now come on out."

Annabel's face disappeared for a moment, there were a couple more thump-thumps, and the girl teetered into the worship hall, atop a pair of hazelwood stilts that swamp witch thought she recognized.

"Those your brother's?"

Annabel thrust her chin out. "I grew into them."

"You're growing into more than those stilts," said swamp witch. Like the rest of the Balchies, Annabel was a blond-haired specimen of loveliness whose green eyes held a sheen of wisdom. Looking at her, swamp witch thought her brother Tommy would no longer hold title as the family's number-one heartbreaker. Not in another year or two.

"We got your dragonfly," said Annabel, teetering over a little slithering pond of shadow. "He brung you here, in case you didn't know."

"I didn't know," said swamp witch. "I'm not surprised, though. He's a good dragonfly. Is he all right?"

"Uh huh. We got him at the house. Figured you could take care of yourself, big old swamp witch that you are. But we didn't think he'd be safe among the Blessed Serpents of Eden."

"They're just plain corner rattlers, hon, and I'm no safer than anyone else when one decides to bite. But thank you for protecting dragonfly. Did he say why he brung — brought me here?"

"Figured it'd be the one place where the angel couldn't come."

"The angel."

"In the yellow suit," said Annabel. "With a vest underneath black as all damnation."

"Him. *Huh*. He's no angel."

"That's what you say. He's huntin' you, and you're a swamp witch—"

"—so it follows he's got to be an angel." Swamp witch sighed. "I see."

"Papa said you'd probably be wondering why we didn't give you up to that angel."

"Your papa's a bright man," said swamp witch. "The thought did cross my mind."

"Papa said to tell you he don't like the competition," said Annabel.

Swamp witch laughed out loud at that one. "I believe it," she said. "Oh yes."

Laughing felt good. It may not be the antidote to regret, but it sure helped the symptoms fine. All the same, she took a breath and put it away.

"He sent you to see if I was dead, didn't he?"

Annabel looked down and shook off a rattler that was spiraling up toward her heel. "Yes ma'am," she said, a little ashamedly. "But he said you might not be. If, I mean, you was righteous."

"So I'm righteous then?"

Annabel crooked her head like she was thinking about it.

"I expect," she said. "Yeah, good chance you are."

"All right," said swamp witch. "But if you don't mind, I'll take no more chances. You still got that spare set of bamboo stilts I know Reverend used to use in back?"

Annabel said she did, so swamp witch held out her hand. "Think you could toss 'em my way? I'd like to go see my dragonfly and maybe your Papa too."

∗∙╂∙╂∙╂∙∗

A moment later, the church hall was filled with a racket like summer's rain on a metal shed. Swamp witch was making her escape, and that pleased the corner rattlers not at all.

∗∙╂∙╂∙╂∙∗

Swamp witch dropped the two stilts by the Reverend's porch and went in for her meeting. The porch was screened in and the Reverend was there, sitting on an old ratty recliner covered in plastic. Dragonfly was sitting quiet on the table beside him, in a big pickle jar with a lid some-one had jammed nails through, just twice. Reverend looked as smug as he could manage, his face stiffened like it was with all the rattler venom.

Swamp witch understood there were days he'd been different: all stoked with holy-roller fire, straight-backed with a level gaze that could melt swamp witch where she stood. That was before he'd found the serpent spittle, before swamp witch had found her own calling.

Did *he* have any regrets? she wondered. Maybe taking the snake-tooth into his arm, letting it course through him 'til he couldn't even sit up on his own? Raising his young by nought but telepathy and bad example?

Did he regret any of it? She thought that he didn't.

"Papa says you look like hell," said Annabel.

"Thank you, Reverend. You are as ever a font of manly righteousness."

Reverend lifted his hand an inch off the arm-rest, and his lips struggled to make an 'o'.

"Papa's cross with you," said Annabel. "He called you a temptress."

"Well make up your mind," said swamp witch, laughing. Then she made serious. "We got problems here, Reverend."

The Reverend agreed, making a farting noise with his mouth.

"This tea drinking angel," said swamp witch. "You reckon you know what he's here for?"

"You," said Annabel.

"You answered too fast," said swamp witch. "What's your Papa got to say?"

The Reverend's hand settled back onto the arm of his chair, and he sighed like a balloon deflating. Dragonfly's wings slapped against the glass of the jar.

"Angel wants Okehole." Annabel put her head down. "All of it." She looked up between strands of perfect blond hair. "Its souls."

Swamp witch rolled her eyes. Everything was about souls to the Reverend. Flesh to him was an inconvenience — a conveyance at best and lately, a broken down Oldsmobile. The tea-drinking man wasn't an angel and he didn't want souls. But she nodded for the Reverend to keep going.

"He's aiming for you," said Annabel, "because *you* got all the souls."

Which was another thing that Reverend believed. This time swamp witch would not keep quiet. "I do not have all the souls, Reverend. You know what I done here and it's not soul stealing."

"Ain't it?" said Annabel. "Puttin' us all an a jar here — just like your bug! Comin' to visit each Saturday and otherwise just keepin' us here? Ain't that soul stealin'?"

Swamp witch sighed. "Tell me what you know about your soul-stealin' angel."

The Reverend sighed and coughed and his head twitched up to look at her.

"He came by here this afternoon," said Annabel. "Annabel — that's me — brought him some iced tea made like he asked. He talked about the Garden — about the day that Eve bit that apple and brung it to Adam. He asked me, 'What if Adam had said to Eve: I don't want your awful food; I am faithful to Jehovah, for He has said to me "Eat not that fruit." What if Adam had turned his face upward to Jevovah, and said: 'I am content in this garden with Your love, and want not this woman's lies of knowledge and truth. She has betrayed you, O Lord, not I. Not I.'

"If that happened, would you sustain on serpent venom? Would *she* be the keeper of your town's souls?'" Annabel nodded and looked right at swamp witch. "By 'she' I took him to mean you. That's what Papa says."

"So what did you say to that, I wonder?" said swamp witch.

The Reverend's lips twitched, and Annabel hollered:

"Begone!" The Reverend's eyes lit up then as his little girl spoke his word. "I am not some shallow *parishoner*, some *Sunday school dropout*, some holiday churchgoer — oh no, the venom as you call it is holy the blood of the prickly one and I am His vessel! Begone! Git now!"

"Your faith saved you," said swamp witch drily.

"Papa ain't finished," scolded Annabel. "He says the tea-drinking man got all huffy then. He was calm up 'til then and suddenly his face got all red. The rims of his eyes got darker red, like they was bleedin', and the lines of his gums got the same colour as that. And his teeth seemed to go all long and snaggly with broke ends. And he said to my Papa:

"'*You don't tell me what to do. You don't tell me nothin'. This town will weep for me, like it wept for her.*'"

"Her being me," said swamp witch.

"Ex-actly," said Annabel.

"So how'd you best him?" asked swamp witch.

"Didn't," said Annabel. And the Reverend grinned then. "Just agreed to keep you occupied. 'Til the tea drinkin' angel were ready to finish you off."

The Reverend's hand rose up then, and fell upon the jar. His fingers covered the two air-holes in the lid. Dragonfly fluttered at that, then calmed down — no sense in wasting oxygen.

Swamp witch reached for the jar. But the Reverend found the rattler's quickness in his elbow and snatched it away so fast dragofly banged his head on the side and fell unconscious.

"Why you lyin' deceitful parson!" hollered swamp witch. With her other hand she reached for her pebbles, intending to enunciate peroxide or some other disinfectant canticle. But the pebbles were gone — of course. Annabel and perhaps her brother Tommy had leaned down from the top of stilts and pulled them from her pocket while she slept in the Reverend's church. "You're in league with him!"

Annabel leaned forward now, and when she spoke her papa's lips moved with hers: "You ought never have been, swamp witch. You ought never have come here and shut the world from this place. You say you are protecting people but you are keeping them as your human toys, like a she-devil in a corner of Hell. The angel will drive you from here, madame! Drive you clear away."

"Take your fingers off'n my dragonfly's airholes," she said. She was most worried right now about her dragonfly. For blinking and recollecting conclusions, she saw that she would not be spending long now in the Reverend's company. But her dragonfly wasn't with her either, and that caused her to suspect that the poor creature would soon suffocate if she didn't do something.

The Reverend, to her mild surprise, moved his finger up. Or perhaps it slid. No, she thought, looking up, he meant to. His face twitched and his lips opened.

"You should never have come," he said. In his own voice — which swamp witch had not heard in many years now. And behind her, the breeze died and slivers of moonlight dissolved in the shadow of the tea-drinking man.

The Reverend stood up then, and Annabel cried: "A miracle!" and the Reverend took a step toward the edge of the porch, where the yellow-suited tea-drinking man stood, smile as large as his eyes were sad.

"O Angel," Reverend said, his eyes a-jittering with upset snake venom, "I have delivered her!"

"You fool," said swamp witch. And she stepped behind the Reverend, took hold of the jar that held her dragonfly, and said to him: "Carry me to Albert."

That was when the tea-drinking man bellowed. At first, she thought he was angry that she was getting away —

trying to sneak behind the Reverend, climb upon her still-groggy dragonfly and sneak out through a hole in the porch-screen. If that were the case — well, she'd be in for it and she braced herself, holding tight on dragonfly's back-hair.

But as she swirled up to the rafters of the porch, she saw this was not the case. The tea-drinking man was distracted not by her, but by Reverend Balchy's sharp, venomous incisors, that had planted themselves in his yellow-wrapped forearm.

Reverend Balchy stopped hollering then, on account of his mouth being full, and Annabel took it up.

"Gotchya, you lyin' sinner. Think you can use me? Think it? When swamp witch come to town she took away most of me — you'll just take away the rest! Well fuck yuh! Fuck yuh!"

Dragonfly swung down, close past tea-drinking man's nose, and swamp witch could see the anger and pain of the Reverend's ugly mix of rattler venom and mouth bacteria slipping into his veins. There'd be twitching and screaming in a minute — at least there would be if tea-drinking man had normal blood.

Tea-drinking man didn't seem to though. He opened his own mouth and looked straight at Annabel:

"What," he said, "if you spoke up for yourself? What if you walked the world your own girl, flipped—" he grimaced "—*flipped* your old papa the bird, and just made your way on your own-some."

Annabel looked at him. Then she looked up at swamp witch, who was heading for a rip in the screen where last summer there'd been a fist-sized wasp nest.

"I'd never be on my own-some," Annabel said. "Not so long as *she* protects me."

And then swamp witch was gone from there, escaped into the keening night and thanking her stars for the Reverend's poison-mad inconstancy. The tea-drinking man bellowed once more, and then he was a distant smear of yellow and the stars spun in swamp witch's eye.

→⊹⊱⊹⊰⊹←

Was it cowardice that drove swamp witch across the rooftops of her town, then up so high she touched the very limits of her realm? Was she just scared of that tea-drinking man? What kind of protector was she for little Annabel, the Reverend, all the rest of them? Maybe when the Reverend was faking out the tea-drinking man, when he said "you should never have come," he was right. For when she'd come hadn't she stolen away the Reverend's faith and the comfort of self-determination from her people and hadn't she just kept them like she wanted them? Had she ever thought through what it would be if it had come to this?

— Why'd you take me there? she said. Were you in league with the Reverend?

Dragonfly didn't answer.

— Did you know about the Reverend's double cross?

They flew low through a cloud of gnats, who all clamored — yes! yes!

— Can I trust no one? swamp witch despaired.

— Hush said dragonfly. It swung back through the gnats, and swamp witch could see the mists of her home, the Okehole Wetlands, rising from amid the stumps and rushes. Now let's go home.

Swamp witch thought about how comfortable that would be. And with that, she realized she wasn't scared of the tea-drinking man. She was scared of something else entirely.

Swamp witch dug her knees into dragonfly's thorax and yanked at dragonfly's hair to make a turn.

— Uh uh, she said. After all that, I'm not lettin' you make any decisions. You know where we got to go.

Dragonfly hummed resentfully, and together they flew down — down toward the business section at the east end of town. There, the smoke and book waited for her, orange flickery light from its sign illuminating a patch in front like a hearth-fire.

She reached to the ground by the road, and picked up two pebbles that seemed right, and stuffed them in her jeans, then in she went.

≫⊶╂⊷╂⊷╂⊷≪

Albert Farmer sat in the front of the store, which was the nice section, all scrubbed and varnished and smelling of fresh pipe tobacco. The not-so-nice section, with the girly magazines and French ticklers and the cigars from Cuba — that was in was in the back, and this part was nothing but nice. Just some cigarettes and old-fashioned pipes in a display case, and a magazine rack that held nothing to trouble anyone — Times and Peoples and Archie comic books, Reader's Digests and a lot of magazines about guns and cars and fixing up houses. Albert sat behind the counter, smoking a hand-rolled cigarette and sipping at a glass of dark wine he made for himself.

"Sweetness." He smiled in his way as swamp witch slipped through the mail slot and sat at the counter. "I thought you mightn't come."

"The town is under attack," said swamp witch balefully.

"I know," said Albert. He pinched off the end of the cigarette, and stepped around the counter. "Come here."

He looked guilty as hell. But swamp witch stepped over across the floor anyhow. Dragonfly, traitorous insect that it was, flew in back to sniff cigar-leaf and browse pornography.

Swamp witch said: "You know anything more about that?"

Albert smiled. He had an easy smile — teeth too white to have smoked as much as he seemed to, half a dimple on one cheek only. It broke swamp witch's heart every time she saw it. So when he just stepped up close to her and held the palm of his right hand forward, so it hovered over her left breast, she just let her broken old heart bask in his heat. Her arms fell upon his shoulders, and then crept down his arms, over the shortened sleeves of his summer shirt. O Lord, she thought as he pressed hard against her middle, wasn't this what a Saturday night was for? Couldn't it just be forever?

Swamp witch knew it couldn't. One day a week was part of the bargain.

She pulled back and looked at Albert levelly.

"Why did you bring tea-drinking man here? Why did you let him in?"

Albert frowned. He started to deny it, but looked into swamp witch's eye and knew he couldn't.

"How'd you know it was me?"

"I remember the future," she said. "I remember the ends of things."

"There's no joy in that," said Albert Farmer.

"I know." Swamp witch stepped away and shook the lust from her head. "It's not like the beginnings. Those are the real joys."

Albert nodded. He leaned back against the counter; appeared to think, but it was hard to say because the lights were low.

"Are they?" he finally said. "Beginnings, I mean. Are they the real joys? You ever think much about ours?" Swamp witch looked at him. "You don't of course. Or else you'd never say that about beginnings. Maybe you'd have killed me by now."

It was true that swamp witch didn't think about beginnings but it wasn't that she couldn't.

"I loved you," she said.

"You still do."

"I still do. But we're busting up. I know it."

Albert's smile faded and he nodded. "That's how the night ends," he said. "Will you have a glass of wine with me?"

Swamp witch shrugged, like a sullen teenager she thought, and mumbled, "*Mayuswell*" and leaned her butt against the countertop so she wouldn't be looking at him. She heard the wine gurgling from bottle to stemware, and Albert came around the front of her and gave her the glass. She looked into it, swirled it a bit.

"You knew it had to come," he said. "From the day we made this place, you know this had to come."

Swamp witch sighed. She did know — she did remember. But what pleasure was there, in recalling a game of skill against this — this roadside mephistopheles, during the worst afternoon of her life? That was well hidden away, that memory.

At least it was until this moment — this moment, when she once more recalled the crossroads, just to the south of town near the sycamore grove where she sat, bruised and angry and waiting for a bus or some conveyance to take her away. When she said:

I'd just like to send you to hell.

And when not a bus but a shiny little two-seater from Naples rolled up, and he stepped out and set down the checker board and said, "would you now sweet mama?" and she said, "maybe not exactly," and he said, "well care to play me?" and she said "what for?" and he said "what do you want?"

"I wanted my town back," said swamp witch, bringing the wine glass from her lips, "just my town. And just Saturdays. Just Saturdays. And I won it."

"Fair and square," said Albert.

Swamp witch set down the glass. "I cared for it here," she said. "It was mine and I cared for it."

"Yes," said Albert. "It was yours. And you cared for it all right. But not forever. You knew that."

"Not forever?" she said.

"Only," he said, "so long as I could keep winning."

"What do you mean?"

"Oh swamp witch. I was wandering as I sometimes do the other day — and I came upon a crossroads as I often do — and there who should I see but a sad old sack of a man. And I said to him as I must: Want to play a game? Albert took a long pull from his wine glass. "And he said to me as he was wont to: I'd love a game this afternoon. And so we set down and played."

"Checkers?" said swamp witch unkindly.

"A word game — a remembering game. And oh he was good, and at the end of it—"

"You," said swamp witch, "are a sorry excuse for your kind. You never lose a game you don't want to. And now... You lost my town, didn't you?"

"There are those who've been hankering for it for some time now."

"Yes — but *you.*" She set her glass down. "You ought to know better."

Oh he ought to. But swamp witch saw in Albert Farmer's eyes, the back of them where the embers sometimes smoldered, that he didn't. Couldn't help himself truly. He was a kind man and kind men helped others with the things they wanted. Fine if swamp witch were the other. But nothing but hurt or betrayal, if it be someone else.

Now, swamp witch knew with regretful certainty that she would not only lose Albert this night — but possibly the town as well.

"Others fight him, you know," she said, thinking of the Reverend and his poisonous bite. "Others love me better."

"Oh Ma — oh swamp witch," said Albert, correcting himself, "you think I don't love you well enough? That is a stinger, my dear. I've as much love for you as is in me. Now come—" he draped his arm over her shoulder "—there's little time."

"Is there?"

"Look," he said and pointed between the gossamer window covers to the street. There, sure enough, was the tea-drinking man — his suit was a bit mussed and the skin around his eyes was dark with snake spit, which was also why he was moving so funny swamp witch supposed. He stood a moment in the middle of the road, tried to smooth his hair with his hand and stomped his foot like it was a hoof. Then he looked over to the smoke and book.

Was there a sense in fighting it?

Swamp witch knew better. She leaned over to Albert, and smothered the little space left between them with a kiss. He tasted of salt and wine and egg gone bad, but swamp witch didn't mind. She let herself to it and lived in the instant — the instant prior the end, and when she pulled away, the tea-drinking man was there at the big window, looking in with socketed eyes and a terrible, blood-rimmed grin.

"Why'd you let him win?" she said.

Tea-drinking man's ankles cracked as he stepped away and pushed open the door, jangling the little bell at the top. The sickness was coming off him like a fever now. Swamp witch held onto Albert harder and slid her hands into her pocket.

"I ain' feeli' well," said the tea-drinking man.

"You ain't lookin' well," said swamp witch. "That venom'll kill you."

Tea-drinking man shook his head. "Nuh," he said. "Nuh me."

He reached around them, arm seeming to bend in two spots to do it, and lifted swamp witch's wine glass. Unkindly, he hocked a big purple loogie the size of a river slug, let it ooze into the glass and down the side. It fizzed poisonously.

"This is who you gave me up for," said swamp witch. Albert's shoulders slumped.

"'Twas only a matter of time before they saw what happened here," said Albert.

Swamp witch sighed. She snaked her hand underneath Albert's arm. They stood there at the end now — seconds before it would occur, she could see it clear as headlights, clear as anything. She brought her lips to his, and said: "Goodbye," then added, fondly: "Go to hell."

And with that, Albert stepped away and smiled his sweet smile, and in a whiff of volcanic flatulence, did as he was told and stepped to the back of the store.

And it was just her and the tea-drinking man.

→⊹⊹⊹←

"Why di'— *did* you ever want this place?" asked the tea-drinking man. "I's a rat hole."

"A snake pit," agreed swamp witch. "I agree with your sentiment some days. I wanted it because it was rightfully mine. Why'd *you* play Albert for it?"

"Symmetry," said the tea-drinking man.

"That explains not a thing," said swamp witch.

"All right." The tea-drinking man took a ragged breath. "You took this place off—" he looked into the air for the word and found it in the old dangling light fixture over the cash register "—off the grid. The world ran its course, my dear — ran to dark and to light and good and evil. Why, those of us on the outside took the time we had and made things. There are towers, dear swamp witch — towers that extend to heaven and back. Great wide highways, so far across you can only see the oncoming autos as star-flecks in the mist. We've built rockets. Rockets! We've gone higher than God. And yet this place? Stayed put. All those years. Why?" He gave a drooling little sneer. "Because it's rightfully yours?"

"That's right," said swamp witch. "And whatever you say, it's better for it."

Tea-drinking man shrugged. And although he never seemed too inflated, he seemed to deflate then. He slumped a little, in fact.

"What did you think you would accomplish?"

Swamp witch shrugged now. What did it need to accomplish? She wondered. What was the point of this accomplishment anyhow — of taking your powers and making the world into a place of your dreams? Why look ahead — when all that was there were endings and misery? Why not make a pleasant place now?

"And you fester in your swamp," said tea-drinking man, "wallowing in the muck with your insects and rodents and frogs. I'd drain that swamp, I was you."

Swamp witch looked at him, and as she did, she saw another ending: one in which all of Okehole County was nothing but an embodiment of tea-drinking man's hopes and dreams — victim of his regrets.

It was an end all right — a point too long before she buried her own children and faced her own end. Swamp witch did not like to look upon ends long, but she couldn't look away from this one: it filled up the horizon like a great big sunset.

"You have got the sickness," she said. "The dreaming sick. You won't now give it to me. And you won't give it to our town. You won't give it to this county."

"I already done that," he said simply, sadly almost.

— No he hasn't, said dragonfly, buzzing up from the back of the shop. Hop on.

❖•❧•❧•❖

The tea-drinking man tried to grab her, but he was sore and half-paralyzed now from the Reverend's bite, and he just knocked over a box of chewing tobacco and mumbled swear-words. Swamp witch felt her middle contract and the smoke and book get big and she flung her leg over the back of dragonfly. Tea-drinking man called after her: "You shouldn't have!" but swamp witch already had, and she wouldn't let the itchy virus of regret at her now.

☙❦❧

Swamp witch soared. She climbed again to the very top of her domain — the place where the dome of stars turned solid and fruit-drunk swallows'd stun themselves dead. Dragonfly set up there, buzzing beneath the sallow light of Sirius, and swamp witch leaned over to him and asked him what he'd meant by that.

And dragonfly whispered his answer with his wings, buzzing against the hard shell of the world so they echoed down to earth. Swamp witch peered down there — at her town, her people, who from this place seemed even tinier than she was now. She smiled and squinted: could almost make them out. There was little Linda Farley, her eyes dried up and a big old garden hoe in her hands; Jack Irving, with a red plastic gas can, riding shotgun in Harry Oates' pickup; Bess Overland with a flensing knife and Tommy Balchy, beautiful young Tommy, with a big old two-by-four that'd had a nail driven through it. He was leading the senior class from the Okehole County High School, and a bunch of straggling ninth-graders, down Brevener Street, toward the front of old Albert Farmer's smoke and book.

Swamp witch smiled a little, with sudden nostalgia. The last time she'd seen her folk like that had been before she'd met Albert — just before, when she'd been invited to leave her home town — on pain of death pretty well. She saw that so clearly, she knew, because it was so similar to her recollection of what was about to happen.

Tea-drinking man was going to pick up the telephone in Albert Farmer's shop, dial a long-distance operator who hadn't heard from Okehole County in Lord knew how long, and tell the others that he'd done it. "Symme'ry," he'd say, then repeat slowly, *sym-met-tree*. Is restored. We got it."

And at the other end, a voice that ululated like wind-chimes would laugh and thank him and tell him that his check was in the mail, the board of directors were pleased, there was a new office with a window waiting for him, see you later and stop by the club when you get back. And tea-drinking man would with shaking hand hang up the phone, and step outside to survey his new town.

And then — like before, when swamp witch had come out of the pharmacy, the glamour fresh upon her, two smooth pebbles in her pocket and the knowledge that she could do anything — *anything*! — then, the town would set upon him.

Swamp witch had been faster than tea-drinking man would be. Swamp witch had also known the town, known it like her own soul practically, and she'd cut down the alley-way between Bill's and the Household Hardware and muttered "glycol," and vanished from their sight, leaving them all hopped up and pissed off with nothing they could do.

Slow, sick old tea-drinking man, who'd swapped his dreaming sickness for snake sick, wouldn't have the same advantage.

They'd do to him what they couldn't ever do to her.

And that would be the end.

— Think, she asked dragonfly, once they got that out of their system, tearin' themselves up a witch, actually beatin' one — think it'd cure them of all the regret that fellow'd stoked 'em with?

Dragonfly pondered the question and finally said:

— You don't ask a question like that unless you know the answer.

— You are a wise bug, said swamp witch.

— Not wise enough to know where you want to go next.

— Hmm.

Last time this had happened, swamp witch had figured she'd head straight for the wetlands and wait it out. Then, she'd been sidetracked by a game of checkers and the promise of certainty. This time, as she directed dragonfly down toward the mist of the wetland and past that to her tiny hutch, swamp witch vowed that she would not pause on her way there. She would spend the next six days in the swamp, thinking about what she'd do on the seventh. It would take a lot of careful thinking leading up to Saturday, because for the first time in her life, she'd be free that night.

The Recorded Testimony of Eric and Julie Francis

D. W. Archambault

Click.

"Is this thing on? Check. Check. One. Two. Three."

"Okay. Good. It's working."

"For me, there is no past. I have few ways I can record or revisit it. The only way I really can do so efficiently is through conversation or this voice recorder. I guess you can say that I only live in the moment.

"Anyway, enough philosophical bullshit. My name is Eric Francis, and I'm seventeen years old. Let me tell you what I'm doing right now."

Right now, I'm running up a mountain. When you run up anything steep, it's important to shorten and quicken your stride as I do to keep pace. The air feels cool on my face. For the first time in hours, there is nothing between me and the grey sky. It rumbles like it has for the entire journey. This last leg is the most difficult, but it has been well rehearsed. I am struggling a bit, but I run at a pace which few can match. I don't need to defend myself. Actions speak for themselves. I'm simply the best at what I do.

The sky opens up with hail the size of peas. They carom off my invisible legs in odd directions. The hailstones smart, and I want to swear, but then, they'll see you and take you out. I'd rather stay invisible, thank you very much.

When I start down the top of the mountain, the hail switches to rain. The rocks are slick. My boots feel like they are about to slip, sending me tumbling over the edge of the cliff. It could be worse. I could fall and tear open my suit, or water could somehow find a fold, and I'd drip off thin air. Rookie fears. More likely to cause you to screw up. I keep the same cadence as I pass by the edge of the cliff and start back into the forest. Under the canopy, the path is drier, and the rain crackles against the leaves above.

I feel a light breeze halfway down. It's strange to feel the wind blow here, being the most sheltered part of the run, but I ignore it. I don't think much of it as I pull into the drop-point. It's a wooden cabin in the middle of nowhere. It always looks empty from the outside, but if you knock the right way, they'll let you in. When inside, I shut down the suit and pull out my mouthpiece. I'm visible again, covered in thin OLED film, CCD chips, and Peltier devices. That probably doesn't mean much to you, so let's just say I look like a ninja who can be invisible in light and infrared at the flick of a switch. I pull back my hood and give Ron a big smile.

"Hey, Eric." He's looking at the floor. This isn't like him.

"Hey, Ron." I hand him my bundle. It's a couple pounds of books that I stopped noticing after the first mile. Same sort of stuff I've been handling for years. He accepts it and bites his lip. He just goes back and puts it on the shelf next to another package. Ah, things are running late. Stuff's not being delivered on-time. Not my problem.

"Antoine's running late again?"

"Uh, no. He came by an hour ago."

Come to think of it, it seems strange that there was only one other package on that shelf. I look at my watch. I was on pace. In fact, I was even close to breaking my best pace.

"Stragglers who can't do their job? Is that what's getting you down?"

"Eric." The way he's talking sounds like he's selecting his words very carefully. It's so annoying. "Did anyone ever say you are...difficult to talk to?"

I smile. "Only jealous losers. Why?"

"Your sister beat you down the mountain today."

I laugh. "Quit kidding around, Ron. That's like, impossible. I could…"

But when I looked over at the fire, she's already there with her back to us. Julie's sitting cross-legged on the floor, reading a book in her ninja suit. I hadn't seen her in a while. I guess she's been running different routes.

"She's been sitting there reading," Ron says. He looks at me sort of confidentially and is twisting the hem of his shirt. "She read a lot, Eric?"

Asshole. How the fuck should I know? I ignore the question. "Yeah, well, I had a bad run today, Ron. Was feeling tight out there. Had some tough luck. Man, but Julie, she must have been kicking ass. Hey, Ron. Anyone in the shower?"

"Uh, no one else has made it down yet, and Julie's done with it, so you can go ahead if you want to."

Real mature. Showering real fast to show me up. "Um, yeah, great, thanks. When's the run back?"

"Tomorrow morning at five."

"Morning shift. Got to love those."

"It's a long one," Ron says. "They're putting Julie on it too. Probably take you guys a few days."

"She better not slow me down."

He grins in a way that's pissing me off. "Guys at the office think you'll be the one having the problem keeping up."

I pat him on the shoulder. "Yeah, true. I've been feeling off the past little while. Thanks. I'll be back in a second."

I slip into the shower room and softly shut the door. I turn on the water and make it real hot, so that it's steaming up the room. I don't know why hot water has such a calming effect.

I pull off my boots and chuck them into the corner. I peel off the black fabric off my skin and drop it on the floor. The ceramic in the fabric clinks against the tiles. Hot temperature isn't good for it, but I don't care. I step into the bathtub and flip on the shower. I punch the wall. Not hard, but just hard enough so that my hand aches a bit and silent enough so no one hears. For a good couple of minutes, I stand there and let the hot water run over my face as my emotions pickle my mind.

I turn off the water, grab a towel, and dry off. I don't have, or really need, a change of clothes, so I pull back on my running stuff and click closed the buckles of my boots. Kinda hard being all one piece and now sticky because of the steam in the room. I could go invisible if I wanted to right there. It was such a feeling of power at first, but it gets boring after a while. I reach for the door and push it open.

"Hey Eric, what took you so long in the shower?"

It's Nate. He's grinning. If he knows that Julie kicked my ass, he'll make me wish I went invisible.

"Sorry guys. I figured you were far behind as usual, so I took my time."

"Got in... maybe ten minutes after you?"

"Ten minutes is still ten minutes."

"Yeah, but it's a lot shorter than other times, bud. Gap's closing."

"Lota lip for someone who sucks. Besides, it's not a race the last time I checked."

Nate frowns. "So says the man who got his ass handed to him by his sister." He grins and taps my shoulder. He steps past me before I can say anything and shuts the door behind him.

Fuck, he's still slower than me! Hell, he's even slower than my sister! The irony isn't lost. I'm not that stupid or emotional. I head back to the fireroom.

Julie and Ron are setting up the beds. Julie's already changed into her flannels, and Ron is, well, Ron, in his dirty jeans and red plaid lumberjack shirt. They're making five beds. Julie's pulling covers over the mattress as I walk over.

"Need help?"

"Hey, Eric. Sure," she says. I help tuck some of the blankets underneath her mattress.

"Why did they put you on this run? You usually aren't on it."

"I think they just wanted to get me here for the long run we have to do. They tell you about that?"

I nod. "Yeah, they're saying it'll take a couple of days. I'm glad I'll be having you along."

"Really? Because I could swear..."

"Julie. I was just getting upset, that's all. Try to forget about it."

"All right."

"Besides, I'm glad I'll have you around and not that slowpoke, Nate."

"Same here."

"Have you run with him at all?"

"Not really."

"You see, Nate uses all that shit he spews out of his trap as propellant. He insults you while talking over his shoulder. The key to beating Nate is to get him to look at you. If you get out in front early when he looks at you his mouth knocks him clear on his ass."

She smiles and laughs. I can't help but do the same.

I pick up a pillow and jam it into a case. "But, you don't need Nate to knock himself on his ass. You're probably a hell of a lot better than him."

She shakes her head and starts on the next bed. "Is there anything else you want to talk about other than work?"

"Is there anything else worth talking about?"

She finishes tucking the sheets under her pillow and picks up a book from her things. "I guess there isn't with you." She turns and goes to sit by the fire and starts to read again.

I know she's just acting like this to piss me off, but I'm not going to fall for it. I go over to my stuff and put on my flannels.

→•I•I•I•←

We wake up at four the next morning and suit up. There's something really cool about getting up so early in the summertime and looking at the last stars disappear. The sky's all navy with dawn, and you can feel the chill of waning night on your skin. Then again, I'm a runner so maybe it's just my inherent masochism talking again.

I pull up my hood and pull my mouthpiece over my nose and mouth. The mechanism cools my breath. The only thing that's showing is my eyes. Now you see why I call it a ninja suit. I flip on the cooling system. The suit inflates a bit as nitrogen begins circulating. It feels cool against my skin, but it will soon find a balance so that the Peltier devices keeps the outer surface of me at ambient air temperature. IR invisibility in T minus five minutes.

Time to go find Ron.

He isn't hard to find. Ron's in the fireroom with Julie. She's already suited up. As she heads for the door, Ron motions for me to approach. When I get there, he clunks two fuel cells into the sockets at my hips to run the optical camouflage, and two into the reserves on the back for emergencies. He takes a long drag from his cigarette before speaking again.

"You're wearing contacts for this one."

I glare at him.

"Sorry, bud. No arguments. Them's the rules."

I begrudgingly take a pair from the box and slip them into my eyes and put their five control caps on my fingers. I press my thumb and middle finger together. An amber dot appears in the middle of Julie's chest a few feet away.

"Transponder's working."

"Good. These contacts have a new feature. Press your thumb and index finger together."

I do and an amber GIS appears in front of my eyes. It's a electronic map showing elevation contours, and our route through the mountains. There's also a pair of dots for Julie and I blinking at the start of the course.

"Julie just sees some text with written directions because, you know, she likes to read and all. We know you can't handle that, right?"

He's looking funny at me again like I'm hiding something from him. What's his problem? "Thanks." Asshole.

"Not a problem."

Julie flips on her optical cam, shimmers, and disappears. I do the same and she opens the door.

"You kids stay together," Ron calls after us, "and don't forget to have fun."

When I get to the bottom of the steps, I can't see Julie. It's not a problem. I press my thumb and forefinger together to get her transponder up again, but nothings comes up. I open an encrypted channel.

"Is Julie live?"

"Julie's live."

"Where are you?"

"Wouldn't you like to know?"

"Quit playing around and switch your transponder back on. We need to get started."

I feel a hand on my shoulder and turn to see a pair of smiling eyes and a nose hovering in mid-air.

"Gotcha," she says over the channel.

"Very funny. Should we stop fooling around and get started?"

"Roger, that!"

She takes off for the forest. I have to run hard to catch up, but when I do we settle into a tough pace. There's no way she'll be able to keep running this fast. I keep up with her stride for stride, struggling a bit. The start is always the worst. Soon, I hope that the endorphins take over and I forget that I'm running.

"Is the pace good for you, Eric?"

"Yeah, fine."

"We're going off trail soon. I have a good memory. Do you remember the map?"

"Remember the map? I have a soft copy on my contacts."

"Oh, good. It's handy to have just in case I lose you."

"You're not going to lose me."

She begins to pull ahead just a little. I pick up to draw even. We turn onto a narrow path in single file.

"Let me know if I'm pulling too far ahead?"

"In your dreams."

She picks up speed and I pull even, but I can't hold the pace. A ridiculous distance grows between us throughout the day. At intervals, I pick up the pace managing to keep the gap even for a few minutes, but I could never hold it.

→⊹•⊹•⊹←

Around seven, she stops running. It takes nearly an hour before I finally catch up to her. She should be somewhere nearby this grove, but it takes minutes to find where she set up camp. There's a foil package which has been already open and eaten. It looks like she's cooking another under a foil dome with a heating cube. One for me I suppose.

I look all around the grove, but I can't see her anywhere. She obviously still has her suit going, but it's frustrating as all hell that I can't find her. I try the transponder, but she's turned it off again. I act like I know where she is, but I know that I'm doing a shitty job of it.

"I've put some dinner on for you. I've already had mine." It's like her voice comes from nowhere. I can hear her laugh softly.

"I'm by the big tree," she says.

"That's helpful. There's about fifty."

"See the felled log."

"Yeah."

"Look at the stump."

I squint. In the low light, its hard to see anything. After what felt like a minute or two, I finally see her thin lips. They are smiling, hovering just above the edge of the log. Her black eyes float just above them, twinkling. The rest of her is invisible. Just keeping her eyes and mouth in sight is taxing and so fucking annoying. I step forward slowly, not wanting to trip over her. When I think I'm clear of her, I plop down carelessly like I knew where she was the entire time. Her eyes and lips are so close that it gives my mind a rest.

"Your food is almost done."

"Thanks."

There's a long pause.

"If you don't take it out, it'll burn," she says.

"How long has it been there anyway?"

"Twenty minutes."

I push myself off the ground and lift up the dome. The surface of the foil is searing hot, so I pick up the package by the corner and chuck it down next to her.

"You should watch where you throw that."

"I knew where you were."

A grin is her only reply. It says bullshit. I don't answer. I sit down and start eating.

"I never thought you were going to get here," she says. "It was like an hour before I saw you."

"I pulled something."

"Hmmmm. I didn't see you limping."

"Yeah, well, it wasn't that bad. Slowed me down a lot, though. I was all tight."

"It slowed you more than a lot."

"Yeah, it did."

She smiles, pulls a book and light out, and starts reading.

Fucking bitch. I slap it out of her hand and I should have clocked her one too.

"What was that for?"

Feigned surprise. She knows exactly what that was for. "You think they won't notice a levitating book? They see that, and we're both fucked."

"And your screaming won't draw their attention over here? It echos for christsakes."

"Just put the book away."

"And do what? Just stare into the night."

"If that's what you need to do to entertain yourself."

She walks over and picks up the book again, fingering the pages to find where she's left off. "I'm going to read. If you have a problem with that, just don't look."

⇥•⟊•⟊•⟊•⇤

Julie hasn't moved in an hour. She's probably been asleep for awhile. I've been watching her. Although it's boring, it isn't hard to do when your gut aches since you've eaten too many of those bad memories again.

Whenever I get into these moods, I fixate on a time when I was nine years old on the playground. There's a sign above the door which a six year old can read. Through observation over the years, I've learned that the sign asks us to take off our shoes before entering the building. It looks like this to me:

Kidly Kinly Kibly Kimly Kinbly Kindly leaes leaves leave your shows sows sheos shoes poor boor roob odor door.

I still don't know what it means. The more I stare at the words, the more the characters are restless, changing positions, nearly vibrating. It takes me several hours to read a sentence. How the fuck am I expected to read a novel in three weeks?

That day, I decided I had enough bullshit. Oh, they tried to teach me how to overcome my learning disability, but I finally decided I wasn't going to fucking let them. It was their fucking problem if they didn't understand what I saw. Who needs any of that shit anyway?

When I surface from my thoughts, my eyes are adjusted to the dark of the grove. I get up and walk towards her. Julie's book is lying on the ground close to where she should be. It calls, like it always does. I want to go over there and pick it up. I want to be able to decipher its code right now. However, I don't. I've decided that between the covers only lies frustration followed by rage. That's the way it always has been and that's the way it always will be.

And why the fuck did *she* have to remind me of that? I was fine until she came back from whatever training they gave her. She must've learned to read there. She probably even knows the purpose of our runs. Who we're working for. I can deal with that. But, why did she have to kick my ass at the only thing I'm good at?

That's because she didn't. She must be fucking cheating or something. I worked hard at this for years while she was sitting on her ass and was reading books and shit. There's no goddamn, fucking way she went from being a lard ass to beating me twice in like three months flat.

I'm going to teach her a lesson. There's a story among runners that if you want to pull a prank on someone faster than you, use what I have in my hand. I bought one a very long time ago, but I've never had the need to use it. The device sorta looks like a pair of ear-bud headphones, but instead of speakers they are two electric plates. Without making any sound whatsoever, I cut two small holes in her hood, one above each ear, and slip the buds in. They're small enough so that she won't notice them brushing against her hair. However, what she will notice is the disorientation she feels when she pulls far enough away from me. The transponder will cease receiving a readable signal and the buds will yank a small current through her head. The worst thing that'll happen to her is she'll puke. At least, the dizziness will slow her down until I catch up.

It isn't cheating. It's getting even. She's the one whose cheating in the first place, and I have to resort to technology to level the playing field. It serves her fucking right.

⊹⊹┃⊹┃⊹┃⊹

When I wake up the next morning, she's gone or hiding.

From the look of the sky, it's about five in the morning. It's dawn, but there still isn't enough light coming through the trees to see anything. I try the transponder, but of course she's turned it off again. Julie's probably got an early jump on things and has taken off down the trail — not that she'll get too far.

I flip on the GIS and try to get a feel for where I am along the route. It looks like I'm about halfway. I'm about two or three mountains away before the drop-point. I chew on a granola bar for breakfast. There's no point in rushing. She hasn't gotten far, unless, of course, she's found the buds and turned them off.

Just to make sure, I send the output of the buds' transponder up on my contacts. This involves messing with the comp on the waist of my suit. The interface is kinda tricky and I'm not all that good with electronic stuff, but after a few minutes, I think I've got it sorted out. I flick the switch.

Immediately, it's obvious that she, or whoever has abducted her, hasn't found the buds yet. Her beacon comes up on the GIS with a nice, strong signal, and surprisingly very far off course. Then I notice that she's traveling at over ninety kilometers an hour.

She's in a truck or something.

Fuck! They took her. How's that possible? We were practically sleeping on top of each other. Maybe they picked up the signal from the second transponder I implanted on her last night? Maybe she ran this morning and fell ill when she got far enough away and they picked her up after that? Oh my fucking God. I got my sister killed. No, I don't know that yet. I need to get her back.

I take off into the woods without caring about pace. The whole day is like that. Running so fast I know that my lungs and legs should be hurting, but they're not. Knowing that I should eat or stop to drink some water, but I don't. Concentrating on the physical act of running calms the mind. There's just me and the pounding of my feet on the trail. I find comfort in the monotony of a constant stride. When I'm not thinking of Julie, I almost regain my own personal zen.

It's late afternoon by the time I get to where they've taken her. The car arrived here several hours ahead of me. I'm only able to get here so fast is because I'm not confined to roads, but I won't tell anyone that. It's important to screw with the competition's psyche and lead them to believe you're a machine without desire or need for rest.

Anyway, the building is a white, concrete block, surrounded on three sides by the same woods I've been running through all day. Out in front, is the service road which leads God knows where. I've been watching for a couple hours now. A bunch of trucks have come through the front gates. They're not given that thorough and inspection. It shouldn't be trouble at all for me.

It's dark outside, which I hope will make this easier. The only way in seems to be through the front gate. That wouldn't be so bad if it wasn't for the six or seven heavily armed guys patrolling every few minutes. I thought that these assholes we're trying to avoid were pretty low-tech? Then again, why would the boss throw all this technology at us if they were? They've got a simple checking procedure for trucks, which I figured out hours ago. Another one's coming by, and its time to put my clothes to use in the way I was trained to use them. I make sure my transponder is off and run towards the gate. I know I do this without making a sound.

The truck parks out in front and some of the guards there are inspecting it. I'm a few yards away, basically looking over their shoulder when they open the metal doors. After they finish checking out the load, they hop out of the back and I run towards them at full steam. They don't notice me as I weave around their shoulders. I slide between the doors as they close them. The crowd goes wild. I am simply the best at what I do. After the doors close, I let out a huge breath and lean against one of the barrels. The truck lurches forward.

The ride into the loading bay is no more than two hundred metres, but the drive in the dark feels like it takes forever. It gives me time to think, but there really isn't much to think about. I'm winging this one. I royally fucked up, and Julie has to pay for it. Fuck! They could've executed her by now! I'm just going to get my ass killed. Too late for those thoughts.

The hold doors flying open interrupt my mental castigation (For the record, I fully aware of what the word 'castigation' means, assholes.). I didn't even realize we had stopped. I make my way to the back corner of the truck as they start unloading with some sort of robotic arm. That's when I realize the truck is full of oil. Holy shit! There must be a million dollar's worth here. Where did they get that much? No wonder our guys are interested. When I feel my flat being lifted off the ground, I realize that I should have been paying attention to the roboarm instead of gawking at barrels of oil.

It's all moving so fast. I don't want to make a sound, but I know that I have to jump off. The hydraulics let out a loud hiss. I hop off, absorbing my impact against the metal floor by crouching. There's hardly a tink, but I hold my breath and wait. It sounds like the arm is going to continue working and I creep to the back corner of the truck again.

After the last flat is unloaded, the crew leaves the truck's hold open. Their chatter disappears behind some door somewhere. God, they're stupid. I let out a long breath and start toward the doors. There's nothing that I can do except get out and see what's there. It's not like I have any experience infiltrating places like this. I slip my invisible feet down to the concrete floor of the loading bay and push away from the back doors.

Before I have a chance to get a look at the place, all the lights turn off and an alarm begins to sound. I look down and my, once invisible, suit to see that it's flashing more bright colours than a discotheque. The Peltier devices have also started working overtime, making me feel like I'm standing in a broiler.

Maybe they're not so stupid after all. Evidently, these guys expect my type of intrusion.

I panic. There are voices calling from the hallway. I look around the room, but there are few places to hide. I need to get this goddamn thing off. An army is about to come through the doors with flashlights, so I strip faster than I have in my life and transfer my contacts' control caps to my fingers. I chuck the disco party into the back of the truck, shut the rear doors, and hide under its cabin. The doors into the rest of the building are a few feet away. They're in now. Flashlights sweep the room, looking behind the boxes and in the truck windows, and I know I need to get out of here. I make a break for the door. Even though I'm sprinting flat out, I do not make a sound. Fortunately, they haven't turned the lights back on. At least, I'll have darkness on my side while I take on this fucked-up, excessively-armed base solo and barefoot in my under shirt and boxers. I wouldn't want to give them too much of an advantage.

As I'm skulking (Yes, I know what that means too, assholes.) down the hallway, I remember the contacts. I flip them on and they haven't found the transponder yet. My sister is blinking like a Christmas tree in the ceiling. This is how I get to her so fast. I run up a few flights of stairs until I'm at the level she's at. Her dot's at the end of the hallway, and, fortunately, the door she's behind is open a crack. I slip inside the room and hide behind a couple of machines near the back. There's a couple of guys standing back onto me and I can see Julie through what I think is a one-way mirror. They've got her strapped into a chair and she has all this weird headgear on. She's fucking pissed. Tears are streaming down her face and she's screaming at them.

"I told you that I can't fucking read. I was just acting, okay? I don't know shit about any codebooks. Even if I had one, I couldn't fucking read it. Just take them all and stop fucking hurting me, all right?"

I'm embarrassed to say that my first thought is: *you fucking poseur*, but after what I put her through, I realize that it just isn't fair. Besides, thinking that sorta shit got us into this mess in the first place. I quiet my breathing and concentrate on how we're going to get us out of here. The two men ignore Julie's cries and examine her like she's some sort of experiment. I think that's a picture of her brain on the screen in front of them.

"Her language centres appear to be normal in response to the text. No activity there. I think she's telling the truth."

The second guy shakes his head. "I'm not satisfied. Other areas of her brain could be compensating. We should check here out fully before killing her, just in case we have this problem with other runners."

And that's when I make my move. It's not like I have a whole lot of time. Noise is beginning to come up through the floor and those guys are going to hear it soon. Besides, at this point, I really want to hurt the bastards. With surprise on my side, I wham their foreheads against the panel a couple of times. I'm not going to describe any of this part because it's fucking gross. Fortunately, I don't have to do it for long before both of the geeks are out cold. I head into the other room and begin working on Julie's straps.

It's not flattering, but the only way to describe Julie is that she looks like shit. She can barely keep her eyes open, she reeks of sweat, and she's shaking all over. However, I've never seen someone so happy to see me in my entire life.

"Eric? Is that you?"

"Yeah, it's me."

"Why are you in your underwear?"

"I didn't want too much of an advantage." Even though she's basically out of it, I swear she smirks. I begin to undo the buckles on her ankles. "The suits don't work here," I say. "They flash all these bright colours and shit. Don't turn yours on."

"You know how to get out of here?"

I do. After Julie's finished puking on my boots, we're in the hall. She's slow at first and is leaning heavy on me, but soon she's moving at a good pace, despite having the living shit kicked out of her all day. I'm paying so much attention to her that we get lost.

"You know where we're going?"

I'd better. "Yeah, I do. We gotta go this way"

We keep to the stairwells and dark hallways, but it's obvious the lights are back on full blast. Fuck! They figured out that I ditched the discotheque. If I wasn't freaking out before, I'm freaking out now. We pick up the pace. Somewhere from the recesses of my memory, I remember how to get to the loading bay. When we get there, it's all locked down because these guys aren't stupid. They're probably upstairs now, but they'll be back here in a moment.

Julie takes one of the fuel cells off her hip and starts fooling around with the connector.

"What are you doing?"

"Making a short. I need some wire."

I pull back her hood and tear out the buds. "Here."

She huffs. "No wonder I was puking my guts out."

"Just finish doing the short or whatever."

She ties the plates to weird places on the connectors and throws the whole thing against the door. We run to the other side of the room and I see why a few seconds later.

The cell goes off with a nice ball of flame and takes a chunk out of the door. We do what we do best: run through the hole and out to the fence. We clumsily scale the fence and are sprinting into the woods as fast as possible. Engines are turning over behind us. We're going to have a tail to lose in a few moments. A tail with a whole lot of guns. I'm embarrassed to say that despite being through hell, Julie is still kicking my ass.

"Hey, slow down. I can't keep up."

"Eric, they're going to kill us."

"We have to stay together. It's not like we have anyone else anymore."

She slows down and we run side by side. Honestly, it's not like she slowed too much.

Screw the ego. I'm going to just have to deal.

God, this recording is going to be so fucking embarrassing, but I'm going to describe everything that happened to us anyway.

→•I•I•I•←

"The clink you hear in the background is Julie and I chucking the transponder from her suit into the bush. We've just started running away from the device."

"Eric, who are you talking to? Hey, get that thing outa my face."

"It's a voice recorder."

"A what?"

"A voice recorder. It's not like either of us can write a note or something. It's the only way we can record our side of the story, if they find us and blow our brains out."

"So that's what you've been talking into all this time?"

"Yup."

"Well, just get that box out of my face."

"Not until you tell our lovely audience what is really going on."

"Eric, they fucked with the language centres of our brains. Made it so we couldn't read or write and couldn't understand the books we were carrying for them all these years. You know, Ron?"

"Yeah?"

"Well, he tipped them off. He thought I could read. Those were our guys back there."

"Thank you for putting that so concisely, Julie Francis. Now let's just hope someone finds this."

Click.

Rainmaker
Kim Goldberg

She had not intended to eat her keyboard
but no better option presented itself on the thirty-
    second
day of the longest dry spell
in the shire's history. Her consumptive act,
while not pre-meditated, was not entirely random
either. She had systematically deployed lesser tactics,
hammered out whole battalions of

r-a-i-n-w-a-t-e-r-f-l-o-o-d-t-i-d-e-s-t-s-u-n-a-m-i-s
o-l-d-t-e-s-t-a-m-e-n-t-d-e-l-u-g-e-s-o-c-e-a-n-s-p-e-w

only to watch them crumple
like unarmed soldiers, like tumbleweeds in heaving
dustbowls, leaving nothing but lime-colored
scum and two flies lining the floor of the shire's
well. It fell to her, the definer, to vanquish
the unbounded drought. While fingering
last night's chopstick, she began prying out the "o"
knowing this one was somehow at the root
of all the trouble — its exuberant circumference
    mocking
droplets and well holes and open mouths.

It went down easier than it let go, and she moved on
to the "w". By the time she got to the
punctuation, she discovered the merits of mango
chutney. Numbers were toasted with peanut

sauce, function keys floated in miso broth. When her

meal was complete she belched up the asterisk and
ampersand, shoved the skeletonized keypad back
under the desk and went for her after-dinner
ramble, having altogether forgotten
her societal mandate. But an imperceptible shift
in her gait, a whisper of alien fragrance, a glimpse of
seashells, gave her away. And the villagers
all scurried home to set out buckets and kettles
and washbasins.

The Azure Sky
Lisa Carreiro

I crept barefoot through the cold, dim Station. My breath puffed out in tiny clouds. I believed I saw moisture on the pocked steel walls although it was actually the uncanny sheen the low lighting cast. I believed, too, that I could hear the aging Station creak and moan, but I was unafraid. For the eerie artificial night when the others were asleep was the ideal time for theft.

I tiptoed into Marcia's memory bank and pilfered a thumb-sized gel, then scurried back to my bedchamber.

Memory gel works quickly. Instantly, sparks flared in my peripheral vision — stars, I thought, accompanied by bone-chilling cold and vertigo. Marcia — whom I became in the memory — walking in space to repair a satellite. That memory, though, quickly became a flight deck, metal and squared, where space loomed before me through a wide curved viewing pane set above an operations panel. Marcia's unrefined memories did that sometimes; images overlapped and sensations merged.

I saw Marcia's strong hands — now mine — capably key in coordinates, but that image blurred too and I suddenly fell. The stars I'd initially seen sped by me so quickly I knew I was falling through space. I grasped at air while I fought nausea, then the stars disappeared like an idea that slips away before you can fully realize it. My own steel-walled room was all that surrounded me.

"Marcia?" I whispered, still belly down on the floor. I tasted blood in my mouth where I'd bitten myself.

"If life was always as exciting as you wish it were, Riley, you would be dead." The Marcia Program had woken me and ended the memory, but it was human Marcia who spoke.

I knew better than to steal Marcia's raw memories. But the brief, refined ones I was permitted — a glimpse of azure terran sky or taste of freshly picked sweet berries — were so diluted they couldn't satisfy my craving for adventure.

"I was..." No point in lying. The Kuiper Belt's Marcia Station Program was omnipresent, and human Marcia learned what she needed to from her Program. In a symbiotic relationship, the Station sustained Marcia's ailing body while Marcia — or what was left of her — operated the Station. Marcia's memories ceased hours before she was nearly killed by pirates who'd stolen her vessel. A cerebral reburn had deleted that traumatic experience, and her memories resumed after her rehabilitation.

Marcia packaged thousands of her life's memories in gels, which, smeared on skin and absorbed, enabled anyone to experience them. She also stored her memories into chips used as training programs or games. The raw memories, those I preferred, had a disjointed and sometimes nightmarish quality to them. And even many of her finished memories were so intense, she had to dilute them. Marcia's packaged memories were of an exceptionally vivid quality, and were in high demand from those who passed through the Station.

Through most of my youth, Marcia Station provided respite to thousands of weary travelers bound for the Belt and beyond. As far back as I could remember, tourists, merchants, and scientists had filled its corridors. Regular visitors vied for my attention, brought me gifts from outstations, or captivated me with tales of other worlds, including the earth of my ancestors. By my fifteenth year, however, the steady stream of humanity had dwindled to a trickle. The new QLS ships didn't need to dock at Marcia Station.

⊹⊱⊱⊰⊰⊹

"The ships don't literally travel at quarter-light-speed. People come up with the most inane short forms." I sat cross-legged in a chair linked to Marcia's schooling program. "But a supply ship is coming. *Maman* says it will be the last large ship to dock here. Rijwik is on it, too."

"I know," Marcia said. "Did you read all the specs on QLS ships?"

I groaned aloud, although Marcia's lessons enthralled me. Enhanced by sensations from her memories, everything from quantum physics to an ancient tea ceremony were brought to life. But that day, I could think only of Rijwik. Terran-born, her life was so exciting, Marcia's adventures as a satellite engineer paled in comparison. That a supply ship was finally going to arrive was celebration enough; that my old pal Rijwik was also en route was double celebration. Within days my all-consuming boredom would be alleviated. I hoped to persuade Rijwik to remain on the Station until we moved to a busier outpost. On Rijwik's previous visit nearly a terran year earlier, she arrived bearing two fresh purplish scars across one cheek.

"Nasty boys," she said in response to my horrified stare. "Stole my last dry goods and tried to tap into my water bin. I said, 'You take the dry goods, but I keep the wet.'" She pointed to the scars, and winked wickedly. "They both look far, far worse than me. Their ship is barely fit for salvage. If anyone finds them floating outdoors," and she chuckled chillingly, "none of my goods will be with them." Rijwik leaned closer and whispered so that my mother wouldn't hear. "Perhaps a gaddfal will find them." Gaddfals, Rijwik told me, ate human remains. She even claimed she'd hunted gaddfals, although my grandfather said she was joking. No one in their right mind, he said, deliberately sought out gaddfals.

On that same visit, Rijwik beckoned me into her docked vessel tethered just outside the Station, the only place we could escape Marcia's omnipresent watch. We squatted among storage cubes and sacks, our feet in stirrups to keep us grounded in zero-G. Rijwik withdrew a tiny laser knife from a pocket in her vest.

"A few are born into the tribe of Rijwik, others are initiated." She flicked the wee laser beam on and grinned at me. Her graying hair floated slightly above her shoulders, lending her a Medusa-like quality. She pointed to a scarred symbol etched on her upper left arm, then pointed the tip of the knife at mine. "If you're going to be a pilot, you're going to have to be strong."

I held my arm out and drew a deep breath in. The knife stung, and my arm ached for a few days, but I was left with an impressive stylized scar. It was worth my mother's ensuing scolding. I stared at the scar in my mirror and imagined myself years older, disembarking from a vessel at some distant outstation, arms bared, flaunting the scar.

→•┼•┼•┼•←

"Looking for entertainment or education?" The Marcia Program had developed an acute sarcasm. I hissed at it, and resumed searching through Marcia's memories.

"What would keep you out of my memory bank?" human Marcia asked. "What could I design in exchange for your word that you'll never go in there without asking?"

I stared at the gels and chips arrayed on a shelf. I licked my lips and turned to the steel wall. "Gaddfal hunting," I said.

"Oh, if there are gods may they be sure to deal with the likes of Merchant Rijwik."

"It's my own idea, Marcia."

"Born from the cowboy dreams of herself."

"Could you create it?"

"I could. Why should I?"

"It will prepare me for an emergency. Gaddfals could attack us."

"Not so long as I operate this Station!" Marcia replied with uncharacteristic fury. She was silent for several seconds. "Why gaddfals?"

"I'd have to be at my best to catch one. Humans can't match them in battle." I kicked the wall for emphasis.

"Gaddfals *are* human."

I ignored the tone in Marcia's voice. The crumpled spot on the wall repaired itself. "But they can survive better than us. Gaddfals hardly feel the cold, they're not affected by radioactivity..."

"All living things are affected by radioactivity."

"I've heard they hibernate on long voyages, but at other times don't sleep at all. They eat dead humans they scavenge from wrecked ships."

"Riley, gaddfals say all those things, but no one has proved any of it to be true. And their claim to eat human remains is no doubt part of their self-propagated folklore. Gaddfals are a particularly nasty group of pirates. That is all. And that is bad enough."

The discussion was ended.

"Come visit me," Marcia said then with more characteristic warmth. "I have something for you."

Two glass doors slid open, one after the other, permitting me entry to Marcia's room. Seated, she had her back to the doorway, and turned cautiously as though she might break. Her arms rested inside clumsy oversized gloves. Wires ran from her temples and a flat metal plate that lay across her chest. Her body was skeletal and her skin colorless. Marcia's face was lined and bluish under eyes that still sparkled with intelligence and wit. Her short-cropped hair was gray and thinning. Flat photos decorated one wall: smiling family pictures, me as a toddler, a beach where bright sunlight reflected off of white sand. On a screen beside Marcia was an image she projected to strangers who came to visit: a robust, young Marcia. The projection was not used because of vanity on Marcia's part, but for the comfort of visitors. Most couldn't bear the sight of the real Marcia. Not in her last years.

"You're going to begin a new subject tomorrow," Marcia said in greeting, a hoarse whisper from a taut dry mouth. "I have a file of Mandarin lessons for you."

"Mandarin? That's hard."

"Your mother finds it difficult, but she has mastered several important phrases. You are adept at learning languages so you will not find it as difficult. The crews of the QLS ships are primarily Mandarin speaking. Of course they know Sol and Mars Standard, but it would be diplomatic to speak some Mandarin."

"The QLS ships aren't going to come here."

"No, Riley." Marcia licked dry lips with a papery tongue. "Wherever your family works next will serve QLS ships. Charon perhaps."

"You won't come."

Marcia smiled at me indulgently. "You know I can't. I have to run this little place. The creeper vessels still need a place to stop."

"All alone. You'll be bored."

"I've my compatriots at other Stations to swap tall tales with. Hugo is much more interesting since he merged with his Station."

Hugo had been dead since before I was born. He and Marcia used to drink together when they were young and whole.

I sat cross-legged at Marcia's feet. I couldn't lean on her anymore, not like when I was a small child. Marcia was in too much pain and human touch was nearly unbearable to her. The comfort was the same though, to sit beside her in the quiet Station. Listening to her breathing, to the hum of machines, the heartbeat of the Station. Occasionally to glimpse up at the still image of a healthier Marcia on the screen, waiting for whenever she would need to project it.

"Even if we weren't going to Charon I'd leave soon. The closest pilot training's in the Proteus colonies," I said.

"I'll create some flight training programs for you."

"Give me your training memories."

She shook her head. "Not worth your time practicing on those. That technology's ancient. Dinosaurs still roamed the earth then."

"They must be more exciting than those blighted holos I have."

Marcia wordlessly handed me a gel, which I eagerly smeared on my temples and hands. A blue dot appeared and blossomed into a pinwheel of colors: blue spun into a sky, green a sea, yellow into people dressed in vivid colors. White sands stretched out on either side of me. Salt water rolled across my bare feet.

The sea skimmer that appeared could hold at least three people, certainly Marcia and her two brothers, who eagerly clambered into it. Marcia held the sides of the skimmer with a comfort borne of years of similar rides. Her fingers — mine — nestled easily within grooves near the skimmer's prow where I knelt. The green sea stretched before me. The skimmer rode the waves, rising up until the prow seemed airborne, then fell from the azure sky into the green sea. My stomach too rose and fell. Water slapped the skimmer's sides; saline spray moistened my hair. Overhead, the hot midday sun disappeared behind huge clouds; thunderheads. The waves grew wilder; the strengthening wind blew water across us until we were soaked. We bailed water with bare hands and called to each other in panicked voices until an enormous wave rolled over the skimmer and capsized it. I tasted salt water, felt my stomach heave as I rolled under the wave and up again. I grasped the edges of the overturned skimmer and sought my brothers through the gray downpour.

Marcia woke me.

"I wasn't ready to stop," I said, gasping for breath and spitting out water that existed only in the memory. The nausea would soon have been more than I could bear, though. The dried gel flaked off my skin and I scrubbed at it. Even in its dormant form, it sparked with memory.

"You forgot to breathe," Marcia said. "You beg for wild memories, but you haven't mastered the concentration you need for the intense ones. The memory becomes your reality, and you are unable to escape." Marcia was momentarily silent. "One of my brothers fell overboard."

"Did you rescue him?"

"No, Riley. He drowned."

>+I+I+I+<

Another too-quiet night when I couldn't sleep, I headed for Marcia's memory bank. As I snuck past her doors, I saw that someone was projecting into her room. Rijwik. Her projected image could only "see" a meter or two around her and Marcia had her back to me, so neither woman noticed me peering in through the glass.

Rijwik's projection itself didn't concern me. When we were asleep, she often recorded a message for us to see on awakening. But for Rijwik to project into Marcia's room was unusual. Their cool indifference to one another had been apparent to me for years.

I watched them. Rijwik gestured with wide sweeps of her arms and rapid hand movements. Her expression was earnest. One of Marcia's thin arms slowly rose and fell, a languid mirror image to Rijwik's frantic gestures. Rijwik's projection faltered, disappeared, then reappeared. I leaned against the glass to try to hear the conversation. I could discern Rijwik's voice, but not the quieter Marcia's. The Marcia Program startled me, whispering, "Go to your room now. The cold is aggravating you."

Not the cold. The sight of Rijwik in Marcia's room, flickering as if she were unable to project.

The Marcia Program was trying to block Rijwik's projection while human Marcia weakly gestured her away. When Rijwik's projected image finally dissipated, Marcia's gloved arm lay limp at one side of her chair. I exhaled, not realizing I'd been holding my breath, and returned to my room.

>+I+I+I+<

Hours before the supply ship finally docked, I slathered stolen gel on so thickly that Marcia wouldn't be able to easily wake me if — when — she found out I was again pilfering her memories.

I saw a flight deck again. The operations center dominated the view. Bulky material was stowed along the ceiling, and pipes and wiring ran liberally along walls and floors. Handles lined the sides. The vessel moved through space slowly but perceptibly. A disembodied voice called for help, identifying himself as a refugee.

Delight and terror coursed through me. Marcia *was* creating a gaddfal hunting program, and the refugee's disembodied voice added to its realism. I nearly jumped when I heard a second voice within the program reply: Marcia. The refugee spoke poor Mars Standard and I could barely understand him, but Marcia's reply was clear. She gave him coordinates to her ship.

I focused on the text that crawled by one corner of my eye: Marcia's heart rate and temperature, as well as environmental indicators. The text was disconcerting, but my grandfather had told me people became accustomed to it.

The radio voice crackled, still sputtering bad Mars Standard. Marcia reassured him that her vessel was secure, but emphasized the urgency, repeating, "You have to hurry," in both French and Mars Standard.

She rose from the operations center and floated the length of the chamber and through a door. The shiny metal walls reflected Marcia, and I looked right at her as if looking at my own reflection. Tall, in her late thirties, wearing a blue-gray one-piece suit with a black thermal vest and knee-high black boots. A glimpse of Marcia's face: intense fear in dark eyes, wisps of short black curly hair, olive skin flushed by her panic, so unlike the wan visage I was familiar with.

Marcia spoke into a panel. Mars Standard, heavily accented with the vowels of her native terran language. A previously unseen door slid open. She reached in, grabbed a piece of material, and shook it open.

A survival suit. A human could survive for days if she connected its lifeline tether to a vessel. Marcia donned the suit, and checked its functions. I read the text in my eye: heart rate normal, vessel's temperature fifteen degrees Celsius.

Marcia sealed herself inside a clear booth. Her voice jarred me: "Okay, you may enter on my GO." She pressed three buttons that after a few minutes slowly opened a portal to the vessel's exterior.

Oh gods! I saw space as I could only glimpse it through the too few windows of the Station. My heart beat harder. Marcia Station had such a vast system of airlocks and chambers that it would take deliberate and concerted effort to be pushed into the void. But on Marcia's little vessel, only the door of that booth stood between her and the outdoors. A tiny craft that looked as though it couldn't hold anybody squeezed in through the open portal. I felt Marcia's vessel shift slightly when the small craft set down. Three or four minutes ticked by after the portal had shut completely before Marcia exited the booth.

"Remain inside your craft," she told the refugee. "Emergency Solar Regulation sixty-two. When I cue you, you may leave your craft, but remain in this chamber until we arrive at Sat Base Ten."

Marcia returned to the flight deck before she allowed the refugee to exit. Overhead, one corner of the screen showed an image of the chamber she'd left him in.

I was shocked to see two people emerge from the craft. Their backs were to the screen. Marcia touched the image to enlarge it. The pair donned some kind of suits. *Perhaps*, I thought, *they also have survival suits. That would be sensible.* But Marcia hooked her radio set over one ear and spoke in urgent whispers.

"Sat Ten. *M'aidez*. Refuge seekers are pirates."

I was startled to hear a blurred reply in my ear. The two spoke for several minutes, but when Marcia looked up at the screen, the pirates were no longer in the chamber. She jumped so suddenly that I myself fell on the floor. Marcia gasped an explanation into her radio and sealed the doorway to the flight deck. She pulled her suit's hood up and locked the faceplate, then floated to the ceiling over the operations center. There, she reached overhead, pried open a panel, and hauled herself into a crawlspace so tiny that I could hardly breathe. She replaced the panel and, belly a few centimeters above the floor, floated through the narrow space. Her heart rate was too rapid, and her breathing was shallow — as was mine. I could no longer see my own room, only that crawlspace.

Marcia wriggled through the confined area avoiding wires and plates of chips. The text in my eye alerted me that the temperature on the vessel had dropped to ten Celsius.

When she reached the end of the crawlspace, Marcia kicked her strong legs upward until a wire-covered panel was ajar.

"Sat Ten, do you have a lock on me yet?" Marcia's whisper was breathless, and I spoke the words even as she did.

"You're spinning," the voice replied. "We can't find you."

Marcia floated into another chamber and tried to grasp a ledge. She slipped, and hit her head with such force my own teeth gnashed together. I muffled a cry as she bounced off the wall, and flipped in a languid mid-air somersault before she was able to grasp the ledge properly. My stomach heaved in protest. She reached awkwardly over her head to open a hatch and climb through, sealing it behind her. The space was so dark I could not see anything, but felt us press the keys of a pad, and then heard the sibilant shushing of another hatch opening.

I gasped: space loomed just beyond the small hatch.

Marcia tethered herself to the vessel's exterior. She grasped handles and hauled herself out, braced her feet in grips, shut the hatch, and clung to the handles.

Above her, space, terrifying and breathtaking; like nothing I would see again until I became a pilot myself. That day vertigo knocked me to the floor a second time: Marcia's vessel falling, blue and white stars rushing by overhead.

I could discern slight whispering in my ear, and Marcia's familiar voice, tinged with urgency, reply. "*M'aidez*. Pirates. One and one-hundred-forty from Sat Base Ten. *M'aidez*."

Overhead, the stars suddenly sped faster and Marcia's arms flailed. She had fallen off the vessel; no, she was being dragged back into it. I saw her booted foot kick, but one unarmed engineer was no match for two well-armed pirates. Marcia was pulled into the vessel roughly and dragged back to the vessel's main chamber.

The two began to shout in Sol Standard. Liberally cluttered with vile epithets and threats of torture, the two demanded that Marcia pilot them to Aurial Colony, a gaddfal outpost. She refused.

On my floor, able to taste real blood in my mouth, I was weeping.

One of them kicked Marcia viciously several times, and shouted, in far better Mars Standard than he had spoken earlier, that they would gladly take what they could as scrap. The second banged Marcia's head against the wall and I felt the pain too. Marcia's memory faded to a blackness; only then could I see, finally, my own room as a ghostly backdrop to her memory. My hands were shaking as I tried to rise from the floor when Marcia's unconsciousness flared into a shimmering brightness. For a moment, I saw exactly what Marcia saw after she had slipped out of consciousness: an azure sky, incomprehensibly beautiful. Bright hot sun high overhead. The sun-kissed beach of her childhood, white sunlight glinting off sand. Marcia attempted to stand up and run as she did in her youth, her toughened bare feet kicking up hot sand. Two dream-like figures, her brothers, cajoled her to follow them into the rolling waves. The sun was so hot, but she was so cold.

Marcia snapped into awareness. The vessel's temperature was below freezing, the oxygen dangerously low. Marcia lifted her head and saw one of the pirates take off her mask to wipe away perspiration.

Marcia and I looked into the face of Rijwik.

Oh gods. My beloved Rijwik, who tugged the mask back on when Marcia saw her. A glimpse only, but enough to recognize Marcia's torturer. I tore the gel from my face, my fingernails scraping skin with the effort. The memory shattered; the taste of blood and smell of fear lingered in my room even after the last of the image had dissipated.

I knew the rest of Marcia's story. Three days later a fellow engineer found her drifting through space, tethered to the remains of her vessel, much of which had been taken by the gaddfals. Marcia had been tortured and left to die.

Silent drifting through cold dark space. Stars barely pinpricks of blue light through black. Cold colder than humanity was meant to know. Marcia never forgot. Mood enhancers and cerebral reburns could not change what Marcia remembered. Marcia was a master at subduing pain and controlling her emotions. She had work to do. She had that damned Station, her pitiful pension, to operate.

I could not control my sobbing. I entered Marcia's room and fell at her feet unable to speak. Marcia's left hand withdrew from her glove, drew my head to her knee, and stroked my hair.

"What can we do? She'll be here soon," I said when I could finally speak.

"Nothing, Riley." Marcia's human voice didn't quaver. "When she is here, you will act as though you know nothing."

"But..."

"Nothing." A whisper. "Not to your mother nor grandfather, either."

⋗⊹⊹⊹⋖

Rijwik knelt down to embrace me as if I were still small. "C'mere and stand beside me, you must be as tall as me now."

My cheeks burned and I could not speak. My mother mumbled something about my moodiness and the Station closing, then frowned a warning at me to be civil.

Rijwik winked at me, but her brow was furrowed. "Oh, Charon will be an adventure after this box! When you get there, I'll procure a proper survival suit for you, and we'll race across the surface. What d'ya say, child?"

"Impossible." I choked the word out.

Rijwik blinked, chuckled, and tried to wrap a bare arm around my neck, but I slipped away from her and grunted. She wore, typically, a sleeveless vest even though the Station's artificial-night temperature was freezing.

"Aren't your arms cold?" I stared directly into her ice blue eyes.

"Terra has many frosty zones. My mother would toss us into a snowbank when we were mere babes, and if we crawled home, she kept us." Punctuated with her characteristic wink and manic laughter.

"Marcia needs to see you," my mother interrupted, speaking to Rijwik. "She has a program you requested. Take her to Marcia, Riley." My mother, still believing I wanted to spend time with Rijwik and attributing my sullen demeanor to the pending move, gave me a not-too-gentle shove to accompany her order.

Rijwik shrugged, and clapped me on the back. I shied away from her once-loved touch and led her to Marcia's room. There, Rijwik belied not a hint of regret or concern.

"Here's that program you wanted," Marcia said, holding out a packaged chip. I stared into her eyes to try to detect hidden rage or fear, but she was characteristically placid.

Rijwik took the chip and stuffed it into a vest pocket. "Good. I'll run it later," she said and left the room without another glance at Marcia. "Come, child," she called back to me. "I was in the Uranus colonies. You'll never believe what I did there..."

I glanced back at Marcia as I left her room. Marcia winked wickedly.

⋆⊱┈┈⊱⋆

I managed to avoid Rijwik during most of her stay by helping a tech on the supply ship run maintenance program checks. But my mother's command to see Rijwik off left no room to argue. Someone had to stand by the docking area to supervise the ship's departure, a task I had in the past happily done. It would be quick. The ship's crew had already boarded, and was waiting impatiently for Rijwik.

She tossed her bulky bag into the chute to the ship. "That damned boring crew," she muttered, not for the first time. "You're sure you don't want to come along?" She entered the adjoining chamber where I stood. "We can drop you at Charon in a few months."

I shook my head wordlessly.

"It's your chance to escape this coffin early." Her ice blue eyes met mine. "Tell me girl, have you forgotten you're of the tribe of Rijwik?" Her fingers traced my now-detested scar and I jumped back. Rijwik grinned, slipped a hand into her vest pocket, and withdrew the chip that Marcia had given her. She held it up, waving it near my face.

"Aye, child, you hate me now." She clasped a freezing hand on my arm and held it so tight it would leave a bruise. "And just whose genetic material do you think your *Maman* used when she made you, eh girl? Marcia's?"

I sputtered, trying to speak.

Rijwik loosed her grip and stepped back. "Your *Maman* needed a strong child for this environment. A regular human can't possibly survive the conditions we'll meet if we're ever to move beyond this system."

"Marcia survived." I whispered for fear I would scream.

"You call that survival? Stupid girl! Survival belongs to the likes of you — bare footed, bare armed, near to six foot tall and still growing at fifteen! Your future is out there," and Rijwik pointed past the portal of the docking area, "beyond this system. The old human species is stagnant!" She lifted up the chip, held it briefly high enough that it caught the light. Its enclosed memory seemed to wink at me in the glint. Marcia's memory. Rijwik popped the chip into her mouth and swallowed it. "Like it or not, you're a member of the tribe of Rijwik — of the tribe of gaddfal. And sooner or later you'll have to accept that."

She cupped one strong hand under my chin, something she'd done when I was a toddler. Her touch was gentle. Briefly, I saw my mentor and friend — the woman who'd carried me on her shoulders, told me outrageous stories, and fueled my desire to become a pilot. But just as quickly, that awful moment in Marcia's memory returned to me as vividly as my own: Rijwik wiping perspiration from her face.

I furiously slapped her hand away and stepped back.

Without another word, Rijwik turned and stepped into the chute to the ship. The partition slid shut and I slid slowly to the floor, my last meal rising in my throat.

❖❖❖❖❖

I returned to Marcia Station only after I'd earned my higher ranking Sol pilot, entry into the pilots' guild, and the two silver wings I wore on the sleeve of my blue uniform. The wings sat directly over where the scar had been.

"Marcia," I whispered into the dim corridor after I disembarked. Lights flickered and brightened.

"Riley." The Station spoke as I walked. "I am very proud of you. Where are you going next?"

"Pado Six Station."

"Ah, Pado Stations are good... nearly as good as we are."

I chuckled, and Marcia too, laughed her rare, lilting laugh. I strolled the familiar corridors, lights brightening ahead of me and dimming behind me. As I neared Marcia's room, her projected image appeared in front of me. Instead of her youthful whole self, however, she projected the Marcia I'd grown up with and loved; the woman who'd helped raise me, seated in her chair, wires in her temples and the plate across her chest. I wanted to hug the projection. Ahead, the lights brightened.

"Riley, I'm glad you're here. I need a few favors from you." Marcia slipped her thin gnarled hands from her gloves and stood up.

"Marcia?"

"Sit down," Marcia said. "I have so much to tell you."

I squatted on the floor with my back against the steel wall. Marcia's image squatted in front of me and clasped my arms with her phantom-like projected hands. I knew suddenly what she had to tell me, and I choked back tears.

→‖◦‖◦‖←

The glass doors slid open. The room's temperature was well below freezing. In spite of what Marcia had said though, I still expected her to turn in her chair and grin at me, but when I reached her, her cold body was slumped over.

I stroked her hair, and wept. "How long ago?"

"Several months." Her projection was standing behind me, so I turned to face it.

"But we've spoken so often. Merchants have been here and... and talked to you. They stop at Charon, and tell *Maman* that they saw you."

"I knew you'd come as soon as you received your second wings. If I'd told you at the time, you'd have interrupted important training."

"This is more impor..."

"No, Riley. It didn't matter. All I did... all that body did," and she pointed at her cold corpse, "was sleep. I am here now."

"But sometimes the merge isn't permanent. You might have... disappeared before I got here."

"But I didn't. I seem to have an exceptionally vivid consciousness. We all do, all of us who run these Stations. We have to. That's why so many of us merge when our bodies die."

"I shall have to break it to *Maman*."

Marcia nodded. "Riley, I've started the oven for my cremation. And I need your help to distribute my belongings. But I have another favor to ask of you."

"Anything, Marcia."

❖❖❖❖

A public, bloody battle among a group of gaddfals on Aurial Colony made news regularly. Among its victims was Rijwik, whose face appeared on a broadcast I stopped to watch while preparing to reboard my ship. She had been tossed into the void without protection. She had, apparently, lived for nearly six minutes.

I am sometimes haunted by the echo of Rijwik in my aging face. But a gaddfal I am not. The stagnant old humans did edge out beyond the known system. I, however, stayed within its limits, venturing only a little farther out than my childhood home in the Kuiper Belt. And wherever I flew, Marcia accompanied me to all the places she should have gone — her cremains in a small ornate box I kept beside me on my craft. And a little bit of her consciousness in a minute chip I wore like jewelry on one ear.

"Everywhere," she had said, "every steel station, every stone moon, whether beyond the Belt or back to the Saturns." I had nodded, crying too hard to properly speak, wet childish tears falling on my blue uniform.

"Everywhere," I had promised. "You will not leave my side."

"I knew you'd agree. But there's more. It may be many years away, but a woman who could so deftly steal my memories can manage this small crime."

❖❦❖❦❖

In my sixtieth year, I finally visited earth. And with me came Marcia, as I'd taken her to every other place I'd gone.

My bare feet, accustomed to chilly steel floors, burned on the hot sands at the beach of her childhood. The bright sunlight brought tears to my eyes.

In my pocket, I carried Marcia's cremains. I squatted at the shoreline and waved my hand in the cold water. After a surreptitious glance around, I discreetly poured Marcia's cremains out through a tube that ran from my pocket to my ankle. The coarse gray and black mixture blended into the fine white sand. Standing up, I stirred the cremains well into the sand with my bare toe. Within minutes, a wave rolled across my feet, and swirled the displaced sand and cremains. I snapped the chip open, imagined I saw a brief spark as Marcia's consciousness dissipated.

I squinted up at the dazzling azure sky. I could not see Marcia Station as I sometimes did when piloting near the Belt. But when evening fell I stared up at the first stars, and knew Marcia looked back at me enjoying the feel of the sand between my bare toes.

"You survived, Marcia," I whispered.

Persephone's Library
Khria Deefholts

This morning, I walked up past the new subdivision to the end of the world. Or at least, to the beginning of the end, just at the edge of the mud flats.

It's deceptive, when you stand there, where the asphalt breaks off in that jaggedy line and the flats begin. They look like they spread out forever, but actually, it's just a couple of hundred yards. And then the world ends.

They've set up patrols along the edge at night, so people don't wander out there accidentally and fall off. They also try to catch the jumpers when they can, but they don't always succeed. People still slip through.

Take this morning, for instance. I mean maybe I just got lucky, but there was no-one in sight when I walked up. Even the watchers in the houses along the edge weren't around. I could've just kept right on going and maybe even jumped if I wanted to.

But I didn't. I just wanted to see the flats.

They look a little like I imagine a beach must have looked, back in the day, except of course there would have been ocean, instead of nothing.

→⊹⊹⊹←

I remember reading about beaches. Seph showed me a book.

She said, "They don't want us to remember the beaches. But I remember. I remember walking on the pebbles and they'd poke into the bottoms of my feet. It kind of tickled-hurt."

She closed her eyes as she spoke, wrinkling her nose and grinning, her shoulders pulling up and her bare feet curling as if her body were experiencing the sensation all over again.

"And the water would creep up over my toes, all cold and slithery. And the waves would growl and roar and sing to me." She glanced over at me, her eyes the colour of cocoa, her freckles dark brown against the pallor of her skin. "But the ocean wasn't the end of the world. It was the beginning of a different world."

"I suppose." I looked down at the picture on the cover of the beaches book. A small brown rock outcropping, with a wave smashing against it and spraying water everywhere.

"No, Mina, this is important." She frowned at me. "It wasn't the end of the world."

I looked at her. "So what — you're saying the world doesn't really end at the mud flats?"

"They want us to believe it does."

I rolled my eyes. "Because we're dying, Seph. Our numbers are dwindling every day and you know it. If we keep losing people like this, we're not going to survive."

"Our numbers are dwindling because people are getting sick of hanging out here, living under the thumb of the Führer and his thought police."

Seph was always using crazy words like that. She was a history buff.

We used to go out to her library, which was actually a stash of about twenty or so books — the ones she had been able to save. We had to go out, past the pond and into the forest to get there.

She tied them in plastic bags—" I never thought I'd say this, but thank God plastic doesn't biodegrade "—and a piece of heavy, camouflage-patterned tarpaulin she had managed to scrounge from somewhere, then hid them behind a particular clump of bushes. So far, no-one had found them. But then, people didn't really go into the forest much anymore. Not since they found the body.

"You really should show your father more respect." I looked over at her, where she sat, peering at her assortment of books.

She shrugged. "I'll show him respect if and when he actually earns it."

✦•I•I•I•✦

In Seph's eyes, it was her dad's fault that she got marooned here in the first place — her word, not mine.

He convinced the courts — this was back in the old system — that her mother was unfit. And so she had to leave her mother and the beach and the ocean and come live here.

She hated it at the time, and then when we became the Chosen Few, she hated it even more. I never understood her rage — just like I never understood why she couldn't just accept the facts: we were all that was left of the world.

Her father — Teacher John — was right. He had to be, because nothing else made sense. Maybe we wouldn't have believed it before, but how else to explain why the rest of the world had just broken off and fallen down, deep down and away, before smashing into tiny pieces like a crystal vase?

God had punished the others because of all the corruption that had seeped into the lives of man through the centuries. Our little tiny outpost was all that was left of His second chance. Those who were unworthy became jumpers, unmourned, unacknowledged and unnamed. They jumped off and fell and shattered on the remains of the world.

And the rest of us... well, Teacher John rightly pointed out that we'd have to play our cards very carefully if we didn't want to lose our second chance.

"For now, God's letting us settle in," he'd say. "We're still adjusting to the new state of things, and He's allowing for that." Teacher John never hesitated to remind us, though, that we had to start looking to the future and "get our act together."

And we believed him. Everyone, except Seph.

"It's all a load of bullshit." She shifted her position, lying back on the mossy ground between the ferns and squinting up at the leaves and sky above.

"Seph, we're floating in the middle of a vasty nothingness. It's just empty, past the flats, or hadn't you noticed?"

"There's something out there, Mina. It's like the ocean. But the Führer has everyone brainwashed and so no-one dares take that step into the unknown. Well, except for the jumpers."

"Maybe the ocean was another world, Seph, but as I recall, if you went into it, you drowned."

She gave me an impatient look. "It's a metaphor, Mina. Maybe the parallel isn't completely accurate."

"Besides, the jumpers go there, and that's the last we see of them."

"Why the fuck would they come back here? They've escaped. Of course they're gonna say 'hell with them' and get on with their lives."

"My dad would have come back if he could have, Seph. He promised."

"Shit. I forgot. I'm sorry, Mina."

A pause. I looked down at my hands. They were balled into tight fists, the knuckles poking out like pebbles on a beach.

I swallowed. "If you're so sure there's something out there, why don't you just go?"

She gave me a brooding look, but didn't answer my question. Instead, she rolled over to look at her books, her head propped up with one hand.

Reaching out, she picked up a battered paperback and hefted it. It was called *Passion's Slave* and had a painting of a man and a woman wearing wispy clothes that fluttered in the breeze as they held each other close. The woman's head was thrown back, while the man's tilted towards her amply displayed cleavage.

"I wonder if I'll be able to sneak out some tape for this one," she murmured, sitting up so she could take a closer look at the spine. With the tip of her index finger, she pressed the peeling paper into place.

When she lifted her finger, it curled back up.

She glanced over at me. "If nothing else, I'd hate him for what he did to the books."

I wouldn't be surprised if Seph had her entire library memorized. All twenty-two books.

As for me, I've never been much of a reader.

I stood up. "I have to go. There's a meeting tonight, so we're having an early dinner."

"See ya." She had returned her attention to her books.

"Are you gonna be there this time, Seph?"

She shrugged. "We'll see."

Teacher John had been furious the last time she had missed a meeting. I didn't see her for a few days after that, and when I did, she looked strangely fragile, her movements stiff and her eyes sunken. I'd walk out to the forest every afternoon, but she didn't return to our spot for almost a week.

Now, I swallowed, remembering that. "Come to the meeting, Seph. What'll it hurt?"

She gave me a pitying look. "That's a really good question, Mina."

☙❧☙❧☙

That evening, it was standing room only. I even saw Kendra's mom there — and she almost never came out to the meetings. Teacher John or one of his helpers usually visited her at her house.

I suspected, when I saw her, that the meeting had to be pretty important. When I glanced at the entrance to the gym to see Seph slipping in at the back, her lanky body all angled and tense, I knew.

There was something going down — something big.

"I'm just gonna say hi to Seph," I told mom in an undertone. She nodded, her attention fixed on the stage. Teacher John had just arrived, and he was conferring with his helpers and protégés on the sidelines.

I walked to the back, where Seph was standing.

"You made it." I grinned at her.

She shrugged. "In a manner of speaking." She paused. "We shouldn't be talking like this."

I shook my head. She never wanted us to be seen together, like somehow being friends with her was a big crime or something.

"I'm serious, Mina. He might see us."

"Your dad is what's kept us from self-destructing, Seph." It was true. In the months after everything disappeared, it was chaos. Teacher John and his helpers were the ones who brought order back and helped us make sense of what had happened — why the world had disappeared, but the lights still worked, the toilets still flushed and supplies appeared in the loading docks at the grocery stores.

Sometimes we'd get a few wonky shipments — one time, we got a whole flat full of plush purple toy elephants instead of eggs and bread. That was when the rationing began — and everything actually worked out very well. We were never overstocked with food, but neither was anyone going hungry, and the rations meant that we were never too short, even when there was the occasional glitch in the mysterious supply chain.

Teacher John was right — the only thing that made sense was that God was providing for us. He had given us a second chance and we'd best not fuck it up. Given that, I could almost see why Teacher John was so hard on Seph sometimes — it wasn't just a matter of having a wayward daughter. The entire future of humanity — what little was left of us — was at stake.

I cleared my throat. "I think he's acting for our best interests."

She looked at me, one brow raised.

"No, really."

She swallowed. "Just go sit back down with your mom."

But it was too late. Anvil Dempsey was already introducing Teacher John.

"Shit," she muttered, glancing around. "Look, just—" She pulled me closer so that I was standing behind Trent Norton and Anders Lavine.

"Great. Now I can't see the stage," I whispered as everyone started applauding.

"And he can't see you."

The speech was beginning. I peeked around Trent's shoulder.

"Thank you all for coming tonight." A pause, as Teacher John allowed the audience to settle and his expression turned grim. "We have lost many in these past six months. Friends, husbands, children."

He spoke at some length of all the setbacks we had suffered. He reminded us of all the crazy things we had tried, back at the beginning — and of how many good people we lost in the process. Like my dad.

⋇⊹⋇⊹⋇

"If I can come back, I will." That's what Dad had promised mom and me. But he hadn't come back.

This was still in the early times, before Teacher John had any of his visions, and so we hadn't known what was going on. Because of that, Dad wasn't considered a jumper. We were still allowed to talk about him — to name him — because he had sacrificed himself to help us better understand what had happened. He was a hero.

Frankly, I'd rather have had my dad back than be the daughter of a hero. Maybe then mom wouldn't sit around all day staring at nothing and then start crying for no reason.

At any rate, after that, they had tried other things, including lowering people slowly, on a rope, the way mountain climbers used to do it. But not long after the volunteer disappeared from sight into the surrounding nothingness, the rope would go slack and the person would be gone.

Then the visions started coming, and Teacher John was able to tell us the truth about what had happened. We were the lucky ones. The Chosen Ones. The final hope for humanity.

⋇⊹⋇⊹⋇

"The Great One has not seen fit to gift me with the vision of what is to come, should we win back our redemption. That is for Him to know and us to learn. He has only shown me what is now, and why it is. He has shown me what we must do, if we are to survive. We must be patient. We must be faithful and good." Pause. "And we must do whatever is necessary to rebuild our numbers, for did he not say, 'be fruitful and multiply?' And so we must do just that."

Seph threw me a look.

I knew she didn't believe a word of it — which always puzzled me. It just seemed pure stubbornness on her part.

After all, how else could it be, but as Teacher John said? I asked her about that once. She said, "The reason we still have an infrastructure is because there's something else out there. That's what I keep saying. It looks like nothing, but it isn't. We're still on the grid, somehow. I'd think that should be obvious."

"So it's all some big conspiracy theory?"

She thrust out her chin. "Why not? What better a way to control people than to make them believe that they're God's chosen? That they'll only get their second chance if they play their cards right?"

"And why go to such trouble? Didn't you tell me something about the simplest explanation often being the one that fits? I mean, it seems to me you're jumping through hoops to make this complicated theory of yours fly. You may not like the idea, but maybe God really did do all this. It's simple and it makes sense."

She shook her head. "It's nonsensical superstition. Back in the old days, before science, I suppose it was forgivable to believe that the gods were behind all the things we couldn't explain. It was easier to say the gods started a storm because they were annoyed, than to investigate meteorology and figure out why clouds move the way they do."

"Yeah, but maybe meteorology was just the scientists' way of naming their own gods."

"Holy motherfucker!"

Seph's explosive mutter brought me back to the moment.

"What?"

"Weren't you even listening?"

"I was thinking about something else."

She closed her eyes. "Sometimes, I almost hope there is a God, Mina — otherwise, you've really got no damn hope in hell."

"Yeah, thanks. So what did he just say?"

We were getting nasty looks from the people standing around us.

She shook her head. "I'll tell you later."

>•I•I•I•<

I didn't get a chance to ask about it that night. When I rejoined my mom, she didn't seem in the mood to discuss whatever Teacher John had been talking about. She had that distant, misty look she gets when she starts brooding about dad. I wondered how much of the speech she actually heard.

Seph was waiting for me the next day, in the forest.

When she saw me coming, she started singing, to the tune of "here we go 'round the mulberry bush", "'This is the way the world ends, the world ends, the world ends. This is the way the world ends, not with a bang but a whimper.'"

Her eyes glittered with a feverish light as she sang, yet she seemed in high spirits.

I returned her grin, choosing to ignore the febrile intensity of her gaze. "What are you going on about?"

Her smile widened. "It's a poem. I can't remember most of it — though I wish I could. That's just the final bit. How it ends. 'Not with a bang, but a whimper.'" She laughed. "Not bad, hey?"

"Sounds kind of stupid to me."

She tilted her head, still grinning oddly. "Did it ever occur to you, Miss I-believe-in-our-mission-from-God that this might actually be Hell that we're in? That this isn't a second chance, but a closed circuit, like in the play?"

She looked paler than usual — her dark brown freckles stark and somehow disturbing. Her eyes were raw and bruised-looking, as if she hadn't slept much that night.

I sighed, feeling a twinge of worry. "I never know what you're talking about half the time."

"That's probably not a bad thing."

"So you think we're in a play, now? Or Hell?"

She shook her head. "Naw. I'm going with the rats in a maze theory. I'm sure there are scientists watching us even as we speak, and making notes about our behaviour patterns. And if we leave and find out about the experiment, they can't let us back in or we'd mess things up royally." A pause. "So what do you think of that?"

"Cuckoo," I said, pointing at my head and she laughed.

"Yeah, maybe. I'm starting to wonder, actually." Then, she grew serious. "I don't think we should hang out together anymore, Mina."

"But there's nothing else to do!"

"Dad's starting to take an interest, God forbid. He's noticed that we're friends. He's noticed you. I don't want him—" she broke off.

"What? What don't you want him doing?"

She was silent, staring into the distance. Then, she shrugged. "You know. What he said last night."

"What did he say? I told you, I missed it."

She looked over at me, her eyes troubled. "About there being fewer men than women and how we need to grow the population."

"But he means the adults."

"Stop being so naïve. We're young, strong — prime breeders. They're going to lower the age of consent, Mina. That'll be the next step."

"You're so paranoid."

She gave me a cool smile. "You're forgetting, Mina. I know him a lot better than you do."

✦┤✦┤✦┤✦

When I went to the forest the next day, she wasn't there. She had left a note under the rock that served as our secret bulletin board, "Stop coming here, Mina. I mean it. He's had someone following me this past day — I managed to lose him, but I'm not coming back here for a while. I can't risk losing the library."

On my way back home, I paused by the muddy pond at the edge of the forest. That was where they had found Kendra's body — or rather, Seph had found Kendra's body. The two of them used to be friends, before the world disappeared. And then came the change, and Teacher John, bringing order out of chaos.

One morning back in those early days, Kendra drowned herself. Her note said, "I didn't want to become a jumper, only to find there was something more out there — some other kind of life I'd be stuck with. I just wanted it to be over."

Seph took it hard, I think — but I'm not sure, since she never talked about it. She and I only started hanging out more recently.

Before that, I used to think Seph and Kendra were kind of strange. Kendra was actually pretty popular at school, back when we still had school, but she and Seph were inseparable, and everyone knew that Seph was a weirdo.

But then after the change, mom started to lose it — her office in the city had disappeared, along with the rest of the world, so she had nothing to do. No work to go to.

Besides which, we had food and stuff and it's not like we had to pay the mortgage anymore, so there wasn't any real reason for her to work. Between that and losing dad, she started zoning out more and more. So I had to do everything — shopping, cooking, cleaning. All that stuff. And sometimes I began to have these weird panic attacks when I sat around with her at the house. Like I suddenly couldn't breathe.

That's when I began walking — and found that because of Kendra and the suicide, people didn't like to go down to the forest anymore. I think they didn't like the

idea that after everything else that had happened, someone young and beautiful and smart had actually chosen
to end it rather than become a jumper and hope there
might be something more.

So one day, as I was walking in the forest, I found Seph
and her library.

"What the fuck are you doing here?" She sprang up
from where she was crouched, looking at one of her books,
and cornered me, an unwavering, feral intensity tight-
ening her face.

Teacher John had declared the irrelevance of all prior
knowledge a few weeks before and had convinced people
to throw their books off the edge. "They're deceptions
— they give us false hope and foolish distraction," he had
said, his speech rising and falling in a mesmerizing
cadence that pulled you along with it, whether you
wanted to be pulled or not.

And before anyone knew it, they were rushing off to
throw their books into the void.

I'm sure a few people kept some here or there, but like
Seph's collection, they became contraband and anyone
caught with books was subjected to severe punishments
in the form of rationing restrictions.

Seph said that was because an idea was the most in-
sidious and dangerous threat to any kind of oppressive
regime, and so her father didn't want people reading
books and coming up with alternate theories.

"But at least we're all able to live peacefully this way.
Would you prefer that we revert to the chaos of the early
days?"

She shrugged, clearly unsure of where she was going
with her protests. "Maybe I would."

⋙⋅⫶⋅⫶⋅⋘

After I found the note, I went back to the forest from
time to time, but she was never there. Even if I didn't
understand what Seph went on about half the time, I
missed her.

Hanging out with her helped to break the tedium of the everyday, with mom, and the house and the usual routine. Seph was crazy and funny and fun, though I wouldn't have guessed that before I got to know her.

Sometimes, I'd even fish out one of her books and read for a while — though I was always careful to re-wrap it and put it back away after I was done. I knew how important they were to her.

+•I•I•I•+

A few days later, I woke to a loud knocking on the front door in the middle of the night.

It was Seph. She stood unsteadily on the front steps, her crazy grin pasted on and her eyes glittering.

"They've been following me, Mina. And he's noticed you, too. I think he's got someone following you," she said in a stage whisper. "You haven't been going to the *you-know-what* lately, have you?"

I assumed she meant the library. It had been a few days since I last went. I shook my head.

"Good. You're gonna have to watch your step though. I mean, he thinks you're..." She swallowed. "I can see it in his eyes when he mentions you."

I experienced an odd flutter — something between pleasure and fear. "He mentions me?"

She ignored the question. "I snuck away tonight. I think I might move the books. They're too easy to find there. Do you want to help?"

"Didn't you say you were being followed? Maybe you should come inside, where they won't be able to hear you."

She shook her head. "I've lost them for now. It's okay."

A pause, then she ran a hand through her hair. "So are you coming?"

I hesitated. Moving the books didn't seem like a great plan to me, especially given that she seemed kind of out of it.

"Look Seph—"

But I had waited too long. She raised her hand. "Never mind. You're right. There's more chance of them finding two of us than one."

"That's not—"

"I'll see you around, 'kay?"

⊹∘⊹∘⊹

She was right. I was being followed. I spotted him the next day, when I went shopping. I hadn't noticed before, but now that I knew, it was driving me nuts.

That's probably what made me do it, even though I'm not normally the rebellious type — I just had to get away, if only for a little while.

I snuck out the basement window in the back and cut through the house behind us — the entire family had been jumpers, and so it stood empty for the moment.

Once I made sure he wasn't behind me anymore, I headed over to the forest, to find Seph's library. I figured I'd read for a little while — and who knew? Maybe Seph might show up at some point too.

I couldn't believe I was actually looking forward to sitting around reading a book.

Except that they were gone. I thought at first that Seph had succeeded in moving them.

But something wasn't quite right. I looked at the little circle of trees more closely. There were bits of moss gouged out of the ground, as if there had been some kind of struggle. Some of the fronds of fern were broken.

I took a few more steps — and then I saw it, a short distance away, amid the ferns. The swatch of camouflage tarp in a crumpled heap, all but lost in the dappled afternoon light.

I walked over and picked it up. Two empty plastic bags and several torn pages fluttered to the ground.

I swayed slightly, feeling winded, as if someone had punched me in the stomach. And I didn't even really care for the books all that much. Or so I had thought.

⊹∘⊹∘⊹

No-one saw Seph again after that. Teacher John never mentioned her and I didn't dare ask too many questions — not even after I became one of his wives. He didn't have any photos of her in the house. It was as if she had never existed.

She was right about a lot of things, was Seph. It sometimes keeps me awake at night, worrying about what really happened.

But I like to believe she got away — and that she managed to discover that place she always claimed existed beyond the appearance of nothingness.

I still don't know if I believe that theory of hers. But these days, I find myself walking up to the end of the mud flats more often than ever. I stand, peering over the edge of the world, and as I feel the baby shift restlessly inside me, I can hope Seph was right — that somewhere out there is another place for us to discover and escape to, when things here become truly unbearable.

If Giants Are Thunder
Steven Mills

They beat him with sticks and fists about the head and
back, tearing the thin flesh of his wings, then left him to
bleed in the yard behind the bone-sawyer's hut as they
ran and flitted away, laughing and shoving each other. Tika
spat blood onto the dry ground and rolled onto his knees.
More blood dripped from his face, and his wings hung like
gnawed leaves against his arms.

He shouldn't have lied. He knew Kwist and Yarko
would chase him down and beat him if he lied; yet he
couldn't help himself. It was Kwist's sneering — Kwist's
mothers were being granted a giant's head house by the
judges after this season's Lightning — that made the first
lie leap out of Tika's mouth. Families didn't get giants'
heads granted to them for no reason, Tika knew that and
Kwist knew that, so when Tika lied and said *his* mothers
would be getting a giant's head house *next* season, Kwist
turned on him. Instead of backing down and saying what
his mothers had always told him— "Maybe some day, Tika,
if the fates face our direction, maybe then" —what came
out of his mouth was that stupid lie, big and ugly as a
giant's scrotum.

"Hup, Tika, is that you?" Doskin, the bone-sawyer, took
him by the arm and helped him to his feet. "Who did this?"

Tika clamped his mouth shut, stared past Doskin at the
heaps of bone-dust beyond the mill, on the far side of the
work yard.

"So that's the way it's going to be, is it?" Doskin led him
inside his gleaming bone-log hut and sat him on a stool

by the sink, where he dampened a cloth with cold water and set to cleaning Tika's wounds.

"Don't tell," Tika said suddenly, knowing that if his mothers found out there'd be a big fracas before one of the judges by day's close. He winced as Doskin inspected the laceration above his left eye.

"This one'll need a physician's attention," Doskin said by way of explaining that there was no keeping his mothers out of this one.

"I've had cuts before."

"And your wings, well, they'll need attention, too."

Tika let out a long, slow breath. Without thinking he looked up into Doskin's face. Doskin bared his teeth, and Tika quickly averted his eyes. His mothers were more lenient than most in their township, so sometimes Tika found himself forgetting his manners. More than once he'd been threatened with abandonment in giantland for being insolent. He knew it to be an idle threat used on children, and he was no longer a child, or at least was close enough to his Lightning to believe so, but it quickened his heart with fear anyway.

Why should he be afraid of giantland, anyway? he thought sourly. Did the True People not kill a giant or two or three every season and dry its meat for food, saw up its bones for building, and scour out the massive skull to gift the families favored that season by the judges?

Tika had never seen a giant killed, but had traveled all his ten seasons with the whole township to the kill site and seen the slain giant, as large as a river, a river of flesh, laid out on the ground, and he helped with the drying of the meat — his mothers, both physicians by trade, worked as butchers at the kill — by taking the lizards out into the forest day after day to load them up with firewood to keep the smoky fires burning.

"You might not make your Lightning with wings like this," Doskin said as he finished bandaging Tika's head.

Tika's heart fell. He couldn't remain a child, he just couldn't. He wanted his ceremonial hunter bag. He was tired of the fighting, the gameplaying, the endless dreary lessons from the judges — he wanted to be an adult, to start his training as a scouter, so that one day he would become a giant slayer.

That was the other lie he'd told Kwist and Yarko. It was the lie he'd been telling himself his whole life. He was going to become a giant slayer, not just a scouter, but a slayer. A legend among legends. *Anybody can become a giant slayer if they want to*, he had yelled at them, which seemed, in the end, to be the culminating taunt, for that was when they lunged at him and he ran and flitted, but they caught him anyway and beat him.

Giant slayers were chosen by the giant who comes to give up his life for the True People. That was the plain truth of it. As proof, the judges towed out the story of Keshlar, wing-mother of Toh, who had been wrangling lizards near the bogs when a giant swirled out of the morning mist and fell to her knees, crushing the lizard Keshlar had been lunging. Keshlar, understanding instantly the gift that had been granted her, flitted and climbed the giant's jerkin until she crouched easily on the giant's shoulder, half-hidden by the ropes of dirty hair. She retrieved her ceremonial hunter bag from her pouch, lit the stem with a sulfur match, and as the giant took in a breath, Keshlar flitted around her face and lobbed the hunter bag into the giant's mouth.

Tika understood the flip side of that truth, too, the moral lesson: if one were greedy, the giant would never appear. The judges had made that lesson abundantly clear. But Tika choked on that moral as if it were a mouthful of putrid fish. Doskin was not greedy, yet he lived not in a giant's head house, but in a bone-log house he made for himself, and he had been a celebrated scouter, too; Judge Yanti clearly was greedy, and mean, but she had two head houses, one for herself and one for her mothers. Tika did not feel greedy, even though he coveted a head house and the glory it came with, instead he felt cheated. Why hadn't a giant offered itself to one of his mothers? Why had not their service to the township as giant-butchers and physicians been honoured? It wasn't fair.

What Tika had come to believe was that that if you were not near where there were giants, you could never be chosen. He had come to believe that being chosen had nothing to do with a fullness or a lack of greed — he wasn't completely certain of this, but it felt true, like a good meal sitting in the pit of his belly. But it was a belief he usually kept hidden under his wings. He so badly wanted to be chosen, though. That is why he could not delay his Lightning, for it involved ten days' journey through the world-tides into giantland with a master scout, to hunt and to learn, and if the fates faced your direction, to trick a giant out into the True World and slay him, something that had not been done in so very many seasons. Tika intended to be the next one to do it. The sheer delight of the thought of all that glory made Tika quiver, even though Kwist had hit him especially hard when he had said that.

"Hold still!" Doskin admonished. "Or I'll end up tearing this wing of yours further."

⋆⋅⟊⋅⟊⋅⟊⋅⋆

Tika traveled with Lef in the fifth canoe — second to last. Lef was a master scouter, twice a giant slayer, with a head house for himself and another for his mothers, and he was barely twice Tika's age. Tika had hoped to have the mythical Toh; however, the judges placed Kwist with her instead. They were to travel a full day down the Kar River to the place where the True World mingled with giantland, just before the Kar River threw itself off the plateau into the Karlat Sea a dozen giantlength's below.

Lef didn't seem to like Tika much, saying little the whole morning, except to correct him on his paddle stroke. Tika tried not to be sullen, but he couldn't help it. He had looked forward to his Lightning for forever! And now he would have to spend it being criticized by Lef and taunted by Kwist and Yarko. It wasn't fair.

His wings had healed, though a long scar on the left one impeded his turns a little, and the cut above his eye was almost invisible. His hand-mother had threatened to beat him herself for being so foolish as to taunt Kwist. She was mostly wind, and Tika knew it, but it did take some determined begging to keep her from going to the judges.

His wing-mother argued in his favour, saying the judges'
intervention would only make matters worse for Tika.

As they paddled around the next bend, their canoe
almost struck the canoe in front of them, which had come
to a dead stop in the middle of the river. The other canoes
were scattered over the water like a hatch of skimmers. No
one was paddling; instead, they were staring as if
giantstruck.

On the marshy shore on the right side of the river, a
giant's body lay fallen, half submerged, a flood of rich, dark
blood discoloring the sand. Further downriver, a second
giant, also fallen, this one on its back, something impaled
in its chest, a long pole pushing into the sky. Then a third
giant. And a fourth. Several more on the far shore. In the
distance Tika could hear the crash and roll of thunder, or
what he imagined was the Kar River falling to the Karlat
Sea. Then the ground shook and seconds later the river
bucked, jostling the canoes. The banging of metal on metal
followed, like the everyday sound of the forge up the street
from Tika's bone-log house, but strangely bigger, louder.
And suddenly there was roaring in the forest to Tika's right,
the blood-drying howls of giants.

Lef shouted, "Hup! Toh, Jhemp! Turn back!"

Toh twisted in her canoe when Lef called her name. He
waved her toward him. Jhemp was already yelling at her
underling: "Paddle, you worthless lizard-turd!"

Tika dug his paddle in hard, pushed backwards, and
sculled his wings as well. Terror burned through him, and
all his giant-slayer fantasies, all his braggart lies, blew away
like bone-dust in a windstorm.

They thundered out of the forest on the right, coming
straight at them. The ground shook and the water trembled.
The sheer bulk of them made Tika cringe. Seven giants,
smashing through the trees, metal armor flashing like
lightning in the midday glare, swords — as long as the
street Tika lived on! — crusted with blood, dented and dull.
They grunted with effort as they ran. Seven mountains of
flesh and metal bearing down on their six tiny canoes.

The giants leapt over the fallen giants on the beach, the
closest landing on Toh's canoe, crushing Kwist underfoot

right to the bottom of the river in an instant. Toh flitted up and away from the remains of her canoe, throwing down her paddle and reaching for her ceremonial hunter bag. With her other hand she grabbed at the legging of the next giant. The last Tika saw of her was her wild yellow hair flowing straight out behind her, wings tucked tight into her back, legs splayed as she was jerked through the air, her one hand anchored to the giant's legging.

Waves higher than houses swamped canoes as the giants plunged across the river, the water barely touching their knees. They pounded up onto the far shore and thundered into the forest. Tika and Lev somehow managed to keep their canoe upright. "Forward!" Lev yelled at Tika. They were going after the survivors thrashing about in the water. Kwist would not be among them.

✢⊹╋⊹╋⊹✦

They erected only one of the giantskin tents, and built a small fire inside. They needed the fire to dry out their clothes and gear, otherwise they would have done without for the sake of avoiding detection, but wet clothes meant almost certain death in the cold nights near the Sea's edge.

They had floated quite a ways downriver by the time Lef had managed to wrangle the last canoe out of the water and gather everyone on shore. Giant carcasses were strewn everywhere, a treasure trove of mythic proportions of metal and bone and cloth, even if the meat was worthless. Giants' heads for whole townships! But Kwist had been lost. Toh had not returned. Ardree's leg was broken, although Jhemp managed to get the bone pulled back insideand realigned by pulling on her ankle while Tika and Lef and Yarko held her down. But the bleeding wouldn't stop. She needed a physician. And some of their food had been lost in the water, or ruined. The night cold, hard as metal, frosted the sand while the stars tossed bright light across the river.

With Toh gone, Lef took charge, and Tika found himself giantstruck by his mentor's calm in the face of all that had happened to them.

They shared a thick stew around the fire, sitting naked and close to the flames. It was the best food Tika had ever tasted. With hot food in his belly, though, he was suddenly so tired his wings trembled. But Lef was about to speak, so Tika forced himself to pay attention.

Lef rubbed his chin with the back of his wrist, then wrapped his long arms around his bare knees. He offered up a wry grin, gave a little shrug with his wings. "This is not a typical Lightning," he said. No laughter. "Giantland seems to be moving somehow, spreading out over the land of the True People. There are stories that speak to changes in the world-tides in the past — the story of Lith, for example, who went searching for giants after the True People had not slain or even seen a giant for twenty seasons.

"But I don't think giantland has ever flooded over like this. Something is wrong, and the judges must be forewarned. We will divide into two parties. The first will paddle back to the township, take Ardree to the physicians, and report to the judges. The second party will follow the giants, to see how far giantland has flooded, and to find Toh. Be prepared to leave by first light."

Tika so desperately wanted Lef to pick him to follow the giants that he could barely contain himself. When Lef suddenly bared his teeth at Tika and growled, Tika realized that he'd been staring at Lef in his desperation, and that clearly he'd ruined any chance he may have had for being chosen. Indeed, Lef did not pick him to follow the giants, and Tika was angry, at himself for forgetting his place, and at his mothers for teaching him poorly, and especially at Lef for not seeing, not realizing, how badly he wanted to go.

Tika sulked through cleanup after the meal, and twice pretended not to hear Jhemp when she asked him a question. He just didn't see why Lef wouldn't have chosen him — Lef was his mentor, he was supposed to teach him scouter skills, and how could he do that if he sent Tika away with Jhemp back to the township?

Before they had settled in for the night, Tika found himself at the end of Lef's hard grasp being dragged unmercifully to the river. Ice traced the edges of the water while starlight turned Lef's face into ugly hard lines. Lef threw Tika down on the sand, barely a canoe's length from the elbow of a dead giant.

"Now you listen to me, you puddle of lizard piss." Lef's voice was barely above a whisper but it roared as loud as a giant's in Tika's head. "I asked the judges to make me your mentor. I *asked* them. Do you understand? But I won't stand for your insolence, or for you going about feeling sorry for yourself, thinking you are ill-treated. Yes, Kwist and the others were unfair to you — but you couldn't keep your lizard tongue to yourself either, could you? Now Kwist is dead, so that's the end of that, isn't it. You want so badly to be an adult, well, here's your chance. You're twice as bright as Kwist ever hoped to be, and you've proven today that you can follow instructions. Jhemp will need someone like you to get the rest back alive. You want to be an adult? Well, then, adults do what *needs* to be done, not just what they want to do."

Tika's heart flipped about in his chest like a netted fish.

Movement caught the corner of his eye and he cringed. "Keep your voice down, Lef, or you'll awaken the dead."

"Toh!" Lef's wings carried him over the six strides of sand to drop right in front of her. Tika flitted to his feet, but kept his eyes respectfully lowered.

"We need to leave this place," she said to Lef. "As soon as we can."

Lef nodded, his wings trembling a little.

"Did he live?" she asked quietly.

Lef shook his head. "His body never surfaced."

Tika stole a quick glance at Toh. Her eyes were soft, sad even, and she looked tired. Her wings drooped until she shrugged them upright. "I rode the giant to an encampment. A thousand tents, Lef! Maybe five thousand giants in all. Spread out across the Jhitan Plain. The Jhitan townships are no more, trodden to dust."

"Five thousand giants?" Tika blurted, his heart racing with an uncontrollable fear.

"Be quiet," Lef said to him.

"The giant I rode, she and the others conferred with a group from among the tents. It was all roaring and thunder to me. They do speak to one another, and understand one another, and clearly they kill one another" — she nodded at the corpse lying behind them — "but they do not know of us, or care... or so it seems. A second band of giants left the camp as daylight abated. I was able to ride most of the way on one — however they wanted to cross the Kar River closer to the Sea than I wished to be, so I left them, hoping to find you somewhere along the shores. Your yelling was an easy light to follow."

"I was not yelling."

"In the still of a frosty night, it becomes yelling."

Lef grunted, and turned to Tika, who made sure to keep his eyes sewn to the sand. "Go," Lef said. "Tell the others Toh has returned, and that we all travel home by starlight. This Lightning has been overshadowed."

Tika flitted to the giantskin tent, shaking from the cold and from the vision Toh had shared, of a thousand giant tents across the Jhitan Plain, and of the Jhitan townships trampled to dust beneath the boots of five thousand giants.

⇥•⊦••⊦••⊦•⇤

The judges could deduce no reason why giantland had flooded into the land of the True People. Certainly the world-tides had always been fluid, moving a few giantlengths this way or back that way, but the border remained more or less steady along the north side of the Kar River in the Great Rising Forest. It had always been thus.

To Tika's ears the judges seemed more stunned by the loss of the Jhitan townships, and their trade with them, than by the presence of this army of giants. Tika tried hard to keep his eyes lowered as he listened, but it was difficult. At times he wanted to shout out at them, to give words to the fear in him that the end of everything was a wing's breadth away and they were fools to be immersed in discussing the loss of trade!

His wing-mother gripped the back of his neck and gave him a gentle shake. He let out a long, low breath and shrugged his wings tight against his back, then reached up and whispered: "How can trade be more important than the giants?"

She put her mouth to his ear. "Most of our foodstuffs come from the Jhitan Plains — we trade our giants' bones and meat for almost all the food we eat or cook with."

Tika frowned. "Why don't they kill their own giants?"

"Have you not been paying attention during your lessons?"

He scowled at the ground under his bare feet, kicked at a stone. Another hand replaced his mother's on his neck, and he found himself being pulled backwards through the crowd that had gathered in the main circle to listen to the judges. Tika stumbled, used his wings for balance, then craned to see who had hold of him, but saw nothing except angry adult faces and bared teeth.

He was spun about, then, once they were beyond the crowd. It was Toh pulling him. "You are needed, lizard-turd," she said and shoved him ahead of her. He flitted his wings now and again to keep ahead of her, his shorter legs unable to match her long stride. Some day he would be as tall as her, taller maybe. And he would have his own Lightning underlings to shove around.

"You are apprenticed to Lef," Toh added as if it were an afterthought and not the most important piece of information of his whole life. He flitted up and spun about to say something, but she bared her teeth and growled, and so he spun back in the direction they were marching, keeping his elation — and his fear — to himself. Apprenticed to a giant slayer! But Lef had thrown him across the sand. Not that he hadn't deserved it — he *had* been behaving like a child.

They met Lef at the lizard corrals. And Yarko, Toh's new apprentice. Doskin, the bone-sawyer, was there, too, mounted already on a lizard, and another adult, a female, whom Tika did not recognize.

Lef handed Tika a ceremonial hunter bag. "There will be no festival this time, although, truly, it was a Lightning that will be the fodder of stories for generations. If the True People survive." Tika fingered the bag, a simple giantskin tote, with the letters of his name drawn on it by his mothers. Inside the bag was a mixture of saltpeter, charcoal and sulfur, compressed inside a bone jar, with a burning stick in the top. When lit with a sulfur match and placed inside a giant's mouth, nose, or ear, the explosion would slay the giant. Tika slipped the hunter bag into the pouch of his jerkin. He knew now that he was an adult, even if he didn't feel like one.

Lef reached his claws under Tika's chin, lifted his face until their eyes met. "Say the Lightning," he said, then waited.

Tika stared hard into Lef's dark eyes, then said the words he had been yearning his whole life to say:

> *"If stars are snow, we are hail.*
> *If world is wind, we are storm;*
> *If fates are rain, we are deluge;*
> *If giants are thunder, we are lightning."*

Lef cut Tika's cheek with a claw to mark him. Blood dripped onto his jerkin, not the shameful blood from cuts after a beating by Kwist and Yarko, but the blood let for Lightning. Tika was no longer a child.

They rode lizards and pulled wagons far into the west and south, following the trade route to the southernmost Jhitan townships. Dust filled the sky to the west and north where the giant army camped; at night a forest's-worth of firewood was consumed in campfires, dimming the swirl of stars. When they reached the Jhitan River, they found they had come to the end of the giants' encampment. But the mists that denoted the world-tides, the boundary between giantland and the land of the True People, could not be found.

Maybe, Tika thought, the boundary was no more. He wondered, then, sitting low in the seat on the lizard's back, if there had ever been a boundary. Perhaps the world-tides were not, as the judges had described, like the boundary between the land and the Sea, discernable, ever shifting, but not able to move in any significant way. Perhaps it was like the boundary between townships, merely a line of the imagination: Kar township here, Mir township there. Perhaps, there had simply never been any reason for the giants to cross the imaginary line in such numbers before, just as the True People had no discernable reason to want to fill up giantland. Both had enough of what they needed where they were.

If so, what had changed?

Tika mothered these thoughts, fussed with them, while the lizard rocked him in the seat. He was not party to the conversations between Lef and Toh and Doskin, and the newcomer, Khee, a Jhitan trader. And Yarko had made it clear that she was not interested in any conversation whatsoever with Tika. She had been Kwist's friend, and seemed to look upon Tika as if he had somehow been responsible for Kwist's death. Tika did his best to ignore her.

They camped east of the final row of giants' tents, ate cold food, then curled up in their sleeping pouches underneath the wagons behind a large rock outcropping. In the morning they would search for survivors beyond the Jhitan River, while afterwards they would move among the giants gathering intelligence. If there were no Jhitan judges who had survived, then they were to return to Kar township so that the judges there could formulate a plan.

Tika lay awake. Soon they would move among the giants to learn where they kept their food, their water, what their tents were made of, whether or not they had pack or travel animals. Tika hoped not — animals large enough to carry giants would be a frightening sight indeed.

What plan would the judges make? How could the True People, even if they amassed together every last one of them, drive five thousand giants back from whence they came? Or should they simply kill them? Tika almost laughed out loud at the silliness of such a thought. Slaying a single giant made a legend of you! How could they, each only the height of a giant's eyeball, slay five thousand giants?

With five thousand hunter bags, of course.

Tika held his breath.

In Kar township there lived almost a thousand adults. Each carried a ceremonial hunter bag. Clearly, five townships the size of Kar contained enough adults to slay five thousand giants.

Tika sat up, banged his head on the bottom of the wagon. The lizards, tied to the sides of the wagon, didn't move. Tika wanted to shake Lef awake — but that is what a child would do, he told himself, an adult would wait until morning. So Tika shook out his wings, retucked them, and squirmed back down inside his sleeping pouch. Morning, however, couldn't come fast enough.

Try as he might, though, he couldn't sleep. He would doze and the thunder of giants running across the river, crushing Kwist without a thought, would jar him awake and leave a storm of fear whirling inside his chest. It was difficult to believe Kwist was dead. Tika had known people who had died, several just this past half-year from some kind of breathing sickness that his mothers could not cure. He remembered the reek of fear that blew through the township like the stench of sulfur, each one fretting that they or their loved ones would be next. And even though only a few died, the fear lived on. Just like with Kwist's death: only he had been killed, but the fear they all felt, then and after—

Tika sat up again, but slowly this time, so he didn't bang his head.

Do giants feel fear? he wondered. They slay each other — they must at least be afraid of their enemies.

Are we not their enemy?

But how could they fear an enemy too small to even notice, an enemy almost invisible to them, seemingly as harmless to them as the tiny eaters that lived in the cracks of a lizard's skin were to the lizard?

Tika lay down for the third time, but craned his neck to look in the direction of the giants' camp. "*We are lightning,*" he whispered to all five thousand of them spread like dung on a field across the far-flung Jhitan Plains.

❖❖I❖❖I❖❖I❖❖

Lef listened to him as if he were an adult.

I *am* an adult, Tika reminded himself, tracing the cut Lef had made on his cheek.

Then Toh divided their group into two parties: Doskin and Khee went south, across the Jhitan River in search of survivors; the rest of them were to visit the giants' encampment.

Tika, Yarko, Lef and Toh spent the daylight each making their way about parts of the giants' camp, hoping to make sense of some of their ways. Great and terrible animals, some smaller, others clearly so large they might indeed carry a giant, were corralled in several places among the tents — the stench of them so overpowering Tika feared becoming faint while flitting amongst them. Even the stink of the giantflesh! Tika feared he might never be able to eat meat again. And the great long pits they dug for their dung, deep rivers of putrid waste.

As far as Tika was concerned, giants lived a disgusting and reprehensible existence, bellowing at each other, pissing wherever they stood, their huge waterfalls of rank urine splashing the ground and everything else nearby, and eating mountains of meat torn from the cooked carcasses of some of their smaller, more revolting corralled animals.

❖❖I❖❖I❖❖I❖❖

They met back at the wagons at nightfall. Doskin and Khee had found numerous camps of families — more than three townships' worth — who had fled the Jhitan Plains when the giants thundered into sight, and so brought with them three judges, each representing a region of the people of the Plains.

Tika, although exhausted from the long, tense day among the giants, his wings drooping behind him, sat and ate the cold supper heartily and almost trembled with excitement when Toh addressed the Plains judges.

"This encampment of giants is temporary," Toh said as they sat in a circle hidden from the giants' view behind a fall of blood-coloured boulders. "They appear to be waiting for something to happen. Several come and go from the north end of the camp, but mostly the giants work about the camp or do nothing. I have seen a township of giants in giantland, and this is not one of them. Nor are they building any significant structures or dwellings in order to make this camp into a township."

"Well, if they get up and move, where might they move to?" one of the judges asked. "Why have the world-tides not kept them away?"

Toh shrugged her shoulders, gave her wings a little shake. "We don't know. What we fear, though, is that this camp may be waiting for an enemy, whom they plan to battle. Lef has seen giants battle one another in giantland, but not on this scale. A battle of giants is a terrifying sight to behold. In giantland, they can do as they please, but when they flood over to our land, that is another matter. You have seen the destruction caused when these giants simply marched in and set up camp. Imagine the destruction if another five thousand giants invade and the two sides clash."

Tika's breath came in short, sharp gulps at the thought of ten thousand giants in battle on the Jhitan Plains. Easily they would flood over to where Kar township lies, and his mothers, and all the other townships that sit on the river's edge and throughout the Kar Forest, which cups the eastern rim of the Jhitan Plains.

Another of the judges nodded, then said quietly, "Truly, such a battle could mean the end of the True People."

Lef leaned forward. "How many adults are camped across the Jhitan River?"

The judge shrugged one shoulder. "Nearly three thousand, by last count, but not for long. Our food supplies are low and the nights are far too cold for living outdoors."

"A thousand adult volunteers, that is what we ask." Without hesitation the eldest of the judges, a woman with a crinkled face and swollen hands and feet, nodded. "You shall have them."

✢✤✣✤✣✤✢

Despite his exhaustion, Tika couldn't sleep. His left wing itched along the scar he got from Kwist's beating, and the cold seemed to reach right through his sleeping pouch to pinch his skin. Under the Plains judges' authority, Toh set him in charge of fifty adults. Tomorrow they would mark out which part of the camp each of the three scouters and two apprentices would oversee. Then, when the Lith Constellation had risen directly overhead, they would strike. Like lightning in a storm. Two hundred and fifty strikes of lightning, a thousand if need be.

✢✤✣✤✣✤✢

Lightning struck.

Each adult flitted inside their designated tent with instructions to move among the four or five sleeping giants to find one with an open mouth or readily available nostril, then strike the sulfur match, light the stem, and toss their hunter bag. Each adult was to report to the scouter or apprentice in charge as to the success or failure of the slaying. Should an adult be slain by a giant, or lose his or her nerve, or fail to detonate their hunter bag, or simply be seen by a giant, the scouter or apprentice would finish the attack.

The pops of exploding hunter bags rattled across the giants' camp like gaming pebbles thrown onto a bone tabletop.

Morning found the giants' camp in a state of panic. There was much bellowing, and giants rushed about in all directions in bands of six and seven, apparently searching for something beyond the perimeter of the camp.

That night, Tika and the others led their respective bands of fifty more adults to their next designated region of tents. And again they struck like lightning.

One of the adults under Tika's leadership missed when he tossed his hunter bag, his fear making him rush the throw. The bag exploded on the giant's shoulder, waking him, and he in turn woke the others in his tent.

Tika flitted to the tent in question. Outside, two giants clambered about, bellowing and roaring, as if to rouse the other giants. Tika scrambled up the tent flap and flitted inside, his whole body quivering with fear. One giant leaned over another, examining his shoulder where the exploding hunter bag had burned him, using a round light that he held in his hand. Tika could smell the cooked flesh as he scrabbled up the inside of the tent, feeling for purchase somewhere. He found a seam and held on with his feet and hands.

A giant burst into the tent, making the fabric shake so hard Tika could barely hold on. The giant planted her feet like twin mountains and roared at the other giants, who seemed to simply ignore her. Tika dropped onto her shoulder, flitting his wings just before landing to break his fall. He was shaking so hard now he thought he might be sick, but he pulled his hunter bag out of his pouch, lit the stem, took a breath. He flitted in front of the giant's face and threw the bag as hard as he could into her mouth, then dropped fast toward the ground. He heard the pop of his hunter bag exploding, and the giant flailed her arms, clawing at her throat, which was leaking blood through a gaping wound. Tika scrambled on his hands and knees out into the safety of the night as the giant crashed to the floor of the tent.

The fracas caused by waking the giants with the missed throw cost the lives of four adults and resulted in a rapid withdrawal by many of the volunteers who hadn't yet found their marks. Only a hundred and seventeen confirmed slayings.

"One of them was Doskin?" Tika repeated as he pushed more stew into his mouth. They had retreated to their camp among the Jhitan families.

"You don't see him anywhere, do you?" Lef answered with a snarl. Then he softened a little, stood to refill his bowl from the pot. "He crawled into one of the tents, having lost track of a volunteer. The giants had all roused and he was stepped on — initially just his legs were crushed, then a second giant finished him. They didn't see him though;

it was simply an accident. The missing Jhitan had hidden in some clothing when the giants woke and had been unable to make his escape until then."

An insult mounted inside Tika's mouth, but he clamped his teeth shut, trapping it inside. Instead, he said, "We would be more effective if we didn't keep using new volunteers, but instead used those who had already slain giants the night before." He joined Lef in front of the stew pot.

Lef nodded. "Each only has one hunter bag."

"Then each should have two, or three, or ten. We are no longer hunting giants, Lef, we are slaying them."

→►‡•‡•‡•◄

On the morning after the fourth strike, the giants broke camp, and there was nothing orderly about the process. Many tents were left behind, along with much gear and a mountain of debris. The sound of their leaving was unlike anything that Tika had ever heard. The ground shook and quaked with the thunder of so many giants and their animals on the move.

Tika rode a lizard to an outcropping a short distance from where they had camped that night out under the wagons. The others remained in the forest, dancing and singing and preparing a feast. Tika wanted to watch the vanquished giants as they abandoned the Jhitan Plains. He wanted to be able to recount this day, this moment, this victory, for as long as he lived, to carve it deep into his memory. He dismounted, stood for a long time on the stone, buffeted by wind and dust. A storm brewed in the distance, beyond the Plains, far out to Sea, so it appeared as if the wind blew the giants northward. Tika watched all morning in the growing wind as the giants shrank away, driven by fear, fear of what they didn't know, couldn't know because they hadn't really looked.

A shadow swallowed his outcropping. His lizard bolted. Tika spun as a giant's hand encircled him.

Tika flitted up and away, reached into his pouch for his last hunter bag, but the giant's other hand knocked him hard, all the way to the ground, tearing skin off his shoulder. The giant's foot came up, high, the boot monstrous above him. Tika scrabbled across the dirt. Fingers thick as bone-logs pinched his wings together and lifted him off the ground. Pain tore through Tika's back and chest; terror gripped him tighter than the giant's fingers.

He knew he would die now, and that knowledge struck him as both fitting and irritatingly unfair. He was a giant-slayer, the lie he'd spouted at Kwist had come to be; but now, on the very mountaintop of his glory, he would be crushed into nothing as Kwist was before him. Crushed, or eaten, or torn apart.

The giant raised him up, held him high against the darkening sky, as if inspecting him, then pushed him down into a container of sorts, like a bone jar, but as large as half a bone-log house and with clear sides all round so Tika could see out. And then the giant twisted a lid onto the jar. Tika could see the stormy sky through holes in the lid the size of his fist. The jar jerked sideways, Tika tumbled around the slippery floor, hitting his head on the clear wall. The giant, his face distorted and grotesque outside the jar, peered in at Tika. He shook the jar a little, making Tika tumble all over again, banging his head yet again. Other giant faces appeared, distorted and gawking.

Ah, yes, Tika, the incomparable giant-slayer, he taunted himself in order to quell his fear, *I heard he slew seven giants in four nights.* He reached into his pouch, but his last hunter bag was gone — only a handful of sulfur matches remained. He must have dropped it when the giant struck him out of the air.

Rain spit against the sides of the jar. The giant stuffed the jar inside his jerkin, and Tika was plunged into a gray twilight and assaulted by the giant's overpowering stench.

⟐⟐⟐

He had no idea how long he traveled like this, yet as he traveled the immensity of what had happened overpowered him. He realized that the giant — with jar ready in hand — had known to look out for him, for his kind. *They've noticed us*, Tika thought to himself. *They've seen lightning, but now they know it can kill.*

✦•╬•╬•✦

When Tika thought he would die from the smell of the giant, he set his mind to escape.

Even if he had no hunter bag, he still had a handful of sulfur matches in his pouch. He pulled off his jerkin, tore several strips from the bottom of it, then flitted to the top of the jar and anchored his feet and one hand in some of the holes. He used his wings to stabilize himself against the rocking of the giant's stride while he reached out with his other hand and scratched at the inside of the giant's jerkin with his claws until the fabric became quite frayed.

Tika dropped to the bottom of the jar, grabbed the strips of cloth and the matches, and flitted back up to the lid. The strips from his jerkin caught fire easily. He held them against the frayed fabric of the giant's jerkin. Tiny flames erupted. Tika flitted back down to the bottom of the jar, pulled his torn jerkin back on, and stored the remaining matches as the tiny flames crawled up the giant's jerkin, burning and smoking.

Tika crouched and waited. Barely an adult, he had slain seven giants; he had helped rid the Jhitan Plains of five thousand giants; he had been captured alive and imprisoned inside a giant's jar; and now, as truly befit only a legend among legends, he would escape his captor and return to the True People.

Soon the giant would stop to slap at his burning jerkin, cracking open or dropping the jar in his panic. And Tika would make his escape, then, rising from the shards of the broken jar to flee, unseen, into the growing storm.

On Company Time
Nancy Bennett

Work fast newbie, you'll get the bosses' wrath
    if you waste your time
expanding your dreams into viable visions.

    So the axles aren't straight
    and the core is kinda melted molten
    leave it up to the quality control team!
    They'll take it off if they figure its bad enough
        down the line.

So this one on spinning loses a few seconds a century?
    So what? Not like they'll notice
    people will just have to adjust that's all
    and that desert, still expanding
Oh hell, make another Las Vegas, you can't have
   everything perfect.
    I don't CARE what the training film said!

    OH Damn! Now I've done it!
    put my finger right through the old ozone
    Hey. think anyone'll notice?
Slip me some clouds to paste over it and whistle, look
   the other way.

    Why are you taking so long, newbie?
        Better pick up the pace
    Sure, you could create a PERFECT world
      but you have the time to be a perfectionist
    When you're working on company time.

Vampires of the Rockies
Randy McCharles

"This is stupid!"

Bram slammed his foot on the brake, bringing the dusty '94 Buick to a jerking stop. "We've been driving this loop for hours and haven't seen a blasted thing!"

Mina looked up from her guide book and peered through the windshield. Up ahead, the road meandered through a forest of sturdy Jack Pines then turned sharply near a section of chain-link fence that brandished a park-green sign with large white letters: *Please Do Not Feed the Vampires*.

Bram stuck his head out the car window and shouted. "If there's a vampire within fifty miles of here, then I'm Count Dracula!"

"Oh Bram," Mina sighed. "Don't be so melodramatic. You'll have another stroke. Remember what the doctor said about your heart."

"Doctor, schmoctor," Bram grumbled. "That quack will say anything to keep our monthly appointments. Just so's the money keeps rolling in. There's nothing wrong with my heart." He winced and pressed a hand against his chest, then took a pill from his shirt pocket and swallowed it dry.

Mina pushed the guide book under his nose. "It says here that vampires are mostly nocturnal. That to spot one in the daytime is rare."

"Rare," Bram echoed. He waved his hand out the window. "That's why they have a *vampire paddock*. To keep the vampires fenced in where people can see them."

Mina flipped through the pages in her book. "I'm certain it says in here that vampires can fly."

Bram let out a weary sigh and shook his head. "Of course vampires can fly. It'd be a pretty useless vampire that couldn't fly. It'd be a blood-sucking penguin! This is a National Park, Mina. With professional wardens. I'm sure they clip the vampire's wings."

Mina looked up into the trees, searching for roosting vampires. "Mmmm, smell that air," she said. "You can almost taste the pine sap and mountain snow. Toronto air was never this good."

"We didn't drive three thousand miles across the prairies for the air," Bram said. He pushed his foot on the accelerator and drove well beyond the fifteen kilometer per hour speed limit toward the paddock exit. "If we wanted air we could have gone to Yellowstone. At least Yellowstone has werewolves!"

"Where should we visit now?" asked Mina. "The waterfall at Stoker Canyon is supposed to be nice. Maybe there'll be some vampires along the trail."

"We're going back to town," Bram said. "Give that Information Center another try."

⊹⊱†⊰⊱†⊰⊱†⊰⊹

The Information Center was a large, sandstone building on Main Street with no parking and lots of windows.

Bram wheezed as he trudged up the concrete steps to the main doors. Inside they entered a dark foyer with yet more stairs.

"This building is just like City Hall,' Bram complained. "All intimidation and no substance."

"I like the drapes," said Mina. She ran her fingers across the thick, purple cloth.

"Drapes!" muttered Bram. "They build this place with plenty of windows. Then cover them all up and fill the ceiling with pot lights. Is sunlight not good enough for them?"

Mina knew better than to answer.

At the top of the staircase their path was blocked by an enormous, stuffed vampire. It stood ten feet tall. One razor-nailed hand flung wide a magnificent black cape while the other was clenched in a fist at the vampire's chin. Long, white incisors dripped blood into a small cavity in the top of the fist. The creature's mouth was a twisted snarl. It's painted glass eyes glowered.

"Don't know who they think they're fooling," said Bram. "Vampires don't grow ten feet. Not even those big what-cha-ma-call-ems.

"Grizzly vampires," murmured Mina, staring steadfast into the creature's glass eyes.

"Right. Grizzly vampires."

Bram left Mina to her vampire gazing and headed for the information counter. Souvenirs. Post cards. Roadside attractions. None of that tourist junk meant a thing. Bram had come to the mountains to see one thing: a vampire in the wild.

"*Good e-evening,*" said an emaciated waiter-type from behind the counter. He spoke with a thick, Balkan drawl, had dark hair combed back in a greasy 'V', and there was white powder on his face. Your typical Hallowe'en vampire.

"It is not evening, and it is not good," Bram retorted. "We're here to see a vampire."

The tourist guide smiled, displaying swollen, rouged lips and white, plastic incisors. "*Have you tried the Vampire paddock? It is just outside of town.*"

"Yes, we tried the paddock," Bram snarled at him. "You sent us there this morning. And if there's a vampire in that cage then he's got brown roots and evergreen arms."

"*Ahhh,*" nodded the guide. "*Ze elusive Rocky Mountain Vampire. Did you know that some people don't even* believe *in vampires?*"

Bram pulled a twenty from his shirt pocket and pushed it into the mock vampire's hand. "Save your speeches for the Japanese. We came here for the real thing, buddy. How about helping us out?"

The tourist guide squinted his eyes, and his fingers closed around the bill. He glanced to the left, then to the right, then leaned over the counter and whispered into Bram's ear.

Bram nodded. "Now that's more like it."

"Look Bram," said Mina. She had torn herself away from the stuffed vampire and was standing in front of a wall-size diorama. "It's our hotel."

The diorama contained mountains and trees and lakes and streams. It was night. Bats filled the air and a mob of peasants armed with torches and wooden stakes marched toward the very hotel where they were staying: the Banff Springs Castle. Atop the castle ramparts, a tiny, black-caped figure glowered down at the mob. The caption below the display read: 'Local Indian tribes maintained good relations with the vampires until the White Man came with his wooden stakes and wreathes of garlic and hunted them to near extinction.'

"No wonder the hotel bedrooms are so small," said Bram. "They're built to hold a coffin and nothing more."

"What did the information man say?" asked Mina.

Bram took her elbow and led her toward the exit. "He had a couple of ideas."

They drove up Main Street and across a bridge, up around the back of a hill and into a parking lot. There were lots of cars and wastepaper cans, and small children with bathing suits and towels.

Bram frowned.

"I think this is a swimming pool," said Mina. "Did you want to go for a swim?

"No," said Bram. "I do not want to go for a swim. There's supposed to be a cave here. With bats. And vampires."

Mina pointed out the window. "That sign has a picture of a cave.

Bram squinted into the afternoon sun.

"I can't see it," he grumbled. "We'd better go have a look."

The girl behind the counter looked nothing like a vampire. She had black hair. A pale face. Rouged lips. And bits of metal sticking out of her ears, eyebrows, and lower lip. Her eyes were lifeless. Bram believed she might be dead. But a vampire? No.

The creature stirred, emitting a moaning sound that sounded vaguely like the word: "*Ten.*"

Bram scowled and handed her ten dollars.

The lifeless eyes stared at him. The lips moved. "*Each,*" they said.

"You've got to be kidding," said Bram. "We just came to see the cave. We're not going to swim."

The counter girl thrust out a pallid hand. The nails were painted black, and there was a vampire tattooed across the palm.

Mina passed the girl a second ten and pushed Bram through the turnstile. "The cave is this way," she said, pushing him down a tiled, hospital-white corridor and through a glass doorway that led back outside.

Bram's anticipatory smile drooped. "You call this a cave?"

Before them stood a small wading pool surrounded by paved concrete. Rough stone walls rose up to meet a jagged ceiling. It was very dark, the only light coming from the large, Olympic-size swimming pool just outside the cave. Above the wading pool, suspended from the ceiling by a length of string was a large, rubber bat with floppy wings.

Bram swallowed one of his pills. "A rubber bat." he said. "A fake cave with a fake bat." He looked at Mina. "I'm going to kill someone."

"Bram," said Mina. "Remember you heart."

"Twenty dollars we paid," said Bram. "Twenty dollars!" He reached out over the pool.

"Bram, Don't."

⊹⫞⊹⫞⊹

"Look on the bright side," suggested Mina. "The towel rental was just two dollars. And the hotel was only five

minutes away. It could have been worse. You could have
got hurt."

Bram stepped out of their hotel room bathroom wearing a fresh shirt and pants. He pulled a black comb through
damp, graying hair.

"My pills got wet," he said. "There was bromide in the
water and it ruined them. Those pills cost four dollars
apiece."

"You could have got hurt," Mina repeated.

Bram slid the comb into his pocket and picked something black and rubbery off the dresser. "I got my bat,
though. Didn't I?"

Mina shook her head. "And for what? What are you
going to do with a rubber bat?"

Bram's face lit up in a cold grin. "I'm going to stuff it
down a certain Hallowe'en vampire's throat."

⋙⋅⫶⋅⫶⋅⫷

They had planned on eating dinner at the hotel, but after
seeing the prices on the menu Bram took one of his dwindling supply of soggy pills and they went to *Transylvania
Chicken* instead.

After eating, they drove back to the Information Center.

Bram wheezed as he climbed the mountain of steps. At
the top he steadied himself and rattled the doors. When
they wouldn't open, he hammered on the thick wooden
beams with his fist.

"I think they're closed," said Mina.

Bram pressed his forehead against the door and his body
sagged. "Yes. I can see they're closed."

"Then why are you banging on the door?"

Bram looked at her. "Because I was looking forward to
murdering a vampire. That's why. Now I'll have to wait
till tomorrow."

"Let's go see Stoker Falls," suggested Mina. "The sun's
going down, and my guide book says they have fireworks
in the evening."

Bram looked up to see the sun descending between two mountain peaks. "Come on!" he cried. He took Mina's hand and dashed for the car.

⊹•ӏ••ӏ••ӏ•⊹

"This isn't Stoker Falls," said Mina.

Bram turned off the ignition and got out. He had parked by a paved trail that led from a parking lot into the forest. A sign read: *Nature Walks. Guided Tours at Sunset.* Bram set a fast pace down the trail, his breath coming in ragged grunts.

Mina caught up to him and took his hand, slowing his gait. The sun was mostly gone, and thick shadows filled the forest. Something, possibly a bat, darted through the foliage.

"This is spooky," said Mina.

Bram said nothing.

They came out in a small, secluded clearing. Beyond a row of empty benches and a couple of wastepaper cans, a lone figure danced in the twilight gloom. It wore a black cape that weaved and fluttered as legs glided and arms swooped. It made a soft humming noise, an eerie melody. Music, some might call it.

"Oh," said Mina.

The figure spun and faced them. *"Good e-evening,"* said the man from the Information Center. *"Velcome to the Nature Valk."*

"Oh, for the love of!" said Bram. He took a pill from his pocket and forced it down his throat.

"Wow," said Mina. "A real, live vampire."

Bram pulled something black and rubbery from his coat and stalked toward the *real, live* vampire.

"Don't," cried Mina, tugging at his arm. "It may be dangerous."

"I'll show it dangerous," Bram growled.

"Don't I know you?" asked the vampire.

"Not half as well as you're going to," said Bram, raising the rubber bat in his fist.

✦·I·◆·I·◆·I·◆

"We'll," said Mina. "I hope you're satisfied."

Bram flicked the signal to change lanes and sped past a rusted Honda Civic.

"I've never been so humiliated in my life," Mina continued. "Imagine being banned from a national park. How many people can say that?"

Bram adjusted the visor to keep the sun out of his eyes.

"We can never go back, you know."

Bram squinted then pulled his sunglasses from the dashboard and pressed them against his face.

"You're looking a little pale," suggested Mina. "Have you taken your pill?"

Bram reached into his shirt pocket, pulled out a handful of pills, and tossed them out the car window.

"Bram! Have you lost your mind?"

"Don't need no pills," said Bram. "Never felt better in my life." He scratched at a welt on his neck where the vampire had bitten him, then flashed Mina a toothy grin.

"Must be the mountain air."

Recursion
John Mavin

```
int Iteration(i)
{
   if (i=1)
     break;
   else
     return Iteration(i-1);
}
```

✦⊱⊰✦⊱⊰✦

i=9

A uniformed ship's steward comes to your women's resistance training class and tells you that your nine-year-old son, Charley, is not registered with Child Services today. You give him a smile and thank him. You unstrap yourself from the double-grav bike and wipe it down with a towel. You leave the Fitness Centre and take the lift to the port gangway on deck sixteen.

You think Charley is probably in the aft airlock, looking out the eyeport again. A cargo handler you slept with your first week out gave you the access code. He said it was the only porthole with real glass in the public section of the ship. Sometimes you take Charley there to look at the stars. While the electronic flat-panel in your stateroom has zoom features and ultra-high definition resolutions, Charley says he'd rather look with his own eyes. He isn't interested in how the constellations are changing the farther you get — he just wants to know where Earth is.

As you approach the airlock, you see Charley inside, his hand hovering over the control console.

He sees you and pauses, "This is all your fault, Mom." He presses a red button and the outer hatch opens.

You collapse on the deck as your son is sucked into space.

→•I•••I•←

i=8

A uniformed ship's steward comes to your resistance training class and tells you that your nine-year-old son, Charley, is not with Child Services today. You leave the Fitness Centre without bothering to wipe down the double-grav bike and hurry to the aft airlock.

This stupid move was your husband's idea: Thomas was the one who came home with the glossy brochures for the newly terraformed Antares III; Thomas was the one who submitted your names to the Colonist Application Committee; Thomas was the one who failed the physical exam and had to stay behind. And now all Charley wants to do is look back at Earth through the eyeport.

Sure enough, you find Charley in the airlock: he's pacing back and forth like he's been waiting for you.

"Charley, how many times have I told you — don't go in the airlock alone?" You open the inner hatch and reach for your son.

He slips away and presses a red button on the control console.

The inner hatch closes and you manage to grab the sleeve of his jumpsuit before the outer hatch opens. As you're propelled into space with him, you wonder why you don't feel cold.

→•I•••I•←

i=7

A uniformed ship's steward tells you that your nine-year-old son, Charley, is not with Child Services today.

You leave the Fitness Centre and run down the gangway as fast as you can.

You should have withdrawn your application and stayed with your husband, but you couldn't; not after Thomas found out about your affair too. You slap the wall switch and the airlock's inner hatch flies open.

"Charley!" You rush into the airlock and the inner hatch closes behind you.

He turns and slaps you. "That's for leaving Dad." Charley wipes back a tear and pushes the red button on the control console.

You hear the whoosh of escaping air as the outer hatch opens and you fly into space. For the first time since you left Earth, you see the ship's outer hull, where her name, the *S/V Île-Saint-Croix*, is painted boldly in black.

→•I•I•I•←

i=6

A uniformed steward tells you that your nine-year-old son, Charley, is not with Child Services. You leave the Fitness Centre and run down the gangway to the airlock.

A boy, older than Charley, but not quite a teenager, is blocking your access to the inner hatch. You duck around him and slap the wall switch.

Charley is looking out the eyeport.

"Get out of the airlock!" you scream. You grab his jumpsuit.

Charley starts to cry.

You push him to the safety of the gangway just before the inner hatch closes, sealing you inside. A yellow light turns red and you hear the whoosh of air as the outer hatch opens. You're sucked off the ship like blue waste down a vacuum toilet.

→•I•I•I•←

i=5

A uniformed steward tells you that your son, Charley, is not with Child Services. You run to the aft airlock.

A young teenager is standing in front of the inner hatch. You move to the left to go around him, but he moves to block you. You dodge to the right.

He does too.

You reach through the teenager and slap the wall switch. The inner hatch flies open and you duck inside.

You run your fingers through Charley's hair.

He laughs and walks out of the airlock.

You turn to follow but the inner hatch closes between you. The yellow light turns red and the outer hatch opens.

→⊷I⊷I⊷I⊷←

i=4

A uniformed steward tells you Charley is not with Child Services. You leave your class, the same as you did last time.

A pimple-scarred teenager blocks the airlock. He looks familiar, but you don't know his name. He looks older than the boy who was here before.

"Stop doing this," says the teenager.

"Where's Charley?" you ask.

"I'm right here," says the teen.

You look over his shoulder and see nine-year-old Charley peeking out the eyeport. You rush through the teen and gather him in a hug.

"What do you think Dad's doing right now?" asks Charley, pointing through the eyeport.

"How am I supposed to know?" You pull him close and smell his hair. It has no odour, which is odd, because you make him wash his hair almost every night with eucalyptus-scented shampoo.

"You've got to stop," says the teen, turning toward you from the gangway.

You look at the teen and young Charley disappears from your arms, fading into the air. "Charley!" you scream.

The inner hatch crashes down. You look at the control console and see a blinking yellow light. It turns red. The outer hatch opens.

→⊷I⊷I⊷I⊷←

i=3

A steward tells you Charley is not with Child Services. You rush through him and run down the gangway.

The teenager is waiting at the aft airlock. He has the same blond hair Charley does, and the same green eyes. His pimples have gotten worse since last time.

"Please, stop," he says to you.

"I can't," you say. "I've got to save Charley. He's in the airlock." You see Charley looking through the eyeport.

The teen steps in front of you. "There's no one in there."

"There is too, you idiot!" you scream. "Charley, get out of there!"

"Mom, I'm not in there," says the teen.

Nine-year-old Charley starts to fade.

You push through the teen. You slap the wall switch and manage to catch your son's arm before he fades completely.

"No!" you scream. You turn and your hand brushes a red button on the control console. The yellow light turns red. The outer hatch opens.

⇥•⊢•⊣•⊣⇤

i=2

Charley is not with Child Services. You leave your fitness class and run to the aft airlock.

The teen is waiting for you. Now, he looks a bit like Thomas, except he's taller and his stomach doesn't bulge over his belt.

"Stop," he says.

You shake your head and rush through him, slapping the wall switch.

"Listen to me," says the teen.

The airlock is empty.

You shake your head again. "Where's Charley? What have you done with him?"

"I'm right here," says the teen.

You hold your hand over the control console. "Tell me what you've done with my little boy or I'll call Security," you say.

The inner hatch crashes down.

The teen looks at you though the transparent wall of the inner hatch. He wipes back a tear.

"Mom, you've been dead for eight years. I've grown up."

"What?"

"This isn't what happened." The teen presses his palm to the transparent wall.

You look away from him and press a red button on the control console.

The yellow blinking light turns red. The outer hatch whooshes open.

⋙⋅⊹⋅⊹⋅⋘

i=1

Charley is with Child Services. You know he'll be there until seventeen hundred. You also know the stewards will take good care of him. You beg off your resistance training class with a feigned injury.

You walk down the port gangway on deck sixteen to the aft airlock. You're crying. All Charley does is ask questions about Thomas. *Does Dad still love me? Will he forget about me? Will I ever see him again?* You can't take it anymore.

The older Charley is waiting for you at the airlock.

You reach out to touch his cheek, but your hand slides through his skin. You notice his acne has cleared up.

He leans close to you and you can smell the eucalyptus in his hair.

You step back and slap the wall switch. The inner hatch opens.

"I don't want to do this again," says Charley.

"I don't either," you say as the inner hatch slams shut.

"I'm not sure I can ever forgive you," says Charley.

"I understand," you say.

You watch your grown son through the transparent wall. He holds his palm up.

You do the same, matching your fingers to his. "I'm sorry," you say. A tear slides down your cheek. You watch as your hand presses a red button and the yellow light begins to flash.

"Me too," says Charley. "I needed you."

The yellow light turns red and the outer hatch whooshes open.

Tomorrow and Tomorrow

Susan Forest

I'm lying on a cot I set up in your office, Jack, and I see the moon through the window, white as milk. It's full and round and smiling, and I wonder if it's an omen.

I'm surrounded by you, by your things. Your computer. Your radio receiver, blank, silent. Your maps of the farm and the county, grain charts, memos on the bulletin board, all silver and shadow. The office smells of you, still. Sweat and dust. I think of the times I lay in your arms, wet with our love-making, and now I lie on this cot, here, in your office, with another man's seed inside me.

Am I becoming pregnant? I'm thirty-eight. What are the chances?

I did what I thought I had to do.

Now I wonder, how much damage have I done? I feel... empty and alone and as far away as that moon sailing in its sea of stars.

Today plays over and over—

The office. Sweltering. Me, scanning radio frequencies. Again. Still. Full to bursting with the frustration of it, stretched thin in circles within circles of vexation.

I was looking out the window, watching Julie wash the thresher, playing the spray over the fenders. She'd been mowing hay all day. Amazing what the children have learned to do. She's twelve, now. You remember how that fine desert dust needs to be rinsed away? It's August, Jack, and so dry, so hot on the compound where the sun's been beating down.

I caught David from the corner of my eye, walking from the generators with his head down in that focused way he's had since he was two years old — working something out, a more efficient way to do the monthly maintenance on the solar cells, maybe — and Julie flicked the spray on him. She soaked him, head to foot, then she laughed, falling over herself, spray flying everywhere. I couldn't help but smile, watching him wrestle the hose from her and chase her to the other side of the thresher. When was the last time they played like that?

I switched off that horrible hiss of the radio so I could hear their laughter. Then, goddamn it, I cried. It made me angry with myself that I couldn't just enjoy a moment of pleasure without tears springing from my eyes. Goddamn it.

Why? I wasn't crying for William, lying in my arms with those horrid pustules all over him. Not even for you, Jack, and your strength, that I've missed, every day, for the last four years.

It's like — how do I explain? Like trying to hold wooden shutters closed in a wind storm. First an image seeped through: William in his coffin. Then a thought: who'll bury the last of us? Then the whole confused jumble of what-ifs and should-we's and if-onlies came tumbling down.

You and I understood — I think — what the loss of all those other people meant, but we never talked about it. Back when the radio, T.V., net, first went dead, remember? We wondered what happened but *we didn't prepare*. Even in that time that followed, when the farm became a fortress and there was nothing we could do to help all those people, and our own barley fields became a war zone? We should've figured out what was going on and made plans. But it took time for us to realize we were on our own. Did we ever realize it? We never discussed the future, not in terms of how we would cope when it came. It was left to me to figure out what to do, on my own.

And today, Julie had her first period. I realized, I couldn't procrastinate any more.

"Mom?" Little Sara's voice, calling on the intercom from the kitchen. "Supper."

I looked out the window. Julie and David were gone, washing up for dinner. I wanted to stay in the office, with your smell, with my procrastination, a little longer. I fiddled with the radio.

But it was no good. Sara would only call again. I had to put one foot in front of the other and go down to dinner. I didn't let myself think about what I was doing, but I could do the first step. Go to dinner.

The sun rested on the ridge in a hot, yellow sky.

"Mom?" A knock on the door.

I stood up. I put the headset down.

Sara poked her little face in, panting from the heat. "Supper."

⊹⊱⊰⊹⊱⊰⊹

After dinner, I came here, to the office out behind the elevators where you used to load grain on the monotrains before they stopped running. I love the first cool of dusk, when the warmth of the day radiates back from the concrete, but the desert heat is gone.

Do you remember how beautiful the farm is? I love the way the house rambles, comfortable, with the patios and shady gardens around it. The work compound. The garages for the farm machinery, the tool sheds and the generators and solar cells, and the windmills up on the ridge. The storage elevators, mill and food processing plant, off to the right where they don't block the view of the river and the orchard. The grain fields that stretch for miles to the south where the valley opens out. Some day, I want to tell my grandchildren about the pasture up on the hills that my grandfather kept for his sheep. No. I put the thought of grandchildren out of my mind. If I think too far ahead, I'll never be able to do this.

Weeks ago. Months ago, I found a prepackaged syringe, some rubber gloves and disinfectant in the medical closet in our upstairs bathroom. After dinner, I brought them down here, to your office. It was as if I were preparing for expected guests. I put some blankets on the over-stuffed arm chair and got the cot ready. I sterilized a small glass bottle and stopper in the autoclave. It was like I was a robot, following a program I denied writing. Then I returned to the house.

David was on the couch, reading. Julie and Sara were on the floor, hunched over the old pine coffee table you built, playing chess. Sara was studying the board with her finger on the tip of a bishop when I came in. She hasn't started to grow, yet, and she looked so precocious — too young to be taking on this horrid new world. "Want some popcorn?" she asked. I remember, she didn't even look up.

My bowels turned to water. I stood in the doorway, listening to my own voice and wondering how I made it sound so calm. I said, "No. Thank you, Sara. I need to talk to David."

David lifted his head from his book, and I didn't know if he could see the flush in my cheeks or the trembling in my hands. "What?"

"It's about the farm," I said, which was almost true. "I need to see you in the office."

He put a bookmark in his place and stood up. He ran his hands through his hair, and I wanted to weep inside for the little boy I loved. "This may take a while," I said to the girls. "And don't come to interrupt."

"We won't," Julie said. "I'm going to bed." She moved her knight and grinned at Sara.

David followed me outside. The night air was cool and I was glad for the dark. One thing about our farm, it cools down at night.

"What's it about?" David asked as he walked by my side. "I didn't screw up the temperature setting on the grain belts, did I?"

"No, they're fine," I said.

"I was out in the hay this morning and I figure we can start mowing the lower section in about a week if the weather holds."

"That's good. Hay's early this year." Hay, then oats, then wheat. There should be plenty of work coming up to keep everyone busy. Thank God.

We came to the office. I opened the door, and a surge of anger and despair ran through me. "Sit at the table," I said. Control.

David sat and looked at me expectantly.

God, I wished I had a shot of whiskey. I'd thought of it earlier, but I left it back at the house. We both needed to be clear-headed. No misunderstandings later. No accusations.

"David, there's something we have to do, and it is not pleasant." There. Clinical.

I looked him straight in the eye and he was pale under his tan, a look of fright, maybe, at my tone. "All right," he said. David had always been compliant, always wanted to please.

I wanted to say, think about it! Decide for yourself. But, Jack, there was no room for *if he wanted to*, no room for, *let's think about it a while*. There was only one answer, Jack. Only one.

"I don't know if you've thought much about the future," I said to him.

David shook his head a little, trying to read me, I think. He said, "The farm's doing fine. Is that what you mean?"

"Not really."

But David was on a roll. He pointed to the map of the compound on the wall behind him, and I let him go on. He was so proud of himself, like he was whenever he had a school presentation to practice on me. "The storage facilities are all operating one hundred per cent." His finger stabbed the generator station. "There's no way to run out of solar energy, but even if our machines break down so bad we can't fix them, we've got enough food stored to last most of our lives, even if we stop farming tomorrow. I figure the environmentally resistant packaging'll keep the food viable for—"

"Forty years. I know, David. Talk about the rest of our lives."

His finger dropped from the map. "Well... I don't know. I guess we keep on farming. We've got the oxen, and I want to experiment with ploughshare farming in the spring."

"Keep farming..."

"Yeah."

"And grow old."

"Yeah."

"And die."

"Yeah." His expression became distressed. "Okay, I know we're the only ones. We've been the only ones for a long time. It's the shits. Is that what you brought me out here to talk about?"

"So dying, one by one, first William, then the rest of us, until the last one is gone, is the only future you can think of?"

His brows knit in that little boy pout that came on him whenever he'd tried his hardest at something, and found himself boxed in a corner. "No. I don't think about it. I try not to."

"What about rescue?"

"Rescue?" His voice became querulous, as though he knew I was trapping him.

"Do you imagine a future when we may discover others, like us, who are resistant? Survivors?"

David hunched down into his chair and picked at a splinter on the table top. "Yeah. Sometimes."

"You know we've been signaling and scanning the radio spectrum for four—"

"I know! Shit, Mom. What do you want?"

"If you think that there are others—"

"There might be! Somewhere!"

I let silence follow his outburst. Then I went on. "You know why we have no petroleum-based fuel left? Why we have to run the threshers and combines on solar batteries instead?"

"No. Why?" He pushed himself up in his chair and leaned his forehead in his hands. "Yeah. I know. When I was fourteen. You left me in charge. You and dad went looking for other survivors. You didn't find any. Dad got sick and died."

"We used all the fuel because we had to be sure. We wanted to leave no possibility open. David, you need to know this. Maybe there was someone, alive, who didn't have a transmitter."

"There could be."

"Still?"

"There could be."

"David, we found whole cities of rotting corpses. No one could have lived there, even if they had been resistant to the virus, like we are. And we went to isolated places, too. Farms, acreages. A lot of people fled to the countryside in those days. You remember. They took the plague with them. If there are any survivors, now, David, they're too far away to reach. Ever. And they don't know we exist."

"All right." His eyes were still covered by the palms of his hands.

"Do you believe me? Do you know this to be true?"

"Yes."

I reached forward and took one of his hands and held it across the table. "To think otherwise is magical thinking. It's denial, David."

His face was pale, but he nodded, lips pressed together.

I had got this far, the easy part. Now my stomach churned. "But we don't have to stay here, alone, until we die." I forced myself to say it. "There is another way."

He rubbed his nose. "What?"

My mouth went dry and I couldn't speak. My stomach heaved. I looked for a bucket to puke in. I hadn't prepared for that.

"What is it?"

I couldn't do it, Jack. I felt hot. I had to get out of there.

"Mom?"

"We have to start over." I couldn't say it. Not there, sitting across the table from him, holding his hand. I couldn't look him in they eye and say it.

"You're not making any sense."

"There's no one out there. You can never marry. Julie and Sara are perfectly fertile — should be perfectly fertile, for all we know — but they will never marry and have children." I put my hand on my forehead to shade my eyes from his response. "We have to. We have to — make children. Lots of them. Raise them. Teach them—"

David's fingers stiffened in mine and I couldn't go on. I tried to make my brain be logical and think about what to say next, what to do next.

He pulled his hand from mine. "I know."

My stomach turned to water. "You know?"

"Yes."

"How long have you known?"

He shrugged, one shoulder. "Well, like you say. There isn't much to do here. Farm. What's the point? I've thought about... about, well I'm the only boy — man — aren't I? Some day, when the girls get bigger..."

I licked my lips, trying to find the words. "You didn't say anything to me about it."

"Jesus, mom. It's disgusting."

"How long were you going to wait?"

"I don't know." He went back to picking at the splinter. "'Till they were older."

"How old?"

"I don't know! Get off my back."

"'Till Julie was, what, fifteen?"

Again, the shrug. "Sure. Maybe."

"Four more years, David. A lot can happen in that much time. You could cut your finger on a dirty blade—"

"Nothing's going to happen."

I gripped the edge of the table. "We can't count on that. I've put this off too long already. We need to start. Tonight."

He breathed in sharply. "You?"

"For now. Yes."

He paled. "Jesus!"

"What?"

"You're my mother!"

I had no reply for him, Jack. There was no choice.

David slammed his hand on the table and shoved himself toward the door. He stopped, his fingers on the knob. I heard him turn and I could imagine his eyes on me, loathing me.

"Listen to the whole thing." My voice was harsher than I wanted it to sound.

"What more could there be?"

"I've sterilized a glass bottle for you. I've found a syringe. It doesn't have to be as disgusting as it sounds."

"Jesus. You mean it."

"We have to."

"There's no doctor, no midwife, even. If something happens to you—"

"If something happens to me, you still have two more chances. That's the choice. Begin now, you and me, or wait. How long until the girls' hips are wide enough to deliver a baby? Hmm? If we wait and something happens to you, we have no future."

"This is sick."

A wave of irritation boiled through my stomach. "Well, maybe it is, but we have to do it anyway."

David snorted. "And what would we call the little bastards?"

"Children!" I said and anger gave me the strength to look up at him. I swallowed back my other words. *Do you think this is easy for me? Don't you think I'm terrified? What about genetic abnormalities? What about children like William, who didn't inherit the resistance factor? What about complications of childbirth? You're getting off easy.*

He slumped against the wall next to the door. "A bottle for me. A syringe... Jesus H. Christ."

"You can't do it if you think about it."

"I can't do it at all." His lips barely moved.

"Just take the bottle. I'll leave."

He lifted his eyes and they were glistening. "Mom."

"You're the only one who can do this."

He closed his eyes and I made myself move, stand up. I brought the glass jar and stopper out of the autoclave. I pulled the cot and blankets closer to the table.

"Screw you!"

I paused at the door and put my hand on David's shoulder and he flinched. "I'll wait outside."

He didn't look at me.

I stepped out and closed the door behind me.

⊹·┼•┼•┼·⊹

I felt myself collapsing, then. My legs were weak and I threw up, finally, into the weeds. I pushed away from the door, around the corner, and sat down in the wiry grass by the monorail. All I could see was pictures in my mind, flashing by, unconnected. David as a baby, playing with that mangy one-eyed dog. Julie running the seeder, the muscles on her little arms knotted like ropes. You, Jack. Your eyes, reproaching me.

I sat there for a long time. After a while, I wiped my nose on my sleeve and opened my eyes. The cool air touched my back and I felt chilled. The smooth line of the monorail shot straight as an arrow down the valley, finally curving to the right behind the hills, going nowhere. The stars blazed out of the sky, so close I could almost touch them. The moon rose.

I felt flat, numb.

After a while, I heard the door open, and David's boots on the porch. "What you need is on the table," he said. His voice was husky. Then, the sound of his boots, returning to the house.

⇥•⫯•⫯•⇤

I pulled myself from the dry grass and dusted my pants off. I went inside the office. The little jar was in the middle of the table, half full. Promise, for the future. I didn't know if I could store half to use again tomorrow night. I didn't know if the syringe was big enough, or had enough force. I didn't know if it would work.

But. If it didn't work this month, we could try again next month. If we had to, we could do it the old fashioned way.

Then. In four years, maybe sooner, it would be Julie's turn, and when she was fifteen, Sara.

And so I lie here, something dead, gone, Jack; but, something growing, maybe. Jack — we have a beautiful farm, food and energy for a long, long time. With babies, we can thrive. Last.

And maybe — maybe — others *are* out there. Can you see it, Jack? A band of travelers — new world explorers — cresting the hill where our grandchildren tend the sheep.

After He's Eaten...
Nancy Bennett

an elaborate meal
sizzling stars swarming in
 the black hole mouth (having eaten the whole
thing and

 not believing it!)

 watching the late show of force
toy cannons and white shuttles, whizzing in and in
 again.
Never feeling depleted, the metal and mortal bites
   satisfy the function. Drop drop, fizz fizz.

 Antacids for the intergalactic
   whale...

Seven in a Boat, No Dog

Candas Jane Dorsey

They decided to get into the boats at New York, or the place where New York would have been if it were still there. The bovines had been at New York for years and finally had gnawed it down to the ground: the neighbouring farmers had sheep grazing there now, which meant that every hill of rubble was even and hard-trampled and the sheep dung, which is what Zane called it instead of shit, was filling in the rough areas enough to support an overall crop of sturdy, quick-renewing grasses.

Of the seven of them, only one had been to New York back in its heyday. Joycie Karenina hadn't thought much of the transit system, and a scalper in Times Square had taken advantage of her obvious fatigue and low blood sugar confusion to sell her tickets to *The Lion King* at twice the proper price, so she didn't care whether the city survived under its woollen cloak at all, was just as happy to see that it had been its own downfall.

She was a bitchy old woman, was Joycie, and she knew it, but she at least had a past to remember, twelve books in print, and more lovers than Imelda had shoes, and how old did *that* reference make her, Katyann was fond of saying, who was only a year younger but had had only one unsatisfactory husband and was shyly proud of it, as if for a ribbon in canning asparagus awarded by the tired jury of a state fair unacknowledged by the big exhibition circuit. Katyann had wanted to be a writer and have a story published in *The New Yorker*, so she thought that the symbolism, or maybe irony, she could never get irony sorted out, of leaving from the new high beaches of Soho was excellent. Or maybe it was just sarcasm. Maybe irony was just sarcasm too.

Stuart was the practical one, who had found them three Zodiacs in good condition, and a flatbed that ran on alcohol to truck the boats across an unforgiving continent well past its best-before date.

"You told me you wanted grand adventure," he said to Zane when Zane complained, and indeed, Zane had been the one who had insisted on the Outward-Bound extremity of the voyage, and convinced the others.

Land travel is simply tedious, not challenging, he said, but the sea, ah, the sea...

Nasnin suspected that he was simply trying to get them all killed romantically, instead of by feral dogs or starvation. Why, then, did she go along with it? Where was the bite that got her rabid with the notion? Somewhere no-one could see, or was shown. While Joycie and Katyann both had some public merriment (a sure sign of private hungers) related to the notion of unwinding Nasnin from her sari by grasping the heavy embroidered end and snapping it until Nasnin spun out of it like a spin top, the fact is that held by little more than cleverness and determination, Nasnin's sari always remained unwrinkled and undisturbed, by anything — cataclysm and fantasy made no mark on her cheerful spotlessness.

Nasnin was the oldest of all of them, but looked the youngest by at least ten years. She bragged that her grandparents, all four, lived past their hundredth year, which she persisted in calling their millennium, and her parents, all two, were still living somewhere to the undefined west, but she blissfully intended to die as soon as the voyage was underway. So that you others will have something safe to eat and drink, she said, laughing heartily. Rosemary was never sure when she was joking and when she was simply being ironic. Or was it sarcastic?

Of course at their ages the women outnumbered the men, that was a given, though one of them was lesbian and two claimed to be bisexual. Nasnin also claimed to be a virgin but no-one believed her. That hearty humour had not been gained without the sacrifice of at least one hymen. Or so said Sylvaine, who claimed to be transsexual herself, but they were all so old that really, they all looked about the same, vague liplines and thinning hair and the finest of downy moustaches plucked or shaved or depilated from upper lips of spotted crepe. Fetching, Rosemary snarled into her mental mirror, but to the others maintained a mild and generous mien.

Three Zodiacs were needed to hold all the water, gasoline cans, freeze-dried and preserved food, filtering devices, outdated sunscreen (there was no longer any other kind, the breakdown of capitalism progressing about as well as the breakdown of the great coastal cities, that is to say, reduced to artifacts, rubble, and mythology so daringly dubious that two entire generations of disbelievers had already been created) and the other paraphernalia of survival, as well as themselves. The largest of the three had a small engine which ran on water somehow, and there were great lengths of superannuated but still pristine yellow plastic rope for lashing the other two boats to either side to make a great clumsy caricature of a catamaran shell but with the tiny submerged propeller standing in for sails.

On the first day out a great deal of time was spent rearranging things, and finally Stuart said, just as the sun was setting at their backs, I should have taken the fourth one, even if it was patched. Forget it, said Zane comfortingly, and the two men lay down together in their nest of jerrycans and tinned ham. It was only then that Rosemary realised they were now a couple, and she felt she could be forgiven for the rude gust of laughter she made — the sea air will do that sort of thing to a person, give them unexpected moments of exhilaration and abandon, or so Nasnin said, putting her feet up on the gunwale of their boat and admiring for the twentieth time that day the elaborate foot jewellery that she had brought along.

Rosemary thought suddenly that before too many days were over, she would either get dead tired of those feet, or give in and fall in love with them and with the rest of

Nasnin the way the others had: they laughed delightedly at everything Nasnin said, even now when her family's wealth made no difference, their influence was a quarter of a century dead, and Nasnin a shadow of the proud beauty she had been when she learned to swear in English, those many decades ago, so long ago that swearing in women had gone in and out of fashion several times (currently out, where people still gathered), but apparently Nasnin had cared little for fashion's peripeteia. High quality saris and low language had served her well through an adult life longer than Rosemary, who actually *was* the youngest, had been alive.

It gave one pause to think of it — and not tiny delicate cat paws either, thought Rosemary, despite how catty she found herself being, but big barking healthy dog paws from some Newfie or Bouvier who had been out in the mud and was now frolicking across a cream-coloured carpet, with a relaxed swinging motion that Rosemary realised with her last bit of conscious mind was the ocean, rocking her gently to sleep, her last act of the day being to pull her generous straw sunhat across her face in case the sun rose before she did.

Rosemary had been born in a small desert town in the middle of the continent and raised to miniature adulthood on a ranch, or was it a farm? It had hundreds of head of beefalo grazing dryland down to dust, and thousands of acres of sugar beets under vast science-fictional rolling irrigation systems, so she guessed both were correct (a fanch? a rarm?). She had been punished for some hubris in a former life by never growing past four feet eleven inches tall, and she had shrunk a bit in age, sometimes wondered if she had been included because she was neat and tidy and wouldn't take up space better occupied by water bags and Nasnin's spare saris.

The events of decades ago fade into anecdote and index entry, which Rosemary thought a blessing in some ways: how sad it would be to have nothing but an eternal present on which one was unable to act, a list of grudges forever unanswerable and joys eternally unreplicable due all to their unfortunate location in time. But Sylvaine had reached the neurological phase where the present is so murky and unretained that the faded past looks vivid by comparison, and was spending much of her time wondering at her own effrontery at being here in public in this odd picnic party wearing the women's clothing which to him, early in life, had been a fetish more than a privilege. It was touching, in a way, to see how grateful she was for the freedom to wear polyester blends in floral and pastel-plaids: Rosemary had prepared for the trip by looting an Eddie Bauer in Winnipeg on the way, and her only concession to gender was that she had two pairs of Tilley dry-overnight women's briefs: men's were unnecessarily elaborate, and her attire was practical, not a statement.

Sylvaine had transferred over to their boat for a little visit, and was telling Nasnin a long story about the club he used to frequent, and one particular outing in drag to a local mall, he and three others lingering (she seemed unconscious of the pun) in women's wear stores, checking out the other patrons surreptitiously to see if their transgression had been noticed. "And I'm *sure* they knew *something* was wrong, you could tell," she said triumphantly.

Nasnin's father had owned a sari shop, first in Mumbai and then in Canada. "Of course they knew something was fucking wrong, darling," she said kindly, "a bunch of goddamn crossdressers invading their goddamn store!"

Sylvaine giggled.

After Sylvaine was back in her own boat, and napping, Nasnin said quietly, so that her voice would not carry over the water, "Stupid little men. Do they think everyone was looking? But of course they do. My father and mother would never have spotted their like but the silly buggers were always calling them into the fitting room for advice. Hair on their backs, and amateur penis tucks. They loved the thought that they were about to get arrested. My mother used to recommend a goddamn depilatory cream she made herself. She must have supplied half the closet cases of Mill Woods. She had a good goddamn laugh about it with us too, let me tell you!"

"I feel sorry for her," said Rosemary. "How it must feel to outlive all your issues."

"But that has not happened to you, darling," Nasnin squelched her.

"No," said Rosemary. "In fact, I suppose we can thank global warming for our little company being together at all."

"Don't be so fucking tedious," said Nasnin.

"Too late," said Rosemary.

"What is the matter with you? You have your period?" and Nasnin laughed excessively.

Rosemary had to grin. "Just the fucking hot flashes," she said, setting Nasnin off again.

That second day was a little choppy, though the subsidence of the ocean currents had done a lot for private boating. By evening they had made a fair amount of progress, and according to the GPS were right on course, but Joycie Karenina — and heaven forefend one called her just plain Joyce, as she had been when Zane first fucked her when they were both in their last year at that fancy private prep school — said that she was in touch with the Gaian spirit and that according to the harmonic resonances they should be steering a more easterly course.

"I agree," said Sylvaine, who was back in the decade when Joycie had held harmonic convergences at several places on the planet convenient to the assignations she had been having in those years.

"Forget it, old girl," said Stuart. "Your harmonic days are long gone."

"New Age has become old age," said Katyann, provoking Nasnin's guffaw, and so blushing with pleasure. Even Zane laughed, although Sylvaine's laugh was tentative and she looked from face to face. Rosemary imagined Sylvaine was suddenly unsure who all these old people were she was stuck with in these weird boats.

So they set course south according to the GPS, lashed the tillers on course, checked that the Zodiacs were securely roped together, and as the sun set, they all settled down and soon drifted off to sleep, Rosemary awake longest, gazing into the gloaming sky, glad that Joycie K had not prevailed: despite the warmth, Rosemary had always hated the shortness of tropical days.

Sometime in the darkest part of the night, one of the Zodiacs bumped theirs and Rosemary woke. She turned her head and there was Zane, alert in his boat, looking down fondly at Stuart asleep.

"Hi," she said softly.

"Didn't wake you, did we? It's chopping up a little so I thought I'd snub up the lashings a little."

"Sounds very nautical."

Zane snorted. "We try. We try. How you getting on with her colonial highness?" He looked over at Nasnin, snoring heavily in the other end of the boat from Rosemary.

"Not too bad. I've decided I don't need to kill and eat her. Yet."

"Funny, most people wanted to eat her first, and when they couldn't, that's when the urge to kill arose."

"Well, it's true, you kind of have to love her or hate her. But it doesn't really matter any more, does it?"

"Feeling your years, are you? I'm surprised. You're the baby of the family. We're all going to rely on you for the gymnastics and lifesaving if we get in trouble."

Rose chuckled softly. "Well, that should look cute. You're how tall?"

"Two metres. What's that, six-six in your primitive system?"

"Oh, you shrank too! Well, you'll get skinned elbows when I use the fireman's carry on you."

"Do you think we'll be all right when we get there?"

Rosemary looked at him. "You seem to actually want to know. This has to be a first, in about sixty years."

"Oh, don't be a bitch, darling. I'm trying to be serious."

"So am I. Well, if you really want my opinion, no, I think we'll drift until we run out of food, then water, then the milk of human kindness, then sunscreen, then each other, then life. Seven desiccated husks, some the worse for the toothmarks, will someday be found drifting up against some other hull, or even some other shore."

"Why did you come then?"

Rosemary looked away across the water. It was amazing how much was visible by starlight, even with no moon. Had it set, or not arisen yet? Like most of the lore they now depended on for their lives, this was a mystery, to her even more than any of the others. Stuart at least had his encyclopaedias.

"Why did you?" she asked.

"Duh," he said, looking down at Stuart, who stirred slightly, curled up closer to Zane, and began to snore slightly.

"Well, then, same sort of thing. Go to sleep."

From the far boat, Sylvaine whimpered, then called, "Mariah?" Zane sat up slightly to look over, causing Stuart to sigh petulantly and throw an arm across his chest.

Rosemary called softly, "Dorme-toi, Sylvaine. C'est bien, rien de probleme."

"Nice," murmured Zane.

"You too," said Rosemary tartly. But she lay awake for some time more, watching the silver tipped waves of the light chop, and feeling the zodiac swivel and undulate beneath her like the waterbed she'd slept on when she was a child. Something atavistic about that, she thought, and it was pretty perverse to use all that water so frivolously on the droughty prairie, come to think of it. Her parents must have been pretty nostalgic for their hippie youth to even keep the thing in the house, let alone tumble their children into it like puppies. Puppies. I always hated those old dogs, thought Rosemary. So why do I still get dog pause? Nasnin snorted and barked lightly in her sleep. Ah, yes, thought Rosemary, and fell into the rising moon.

Fin-de-siécle was her first waking thought, followed immediately by the irritating need to piss. They'd rigged a little seat and half-tent at the side of the Zodiac but one of the others needed to act as outrigger counterbalance, Nasnin of course never less that fully scatological when it was her turn in either role. Rosemary decided as she wiped her ass that it was time to trade boats for a while, but before she could speak, there was a flurry of motion beneath her, and she instinctively cast herself inboard just as the jaws snapped shut on the platform she'd been sitting on. She heard air begin to hiss out of the boat.

"Stuart! Katyann! Sharks!" she yelled, from her position at the bottom of the boat.

"Awesome!" she heard Zane say, then Stuart shouting, "Zane, no! Stop that!" and the sound of compressed air exploding. The boat was tossed wildly and she felt the lashings of a mighty musculature beneath her, only a membrane away. She struggled out of the bottom of the boat, pulling up her jeans, to see Zane standing like a propaganda poster-boy in the stern of the next boat, holding a compressed-air gun. Stuart was struggling to unlash the Zodiacs to give a thrashing beast room to die — or live. Rosemary heard more escaping air hissing. She hoped she remembered rightly, that Zodiacs were constructed with parallel air compartments so they couldn't sink from even multiple leaks.

The rope trailed. Nasnin and Rosemary's boat was driven away from the other two. Between them the water was whipped to a red foam. They felt more smooth bodies jostling under the Zodiac, and both of them held onto the gunwale ropes desperately. Rosemary had time to note that Nasnin's sari looked crisp and fresh. Then the other sharks began to tear their bleeding comrade apart in the intimate theatre between the boats, their industry driving the travellers to further and further removes.

Soon, Rosemary put her head down on her clenched arms, so quickly the spectacle had palled to distasteful repetition.

"Fucking hell," said Nasnin, and Rosemary looked over to see that Nasnin had been splashed by bloody saltwater and her brilliant green sari was limp and brown on the skirt and trailing end. Awkwardly, because she still had to hang on, she unwound herself from it and pushed it overboard, where it floated on the turmoil for a moment before abruptly disappearing in a swirl like the draining funnel of a toilet. Nasnin lay flushed and panting angrily, a thin old body in a green satin half-slip and tight, short-sleeved blouse, grimly holding onto the ropes.

Rosemary struggled up and found an oar. "Get up, you!" she ordered. "We have to get farther away!"

Nasnin cast about herself for the oar, found it half-under her. "That was my favourite," she said. "I wore it the day

I met my first boyfriend." She fit the oar into the oarlock and snapped the safety-catch. "Real silk. Not like the junk you get these days. Is this goddamned boat sinking?"

"Probably. I though you were a virgin."

"A virgin can have a goddamn boyfriend or two," she panted.

"Ah." Rosemary pulled hard at her oar and the boat began to turn.

"Or a fucking girlfriend or two. What, is this boat to twirl now like a dancer?"

"We have to... get back to the others."

"Oh, too fucking bad. Just when I... have you on our own."

Rosemary puffed a laugh. "As if. You can't stand me, you always say."

"Ah, just my way of speaking. You know me."

"Yeah, for far too long."

"So it is you who goddamn hates me?"

"Decided... this trip... one either hates you... or loves you... haven't decided... which..."

Nasnin laughed briefly, no breath to bellylaugh. "Let me know... what goddamn decision... where are those fucking boats?"

"Can't see them... use GPS when we're... far away from sharks..."

"Goddamn fucking motherfucking sharks. My best sari... in the drink."

Rosemary grinned, breathing heavily through her mouth though, so it might have looked a bit savage. Then suddenly she stopped rowing to laugh and point. "Nasnin. Look."

Two sharks nose almost to flat nose, pulling and flapping wildly, between them a taut rope of greenish silk. They must have each grabbed a stained end of sari, bit, swallowed, and now were married by the strongest natural fibre on earth outside spider silk.

Nasnin stared, then spoke in Hindi, an oath or a prayer, could have been either. She let go her oar, backed up against Rosemary on the bench, shivering. They heard the crash of the airgun again and one of the sharks arched high above the water, blood splaying from its eye. Zane was a good shot, Rosemary thought, aside, as she put an arm around Nasnin and reached for one of their thermal wraps with her other hand. She pulled it around them both. The sharks turned on their new prey, and the ocean moiled again. Nasnin was weeping.

Rosemary turned Nasnin's head gently away from the carnage. "Under the seat somewhere is the flare-gun," she said. "Find it while I... no, I'll find it. You get some clothes on. Something warm."

Without a word Nasnin turned to her cargo bags and undid one of the snazzy waterproof zips. Rosemary, grop-ing for the flare gun, aware now that she too was wet with seawater and who knows what else, marvelled again at the neatness of Nasnin's life. Until this moment, perhaps.

Rosemary fired the flare gun, then had nothing to do but watch Nasnin contrive, with much trembling, but still remarkably deftly, to rewrap herself in a brilliant saffron yellow, then in a soft, woolly shawl — knowing Nasnin, it would be cashmere or pashmina. Nasnin sank back to the bench then. They were both shaking and it was Nasnin this time who pulled the thermal wrap around Rosemary's back and tucked in beside her, wrapping their feet and pulling the wrap up behind their necks.

"I suppose we're in shock," Nasnin said. "Fucking prehistoric sea alligators."

Across the water the sound of the engine on the centre Zodiac, and Rose knew they would not lose their companions — this time. She astonished herself by fall-ing asleep, a fall that took two or three short bounces, then the main drop, so that she had time for a few disordered sensations before she dissociated completely.

"Well," she woke to Joycie Karenina's voice, "*that* was a lesson in Nature red in tooth and claw." All seven were in the central boat, though Rosemary had no idea how she got there.

"As if your love life weren't enough," snapped Katyann.

"Is everyone all right?" Rosemary mumbled.

"All right except for their fucking egos." Nasnin of course.

"You should talk," said, of all people, Sylvaine.

"Don't backtalk me, you goddamn little fancyman!"

"Girls, girls!" said Stuart. "Let us try not to do to each other what the sharks failed to accomplish."

"Why not?" Rosemary was surprised to find this was her outer, not inner, voice as the others turned to stare. "We are the last ones, and we are on this fucking wild goose chase. Do any of us really believe that we will be picked up on cue by the rescuing aliens or whoever is doing that sort of thing? Even if we manage to get to the fucking Triangle?"

"Oh, my dear," said Joycie Karenina. "Do you really doubt my vision?"

"Your vision! That's rich," Zane said. "Stuart is the one driving this expedition. He's done more than all of you put together. Except Rose."

"Don't single *me* out," said Rosemary's new outer inner-voice. "I'm just as bad as the rest of you."

Sylvaine said anxiously, "What is little Mary so upset about?"

"Never mind, *p'tite*," said Katyann, glaring at Rosemary.

"Don't single me out either, darling," said Stuart. "We're all in the same boat."

Nasnin and Rosemary were the only ones who laughed. Joycie K and Katyann bristled identically, so that for the first time in decades their resemblance was obvious, and Zane just hugged Stuart and Sylvaine protectively.

"Time to get some sleep," said Stuart. "If we keep this pace, the GPS says we'll be there just after sunrise tomorrow."

"And what will we do then?" asked Sylvaine.

"We will send our signal, my dear. We will wait."

There was a moment of silence, broken by Nasnin, who was looking back at the slight wake the tiny engine was making, and at the two Zodiacs, one slightly lopsided, in tow behind.

"I saw two dogs do that once, on the riverbank in Mumbai. There was a dead beggar there, well, there were always dead people there of course, it was a goddamn dump for the dead. This one must have had something in his loincloth, you know, because they played tug of war with it. But they seemed to be stuck, they couldn't get loose, and they gulped and gulped until they were at each other's faces. Then..." she shuddered. "It was the same with the children who came through last year, looting the apartments. All the old farts shivering in corners like us, while these wild things thrashed through the air around us, throwing our goods around, looking for food and so on. One woman thought, perhaps they would respond to kindness, they are children after all, so she offered them food and some clothing, holding her hands out. They sank their teeth into her arms. I saw her go down, and blood spray just like that fucking fish. It was the only way they had to kill, you see. They had not found the knack of knives yet. They live under the bridges, out of the rain."

"Did I ever mention how much I hate dogs?" Rosemary said.

"Good thing I am a cat, then," said Nasnin with satisfaction.

"I had to learn to shoot," Rosemary continued. "There were packs of them all around my place. Dogs, people: you shot at anything that growled at you."

"Yes," said Joycie Karenina. "I lost all my books. They burned them. My own books, I mean, my only copies. I myself burnt all the others. It gets cold in Toronto in the winter, even now."

"I'm sorry," said Katyann. "I didn't know."

"Well, I wasn't going to tell *you*, of all people. You hated those books."

"I never," said Katyann, turning her face away toward the sea. "Just was jealous."

"Well, isn't *this* charming," said Zane. "Our basic humanity coming out, as a contrast to the savage continent we left behind. Epiphanies in the wake of adrenaline and disaster. Aren't we the allegory of humanity, then. Instead of seven crazy old..."

"I don't think that's necessary," said Sylvaine with dignity. "We are who we are."

They looked at her (with a bit of surprise if they felt anything like she did, Rosemary thought). Sylvaine smiled sadly. "Whoever we are from moment to moment, of course. Don't think I can't feel it all flickering on and off."

"What does it fucking matter?" said Nasnin. "Stuart is right. We are now in the same boat. It doesn't matter what the goddamn name of the boat is."

"Yes, it does," said Rosemary dreamily. "The *Marie Celeste*, for instance, what a romantic sounding name. Not industrial at all. Or the *Flying Dutchman*. All the will-o'-the-wisps people chase. They have lovely names."

They began to slot themselves into sleeping spaces, like books on a shelf, or spoons in a drawer. We remember so much, between us, that no-one will ever know again, thought Rosemary. Being lost, moment by moment.

"Well," said Nasnin, "I for one don't give a tinker's dam about names. It is the thing itself that pleases me. The person themself."

"How Platonic of you," said Rosemary. Again, only Nasnin laughed, but she saw Stuart smile, anyway, and Sylvaine brought her hands together in an almost-silent clap.

"Well," said Nasnin, "that is a virgin's only option, don't you think?"

Phoebus 'Gins Arise
Kate Riedel

No-one was really surprised when Miss Claudia Parry threw the sans-serif ball from one of the new Selectrics at Dacia Middleton, hitting her on the side of the head and sending her bleeding to the nurse's room.

Not that Miss Parry had ever done such a thing before in her thirty years of teaching typing and stenography at Buck's Crossing High School. Still, it was common knowledge that all of Miss Parry's students were snapped up by offices down in the city, not only because they were highly skilled, but because after going through Miss Parry's classes, they could cope with anything that even the most cantankerous boss could throw at them. Of course, this last was not meant to be taken literally.

Dacia Middleton went to the nurse's room. Miss Parry went right on teaching up to the bell at the end of the hour.

Word had already got round. Mrs. James and Miss Honimacher, who taught social studies and music respectively, stopped their conversation in mid-sentence, raising their cups of coffee to cover the abrupt silence when Miss Parry came into the teacher's lounge. Miss Parry crossed to the hotplate to boil water for tea, the Cuban heels of her plain black leather pumps sounding as firmly and rhythmically on the green linoleum tile as the fingers of her students on the Remington manuals they had to master before they were allowed to touch the Selectrics.

Mrs. James lowered her cup and said brightly to Miss Honimacher, "Were you able to arrange a recording session for the choir?"

"Oh, yes," Miss Honimacher said. "Mr. Smith was quite reasonable. It should be a good fund-raiser for the new robes. And — you'll never believe this!" she giggled. "He told my fortune!"

"Really," said Mrs. James, taking a sceptical sip of coffee. "Cards? Crystal ball? How much did he charge for *that*?"

The water boiled. Miss Parry poured it over the tea leaves in the pot, put the lid on the pot, and the crocheted cosy over all.

"Oh, no money. It was on the sign on his door, and I asked about it, and he said all I had to do was bring a loaf of bread and—" she lowered her voice, giggling again, "a bottle of wine. I was a little nervous, going into the liquor store—" Teachers at Buck's Crossing, the female ones at least, were supposed to set a good example for the students, and not consume alcohol.

"It *is* a rough part of town," Mrs. James said, smoothing over the peccadillo. "So what did he tell you?"

Miss Honimacher's prefatory giggle was interrupted when Miss Hansen, the principal's secretary (who had got *her* Selectric a whole year before any were budgeted for Miss Parry's classes) put her head around the door.

"Miss Parry? Mr. Guillet wants to talk to you."

"I'll be there in a minute." Miss Parry took a cup and saucer from the cupboard and, in the renewed silence, poured tea and took it with her. As the door closed behind her she could hear Mrs. James and Miss Honimacher resume their conversation — *not* the one about Mr. Smith who operated a recording studio and told fortunes on the side.

Miss Parry took the chair in front of Mr. Guillet's desk, the teacup perfectly steady on the saucer. She took a sip of tea and waited.

"Well." Mr. Guillet cleared his throat and tried again. "Well. Ah. Yes. You were, I remember, the unbeatable pitcher on the girl's softball team thirty-five years ago." He laughed, or tried to.

Miss Parry did not laugh. She waited, feet together, plain white cuffs showing an exact half-inch below the sleeves

of her loden-green wool suit jacket, dark grey eyes behind
black-framed harlequin glasses fixed on Mr. Guillet, not
a hair out of place in her precise perm, as black as it had
been when she first started teaching. Mr. Guillet gave up
trying to keep the conversation light.

"Ah. Miss Parry. I've spoken with the nurse. Miss
Middleton appears to have suffered a bruise and a cut, but
no further injury. The cut, however, is severe enough to
require stitches. She has called her parents, and they have
spoken to me."

He paused. Miss Parry took another sip of tea.

"This will..." he continued. "Ah. This incident will, of
course, have to come before the School Board. We backed
you up when you sent girls home to change clothes when
they wore skirts above the knee to school." His voice gained
strength. "We did nothing when you failed Ellen Reimers
in typing because she broke her thumb mid-term, instead
of giving her an incomplete as might have been expected.
We ignored complaints about stenography notebooks, paid
for by your students or their parents, torn in half for in-
adequate work. But this is far more serious. I am having
Miss Hansen phone to arrange a meeting of the School
Board for tomorrow night. Two of the board members have
already asked if the meeting was about Miss Middleton's
injury, although I instructed Miss Hansen not to go into
detail about the reason for calling the meeting."

Miss Parry set her cup on her saucer. "Am I to be at this
meeting?" she asked.

Mr. Guillet cleared his throat again. "Ah. The superin-
tendent prefers to keep the first meeting, ah, private. A
second meeting will then be set which, of course, you will
be expected to attend. Have you any other questions? Do
you have anything to say about this incident?"

Miss Parry regarded him a moment, and then said,
calmly and clearly, "There was a mouse."

"I beg your pardon?"

"There was a mouse in my classroom. I had the ball in
my hand, and I threw it at the mouse. I assure you, no
damage was done to the ball; I checked; they are, as you

know, expensive." She looked at the leather-strapped watch on her left wrist. "If you'll excuse me, I have another class in ten minutes."

She rose and left.

It occurred to her, as she returned to her classroom, that Dacia Middleton looked a little like Katherine. She turned the thought over in her mind, then dismissed it.

Despite an undercurrent of fear combined with curiosity, Miss Parry's students in the last class of the day were even more quiet than usual. Quiet as mice, Miss Parry thought with grim amusement.

Finally the last exercise was handed in, the last dustcover put over the last typewriter, the last student out the door in silence that, as soon as the door was closed, turned into a low, tense babble.

By the time Miss Parry had straightened her own desk, seen that all was ready for tomorrow's classes, and checked and locked the supply cabinets, the halls were nearly empty.

She did not have a coat. Her suit jacket had been quite adequate to the April-verging-on-May weather that morning. She tied a green chiffon scarf over her perm, and left the school. The busses that carried the country students home had already pulled away, and the school parking lot was empty.

Miss Parry walked home under the new leaves, misty green as her scarf, stopping only to buy a loaf of bread and a piece of cheddar at the corner store. The neighbourhood was noisy with children just home from school, teenagers spinning by on their bicycles or giggling on the porches.

They did not greet her, nor she them. Miss Parry did not teach because she loved children. Her students did not love her any more than she loved them. But they had backbone when she was done with them; the ones that broke did not pass. Their parents knew that, and they tolerated no complaints about Miss Parry from their children.

She passed the Presbyterian church she had attended since childhood, and which the Middletons also attended.

The Middletons were new in town. Mr. Middleton had been brought in as vice-president of accounting at the cannery. Mrs. Middleton was already on the executive of the Women's Arts and Letters Club, and the Hospital Auxiliary, and the School Board, as well as several church committees. Dacia would not need to make her living in an office; she had probably signed up for typing because she thought it would be a snap course.

Miss Parry had arrived at the bungalow where she had grown up. It was now hers, clean and tidy, painted regularly, repairs made as soon as they were needed, grass mowed in summer, walk shovelled in winter, all maintained by Miss Parry's salary and efforts.

She had maintained her mother, too, those last years when Mrs. Parry was bed-ridden, and Katherine, for her last three years of high school.

Katherine had pleaded for the piano.

"Mother left the house and furnishings to me," Miss Parry had pointed out.

"But she paid for all those piano lessons for *me*! She must have meant me to have the piano."

"She didn't say so in her will."

"She said you were to look after me!"

"As long as you lived in this house. You have a husband now. He can provide you with a piano."

"You know he can't afford it!"

"You knew that too. If you really think you have a case, you can speak to our lawyer."

Katherine never had.

But the Middletons might, to *their* lawyer. And Mrs. Middleton was on the School Board.

Miss Parry had never doubted the house, furniture and piano were morally as well as legally hers, nor did she doubt it now. But right now she had no desire to go up the walk and enter the bungalow, where the piano, dusted regularly but untuned since Katherine had left, sat in the front room.

She walked on.

The trees hung misty-green overhead, the air was mild, the sun still above the housetops. A robin hopped across a lawn, stopped, cocked its head, hopped on.

Miss Parry continued walking.

The sun was level with the rooftops. The smell of cooking dinners drifted from windows opened to the first soft air of spring.

Miss Parry walked until the sun was below the rooftops and the houses cast long shadows across the streets and sidewalks. In the last houses before the railroad tracks, husbands and children were called to supper.

The sound of Miss Parry's heels changed timbre as she stepped from the well-maintained concrete onto the thick wooden planks that brought the spaces between the railroad tracks level with the sidewalks, then back onto the cracked concrete on the other side.

Robins carolled their evening song from the treetops, crowded behind the row-houses built for the immigrants — Poles, Irish, Italians, Greeks — who had come to work in the canning factories earlier in the century.

Katherine had married one of those people, a handsome and charming black Irishman. He had risen to foreman — and fallen into a whiskey bottle. When a young manager brought in from the city had moved back there, Katherine had gone with him. Presumably he could afford to buy her a piano, although Miss Parry had never tried to find out, or even considered trying.

The children of the immigrants had grown and graduated from high school, and their daughters were now secretaries in the factory offices, their sons accountants and junior managers, and new immigrants had moved into the increasingly shabby row-houses. A few small businesses had set up in former residences — a variety store here, a plumber there, a neon sign proclaiming a liquor store.

The street lights came on, and still Miss Parry walked on to where the row-houses ended, to where the canneries loomed foresquare and the miasma of cooked corn, even at this time of year, hung over all.

There was a sign in the window of the last house, lit by a small spotlight to make it legible from the street.

A.P. Smith
Music Lessons
Recording Studio
Oracle

So this was where Miss Honimacher had arranged for the school choir to record.

Miss Parry, holding her bag from the grocery store, stood and looked at the sign for several minutes, and then turned back, but only as far as the liquor store.

As she walked up the steps to the front porch of the row-house, she saw that either Miss Honimacher had mistaken the name, or the sign painter couldn't spell. She sniffed, and, balancing the grocery store bag and the one from the liquor store on one arm, opened the front door and stepped in.

The door gave directly onto an ascending staircase. The stairs were uncarpeted, and her nose wrinkled against the odour of dust and the feces of small vermin.

Somewhere, someone was playing complex runs on a guitar, runs so precise that at first she thought it was a phonograph record, until it broke off, there was a murmur of voices, and it started all over again.

There were two doors at the top of the stairs. The music came from behind one; on the other was a sign repeating the information on the one in the window.

A.P. Sminth
Music Lessons
Recording Studio
Oracle
24 hours - walk in

So the mistake had been Miss Honimacher's. Miss Parry wasn't surprised. None of these younger teachers were as well-educated as they ought to be.

She opened the door and walked through a dim entrance hall, empty except for a spotted mirror on the wall, to a dark room crowded with overstuffed chairs and Victorian side tables.

She sat in one of the chairs, placed her bags on the table beside it, and waited.

Opposite was another chair and table, this one covered with a white linen cloth that must have been meant for a dining table, as it went right down to the floor and lay in folds at the corners.

The guitar in the next room faded into tender riffs, a few discrete notes like drops of water. The tablecloth opposite moved, as if stirred by a draft across the floor. The door opened. Had it been so bright in the hall? Had she fallen asleep?

"Mr. Sminth," Miss Parry stated to the man who stood before her.

The man smiled, like the sun coming out. His face shown with the kind of beauty that cries youth, aloud and joyously, but it was not a young face; his hair was neither gold nor silver, but ivory. He wore jeans, sandals, and a loose shirt that hung in such a way as to suggest that the arms under it were ropy with muscles. He carried a guitar, acoustic, steel-stringed.

"My half-brother recommended a country and western band," he said, gesturing to the wall from behind which the occasional riff could still be heard. "He thinks we're ready for a renaissance in folk music — he may be right."

He seated himself opposite, and tried a few notes on the guitar, casually, so beautiful in the touch that she didn't want it to stop. But he played only a few notes, then raised his hands from the strings, looked at her, and said, "So? What is it you want to know?"

"You're the oracle," she said. "You tell me."

"Ah," he said. "'If anyone hopeth in what he doeth to escape the notice of the gods, he errs.'"

"I also know Pindar," she said. "But I thought you told the future. Anyone can tell the past. And if you're referring to my lie about the mouse—"

"Oh, no," he said. "There was a mouse."

"There was?"

The tablecloth stirred again. "Oh, yes, definitely, there was a mouse. But before we can tell the future, we must acknowledge the past. Although, just for the record, forty years from now the skills you now teach will be obsolete." He smiled, and added, "You can have that one for free. However..." He gestured at the paper bags that sat on the table beside her. Miss Parry half-rose to pick them up and hand them to him, then settled back.

He took out the bread. "And cheese, too," he said approvingly. He took two slices of bread, unwrapped the cheese, cut a slice with a folding knife he took from his pocket, put it between the slices, and took a bite, crumbs falling to his lap. Then he set the sandwich on the paper bag beside the bread and cheese, and took the bottle from its bag. "Nice," he said, examining the label. "Whatever else they may say of you, Claudia Parry, you are not chintzy." He unfolded a corkscrew from his knife and took out the cork with a resonant pop. He produced two wine glasses, Miss Parry wasn't sure from where, poured wine into both, and handed her one. "Yes, very nice," he said, tasting it.

He drank half of what was in his glass. But Miss Parry's glass stopped at her lips. The left sleeve of his shirt was moving. Something was moving down his arm, under his sleeve, around his elbow, down to his wrist. A pink nose, quick whiskers, a hint of tiny, sharp teeth behind a brown-furred muzzle, black bead of an eye, two pink paws. A mouse scrambled from the cuff of his shirt, ran back up to his elbow, disappearing and reappearing among the folds, dropped to his denim-covered thigh, and began eating the crumbs that had fallen there.

She quietly set her glass on the table beside her.

"Now," he said. "You've been a member in good standing of your church for years. Surely you should be turning to God in your crisis. Why do you come to me instead?"

"God accepts us as we are, and His love is not for sale." Miss Parry smiled, but not with humour. "The gods, however, have been known to provide their services for a consideration."

"Indeed. I admire your honesty, as well as your taste in wine." Mr. Sminth took another swallow of wine. The strings of the guitar, propped next to the chair, pinged and resonated. A second mouse, a grey one, scrambled from the sound hole of the guitar, its tail flicking against the strings. It climbed the neck, clinging to the strings, and dropped from the peghead to the table, and helped itself to the sandwich that Mr. Sminth had left there.

"I never tried to escape the gods' notice," Miss Parry continued. "I never had any reason to deceive the gods."

Mr. Sminth lowered his wine glass. A third mouse poked its nose from under the table cloth, ran up his jeans leg, up his shirt to his hand, to the rim of the glass where it hung by its back toes, tail flicking in the air as it drank. It raised its head, red drops falling from its whiskers as it fixed its eyes on Miss Parry. It lowered its head to drink again.

"No," he said. "Only to deceive your mother."

"As for that," said Miss Parry, "Mother thought it was sweet of Katherine to teach her older sister what she learned at her piano lessons. She didn't need to know that Katherine only did it because I told her if she didn't, I'd tell mother what Katherine was really doing when she was supposed to be studying with her girlfriends. Or do you mean all the times Mother called from the bedroom to Katherine to tell her how beautifully she was playing, when most of the time it was me?"

"You took satisfaction in that, didn't you?" he smiled at her. "You were the practical one, the older daughter who had made her way in the big city, and then, when your mother fell ill, came back to look after her and support her and your younger sister by teaching. The younger sister was the artistic one, of course."

"She had talent," Miss Parry conceded.

"And you did not. Skill, but not genius."

"Oh yes, only skill, never genius. Genius is a gift. Skill comes only from hard work."

The table cloth, where it lay on the floor, moved. She could hear faint squeaks. Three more mice scrambled up the folds to join the first at the bread and cheese on the table. Three more dropped from the wall, scurried to the bread wrapper, squirmed inside until only their tails showed, and the wrapper moved as if alive with their depredations.

Miss Parry's arm jerked, unsettling the table beside her. Mr. Sminth reached over with his free hand and moved her glass to the table with the cloth. The mouse on his own glass clung in frantic balance to the rim, then dipped down to drink again once the glass had stabilized. Yet another mouse scrambled up the table cloth and attempted to scale the stem of Miss Parry's glass. It tipped. The mouse clung to the rim as the glass hit the table, rolling, spilling red wine in an arc across the white cloth. As it rolled to a stop the mouse clambered inside to drink what remained there.

"The piano was mine," Miss Parry said.

"It was, indeed," Mr. Sminth agreed. "Keeping the piano was not wrong. In that, you betrayed neither your sister nor your mother. Only me."

"I? I never betrayed you! She was the one who betrayed you! Katherine, to whom you gave the gift of real musical talent, and who wasted it, because she would not work at it!"

Mr. Sminth lifted the mouse from his glass and set it on the table, where it wandered tipsily over to join its companions busily demolishing the sandwich. The table was now nearly covered with mice, a wriggling blanket of grey and black and brown fur, in and out of the bread and cheese wrappers, licking at the wine stains.

He set down the glass and picked up the guitar. "Your sister made her own decision. To not use a gift is wasteful, yes. But is it any less wasteful to pay for something in hard coin, and then throw it away?" He strummed a chord, another, picked out a tune to which Miss Parry thought she remembered the words... The mice paused; some of them raised their heads. "Perhaps my half-brother was right," Mr. Sminth said. "Time for a folk revival."

"Aren't we rather off the topic?" If her voice did not shake, that was only because her voice never shook, and it was too late for it to start.

"It is your question. You are the one who must ask it."

He continued to play, note by soft, single note.

"What is to become of me?" Claudia Parry did not wail; she had never wailed aloud in her life, but if ever she had, it would have been now.

He smiled and moved into simple chords. Somewhere small voices took up the chorus...

> *I won't go to school any more, more, more,*
> *There's a big mean teacher in the door, door, door...*

Over and over, to a squeaking crescendo — "*I won't go to school any more, more, more...*" until Miss Parry raised her hands to her ears, so she could only see, not hear, the mice, singly, in pairs, in circles and lines, dancing to the school yard chant: "*There's a big mean teacher in the door, door, door!*"

But Mr. Sminth continued to play, and gradually she lowered her hands from her ears, to listen... listen... listen... to the Moonlight Sonata, and the Well-tempered Clavier, and Clementi's sonatinas, and all the pieces she had drawn from the piano keyboard with the speed and accuracy of a good typist while her mother lay in her bedroom and believed she listened to Katherine... She hadn't realized they could be played on a guitar. She watched the mice swaying in time to the music, moving in light-footed dances (some, the ones that had visited the wine glasses, were, perhaps, not quite as sure in their movements as the others)... The music moved from the familiar to the exotic, from the exotic to something she could not name except that she had never heard anything more beautiful in her life...

She woke to an empty room. Only the wrappers remained of the bread and cheese, only their droppings remained of the mice. Not even the guitar remained of Mr. Sminth.

She rose, wrinkled her nose in distaste, paused at the mirror in the entry to adjust her scarf over her hair, and opened the door. The sun must just be up; a mote-filled ray cut through the dusty air at the foot of the stairs. Behind the second door a clear soprano voice sang, unaccompanied,

> *Hark, hark, the lark*
> *At heaven's gate sings,*
> *And Phoebus 'gins arise...*

The outside door closed behind her on the lines,

With everything that pretty is,
My lady fair, arise...

The air had cooled considerably during the night, and
with only her suit jacket to keep her warm, she shivered
as she walked back, past the row houses.

The low-angled light lay in gold streaks across the weeds
of the scanty front lawns. When she reached the open spaces
on either side of the railroad tracks, it gained some warmth.
She thought there was movement around her, in the grass
that pushed through the gravel between the cross-ties.

She could smell frying bacon as she walked along the
street, and robins sang to the morning from the tops of the
trees. But the song of the robins above did not cover the
sound of something else below, rustlings, movements just
out of sight in the grass, something that was almost a chant
just beyond hearing range...

She did not go into her own house, but walked on past.
Now mothers were calling to their children to get up, to
get dressed, to eat their breakfasts. The only person she
saw on the street was the newspaper boy on his bicycle.
She did not have to see what accompanied her on her walk
to work, skittering in the grass, skipping through the tulip
beds in front of the Presbyterian church.

The school building was not yet unlocked; the janitor
let her in. She thanked him, climbed the stairs to the second
floor, and walked down the hall to unlock the door of the
typing room. She walked to the front of the classroom and
sat at her desk, hands folded in front of her, and watched
in bemusement as mice scrabbled, seemingly from nowhere,
to the covered typewriters on the students' desks, where
they danced, singly and in pairs and in circles, and, on her
own desk in a high-kicking line like children imitating can-
can girls, while they chanted,

I won't go to school any more, more, more,
There's a big mean teacher in the door, door, door!

The janitor claimed, when he looked in, before opening the doors to the busloads of students, that Miss Parry seemed paralyzed with fear, and he didn't blame her, surrounded as she was by all those filthy critters. He had no idea where all the mice had come from, since he had had exterminators in over Easter vacation as he always did.

They had to believe him, and so they also had to believe Miss Parry: what woman (even Miss Parry!) would not lose control and throw whatever came handiest at an unexpected mouse? It was just Dacia Middleton's bad luck that she had dropped the Selectric ball, and thus happened to be in the way when Miss Parry picked it up and saw the mouse.

This was explained very carefully to the School Board and to the Middletons' lawyer, by Miss Parry's lawyer, at the same time as he explained why Miss Parry expected, and would get, adequate compensation for having to take early retirement after the unwarranted slur on her character and the trauma she had endured in a classroom full of mice.

Miss Parry went home and called a piano tuner.

A year later, she advertised that she offered piano lessons, and soon parents whose children were serious about their music would send them to no other teacher, because, rage against her as they might, not one of those who later applied for admission to the stringently exclusive music conservatory down in the city was ever denied admission.

Bear With Me
Jerome Stueart

Evelyn leaned her suitcase against a camper shell covered in snow. She felt the Yukon burn her cheeks with cold, felt her nosehairs freeze into pins. She savored what she called "the moment before she met Bear face-to-face," where she was prepared to overlook any minor flaws — lack of flossing, hammertoes, belching. She'd lost ten pounds, had her hair cut, took skiing lessons. She felt amazing and prepared herself not to care if he should back away in fear or hold up the sign of the cross to protect himself, or worse, if he should show the subtle facial signs of disappointment. It's the risk you take.

The big moment would have happened at the airport, but he'd asked someone else to pick her up. She adjusted for his lack of sensitivity, hoping it was an unavoidable emergency — some salmon at the Fish Ladder needing directions to the sea, perhaps.

His small house had red shingle siding and a blue roof. If she'd written this real estate ad she would have emphasized "comfortable and cozy," evoking fireplace, friends, wine, and photos on the fridge. *Very attractive*. She flexed her gloved fingers twice and knocked.

The door opened like it did in every horror movie she'd seen, slow and creaky. Muddy boots sat against the wall below a blue parka. A set of Christmas lights draped over a kitchen window in the next room, giving the purple walls a lavender glow.

"Come on in. I'm changing," came his familiar voice. Thank God.

Here she was, like women who had come a hundred years ago, lugging their tons of supplies across a snowy pass into a goldrush town. She hauled her luggage, with no help from the boyfriend, and walked into a potentially heartbreaking house. *Damn, I'm adventurous.* But, with both of them in their thirties, she couldn't afford to be frightened. She'd flown 3,000 miles already, what was one last lug?

Two rooms away, something lumbered into the light of a living room lamp. It was a large brown bear walking on his hind legs. She backed into the door as it closed. She remembered advice she'd read about meeting this kind of bear. *Back away slowly, speaking strongly to the bear. Appear larger with coat and backpack and arms raised. Never run.* Instead, she dropped her luggage. They stood two rooms apart, the ghostly lavender kitchen between them.

Its mouth moved and Bear's voice came out. "You might be startled," it said spreading its arms and claws, pleadingly.

She felt a scream falling like sediment into her gut.

She could see no lines in the costume. She could see the jaw hinge and unhinge. Saliva pearled between his teeth, and she thought she smelled dense fur. No skin between the edge of his eyes and the edge of the mask. Just his eyes unblinking, wild and pitiful, wider now as he tried to explain himself.

"God," she whispered.

He said, "It's okay. Don't be frightened. I'm not always like this." He spoke slowly. He made no moves, not even to back up. His tone was serious but casual, as if he were delivering news that he was, unfortunately, dead. "I didn't know how to tell you, Ev."

Her hand found a very heavy vinyl-backed chair and she scraped that between them, ready if the beast should lunge, ready to protect herself with metal legs. But the voice said it wasn't going to attack.

"How was your flight?" it asked, casually.

It was interested in her flight. She was monitoring her pulse.

"Bear?"

"Not a costume. Real fur. Real me. You might be thinking about the home movies I sent, and those were *me*, but they were me during the day. Night is a whole different creature."

The bear winced at his own words. "If you sit down, we can talk. You can sit in the kitchen, and I'll—" He looked behind him at a couch. "I'll sit here. And I'll explain everything."

He fell into a large comfy chair. The cushions flattened under his weight. They were clearly worn out. He crossed his legs, as if the normalcy of the gesture might reassure her that she was just chatting in a friend's living room.

She sat down, surprised at herself. She wondered what happened to her boyfriend. She felt like crying for the man she thought was here. She stared at him. *This creature is nothing to me,* she thought.

But he looked very lost. He stared at the ceiling for a moment before beginning. "I was eleven." He sighed. "I looked in the window of a neighbor woman's house, and she was having sex with one of the sackers from our grocery store. Red blanket on the carpet. And she saw me. Naturally, she got pissed. I'd heard she was a witch, but no one really believed that." He swallowed. "She changed me." He ran his paw across his chest, as if he were trying to wipe something off.

He looked away from her, across the living room. The knock-off cuckoo clock in the corner ticked.

He turned back to her, breathed out. "There's no pressure, Ev. We can have your ticket changed. I just wanted to have the chance to defend — *present* — myself in person." He leaned forward, tucking his enormous claws in his lap. "I hope you remember all the good things." He smiled, but it just showed his teeth. "We have a lot in common, Ev — music, eight out of each others' top ten movies, plans for the future. I have a good job at the Fish Ladder." He looked around the room. "I'm not always going to live here. I showed you the house I'm thinking about. You said it was a good buy. These are the things to think about. They're what we've built on."

The lamplight highlighted a head of dark brown fur. She had expected *some* difference in the man she met online and the real thing — the same you might expect to find when you meet an actor for the first time in everyday clothes shopping for melons.

He said, "Are you going to say anything?"

She looked at the kitchen floor. It was spotless. He cleaned well.

"I've had about two minutes."

"Right," he said gruffly, "Understandable. Let's sleep on it."

He stood up suddenly. She jumped.

"I should," she said, "stay in a hotel."

"I have a guest bedroom. I won't hurt you. Please, I don't want to lose you in one night."

She looked him square in his small black eyes, looking for signs of common humanity. "I deserved to know the truth."

The bear looked at the floor. "You think I'm hideous."

"I think you look like a bear."

"I'm not a bear inside — only on the outside. I don't attack people or eat anyone."

"How do I know you aren't lying?"

"I'm telling you I'm not lying."

"But you lied about this."

"I omitted."

He looked down because it was a lousy excuse. The walls around him were a trendy orange and yellow, the couch royal blue — dynamic hues — almost comic book colors. And here, a comic book bear stood embarrassed and regretful next to the floor lamp.

"I still deserved to know before now. It's been more than a year."

He didn't answer. He waited as if he hadn't heard her.

"I put fresh sheets on the bed," he said finally.

She picked up her suitcase. Heavier. "A hotel will be no trouble," she said.

He looked agitated. "I promise. I'll be normal in the morning. Different face."

She sniffed back a nervous breakdown. She'd have to call a cab. She'd be alone in a foreign country. She closed her eyes. "Say this to me. Say — Evelyn, it's going to be okay."

She heard him breathe in, and then, they were on the phone again. She had lost her checkbook, her mother had a lump on her breast, she was lonely and making cookies for the office again because no one else baked and she wanted cookies so badly. In that voice, she heard 430 nights of excitement, patience, frustration, all these she had shared on email and, in moments of desperation, on the phone. This time, as every time, she saw his face, his lips, his eyes form the words, "Evelyn, it's going to be okay." She felt herself relax in the presence of hyperbole.

She kept her eyes squinted, said to him, "Thank you," and moved towards the bedroom. She heard him walk back into the other bedroom.

Over the doorway of the guest room were his thinning He-Man sheets, showing muscled warriors, and an evil Skeletor in blue. Wasn't there a power-girl on that show? Where was she on the sheets? She could see how he might identify with being a superhero: one part of you normal but powerless, and the other powerful, usually with less clothing, clutching rescued women. Secret identities: your enemies never imagined your vulnerability; your girlfriend never saw your power.

She opened her suitcase on a high bed of three mattresses. He'd placed irises in a clear bowl in her room. Her favorite. Five of them opened like a hand.

He called out from the other bedroom, "I really do love you, Evelyn."

She didn't know how to answer.

She soon climbed into bed and lay there as the night sounds turned to snorting and subdued growling in the other room. On the ceiling above her were glow-in-the-dark stickers of the stars, in vaguely correct constellations. He snored. He snored like an alarm smothered with a pillow. A steady, soft vibration. She wondered if it shook the bed, and whether she could get used to the sound.

+I+I+I+

In the morning, she saw him pass into the kitchen, and he was a man, as he testified, the same man in the pictures he had sent, only slightly taller than she was with a thick red crew cut and pink cheeks. He was not the towering bear he had been last night. He poured himself some orange juice. He smiled when she walked out of the bedroom. "Did you have a good sleep?"

"I did. I slept long."

"You hibernated. Jetlag and lack of sunlight. It happens."

"You were a bear last night," she said, taking the orange juice from the fridge.

"Yes. You remembered."

She poured herself the glass. "I'm trying not to forget."

"Is it so bad? Is it a terrible handicap?" he asked. "Would you like some eggs?"

She leaned against the counter. She wore her favorite robe over a thin nightgown. Under the covers, she never got cold. The heater kicked in often during the night, a dull roar in the background of her dreams of bears. "I want honesty in our relationship."

"Everyone has secrets."

"Yes, I'll take eggs," she said.

+I+I+I+

He didn't deserve a second chance, but she really couldn't maintain a state of *furious* for two weeks. They walked through neighborhoods with flannel-shirted snowmen like real estate agents representing houses with colorful siding — blues, mauves, greens, very few whites. In a place where the ground was white nine months out of the year, she guessed no one wanted a house that disappeared. They went to an art gallery. She lingered at soapstone carvings of bears, touching their smooth surfaces with her fingers. She ran her finger down a bear's polished stomach, felt the glassy stone curve under her fingertip. Cold even in the warm shop.

They toured Whitehorse while it was light, shopping, sightseeing, crunching snow with the rest of the crowds. Wherever he went, he was greeted by friends with expectant smiles and glances in her direction. "Oh, so *this* is Evelyn!" And they shook her hand, smiling like they knew more than they were saying.

"I've become a saint," she said.

"They're just being friendly."

"What does 'I'm so glad you're with him' mean to you?" she asked.

He ran off ahead of her to a giant paddlewheeler frozen in a surprise winter. He called back to her. "It means you're *lucky*," he laughed.

They stopped and read the historical markers, commemorating pioneers. She'd been doing her research on women in the Klondike. When women came up as wives in the early days, they traded their homes, countries, lifestyles, peoples all for adventure, and maybe a husband. She connected with these women. She wanted him to see her as risky and hardy. She looked at his face thinking she might find traces of the bear of the night, but they had been completely erased by some boy's face. She liked his skin, more now perhaps than before, where it creased when he smiled, where his face smoothed to his ears, the contour of his nose. She watched his lips when he talked, his human, searching green eyes. His cheeks looked pink and vulnerable like an underbelly.

They walked across the bridge over the Yukon River and stopped to admire the crevice between the ice where water flowed. "In summer, it's wide, but as it freezes it slowly closes over until there's just a trickle going through. Just like the light here. In January, we only get four hours of sunlight."

"So you can only look human for four hours," she said, leaning against the bridge railing. "Wouldn't someplace else let you have more of a balance? Like the equator."

He smiled, "Yeah, like a bear's body would be comfortable there."

"Okay, Texas, then." She was thinking practically.

"Here, I can go out at night and everyone knows me. Everyone has a little vice, a little quirk, but we get to be ourselves and no one cares. So I'm the walking bear at night, and everyone just waves and says hi. Where else could I get that kind of acceptance?"

Sea gulls congregated at the bend in the river, laughing at them both. Children tobogganed down the banks and onto the hard river, a river that otherwise would have swallowed them whole. "So, here's a hard question," she said. "If everyone's so keen on you being a bear in the dark, why haven't you found someone...?"

"More local?" He seemed to be looking off for the answer. "I've... I've got standards, too, you know? Just 'cause a woman can take the fur and the teeth doesn't mean she's a soulmate."

⊹⊹⊹

He would not let her see him change. He went into his bedroom, slid the sheet of stars, moons, and suns across the doorway. She thought she might be able to hear the change, but she heard nothing but him stripping away his human clothes and putting on his larger bear clothes. He called out from the bedroom, "I tried one year going to Rendezvous parties as a trapper. I dressed in raccoon and rabbit fur, but they really clashed with mine. So, I go very sophisticated now." He came out of the room a decidedly ritzy bear, with dark maroon, pleated pants and matching vest; a gold watchchain stretched over his belly like a rope bridge. "I know. I look like a children's book. But it's better than the alternative."

She complimented him. He blossomed with pride.

As for her outfit, she'd picked up a sexy, dark red velvety dress with a red feather. It exposed her luscious shoulders. She was peeling up the long black gloves when she came out of her room. The bear eyed her up and down.

"Is it tight?" he asked.

She raised her eyebrow. "*Not* a good first comment. I think you should start over with — 'Yes, you look wonderful tonight.'"

He frowned, scrunching his muzzle. Even in all that fur, she could see that he lingered unfavorably on her chest, tastefully exposed. "I'm just saying that you're going to be moving around a lot tonight, and I don't want you to be uncomfortable."

"You have failed this test," she said, half-smiling. "I look gorgeous. I am going to find three men who will tell me that this evening."

"The men here are not the kind you want to be flirting with," he said as she put on her coat.

"Because you've done extensive flirting with them?"

He didn't laugh. "People use Rendezvous as an excuse to go out and drink to excess and fondle women, and the women here seem to like that."

"Bear, these are your people. If you want—"

"*My* people? What do you mean by that?"

"We can stay at home. I didn't mean to cause a ruckus."

He had his paws on his hips, his all black eyes thinking and thinking. He was right about one thing — he looked like a page out of an Aesop's Fable. "I'm just looking out for you."

She decided she wanted to leave, not argue. "I appreciate that, sir."

He buttoned the top button on her black coat, effectively sealing her in up to her neck. "You look wonderful tonight," he added, grinning, showing those teeth.

"Thank you, Mr. Clapton." Did he mean *now*? Buttoned up to her neck? He walked her out the door, and they did not go in his car, but walked the four blocks to Lizard's Lounge. He was too big for the car now, and would have busted the seats, blown the tires. He got heavy as a bear. She hoped that by the time they reached the bar he would be less protective.

⊹⊹⊹⊹⊹

The night started anew as they entered the room, as if they were making their way for the first time into other people's stories. It was Rendezvous, as Bear had described, a week when everyone re-enacted those winter gatherings of trappers. Some were in costume, long dresses, men wearing red vests; others were in regular clothes. She could tell she'd blown several rhythms. A chorus of approval came in a wave from the crowd. Evelyn had never been the center of so much attention. It was reality TV, where everyone endured thirteen weeks of selection by our lonely hero, until finally, on this night, he brought her to the crowd and revealed his love. Her debut. Great.

The band slammed music into her temples, and she felt suddenly thrown from the very silent world of winter into the rowdy, warm bar. They passed through the crowd to a small booth. Evelyn took off her coat, adjusted her dress. For a moment, she felt naked. Bear looked at her as if she were, and he glanced about the room as if someone might notice her shoulders. She wished she'd brought a shawl.

Greg, the man who picked her up at the airport, and his wife, April found them. April grabbed her by the arms and said she looked *smashing*. She, however, was not in costume. She wore a crinkled light blue cami under a crème top; she was an ad for the Buckle — how Texan, Evelyn thought and smiled. She had short, messy blond hair. They joined Bear and Evelyn, set their coats on the booth seats, and ordered drinks. April, diligent in getting to know Evelyn, asked where they'd met. When she heard that Bear had not put up a picture of his more burly side, she leaned back, reached over and thumped him in the chest. "Bastard!"

She turned to Evelyn. "You have to thump him when he's bad."

They chatted while music played. Evelyn stirred her Caesar — a V8 with a kick. It wasn't so different than the States. Except it was a well-attended costume party in February with no fashion police. Everyone knew everyone else. Ordinary people having a good time. Evelyn relaxed.

Across the table, Bear cleared his throat, scooted carefully out of the booth, and stood beside her, offering his paw. She tried to focus on his eyes alone, but she couldn't help watching everyone watch them as she stood up to dance.

She followed him to a linoleumed dance floor, awash in gold light. For the slow song, he took her hand gingerly and placed it around his back, and took her other hand and held it, trying not to scrape it. His pads were soft. Here on the dance floor, he was considerate. He smiled and she looked in his small, dark inhuman eyes. He asked with those eyes if she was warming up to him. She looked at his wet, black nose. She wasn't sure.

They both warmed to the music and the lights. She felt it pour over her and her shoulders loosened. He shut his eyes, grooved to a bass guitar solo. Flakes of green and pink and gold floated across his Victorian suit, lighting up his watch-chain, as if he had the sun hooked inside his pocket. She swayed back and forth and put her arms in the air. They rolled the negative space between them back and forth, kneading it with their bodies. He opened his eyes. Perhaps the pink light shone on her cleavage, mesmerizing him. She closed her eyes and pulsated towards him. Then she felt his soft paws on her chest, and when she opened her eyes, it was to wink and smile at him, to suggest that they do some of this in private, but his eyes were everywhere else, suddenly, panicky, turning his head, watching who might be watching her. He was not groping her, but covering her.

He yanked her close, covered her with his own body. She thought he was growling and angry, but he was trembling. Through the rest of the lively rhythm, they were oaks withstanding a flood, as he held her still against the music. She knew he had his eyes closed now. Did they look in love? Couples whirred around them, and he held her as she tried to break away.

"Bear, I want to dance," she said quietly. "Just let go a little."

He looked down at her and tried to say something, but she couldn't hear it. The song ended in a blast of drums echoing all over the room. With the last boom, he walked off the dance floor, leaving her to walk herself off. She tried to smile at everyone. She wanted to assure them that they needn't worry — Bear's feelings were being protected, their expectations would all be met.

Immediately Greg thumped him on the chest. Apparently this was the appropriate and usual spot. They pulled back into another corner while Evelyn sat down with April.

"What happened?" April asked.

"I don't know," Evelyn said. "You know him, too. What did you see?"

"He was like diving for your *boobs*. You had your eyes closed, but he was like hungry, slobbery and going right down for them. Not like he was a pervert. He's a man and he saw a nice rack, and this is Bear and he doesn't get out much. He spends a lot of time with the fish in the river. Which is kinda ironic, if you think about it. A bear spending time with fish, but not to eat them. And so he's maybe a little unpracticed on how to be subtle."

But he was shaking, covering her. Didn't April see his eyes all over the place?

"He wanted to see if anyone caught him," April said. "I mean, I saw Greg and he was looking at your boobs too and he didn't need a dance floor."

Evelyn felt exposed. She pulled her bodice up.

"No, girl, it's not you," April said. "Men can be beasts, but we like them like that. And if you can't show some hooters on the dance floor, where are you going to show them? I mean, they only last for a little while, and when they're *gone*, they can't pull a homeless man to his feet."

She watched Greg explain something to Bear in wide, sweeping gestures. She could still feel his trembling body in the hollow of her elbows, where she'd held him. How vulnerable he made himself. He could have brought her up in summer and she wouldn't have known a thing. He brought her up in Winter and exposed himself on purpose. Winter and summer, like two different places up here. He'd told her that sunlight pulled everyone outside, they shed their coats and then, bam!, they went biking, canoeing, hiking, swimming. Tourists flocked the streets and the sun never, ever set. Bear was human for nearly three solid months.

She imagined what it might be like to live here. If not for the women coming up during the Gold Rush, this place would never have become more than tents. Women settled the miners and goldrushers down. Evelyn imagined turning her notice in to the real estate agency, telling people that she was going to be a pioneer in the Klondike; she felt the romance of those words. She felt again the tremble of his body.

A lanky man in a red vest and a black garter on his arm came to their table, introducing himself as Terry. April knew him. He turned to Evelyn, "You look like a girl who hasn't danced enough." She tried to get Bear's attention, but he was still with Greg. She smiled at Terry, standing up, feeling the pleasant weight of his gaze on her shoulders. Bear was capable of cutting in.

He walked her out to the floor. They took separate grooves and she tried to remember the last time she went dancing. She'd gotten to be such a homebody in the last five years. She spent most of her time with her cat, Sioux, and a rented movie. Conditions that propelled her into online dating. She missed going out with friends. She felt like she had inherited good friends from Bear, ones he'd cultivated. While she had turned introverted in a city of hundreds of thousands of people, *he'd* been a social animal in a small town. Certainly, he made a great host. They'd cross-country skied, dined out, visited museums, watched children throw axes, adults chuck chainsaws, cheered on mushing dogs — all part of this social carnival.

Terry looked to his left and waved to Bear, who was now sitting at the table. Bear didn't wave back, just stared at them. He leaned forward on the edge of his seat, as if he might get up on the dance floor and maul someone.

Terry grabbed her hands and pulled her into a jitter-bug. At their table, Bear stood up to a formidable height. He looked across the expanse of the dance floor. Bear didn't walk out or demand to cut in. He pulled out his pocket watch casually, like a cartoon bear, and flipped open the casing. It sparked gold. He closed it shut against his chest, and placed it back in his pocket. Other couples danced in front of him, still he watched Evelyn. *It's just a dance*, she thought.

When she came back to the table, Bear looked away, at his drink. He slurped it through a straw, quickly, noisily, all that vodka going down in one big gulp.

She sat down. "I'm pooped," she said to the table.

Terry followed her to the table, joked with Bear, who grinned with an armada of teeth.

She thought he might say something to Terry. He was obviously feeling possessive, but he just smoldered in polite conversation. She expected him to attack. She expected him to do so many different things with that fur. To be an animal. Instead he was pressed into a smaller box. Being a bear did not expand things for him, she thought to herself, it contracted them.

Someone got on stage and announced the entertainment for the evening: Sourdough Sams — eight men in a contest that would make them the soul of the historical trapper. They entertained every night at different bars doing different contests — drinking, eating, singing, dancing. Tonight's was a striptease.

Evelyn and April woo-hoo'd together above the crowd's shouts. Eight men stripped down to red longjohns to "I'm too sexy for my shirt" and then, together, like a Full-Monty review, down to thongs.

It was so much more than what Bear could stand, she was sure. She patted a place next to her for him, and he obliged. She may have pounded on the table and whistled, but she kept a hand firmly on Bear's thigh. No mixed messages here, she thought. But she wasn't going to shy away from it either. He stripped the remaining hotwings of meat with fastidious teeth. He did not take her hand or even acknowledge that it was there. He seemed distracted and bored. Every other man in the place looked to be enjoying the spectacle and rooting these men on — as they must have been coworkers and friends.

"Do you know any of them?" she asked Bear. She wanted to know who to root for.

"I don't recognize them in their underwear," he said. She couldn't tell if he were sanctimonious or homophobic. She decided a safe bet would be to root for all of them.

When it was over, and the men had swung their last, she put on her coat and told April she was going outside for a breath of fresh air. April said she would join her, but when Evelyn got outside, it was Bear behind her.

"You ready to go?" he asked.

She looked at him. "Now there's the 25,000 dollar question."

"I don't want to fight."

"Me neither. I just want to have a good time."

The cold settled in under her collar, through the threads of her gloves. It came up under her coat to her legs, traveling upwards, leaving a trail of goose bumps.

"Bear, what's with you tonight?" she asked. "Are you embarrassed to be seen with me?"

"No," he rolled his eyes.

"Then what was all that in there?"

He put on his coat. He didn't know what she was talking about. He wasn't much of a dancer in the first place, and naked men weren't his thing. *Good save*, she thought. Besides, the bar was getting too hot for him. He had all that fur, after all.

April came to the door. "Off to get cozy in front of a fire?"

Evelyn smiled and gave her a hug. She didn't think they would make it to the cozy part this week. "We're going to go see the if the Northern Lights are out."

"Oh, those," she said, waving them away with her hand. "Good luck. I can never find them when I want them. Hey, if you do find them, whistle at them. They say the lights will come down and kidnap you."

"Have you tried it?" Evelyn asked.

"Yeah." But she offered nothing else.

⋙⋖⋙⋖

In his emails he had moved to sex first. She'd tease him along the way, give subtle hints, but he always took the first dive, so to speak. They got explicit; they could overheat a hard drive. Bear had a pretty good vocabulary for sex.

She liked that. Oh, she knew he was conservative but his stories to her were very, very effective. She remembered, though, that he wasn't as good on the phone, a little more embarrassed talking dirty out loud.

She watched this face smile, how the black gums thinned, the pale teeth glistened. She watched the eyes, wet along the rims, slivers of white near the corners. The way the fur moved in tiny waves according to the muscles in his face. He didn't look as frightening, or as foreign, as he had the first night. Still, she couldn't connect the two parts of him together, as if separate men were tagteam dating her. She had to work harder with the bear than she did the man. She imagined those two conferred on what they thought about her, about love, about passion. Did he even know what he wanted?

They took another route to his house, through a darkened residential area, bordered on one side by steep clay cliffs. He put his arm around her. He tried to be chatty, as if she were upset. Sometimes he would rub his hairy paw against her neck. The city to their left was quiet. No one was out. The street lights stood majestic in fog. On the way, she shivered, on purpose.

"Cold?" he asked.

"A little," she said.

He took off his coat and put it around her. It was a light trench coat. Not really any help.

She made sure he felt her shiver more as they turned a corner. He asked her again if she were cold and then took off his vest. After all, he said, it was a wool blend. Now he was *bear*-chested in pleated pants.

"You're probably overheating anyway," she said.

He smiled, "I can take it."

"It must be twenty below out here," she said, walking slower.

He thought about it. "At least. But fur is a great insulator." They passed a park with a rock wall frosted by two inches of snow. Evergreens and spruce.

"At least you have the pants," she said. "You need those out here."

He scoffed. "I don't *need* them."

"'Course you do, Bear. You don't have *perfect* insulation."

He stopped and looked at her. "You don't know much about bears do you?" He unzipped his pants, without looking around, meeting her eyes with a spark of defiance. She smiled at him and she thought he was finally catching on. He whipped off his pants and threw them over the park's rock wall behind him.

She thought he was smiling. He said, "Satisfied, you little pervert?"

She laughed. "You were too sexy for that vest, and those pants." She took a gloved hand and ran it down his stomach. He had on Snoopy boxer shorts. But she didn't make fun. He was right about one thing: he was putting out heat like a furnace. Her hand was warm on his chest.

"And I'm not satisfied yet, Mr. Boxer Shorts."

She slipped a hand down his shorts, pulled the elastic wide, slipped them down over his legs. "Now you're a naked bear." She tossed those on the wall as well. But he suddenly reached to grab them back.

Behind her, she heard a rush of panting and scuffling, and suddenly two yellow labs passed her, jumped up on Bear licking and playing. For any other man, this might have been a slightly embarrassing moment, a playful timeout, but for Bear it was anything but. He tried to push them down; he reached for the rest of his clothes, yanking them and a pile of snow off the wall. He looked at her, desperate to get away from the dogs. He argued with them, as if they too would speak English. They barked at him. He pulled on his pants. They were soaked in snow. He strapped on his vest. She took off his coat, knowing that he was coming for it. She watched him stride away from the dogs towards her, talking to them like a master: *Sit* and *No* and *Lay Down*, and there was no humor in his voice as he buttoned up the vest, as he fit his arms into the sleeves of the coat. If he had had gloves, she was sure he would make a point of putting them on over his claws in front of the dogs, too. In minutes he had transformed from a bear back into children's illustration. "People just let their dogs run wild," he said, placing his paw on her back and gently pushing her down the street.

Neither one of them spoke all the way to his house. He was stiff and quick in his strides. The northern lights did not come out, but the street lamps stayed steady on streets to the left and right of them, and they traveled the dark crevice in between.

⇥•I••I••I•⇤

One bright afternoon, near the end of her time in the North, they stayed in to watch *The Wolf-Man*, Bear's request. The TV was in his room; they lounged on his bed, snacking popcorn, watching Lon Chaney, Jr. struggle.

In the middle of the movie, she felt a surprise: Bear's hand caressed her thigh. She wondered where this would go. After the last couple of days, she wasn't sure if he knew, or what to expect if he got started. She placed her bowl of kernels on the nightstand, and turned to kiss him. In the background, you could hear Lon Chaney pleading with his girlfriend not to go out in the night alone. Appropriate dangerous music followed. Bear kissed her with urgency. She lifted his shirt, exposing his pink, human chest, the supple nipples. He pulled off his clothes in advance of her tongue.

She kissed every inch of his body as if they might lose it at any moment. She had the impression she was making love to someone about to go off to war. The sunlight pushed across the room, up their bodies and lit the wall behind them. His lovemaking surprised her. He knew what to do with breasts! How to press his palm on her body, firmly, warmly, slowly. He knew what to do with his tongue. All that he'd written about in emails, he could perform, and this bedroom event, his coming out as a sexual man, seemed to insist that he knew what to do with a human body, though he was uncertain about the other one. Moreover, maybe, he knew what to do with *her* body. What surprised her was how badly she needed his human body to tell her that. But this was sex on fast forward. The sunlight faded behind them. He finished just as the hunting dogs started to pursue Lon Chaney through the forest. Their bays signaled a change in him and she wasn't surprised when he pulled away, covered his face with his hands.

"I need you to go into the other room for a few minutes. I don't want you to see this." He acted like a child hiding himself from her. "I wasn't thinking about the time."

"Bear, it's okay. I *want* to see this. This is a part of you."

He took his hands down, pulled the covers up over his naked body. "No, this isn't okay. You have to go now." She didn't get off the bed. So, he jumped up, pulled on her arms, tried to yank her off the bed.

"No," she said and dove to the other side of the bed, knocking him off balance, pulling him with her to the bed again. She tried to pin his arms. He was stronger than her, but he was upset, nearly crying, panicked. The same look he had on the dance floor. She was going to catch him doing something horrible. She got right in his face. "It's going to be okay."

If he wanted this to work, she had to go back down to Texas knowing everything she was going to be living with. "You closed me out for a year, Bear, but I'm going to see everything."

He pushed her up. He obviously didn't want to hurt her, but the force of his push made her topple into the bookshelf and she steadied herself with her arms. He yelled, "This is my private problem."

"You don't have any *private* problems. You're in a relationship," she yelled back. "That's the whole point."

He got up on his hands and knees on the bed and rushed her, yelling, "You want to see this?"

"Yeah, I want to see this." The glow of light receded from the room, as if they were yelling the light out. After a sudden dramatic crescendo, the TV changed to blue screen. "You're the same man," she said.

"Watching gets people into *trouble*," he bellowed from the bed, positioned like a dog barking at her to stay out of his yard. "I should know."

"You didn't become a bear because you saw something bad. A bad *woman* cursed you. You were innocent—"

"*You weren't there.*"

Darkness fell hard and sudden. She didn't know what to expect. He shrank. Or, the human part of him shrank, as if he were falling inside of a great pit, covered in hair. His outline was smudged with charcoal fur, darker and darker as he fell backwards into the body of the bear. Suddenly, in a wavy movement of fur, the bear left behind leapt off the bed and crushed her against the books, his terrible teeth revealed, his breath hot on her, yelling at her, *"Is this what you wanted to see?"*

It was like a Texas wind, like one of those tornadoes that spiral down suddenly in the middle of your street, tossing everything from in front of you, on its way to toss you. He was every bit a bear at this moment, moaning and roaring at her, but she didn't try to move away. She couldn't really, but she could be terrified if she let herself. She looked down his throat, past his teeth, down to where she thought she might be able to hear the witch telling a boy at his window, "Is this what you wanted to see? This sex. Didja get a good eyeful?"

"I am not scared of you," she told him. She said it again calmly, making it echo off his own throat. He paused for a breath and she said it again, firmly. "I am larger than you. You can't hurt me."

His thick hairy body pressed against her. She could feel the shelves across her back. He stared at her. "I didn't want you to get hurt," he said.

"I didn't. I didn't even change."

He stopped yelling. He eased back a little, though she could still feel his body on her. He looked paralyzed between two actions: holding her and letting her go. She reached around him, and pulled him closer. She stood in a city where everything changed, everything had cycles, nothing was in a permanent state. The sun left; it came back again. The river froze; it thawed. Fish swam south; they returned north to spawn. The man in front of her, with tears in his small black eyes, was a bear; tomorrow morning he would be human, but tomorrow night he would be a bear. No escaping that cycle with him. To accept Bear was never to be able to stop the night from changing him. But damned if she wasn't going to make opportunity out of changes.

She reached down his naked bear body until she had her hand between his hairy thighs. "There is nothing wrong about *this*. This is fantastic. This is good and you, buddy, are good at it." She looked for some hint of recognition. He blinked. He looked down. "Yes, really." She rubbed his arms. "We're two adults. It's okay to enjoy this. Maybe one day you want to find that witch and sock her in the mouth, but I don't mind the bear part, Bear. You wanted to know that." And it was true. She liked the crazy side of it, the adventure that being in love with a man who became a bear at night presented. "I think you're sexy both ways." He looked up at her. "But I gotta know one thing: do you want me?"

"Yes," he said.

"No, I have to be wanted and valued and respected for all that I am too — whether I'm conservatively dressed or naked in your arms. Can you do that? Can you love the wild side of *me*?"

He looked puzzled. Maybe he'd never considered that someone else might need the bear side of her loved — but dammit, she did. And if he wasn't willing to praise that curvy figure she had, well, then, she could find another bear to love in a city of a thousand good things.

"You," he said, clearing his throat and looking her in the eye, "look wonderful tonight."

Any woman of the Klondike worth keeping would have pushed the bear back towards the bed, too. They were not whores, not prostitutes, not golddiggers. They came up for a new life, whether or not they found bears. These women got something for themselves. Trees and mountains and bars and friendly people and wildness. These women would have climbed under the covers with a bear, and when he suggested they just cuddle, they would have turned and cozied up to the adventure.

"I'm as warm as a furnace, aren't I?" he said behind her under covers.

"You're as warm as a house," she told him, feeling his fur against her back. And when he pressed his cold nose against her neck, it sent a chill that melted before it could reach her heart, every time.

little red
Alyxandra Harvey-Fitzhenry

you think you know this story.
you read it as a child
or discussed the meaning of the colour red
and the metaphors of animal instinct
in university classes, when you wore only black
and drank byron, tennyson and keats
in smoky pubs, at worn wooden tables,
with girls wearing eyeliner.
it isn't that kind of a story, not really.
oh, i wore red and lived in the forest
but my grandmother was a bitch
and i never brought her warm cookies in covered
    baskets.
we never went to see her and it wasn't just because
the wolves and the winter were between us.

ii)
i used to crawl out onto the roof at night when
    everyone else was sleeping
to breathe the smoke from the hearth and
    lift my white throat
and sing with the wolves and wild dogs
and all creatures who worship the moon.

iii)
i never had a red cape, satin or velvet;
we couldn't afford such things,
but my moon time came
    the first time i went into the woods
after dark.

i felt powerful, sharp as the stars
with the blood between my legs.
this is what a woman does,
this is the true story of capes and crones
    and handsome men
when the woods are full of silver eyes
like pebbles in the river or rain when everything
    else is dry.
i never saw the handsome man,
the woodcutter or the woodcutter's son
    who were said to speak
the language of the beasts,
though i dreamt about them every night.
that day i bled for the first time
a red apple
was left on the step outside our front door.
i didn't know if it was the woodcutter's son
or the wolf.
i wasn't even sure there was a difference.
it was cold that day and i was barefoot,
running swift as a red deer between the silent trees.
i'm still not sure if i found them or if they found me.

iv)
they stood in a clearing of winter-bitten grass
with their breath white as frost from perfect nostrils,
flared, recognizing the scent of blood and wanting,
the scent of family.
sometimes the nobles from nearby towns
    hunt the wolves,
thinking only of thick pelts, black and silver,
to hang next to tapestries embroidered by
    pale-eyed women
or to lay at their feet and make them feel like kings.
i only wanted to know how it felt to be part
    of such a family
and never to fear winter or lightning.
the nobles always left the forest with broken
    bones and blood
under their nails and wild wild
eyes.

v)
i never really left.

vi)
i slept among them that night
and bared my throat to the moon and licked the stars.
i dripped blood and never tried to see
    if their veins were warm
and if their blood ran blue or silver as the
    northern lights.

vii)
the oldest one, a grizzled female with broken
    whiskers and knowing eyes,
died that night, weakened by the hunt.
the wolves sang and howled and cried
and i wiped my blood over her paws that she might
    run faster into the otherworld.
the youngest carried a sharp edged rock
between tender teeth and dropped it at my feet.

viii)
they formed a circle around me, like mist
    around the moon
or the stone circles in the south.
there was only their hot breath and mine and the trees
whispering.

ix)
the youngest bit my hand when i tried to leave
and blood dripped onto the cold fur and the stone was
    like a knife
or an icicle poised over your head when there is wind
    in the forest.
the sharp edge slid between fur and flesh
and i peeled her like an apple.
there was blood in my mouth.
you'll think this was harsh, brutal even
    for a young girl only twelve

and that such work should be left to men
  with heavy arms or women with scars.
i can only say it was simple and warm
and i never considered making a muff or rugs
  to sell at the market.

x)
instead
i slid into her skin, her body her breath,
and i was finally a woman and a beast and the forest
and i ran
and i lay down among the warm bodies
and dreamt of a girl
  in a house on the edge of the woods,
still sleeping.

Citius, Altius, Fortius
Stephen Kotowych

"I understand you'll soon be leaving athletics entirely," said Akello, as our white-gloved waiter poured steaming tea into delicate china cups.

None of my later biographies would mention that's how my journey to international athletic superstardom began, but that's how it happened. They would mention *where* it happened: the opulent dining room of the famous New York hotel that Akello and I sat in, its vastness empty but for the two of us and the waiter.

"Don't be ridiculous. Why would I do that?" is what I think I said. I do recall fighting to keep my hand from shaking as I raised the teacup to my lips. My denial sounded weak and defensive, even to me. How did Akello know my private plans? Before getting his phone call two days earlier, asking for a meeting, I'd never heard of this Akello person. He'd said he wanted to discuss an endorsement deal, and Lord knows I needed the money — there isn't much in amateur sport.

"There could be many reasons to quit," Akello said, blowing on his tea. "Your showing at the national qualifiers was... less than expected? You'd been favored to win a spot on the Olympic middle-distance team — but to come in sixth?"

"I didn't come here to give an interview. I've talked to enough press about what happened." I threw the linen napkin from my lap to the table, and made to get up.

Akello held out a hand, palm-forward. "And I've read all of those. They were the usual reasons a runner gives when he fails. I know — I gave them all myself when I ran for my country. But it takes another runner, even one as old as I am, to know the real reasons. You lost because your heart wasn't in the race; you weren't focused on winning."

I couldn't read from his face any clue about what he wanted. His dark brown skin was creased and weathered, fine rows of tribal scaring running along cheekbone and forehead, but his expression betrayed no emotion, no hint of motive.

He was right, of course. My passion had never been in middle-distance, even though it's what my physiology best suited. I wanted to be a sprinter, that's where the glory was. Though his stony expression irked me, I was impressed that he could read me so easily.

"You used to run?" I asked, sitting back down.

Akello nodded. "Years ago. I was even in the Olympics, once. Marathon. But I never had your gift for running. A gift, from what I hear, that you have no love for."

"Who the hell have you been talking to?"

"Oh, your discontent is hardly a secret, Mr. Osberg. That I can deduce from the media, too. You've been openly critical of your national Olympic program and vocal about your desire to switch to sprints. Perhaps you'd rather quit than be humiliated again?"

I pushed away hard from the table. Fine china cups tipped off their saucers, spilling tea, and clinked against silver spoons. Who the hell was this guy? I asked myself, stalking away from the table. Who was he to question me like that? The real humiliation would be in joining the ranks of the coaches, one more never-was amongst a bunch of old has-beens. Better to just quit outright. There was always law school.

"You haven't heard my offer, Mr. Osberg," Akello called after me. My only thought, beside anger, was that it seemed a thousand miles from the dining table to the heavy double doors.

"My country will make you a sprinter, if you race for us."

"Haven't you heard?" I shouted back, not bothering to stop or turn around. "I'm a middle-distance runner. I wouldn't cut it in the hundred meters at an elite level. Your country would be crazy to let me be a sprinter."

"But Phillip," said a familiar voice, "he didn't say he'd *let* you be a sprinter. He said he'd *make* you one."

»·|·|·|·«

I don't know if it was the voice or the cryptic promise that stopped me in my tracks, but I turned. There, crossing the room from the kitchen entrance was Dr. Champatsingh. He was their trump card, I realized, kept in reserve in case my reputation as a hothead turned out to be justified.

The last time I'd seen Dr. Champ was in college. He was the varsity track doctor and, though I liked him a lot, we routinely fought over my position on the team.

Our final blow-up, the one that led to me leaving the team, was also over my desire to switch to sprints.

"I'm sorry, Phillip. You're just not a sprinter," he'd said after hearing me out. He'd flipped a metal clipboard shut and handed it across his cluttered desk to me.

I knew what the results would be before I took the cold metal in my hand. I'd seen so many of these reports that I could look past the rows of digits that made up the fiber type composition report, past the mitochondrial content count, past the figures for glycolytic enzyme capacity, to what the biopsy really said: this runner has too many slow-twitch muscle fibers, and not enough fast-twitch ones to be a sprinter.

The walls, bookshelves, and cupboards of Dr. Champatsingh's tiny office in the university's athletic complex were choked with trophies, newspaper clippings, and mementos of dozens of athletes who "Dr. Champ" had helped to victory, including two who later went on to the Olympic medal podium. It smelled of sweat and victory, only reinforcing my own broken dreams.

"You've had biopsies before," Champatsingh said. "I don't know why you expected a different result from this one."

"I've been doing a lot of short-distance training lately. I hoped that maybe things had changed."

"It doesn't work like that," said Champatsingh. "I know you used to compete as a sprinter in high school, and I know you're unhappy that we've moved you to middle-distance. But sprinters are born, Phil, not made. You can change your diet, your equipment, even get some sports psychology and change your mental approach to match a sprinter's, but your fast-twitch-slow-twitch muscle ratio is yours at birth. Training refines what God gave you, hones it into peak form, but training can't make you something you're not. All else being equal, in a race against a sprinter at this level, you just couldn't compete."

"Come on, Champ," I said. "Don't tell me that. I need to be a sprinter — hundred meter dash." And I *needed* to be a sprinter. Do you remember who won the men's 1500-metre at the last Summer Olympics? I didn't think so. Ever hear of a middle-distance runner with his own box of Wheaties? How about a sneaker or sports drink endorsement deal? No? Exactly my point.

The hundred meter dash is the sexy event. People remember who won, remember your name, and see you in countless endorsement deals. You're the rock star, or the fighter pilot of the track world, the one who is the "fastest man alive." I'm not ashamed to admit it; I wanted the glory.

Dr. Champ's response was always the same. "The varsity team has sprinters, Phil. Good ones. You know that. You're not built to be a sprinter, not at an elite level. You're the top middle-distance runner at a Division 1 school. That's hardly something to be dissatisfied with. You have a real shot at the Olympic team. That's what got you your scholarship. Now, I want you back on the training regime we've designed for you, and no more training that distracts. That's what I need from you."

"But that's not what I need from myself." I slammed the door as I left his office. That was the last contact I'd had with Dr. Champ before he showed up in that dining room.

Last I heard, Dr. Champ had been dismissed from his position at the university — officially for failure to produce champion athletes at his old pace, but a friend told me unofficially it was because of Dr. Champ's implication in a doping ring of varsity athletes.

Sitting back down, I listed to the sales pitch for their new "advanced trained program." The program started with a trip to Africa.

＊|＊|＊|＊

Mansoa-Bafata was a little sliver of Africa's western coast that no one had ever heard of until Santamondo Inc. bought the entire country.

They got it for a song, too: Santamondo paid the ruling military junta to turn over authority to the corporation, assumed Mansoa-Bafata's debt to the First World, and promised housing and jobs to the desperately poor nation.

In exchange, Santamondo — one of the world's largest pharmaceutical and biotech conglomerates — got a nation full of cheap labor, unexploited oil reserves off the coast, and a global base of operations free from any government's control.

Now, I know people were aghast at the birth of the world's first corporation-state, and that they decried Santamondo's appointment of a National Board of Governors in lieu of national elections for a government. A number of nations tried resolutions at the UN against such corporate national buy-outs, but none of them passed.

And it is true that Santamondo augmented the rag-tag Mansoan army with private soldiers from out-of-country, and I've heard the stories about crackdowns on protesters, and on rebels in the mountains. But I spent a lot of time in Santamondo labs and factories after I arrived in Mansoa-Bafata and the Mansoans who worked there seemed happy, well fed, and well paid. Yes, many of the managers and technicians were foreigners, mostly European or South Asian, but Santamondo promised that in time, native Mansoans would fill the same jobs.

The morning after my arrival, the handlers provided by Santamondo herded dozens of us foreign visitors into a half-finished building. Yet another new construction project initiated by Santamondo, it seemed like the corporation was following through on the promises made when they assumed control of the country. There was a self-conscious effort to demonstrate the rising standard of living all across the tiny nation. New industry, new housing, improved farming, and all provided by Santamondo, Inc.

Detractors said it was just bread and circuses to appease the populace and distract the rest of the world from the harsh face of capitalism that was sure to rear its ugly head. They said that as more corporations bought their own nations we would see the exploitation, the race to the bottom, neo-serfdom in the twenty-first century. Maybe so, but that was a problem for the future. The only future I cared about was four years away, at the next Summer Olympics.

We were ushered through the construction site to a giant, completed auditorium in the building's basement, equipped with the latest technologies and amenities. A staff of attractive Mansoan women met us, and provided each of us with a clipboard of non-disclosure agreements to sign.

When I'd signed the last of them, I had a moment to look around and see who else had arrived for Santamondo's "seminar."

The banked tiers of seating could have doubled for a mini UN, filled as they were with people recruited from all over the world.

Many were young, probably recruited out of college — star varsity athletes who couldn't hack it at the level of international competition. It was an old story; one I knew too well. The rest were around my age, some older, our common bond a quiet desperation.

Perhaps some wanted one more shot at victory; perhaps others had never known its taste and that gnawed at them inside; for others, no doubt, abilities were flagging too young and they refused to accept the ravages of time and age. Whatever the specifics, our reason for being there was the same: all of us had fallen short in our athletic careers and now we hunted that most elusive of beasts — a second chance.

A trio of men walked into the room. There was a generic looking fellow in a gray business suit who took up a place at the podium, with Akello and Dr. Champatsingh next to him.

The suit introduced himself as some VP of something-or-other at Santamondo Inc., welcomed us all, gave a speech about the corporation's history and business strategy that was all business buzz words like "forward-thinking", "competitive advantage", and I swear he said "synergy" four times in as many minutes. I tuned most of it out.

When he finally finished speaking, a screen slipped down from the ceiling and the lights dimmed as a video began playing.

People watched, enthralled, maybe stunned, as Santamondo's CEO explained the new "advanced training program." And this wasn't an Oscar-caliber performance. It was a typically slick, overproduced corporate video, but the proposal was... *breathtaking*. About fifteen minutes into the film, the guy sitting next to me, (German, by the sound of him) said: "They can't be serious, yes?" It was the first noise I'd heard in the auditorium since playback started.

The CEO's tanned, smiling face faded to black and the lights came up. A murmur rose with them.

When Akello and Dr. Champ made their initial pitch to me, I assumed Santamondo's new training program involved some new drugs. I'm no fool. Santamondo is one of the world's largest pharmaceutical companies, and I'd juiced before — most everyone at his level has, either to win or to just keep up — so that was no big deal. But what was on that video...

Akello took the podium next, but before he could speak a woman near the front stood.

"I'm not interested in hearing any more pleasantries," she said, her accent South African. "I want to know just what you're planning to do to us. Are you talking about making us into a bunch of freaks, with animal genes and viruses and bacteria floating around inside us?" A number of voices from across the auditorium joined in, demanding answers.

Akello looked to Dr. Champatsingh, who moved quickly to the podium, and raised his hand, motioning for calm.

"You misunderstand our intentions," said Champatsingh. "We're not talking about grafting in elements of other genomes. No one will be getting cheetah DNA to run faster, or flea DNA to jump higher. We're simply talking about making use of the best that the *human* genome has to offer.

"And, if you'll forgive me," Champatsingh continued, laughing, "you are already something of a 'freak' — all of you are. Elite athletes don't represent the typical physiology expressed in the population. Far from it. You are a special class of specimens, selected from a very narrow range of the population, with muscles, enzymes, hormones, bone structure, and body build off the normal scale. You've benefited from the best knowledge science has to offer in nutrition, training, rest, and stress management. Your bodies are machines that do one thing very well, and a world-record performance is certainly a rare occurrence — 'freakish' if you will."

Another athlete stood. "Won't we get caught for cheating?"

"Don't look at this procedure as cheating," Champatsingh continued after a moment. "Look at this as cheating," and he held up a shoe. "Who can tell me what this is?"

"A sprinter's shoe," said someone.

"Yes," said Champatsingh. "How many crampons can it have?"

"Eleven," I said.

Seeing me, Dr. Champ smiled in recognition. "That's right," he said, turning the shoe over, showing the spikes to the audience. "By international regulation, eleven crampons each no more than nine millimeters in length, in order to present a 'level playing field' for all athletes. But we all know that isn't the case. There's no regulation stipulating the material composition of the shoe, so athletes get shoes made of ultra-lightweight super-high performance materials, and that gives them an edge. That's how they cheat, those whose Olympic programs can afford such exotic equipment. And shoes aren't the only example. Virtually every piece of athletic equipment used in the Olympics — vault poles, skis, swimsuits — is subject to the same engineering race.

"What about athletes from poor nations? Mansoa-Bafata used to be one. Did their athletes compete on a level playing field with the nations of the First World? Of course not. In less than one hundred years the law of diminishing returns has already set in for international athletics. Sometimes decades pass with records improving hundredths of a second, if at all. In that kind of environment, every advantage counts. All else being equal, equipment will win out. A few ounces less here, an extra gram or two lighter there can mean a gold medal for a lesser athlete; it can mean the difference between world-record and also-ran. Is it fair that two athletes of equal ability can't compete equally simply because one was born in a rich country and the other in a poor one?"

Champatsingh let the crowd's conversation run for a few moments. By his side, Akello and the Santamondo man both grinned widely.

"The race now is between each nation's materials engineers, not their athletes," Dr. Champ continued. "Should genetics be any different? People of Andean heritage pump out more hemoglobin and can carry more oxygen in their blood than other ethnicities. I can give you a single injection of modified genes that will boost your red blood cell count as much as forty percent, increasing your endurance, which will last for an entire season. In competition is it fair your performance should suffer simply because of where you were born, or what ethic group you come from?"

The South African woman stood again saying, "Even if it's only human genes won't they be able to tell?"

"How would they?" Champatsingh asked, and waited. "Drug tests won't reveal anything because you won't be taking any drugs. Most of our gene therapy uses nothing more sinister than the common cold virus to introduce the new sequences. They can't disqualify you for having a cold." Champatsingh paused again, letting the murmured conversation swell.

Every athlete worried about being caught when juiced; one blood sample or failed urine test could end a career. All the benefits with none of the drawbacks...

I stood. There was only one answer I needed. "Look, we're all here for the same reason — to win, no matter what. Now, will these treatments make me a champion sprinter or not?"

Champatsingh smiled, a remembered conversation in his eyes. "Yes, Phil. They will."

→•÷•÷•÷•←

I'm not going to pretend the next three years were easy. They were hard, and painful, and sometimes the program moved too slowly for my taste.

Dr. Champ and the Santamondo scientists devised a whole regimen of trial treatments combined with standard athletic training plans to see how people reacted to the therapy. They warned us that not everyone would respond equally to the treatments, and that some would suffer side effects.

I like how they waited until after we'd signed all the waivers and non-disclosure agreements to tell us that part. I didn't care, though. If this gave me my shot then the risks were worth it.

The program went slowly because of Dr. Champ's careful plans for easing each of us into competition. The 'mods', as the lab techs called them, were completed in stages so that no one's performance was so radically superior to their last as to arouse suspicion. Santamondo wanted us to build a reputation on the international scene before we really began to dominate.

Slowly we started to rack up wins. Even with the mods it was possible for us to lose events; there were still falls, poor judgment, bad starts, and lousy weather to contend with. But we won more than our fair share of events in those early days, especially where raw speed, or distance, or strength were key.

The international media interest in our athletic program was incredible, and exactly what Santamondo had hoped for to gain world attention and credibility as new rulers of a nation. Our success, said Santamondo spokespeople (and I quote), proved that not only athletes, but all "stake-holders" in the Mansoa-Bafata "project" could thrive under the "progressive, corporate-state model of national governance."

We the athletes were held up as examples of how people could succeed in a corporate-state. We, who had either never lived up to our potential, or (like me) had always insisted we were capable of more but been stymied by "outmoded thought systems", could now shine. And to deflect charges that they'd just imported foreign athletic stars to boost their team, Santamondo put native Mansoans on the same mod program as the rest of us, with very similar results. It showed, they said, that direct corporate management of the nation-state meant "greater organiza-tional—slash—national purpose is generated," allowing people to achieve "unequivocal excellence" while help-ing maintain Santamondo's dedication to "corporate-state social responsibility."

The media, and soon the world, ate it up.

Oh, there were rumors and speculation about just how Santamondo, Inc. had made us a winning team but there was never any proof. Not one of us ever failed a drug test, and the mods were, as Dr. Champ had promised, impossible to detect. I think people were still suspicious, but with-out proof what could they do? What could they say?

Soon other companies like the Swedish conglomerate Spärra, or the Chinese aerospace giant Shenzhou Corp. began openly speculating on setting up their own corporate-states. National athletic programs the world over began trying to adapt 'the Santamondo Method' to their teams, trying to see if the "corporate-mental approach" the spokespeople kept lauding would, in fact, produce results.

They could have it; I knew we had the edge. Often imitated, never duplicated. Truthfully, for everything going on around me and around the program, I didn't really pay much attention. My focus was on the next Summer Games.

The mods had worked for me, so much that in many ways I hardly resembled my old self. My treatment derived from experimental therapies to reverse muscle loss in people with muscle-wasting diseases, like muscular dystrophy. Gone was the lean frame of a middle-distance runner; replaced by the bulky, explosive power of a sprinter. My chest and arms and core were more built than they had been, but the biggest change was in the legs. Long groups of slow-twitch muscle in thigh and calf had been broken down and rearranged by the gene therapy, rebuilt into the fast-twitch muscle of the sprinter I'd always needed to be.

I won't lie to you — the mod sessions were the most intense and long-lasting bouts of pain that I'd ever felt. Hospitalized and sedated for each treatment, injection after injection systematically destroyed and then resequenced every fiber of muscle in my legs. My life was a cycle of training and competitions, punctuated by hazes of pain and opiates... At the end of it all, though, I had legs thick as a horse's and speed to match.

The mods weren't permanent, as such. My body interpreted the resequencing of my leg muscles as damage, and was constantly fighting to repair it. I needed occasional "tweaking", as one lab tech put it, to maintain the fast-twitch fibers I'd developed in my muscles.

And what muscles they were.

We'd worked out my competition schedule to slowly climb the international rankings over three years. International meets, the Commonwealth Games, World Championships — I won them all, narrowly at first, but by bigger and bigger margins until, by the time the Olympics came around, people were speculating on which sprinter was going to finish second, behind me.

I'll never forget my championship run at the Olympics. The smell of the track as I got into the blocks, the crack of the starter's pistol, the thunder of the crowd as I pulled away from the field with ease, the stadium exploding in camera flashes when I crossed the finish line...

The feeling is indescribable. It's something everyone should experience.

❖•❧•❦•❧•❖

Hollywood likes to pretend that you succeed by hard work alone. Enough movies will tell you so. Your parents will, too. But I've been around athletes at an elite level long enough to agree with Dr. Champ — you can work as hard, or harder, than an elite athlete works and still not be able to compete. The truth is, world champions, superstar professional athletes are genetically gifted, blessed with the right set of physiological traits and abilities for a particular sport.

I can... I could run middle-distance. But what I wanted to be was a champion sprinter. My genes didn't agree so I did something about it. Simple as that.

You can say that my victories, the world — and Olympic-record times (which I still hold), don't really belong to me, but you'll never get me to believe it. Athletes competing in the original Olympics used mushrooms and plant extracts as the first performance-enhancing drugs, and that was the third century B.C. Doping is as old as the games; we took it one step further.

And you won't get me to cry or complain about the bad break I've had since. I'm not going to.

The way the Santamondo doctors explained it, the resequencing of my muscle fibers eventually warped the DNA in my leg muscles, and destroyed the cells' ability to repair themselves. After my second trip to the Olympics, it became clear that even the tweaking wasn't helping anymore. The muscles in my legs had been so chewed up by the years of alterations that they couldn't tell whether they were supposed to be repairing as slow-twitch or fast-twitch, and eventually stopped trying.

It was a strange thing for me, as someone so used to an active, athletic lifestyle to take to a wheelchair, to watch my legs whither, the muscles shrink and become useless, to watch the tumors grow.

First, they took the right leg, above the knee. Six months later they found cancer in the left leg, too, and took it at the hip. The phantom pain is bearable, but the dreams are harder to deal with. In them I'm always running...

Santamondo's taken good care of the others and me whose mods had "side effects." Some wanted to return to their home countries to receive treatment. But since we'd renounced our original citizenships to join the Mansoa-Bafata team, and since Santamondo wouldn't issue pass-ports for them to leave... I understood: the corporation didn't want their secrets exposed through examination by foreign doctors. Most of the disgruntled came to accept their fate, I think. After all, it was in the contracts and non-disclosure agreements we'd all signed. Still, the resulting suicide of Greg, our champion pole-vaulter, was a real tragedy.

As for me, I was happy to stay in Mansoa-Bafata. The country had been good to me. And Santamondo scientists wanted to keep me close for study, so the corporation made it worth my while to remain. I think they want to find a way to prevent the eventual deterioration caused by their mods. Once they do that, well, I think the next step is introducing elements of other genomes into their athletes. Can you imagine a runner with cheetah genes grafted on? Or a long jumper with kangaroo DNA?

It was easy enough for Santamondo's PR people to cook up a story about a rare late-onset muscle wasting disease to explain my retirement. Because of my confidentiality agreements with Santamondo, I haven't given any inter-views in the fifteen years since the announcement, but I've read a couple of unauthorized bios about me and I find my condition lends a certain poignant irony to the telling, especially in those books that speculate about gene doping behind the success of the "fastest man alive." Phil Osberg — betrayed by the same body that brought him fame and fortune.

I can still wheel myself around, and have help to do most other things around the house. Mostly I spend my time keeping up on the progress of the Santamondo national teams, and watching old videos of my meets. I have one hell of a trophy wall. You should see it.

Right in the middle is a big picture of me crossing the finish line at my first Olympics, arms raised, legs frozen in broad stride. It doesn't matter that the picture was captured as pixels of digital information, illuminated by high-powered flashes. That image could be on a cave wall in charcoal and mastodon fat, some ancient artist painting by flickering firelight, and all peoples across all time would understand.

"Here is victory," says the image. "Here is triumph. I have done it."

Beat the Geeks

Peter Darbyshire

Carl notices the rash during an episode of *Beat the Geeks*. This is the season of the reality science genre. Actors infiltrate science classrooms and seduce the profs with articles secretly written by their rivals and teams of relationship therapists. The actors break up with the profs in their classes by reading their e-mails aloud, until the profs throw their laser pointers at them or run from the room. Other actors pretend to be grant administrators. They drop by labs to tell researchers they've won millions in funding. They say with a straight face nothing is more important than the researchers finding out whether fruit flies can conceive of an afterlife. Hidden cameras record everything. Viewers vote on which actors did the best job. The winners get spots in real movies. Websites keep track of scientist suicides.

Carl watches an astrophysicist hold the hand of a woman in a black dress as they sit on a bench by the ocean. The astrophysicist tells her the latest theory about the universe, that it's infinite. He says this means that anything imaginable — and lots of things that aren't — is out there somewhere. He looks up at the sky and says somewhere the two of them are sitting on this same beach on another earth, having this same conversation. The woman is actually a transsexual, but the astrophysicist doesn't know that. She looks over her shoulder, into the hidden camera mounted in the collar of a black Lab eating a dead seagull, and smiles. The astrophysicist keeps staring at the sky. He says there are an infinite number of them playing out this very scene throughout the universe right now.

By the next morning, the rash has spread across Carl's body. He scratches at it on the way to the shower, tearing off flakes of skin that drift to the floor. He leaves them for the silverfish to eat. After his shower, he checks his favorite porn sites before getting dressed. There are more than a thousand updates since he checked last night. He gets ready to masturbate as he skims through the pictures and movies, but there's nothing he hasn't seen before. He makes scrambled eggs and toast for breakfast.

In the afternoon, he watches a show in which actors posing as lab assistants add chemicals to scientists' experiments to create humorous results, such as explosions that set the scientists on fire, or fumes that cause the scientists to hallucinate and call their department heads to tell them what they really think of their lab space.

Carl wonders if the rash has something to do with his unemployment. He used to work in a lab himself, growing stem cells into human body parts to be used for transplants. Then his job was outsourced to a lab in Brazil. The manager who escorted Carl and his box of personal belongings out to the parking lot told him the new lab was run mainly by robots. It's just skin, he told Carl. It grows itself. The box of Carl's personal belongings still sits by the door, where he dropped it when he came home that day.

Carl decides the rash is probably from a lack of exercise. He puts on a layer of sunscreen and goes for a long walk, past rows of coffee shops full of other unemployed people and bus stops with homeless men sleeping on the benches.

When he comes back, he is sunburned despite the sunscreen. He closes all the blinds and has a cool shower, but it doesn't do anything to soothe the burning in his skin. He goes to bed and has nightmares about a world in which the sun never sets and is always at high noon. He scratches at himself in his sleep. He doesn't see the skin flakes fall to the floor and skitter away. He doesn't see them eat the silverfish rather than the other way around. He doesn't see them join together into a blob and creep under the bed.

The next day, after peeling off more chunks of burned, dead skin and dropping them on the floor, where the blob consumes them when he's not looking, he goes to a walk-in clinic. He asks the doctor for cream for his rash and sunburn. She writes him a prescription to make them both go away. She tells him she saw a show about a rise in solar flares. She says maybe this could be the cause of the rash and burn. She says the sun is going to collapse in on itself and suck them all into it. She says it's going to be the opposite of the Big Bang. She says then things are supposed to start all over again.

Carl doesn't know if that means the world will never end or it will never begin. He asks the doctor if she made the show up, if it's really just a placebo. The doctor adds a note to the prescription and says she's stocking up on drugs for when the end comes. She says she doesn't think it'll be long now. She says Carl should make sure to use all of the cream. Carl thinks about the doctor naked on a porn site.

Carl goes to a nearby supermarket to get his prescription filled. The supermarket is identical to the one in his neighborhood. The pharmacy inside is in the same place as the one in his neighborhood. Even the pharmacists look the same. Carl looks at the magazine stand while he waits. All the same actors are on the covers. He doesn't even need to read the articles to know what they say.

When he goes home, the blob of skin has shaped itself into a small child, a toddler. It hides in the closet while he makes himself a sandwich. It eats little pieces of dandruff, forgotten hairs, a toenail, and grows larger.

Carl takes off his clothes and rubs the prescription cream all over his body. He doesn't want to get any on the couch, so he stands while he watches the latest episode of *Beat the Geeks*. Actors pretending to be government officials present scientists with fake meteorites holding fake alien fossils. The scientists hold each other and cry.

The winning actor is announced at the end of each *Beat the Geeks* episode. The actors thank their agents and talk about how the show was a great opportunity. Videos behind them show the faces of the scientists when the hosts break their disguises as cops or university janitors or homeless people on the street and tell them the truth, that everything is fake.

Carl never watched *Beat the Geeks* when he was still employed as a lab assistant. He was afraid he'd see himself on it one day. But now he can't get enough of it. He'd watch it every waking minute if he could.

When he goes to sleep that night, the creature creeps to the side of his bed and breathes in his breath.

When Carl gets up in the morning, he finds the creature sitting on the couch, going through his box of personal belongings from the lab job. It's fully grown now, but not quite formed. Its skin looks melted, and hair juts out of its body in scattered clumps. But Carl can tell he's looking at himself. It's even wearing the pants and shirt he wore yesterday.

Carl stares at the creature and it stares back at him. He yells at the creature to get out of his place. It yells the same thing back at him. He says he's calling the cops. It says the same thing back to him. He calls the cops. It goes back to looking through the box.

By the time the police arrive, the creature has grown to look like Carl even more. He can't tell the difference between them anymore, and neither can the cops, two female officers. One of them asks if Carl and the creature are twins. Carl says he doesn't know who or what this thing is, but he wants it gone. It says the same thing about him.

The cops ask for ID. Carl pulls out his wallet and shows them his driver's license. The creature pulls out a wallet of its own and shows them its license. Carl recognizes it as an old one he'd put in a box in the closet for safekeeping. The cops give Carl and the creature their business cards. They tell Carl he's going to have to work this out with himself and then they leave. Carl thinks about double dates.

He doesn't know what else to do, so he sits beside the creature on the couch. They look at each other for a while. Carl tells the creature he's not going anywhere. He doesn't have anywhere to go. It says the same thing back to him. They watch the news and a shopping show and a basketball game and more shopping shows. They watch tornadoes destroy trailer parks on a weather show, and they watch sharks attack scuba divers on a travel show. Then they watch the same news shows and shopping shows again.

During all this Carl notices the creature scratching a rash on its arm. His own rash is gone. He wonders if it was the cream or the shower. He wonders if maybe he's the creature, and it's him. Then he wonders if he's on a new show. Perhaps the new trend is making fun of the unemployed. He looks around for cameras but can't see any. But that doesn't mean they're not there.

That night, it crawls into bed with him. It lies on its side, facing away from him, and sleeps. He thinks about rubbing the prescription cream into its skin. He thinks maybe this will make it go away. But he's afraid to touch it.

In the morning, it wakes him up by telling him about the dream it had. The world was empty except for it. It wandered around the city streets, doing whatever it wanted — eating food, taking clothes, driving cars. Never seeing another human being but its reflection in store windows. Carl had the same dream, but he doesn't say anything.

Carl watches the creature dress in one of his suits and put on his favorite tie. He watches it print off a resumé and leave. He stands at the window and watches it go down the street, then goes back to bed. He looks at the cops' cards and tries to masturbate. He thinks about the cameras. He can't get it up. He goes back to sleep.

He wakes in the afternoon but doesn't get out of bed. He thinks maybe the creature is gone for good now, but it comes back in the evening. Its tie is loose around its neck, and its breath smells of alcohol. It sits on the couch and stares at nothing. It's tough out there, it says after a while.

Carl heats them cans of soup for dinner. They don't speak as they eat. They go to bed together after dinner. Carl doesn't dream at all that night.

In the morning, the creature dresses in the same suit and puts on Carl's favorite tie again. It prints off more resumés. It goes out the door and down the street again. Carl doesn't get out of bed. He lies there and doesn't think about anything.

When the creature comes home, it looks at all of Carl's porn sites. Carl closes his eyes. When he opens them again, the creature is sitting on the couch, but it's dressed in a different shirt and tie. Carl must have slept all night and the next day. The creature watches *Beat the Geeks*. Hidden cameras film cancer researchers watching a fake news show about a cure for cancer being found. The researchers cry. An actor comes into the room and says he's the head of human resources. He says the company won't be needing them anymore. The cancer researchers cry some more.

Carl sees the box of his personal belongings back by the door before he falls asleep.

When he wakes, it's night. He doesn't know how long he's been asleep this time, but he's sore all over and thirsty. He tries to sit up but he doesn't have the strength to move. There's enough light from *Beat the Geeks* in the other room that he can see the creature leaning over him, watching him. Its breath smells of alcohol. Its skin is sunburned, patches already peeling off.

It's a special episode of *Beat the Geeks*. The show secretly revisits the scientists it tricked earlier to see what's happened to them. The astrophysicist sits on the bench by the ocean, alone, staring up at the sky. He talks to himself, but the microphones can't pick his words out of the wind. The alien researchers study new meteorites. They keep the fake ones with fake alien fossils on a shelf in their lab. The fruit-fly researchers say fruit flies can conceive of an afterlife, but that doesn't mean they believe in it. The researchers say they'll keep up their tests.

Carl waits for the host of whatever show he's in to step out of the closet or climb in through the window and point to all the hidden cameras.

He imagines a world somewhere out there in the universe where he is alone, with no double lying beside him.

He imagines a world where he's still working in the lab, growing body parts for other people.

The creature leans down toward Carl, and he closes his eyes. He feels its breath on his lips.

He imagines a world where anything is possible.

Nanabush Negotiations: Brantford Ontario

Greg Bechtel

Anastasia Kowalcik is seventy-two years old, and she has invited me in for tea. When I asked her for a bit of change, she offered me food instead. A rare but not unheard of suggestion, typical for those who genuinely want to help but think I'd spend any money they gave me on booze. I haven't eaten today so the food will be welcome, but that's not really why she has invited me here. She might not know it, but this is about something else. I didn't understand this when it first started to happen. I still don't, but that's beside the point. Understanding is beside the point. They need to tell me, and I listen. That's all.

I sit on the white couch in the living room while Anastasia makes her slow, deliberate preparations in the kitchen. The room has that rarely-used look of a guests-only room. Everything is spotless, the room done up in varying degrees of white. There are doilies, embroidered pillows, and lace all over the place. Carpet, couch, and chairs, all white. I try to arrange myself so as not to leave any stains. My boots sit on a mat by the front door, and though I can't smell them, I'm sure Anastasia can. I should have washed my hands, but now she's here with tea and biscuits on a silver tea service without even a hint of tarnish. It's the sort of service so many couples receive upon marriage and so few ever use. (We had one of those, Ellen and I. Never used it.) Too late to wash my hands now. I'll have to remember to keep them in my lap and off the couch.

Once she has settled and poured my tea, Anastasia begins.

>•I•I•I•<

When Nanabush came back, a lot of things had changed. The Haudenosaunee were back, most of the People had moved north, and everything and everyone had new names in new languages: English, French, some Dutch and German. The Haudenosaunee, People of the Long House, were now called *Iroquois*; the Anishinaabeg, the People, had become *Ojibwa*. The land had several new names, depending on who spoke, and there were more white people. Not a lot, yet, but more. They were the ones doing all the renaming.

Lots of things hadn't changed. Trees and rocks and rivers were more or less where Nanabush had left them. The animals were the same, though they were a little harder to find and there were some new ones — *horses*, *pigs*, *chickens*, all new. The People still loved and hated and fucked, as did the newcomers. No one could agree on anything: also not a change. The world was in flux, as it always had been. Nanabush felt right at home.

The first Person Nanabush met when he came back was an old man sitting on a rock by a river. The old man held a stick with a string tied to one end of it, and was trailing the end of that string in the water.

"You're back," said the old man. "Lot of People said you might not come back." He drank something from a clay jug, pulled a face, and stowed the jug back between his legs. "Where'd you go?"

"Around," said Nanabush.

"Hm." The old man watched ripples glint on the river's surface, jiggled the stick.

"What's the stick for?"

"Fishing."

"Funny way of fishing," said Nanabush. "Learn that from the Haudenosaunee?"

"Sort of," said the old man. "Have a drink." He held out the jug. Nanabush, who was very thirsty, took a huge gulp and immediately sprayed a mouthful of the fiery liquid onto the grass in front of him. The old man laughed at Nanabush's coughing fit. He laughed so hard that he ended up doubled over in a matching fit of his own.

"Whiskey," wheezed the old man when he finally caught his breath. "Takes some getting used to. Goes good with this kind of fishing, though. Try it again. Small sips this time."

"Whiskey! I love whiskey! Drink it all the time!" said Nanabush. "It just went down the wrong way!" He took another huge gulp, and this time he managed to hold it in. "Great stuff!" He made a show of grinning and smacking his lips before handing the jug back to the old man. "Just the thing for fishing!" Then he sat down. Sitting suddenly seemed like a good idea, what with the ground all swaying back and forth like that.

The old man took a long pull of whiskey. "So, you're back."

"Mm."

"Not many People around here lately."

"Lotta Haudenosaunee," said Nanabush.

"Yeah," said the old man. "See that one over there?"

"The one with the funny-looking clothes?"

"Yeah, that one. Name's Thayendanegea, but now he calls himself Joseph Brant, all British-like. Figures he's in charge around here. See that house over there?"

"The big finished one, or the one they're still working on?"

"The big farmhouse. That's his. The one they're working on, that's a church."

"Those are pretty big. Must be planning to stay a while." Nanabush laughed. "What's he going to do when the People come back, pick those things up and move them?"

"People aren't coming back."

Nanabush absorbed this for a moment, then closed one eye to squint over at Brant and his entourage. He was having trouble focusing. Brant was surrounded by a crowd of strapping young men, all Haudenosaunee. "Must be one hell of a fighter to beat the People *that* bad." Turning back to the old man, he continued: "Doesn't look all that big to me. Pass that bottle over here."

Nanabush was a bit drunk, so it took a while for the old man to explain about the American Revolution, the British and the French, the networks of alliances and counter-alliances, territorial squabbles, promises given and betrayed. It was 1785, and Nanabush had a lot of catching up to do. By the time the old man was finished explaining, Nanabush wasn't sure if he understood everything, but he understood enough to be angry. By this point, they were running out of whiskey, so Nanabush thanked the old man for the company, the whiskey, and the update and walked as straight as he could towards the crowd of men by the half-church. When he got there, he walked right up to Joseph Brant and spat on his shoes.

"Do you know who I am?" shouted Nanabush.

"I don't know your name, but I know what you are," said Joseph Brant, in English. Brant was proud of his English. He stepped back a few paces. "You are a drunk and a trespasser on Mohawk land." The young men stopped working on the church and gathered around to watch.

"I'm Nanabush!"

"Certainly! And I'm the King of England!" Brant laughed, and most of the men around him laughed too, though a few looked uneasy and turned to hide their faces. "Nanabush is a myth. And you, good sir, are drunk." Brant turned to his men. "You see what we have to deal with? This is precisely what I was talking about." To Nanabush: "Now get off my land before I have you thrown off."

Nanabush was furious. "Your land! Your land? What is this nonsense?" Nanabush understood now that Brant was truly insane, and he told him so. Or rather, he tried to, but the crowd pushed forward, someone shoved him from behind, and he tripped. And something was wrong with his feet; he couldn't seem to get them planted back on the ground where they were supposed to be. Nanabush kept shouting as Brant gave the order, and he was still shouting when the men threw him into the river, where the current carried him, flailing and spluttering, past the cleared fields around the house and deep into the forest.

As Nanabush unsteadily climbed the riverbank, Old Hook Nose, the one the Haudenosaunee call Hagondes, watched and laughed. He laughed as Nanabush tried to climb the bank three times, sliding back down the mud-slicked slope each time. He laughed as he finally took mercy and helped Nanabush to scale the embankment.

"What are you laughing at, Big Nose? Never seen a man go swimming before?"

"Most get undressed first." Old Hook Nose sat down with his back against a tree and watched as Nanabush tried to peel off his wet leathers. Nanabush swayed first to one side, then to the other, before falling flat on his face. "You're drunk," said Hook Nose. Nanabush gave up on the clothes and rolled over onto his back. He would dry soon enough.

"Maybe a little." He lifted his head. "I think I offended your war chief."

"Don't have a war chief. No war on right now."

"Who's this Brant, then? Everyone seems to think he's in charge."

"Oh, him," said Old Hook Nose. He took out a pipe and packed it with tobacco. "Crossed him already, have you?" Smiling broadly, he lit the pipe and held it out. "Here. Don't have much these days, but looks like I owe you for that at least."

Nanabush sat up and took the pipe. "Thanks." He puffed two... three... four times, briefly pausing and turning his head for each puff, then passed it back.

"Brant, as the British would say, is an ass. But he's clever," said Old Hook Nose, gesturing with the pipe. "Too clever for his own good. Or anyone else's, for that matter. And that *ego* of his." Hook Nose shook his head wonderingly. "It's incredible, really. He does the *stupidest* things, but somehow he manages to get away with it every time. It's almost like he thinks he's exempt or something, like some kind of..." He trailed off, eyeing Nanabush.

"What?"

"Oh nothing. Just reminds me of someone I know is all." Their eyes met and held. Nanabush looked away first.

"Yeah, well," said Nanabush, still avoiding eye contact, tearing up a tuft of grass and throwing it towards the river. "All I know is he's got no respect." The tuft landed far short of the water. Nanabush shrugged and turned back to Old Hook Nose. "How'd he get to be like that?"

"Education, I think. Seemed like a good idea at the time."

"Mm. Tell me about it."

So Old Hook Nose did. They talked through the night, and by morning they had a plan.

Nanabush followed the river back towards the Oshweken settlement and found an exposed bed of clay in the riverbank. He took off his clothes and covered himself with a thin layer of moistened clay, which dried to a pale, even grey. Then he took two lumps of clay and put them on his chest, another lump of clay and put it between his legs.

⇢∘⟨∘⟩∘⟨∘⟩∘⟨∘⟩∘⇠

Catharine's first reaction to the white woman at her door was to send her away. With Sophia, Rachael and Jacob, the house was more than adequately staffed. She had no need for a maid. Sophia, of course, had explained all of this, but the woman insisted she wouldn't leave until she had spoken to someone with authority. Catharine normally preferred to leave this sort of task to Joseph, but he had left the day before, hopefully to seek an audience with the English King. There was nothing for it but to deal with this woman herself, Sophia serving as interpreter between Catharine's Mohawk and the woman's English. (Catharine understood English perfectly well, but appearances must be upheld.) This made the entire process even more exasperating, for though Sophia's Mohawk and English were both passable, her translations were less than apt.

And it was more than just appearances. Understanding a language and speaking that language were two entirely different exercises, and this was a line that Catharine would not cross. A language, her mother had taught her, was more than just a collection of sounds or even concepts; it was a way of thinking. To speak English would be to develop certain habits of thought, and those habits, once formed, would be almost unbreakable. If Catharine had ever doubted these assertions, the example of her husband Joseph would have removed them. Fluently bilingual and proud of the fact that sometimes he even *dreamed* in English, Joseph had learned to pass as both English and Mohawk. Catharine saw and understood the effects (and effectiveness) of this fluency, but she couldn't afford to make such a sacrifice. So she endured Sophia's rough mistranslations, the unsubtle massacre of her carefully selected words.

The woman at the door, who introduced herself as Anna Bushnell, explained that her husband had gone out hunting and never returned. She hadn't heard from him for over seven months, and winter was fast approaching. When her newborn son had sickened and died, Anna had made the difficult decision to abandon the farm (which, Catharine couldn't help noting, must have been on Six Nations land if it was within walking distance) and go in search of work. In England, Anna had served as a Lady's maid before joining her husband to emigrate to what she called the New World, and she would be happy to do so again.

Catharine resisted the urge to explain that there was nothing "new" about Turtle Island, that this continent had been here since the beginning of time, or very nearly so. Nor did she explain that her nation, so far as she could tell from her conversations with Joseph and his European visitors, had been around for at least as long as that of the English, likely longer. Henry, Catharine's brother, observed the exchange silently from the parlour and did not attempt to contribute to the conversation.

Years later, Catharine could never explain precisely what it was that changed her mind. Certainly, Anna's story deserved sympathy, and she did have the knowledge and particular accent of a lady's maid. Her qualifications were not in question; her story wasn't in any way unique or unlikely. Within a single day's ride (though Joseph didn't like her riding, she did it anyways when the mood took her), Catharine could have found several women in similar situations, any of whom would have jumped at the chance to serve in a prosperous, prestigious household such as the Brants'. Certainly, Anna could help care for Margaret and Joseph Jr., but this was hardly necessary in a household that already had three slaves to assist Catharine and her brother Henry. Already, Catharine felt she was treated as a near-invalid, her staff tut-tutting every time she tried to take part in any domestic or manual chore.

Perhaps it was the notion of being served by a white woman that appealed to her. Most whites in the area would go out of their way to avoid even talking to their Mohawk neighbours. Or perhaps it was something else. Over the years, Catharine developed a collection of plausible reasons for having hired this woman: Anna could cook food in the English style that Joseph remembered so fondly from his visits to the royal court; she would bring an air of refinement and familiarity to the house for the frequent European guests; she would provide an opportunity for Catharine and Henry to observe the ways of the English at first hand. These were good reasons, all of which she brought out on one occasion or another for various audiences. And yet, in the privacy of her own mind, Catharine was never entirely certain.

In any case, by the time Joseph returned in the spring of 1786, Anna had become an indispensable part of the Brant household. Within a month, her Mohawk was passable, if heavily accented, and she never bridled at being treated on an even footing with the black staff. Anna had a thorough knowledge of what she called "the arts of civilization," but was as adept at animal husbandry and farming tasks as she was at managing a household. When, at calving time, one of the cattle had a difficult labour, it was Anna that rolled up her sleeve, put her arm right up in there and turned the unborn calf the right way round so it could come out. Her humour was quick and genuine, if occasionally scatological, and she quickly learned to absent herself on one errand or another when council members came to discuss sensitive matters with Henry, the meetings often running late into the night. Best of all, Anna rarely asked questions.

Joseph took to the new maid immediately. As Catharine had hoped, he enjoyed having a white servant in the house to parade around when his European friends came visiting. As expected, he loved her cooking, declaring it a fine thing to sample good English food in this "godforsaken provincial backwater." (This was a joke, presumably, since Joseph was always fiercely and vocally proud of his Mohawk heritage in European company. Though sometimes Catharine wondered.) When Joseph returned from the hunt with venison or rabbit or even beaver, Anna prepared it in the English style, but she also became adept with more traditional dishes of squash, beans and corn.

One evening, while combing Catharine's hair in long, smooth strokes by the light of the flickering kerosene lamp, Anna was particularly talkative. Joseph was traveling in the south, rallying support for a unified confederacy of Onkwehonwe nations to oppose the Americans. He would be gone for some months.

"It must be strange," Anna mused, "to be married to such a man. Just think of it! He's dined with the King himself, and even as we speak he's creating a new nation!" The woman couldn't seem to quit chattering. Catharine wished she would be silent. Perhaps it was an English quality to always need to be talking like that. "You know what I heard someone call him the other day?" Anna continued, "King of the Iroquois! Such an important man your husband has become. You must be very proud." Catharine had heard these comments herself, and had cultivated a precise tone for her answer, one appropriate for both private and public consumption. This one time, however, she found she couldn't keep the scorn from her voice.

"My husband is an interpreter with connections. A warrior, perhaps. No more."

"Oh no! He's so much more than that!"

"Joseph is *not* Tekarihoga, much as he might wish it."

"Tekarihoga?" Anna stopped combing to massage Catharine's shoulders and neck. She had strong hands.

Anna was wise in her own way, and open-minded too — even if sometimes she couldn't seem to cease her witless prattle. Yet how could Catharine hope to explain to this Englishwoman the ways in which a Sachem, as the English called the council members, was both like and not like a king? To be Tekarihoga was to be head of a nation for life, but only of one nation in a confederacy of several. Tekarihoga could not accumulate wealth while in office, and he retained his position only at the sufferance of the people and the clan mothers. A nation's leader could give orders, certainly, but the orders carried no formal, legislative force; an individual would always do as he or she chose, though most often (until recently) that choice was compliance. How could she explain that the glorious Joseph Brant, however influential he might become among the English, would always remain Thayendanegea to his own people, and could never be more than a war leader? His cash rewards and stipend from the King, this house, the slaves — these alone would be enough to disqualify him from consideration as Tekarihoga. Neither wholly English nor wholly Mohawk, Joseph was a strange half-way being, a useful tool, an intermediary at one remove.

And how could she possibly explain to this English woman that her marriage to Joseph, though genuine, was also a tool: a means of preserving the confederacy in these difficult times? Could Anna possibly understand how crucial it was for her brother Henry and (by extension) the council to retain some level of influence over this increasingly unpredictable and powerful Joseph/Thayendanegea hybrid? Certainly, it would be impossible for Anna to understand that Joseph, however much he might repudiate his traditional beliefs in favour of the English religion, could never fully abandon these deeply-rooted behavioural patterns. Nor would he want to. And so she, Catharine, a woman of high standing in the Mohawk nation (much higher than Joseph's own) could have some influence, could — to some extent, however small — direct his actions.

Catharine responded as honestly as she could.

"You are English. You wouldn't understand." Catharine received a few blessed moments of silence as the knots in her neck subsided under Anna's patient kneading. "Mmm..." she murmured, head drooping. The two of them had been knitting all afternoon, Catharine becoming more and more frustrated each time she miscounted, ripped back, and had to restart the same row from the beginning. After these lessons, she always had a stiff neck. As the massage continued, she drifted, imagining these hands to be Joseph's. Whatever his flaws (overpowering ambition, pride, acquisitiveness), he had strong hands. And certain other qualities. Catharine hadn't resisted when informed of her intended marriage, though it was to be a political choice rather than a romantic one. She could have refused, but she didn't. Her eyes slipped shut, and under Anna's hands — so much like Joseph's — she recalled why it was that she had accepted her husband's proposal in the first place.

"Tell me about the Tekarihoga," came the question, softer this time.

"It's nothing," said Catharine. "I shouldn't have said anything."

"You don't trust me." Massaging hands shifted to Catharine's upper arms. Anna whispered in her ear. "You keep secrets." The hands vanished, and now Anna's voice came from some paces away. "Perhaps if I share some of mine, then you'll trust me with yours."

When Catharine turned, Anna was pouring water from the porcelain pitcher into the washbasin by the bed. She rolled up her sleeves and carefully washed her hands, occasionally pausing to spit into the water before continuing. Slowly, the water clouded to a milky white, and Anna's hands turned darker. The more she washed them, the darker her skin became, as if she were actually washing in molasses or dark honey. The water in the basin became, if anything, whiter and cloudier as Anna continued to wash. She rolled up her sleeves and washed her arms, then her face and neck, all of which darkened correspondingly. Anna paused and set down the cloth, her body posing a silent question.

Catharine didn't say a word, sat perfectly still, watched, and waited.

Anna dipped her head in acknowledgement then removed her clothing layer by layer, carefully folding each item and placing it at the foot of the bed. Darkened hands moving over skin so pale that it seemed it could never have been exposed before this moment, not even by candlelight, she continued washing. She finished her arms, progressed to her feet and legs, working inwards from the extremities. Catharine silently rose to help Anna wash her back — the skin there also darkening with each pass of the cloth — then retreated back to her chair. Washing her chest, Anna carefully circled the perimeter of each breast. With a slight, moist, sucking sound, she removed them one at a time, revealing flat, dark pectorals, small brown man-nipples. She placed the shed breasts neatly on the floor by her clothes. Disembodied, they looked like lumps of raw dough left to rise. She washed her stomach then reached between her legs. Again, that slight sucking sound.

Catherine slowly adjusted to the reality of a naked, warm-skinned man standing at the foot of her bed.

"What are you?"

"Onkwehonwe, like you. I am Anishinaabeg, as you are Haudenosaunee. My people drove yours from this land not so very long ago. Now you're back. And so am I."

"Who are you?"

The man raised an index finger, stepped forward, and placed that finger on Catharine's lips. "Ah, now that's another question entirely. Perhaps another time." He stepped back to the middle of the room, spread his arms and grinned, displaying his shameless erection. "I surrender. I throw myself on your mercy. A former enemy of your people, I am now your prisoner. What do your people do with prisoners?"

"We adopt them. We take them into our families to replace those we have lost to battle."

And so she did. Joseph had, after all, been gone a long time.

⊶⊷⊶⊷⊶

When Catharine awoke the next morning, the bed was empty. She dumped the basin of grey-clouded water, refilled it with fresh water from the pitcher by the bed, washed and dressed without assistance. She descended to the dining room, where Anna was preparing breakfast as usual. Neither of them spoke of the preceding night's events. Neither did they ever speak of the following nights. It was surprisingly easy for Catherine to maintain the division between Anna, the English maid who served her during the daylight hours, and the nameless man, this Anishinaabeg who shared her bed at night. Though she witnessed the same transmutation countless times, she never lost her original sense of wonder, and it was near-impossible for her to conceive of the two endpoints of that process as the same person. At first, Catharine worried that she might become pregnant, but the man assured her no such thing would ever happen. And, as the months passed, then years, Joseph was never confronted with the embarrassment of returning to an inexplicably bastard child. A balance was achieved, and Catharine was happy, far happier than she felt she had any right to be.

Several years passed in this way. Each time Joseph returned from the increasingly strained negotiations with the Americans, the English, or the various pan-Onkwehonwe councils, the Anishinaabeg's night-visits would cease. Joseph sought the expected solace of his marital bed, and he always found it there. Catharine gave birth to five healthy children, two sons and three daughters, each one indisputably Joseph's child, each the issue of a visit home to Oshweken before yet another departure on affairs of state. Anna helped raise these children, telling them stories and soothing their night-fears. And if any of the children noticed that occasionally Anna was not in her bed when they ran to her room for comfort in the middle of the night, none of them ever mentioned it during the day.

As always, Anna remained a great favourite of Joseph's European guests, and Richard Beasley, a member of the new Upper Canada Legislature, took a particular liking to her. Beasley started visiting even when Joseph was away, and Anna, for her part, did nothing to discourage these visits. Occasionally, having arrived late for dinner, he would be invited to stay the night in the guest room rather than risking such a long ride in the dark back to his own property, and on these nights Catherine would sleep alone. She was never jealous, though she felt perhaps she should be. After all, it was Anna that shared Beasley's bed, not the nameless Anishinaabeg.

In 1798, when Anna became pregnant, no inducement could bring her to name the father. Though the women of Oshwegen whispered, all Anna would ever say was, "I will be her father and mother both. She has no father but me." Beasley, if present on these occasions, would smile indulgently and take his own young wife's hand in his own, even as he regarded Anna's growing belly with obvious pride. Joseph was not so understanding. No fatherless child would be born under his roof. He insisted that as a leader he must provide a moral example to his people, much as the white farmers to whom he was leasing and selling the land provided a material example of European-style progress and industry for those who — whether through ignorance or fear or inertia (for Joseph there were no other reasons) — persisted in clinging to the old, traditional ways. Furthermore, he argued, Anna's single motherhood would undermine the good reputation of the Brant household in the European community, and it was crucial for him to retain the moral high ground in his ongoing land and sovereignty negotiations. As much as he liked Anna personally, Joseph insisted that she must leave — for the good of the Mohawk nation.

Beasley, as an act of Christian charity (and as one of the major purchasers of Oshwegen land), generously offered Anna a choice of whatever hundred acres she might choose from the newly-purchased Block Two. She would not lack for company, he suggested, if she chose a plot near the new German settlement of Ebytown. In fact, the settlement showed every indication of growing in the near future, as Beasley was presently entertaining purchase offers from a group of Mennonites emigrating from Pennsylvania. Anna graciously accepted this gift, along with one dairy cow, two rifles, a wagon, and various other provisions from

Joseph. These were given not as a sign of approval, he said, but in recognition of her years of faithful service to the Brant household. And so, in the spring of 1799, the now seven-months pregnant Anna prepared to leave the Brant household.

Beasley had sent word the week before that the small farmhouse had been completed and was ready to be occupied by its new tenant. The provisions had been packed into the wagon the night before. Anna took her leave first of the slaves whom she had worked with for so many years. The children, five of whom had never known a home without her presence, bade their tearful good-byes to Auntie Anna. The four year olds, Elizabeth and John, began to cry, first the one and then the other. They wouldn't let go of her neck and eventually had to have their fingers carefully pried open and disentangled from Anna's hair before being deposited in Sophia's waiting arms. Anna sent the children and slaves inside (Joseph was away on this particular morning), and the two women faced each other by the wagon. A fresh, warm breeze ruffled the fields. The church bells rang, summoning all devout (and otherwise) Anglicans of Oshwegen to the Sunday service in Mohawk.

"It's Beasley's, isn't it?" said Catharine. "He bought you off."

"If that's what he wants to believe, who am I to disillusion him?" Anna's eyes twinkled. "The truth is precisely what I've said. I am all the father this child has, and I will serve as her mother also."

"Save the virgin birth for the Christians." Catharine indicated the church with a dismissive toss of her head. "Maybe they'll believe you and your child will start a new religion."

"You're a Christian. You converted when you married Joseph. No one calls you by your real name any more."

"I am precisely as Christian as you are English, and in about the same way."

"It's funny," said Anna. "Not a single person has asked about the mother."

"And if they had?"

"I might have told them." Anna tilted her head. "Then again, maybe not. I could have told them the mother is a powerful and devious woman, a traditional clan mother masquerading as a dutiful Christian wife. Much as her brother the Tekarihoga plays the loyal brother-in-law and follower of the so-called Iroquois king."

"A name. Give me a name."

"Adonwentishon. I'll tell my daughter that name. I'll raise her on stories of her mother and her mother's people. She will know that she is a daughter of the turtle clan, and she will speak the language of her mother's people before any other. She and her descendents will never leave this land, and no one will hide her or take away her language, because she will already be hidden among them."

"I know the woman of whom you speak," said Catharine. "She's not nearly so strong or as clever as you make her out to be. Even now, her husband is selling off her people's rightful territory for cash compensation. She is a failure, this woman."

"No one will ever tell my daughter such lies."

"And the father?"

"Ah, the father is a clown, a joker, a fool and a glutton. His appetites are insatiable, and most often he's a slave to them, but he's clever too. No one can outsmart him but himself; he has fought a Manitou to a draw and that Manitou was his father. He respects no one, and the People laugh at him, but he always — sometimes foolishly — protects the weak, especially children. He has many names: Wenabozho, Nanabush, Nanabozho. Some say he's left and won't return until the Europeans are either gone or defeated. But those ones are wrong. I think perhaps they've mixed him up with somebody else."

"Oh Anna," said Catharine. "You tell such pretty lies. Promise me you'll never stop lying." The women embraced.

"I promise," said Anna, stepping back and swinging up onto the wagon seat.

"Miigwech, Adenwontishon."

"Onen ki wahi, Nanabozho."

☀❖❖❖☀

"Anna's daughter was born with the fairest, whitest skin. In the sun, she always burned easily." Anastasia Kowalcik pours herself another cup of tea and freshens mine. "She married a white man, as did her daughter, and her daughter after her." She gestures to the immaculate room around us. "My husband, Henry Kowalcik, left all of this to me when he died. He was a good man, and I loved him. But he never knew my first language was Mohawk. He worried when our daughter Karen spoke first in an invented non-sense language, and he lectured me for encouraging her the few times that he caught me responding in kind. Eventually, I taught Karen English, and she learned not to speak Mohawk in front of her father. But she learned these stories first, and she learned them in her own language."

Anastasia was looking off into the middle-distance as she told me her story. Now, she focuses on the present, speaking directly to me.

"My daughter lives with her husband, a German, over on Strange Street. He doesn't know, as she and I do, just how long we have been here. Maybe one day she'll tell him. Maybe not. But she won't leave. Anna kept her promise. We are still here. We never left."

I nod silently. This seventy-two year old white woman in small-town Kitchener Ontario truly believes that she is the direct matrilineal descendent of Nanabush and Adenwontishon; it's not my place to contradict or question her veracity. Anastasia looks up at the grandfather clock in the corner of the room. Her manner shifts, and she is once again a kindly, slightly over-solicitous, and anglophilic old woman.

"Oh my goodness! Look at the time!" She stands. "I've monopolized your entire afternoon with my rambling! You must be terribly bored."

Although I assure her that I am not bored in the least, Anastasia continues apologizing as she leads me to the front door. As I put on my boots, she instructs me to wait, disappears into the kitchen, and returns with a collection of leftover cookies and sweets in a sandwich bag. She insists that I take these with me. ("Of course you must! I could never finish them all before they went stale.") As the door closes behind me and I descend the front steps, I wonder if she will remember this afternoon. I always wonder if they remember, but I can never tell. The blank look I will inevitably receive the next time we meet, will it mask recognition, collusion, and covert acknowledgement? Or does the encounter somehow slip from their minds, the compulsion duly fulfilled and discharged?

Certain habits die hard. I verify what names and dates I can at the public library. There is no record of an Anna Bushnell serving in the Brant household, nor is there any record of her homestead in Ebytown. Anastasia did, however, get the dates right; several of the principle characters appear to have been in the right places at the right times. Even the names of the Brant household slaves seem to be accurate. But this is irrelevant, a leftover compulsion from an earlier life. I know better now. I take no notes. I write these encounters as I recall them, a mixture of my own and others' words, and I imagine that I am telling the truth.

Urban Getaway
Kim Goldberg

The City was tired
  like a man on death row or a newborn foal — tired
  of waiting, of being legless, nameless, tongue-
  scraped by alien forces.

The City wanted to start over
  strike out, see the world, be roseate spoonbills
  scissoring dark lagoons, taste donkeys gone to
  market along the raveling hem of the Sahara, know
  the difference between past and present tense.

The City consulted the stars
  It brought out elderly bronze tools hidden in
  refugee camps of broken pencils by the duck pond.
  It spent several centuries calculating tangents and
  cosines and parabolic arcs, working like a cookstove
  or a clawfoot tub - sleepless, hair-mussed, thirsty
  for hope. When the formula was complete,

The City whispered the internal secrets
  to all its constituent parts. The secrets were spider
  fists acquiring tiny targets, hissing softly in
  meteorological code that if overheard by invading
  soldiers would be mistaken for an impending
  snowfall.

The City let the plan unspool
  like a slack gut of stagnant water crawling out to
  sea in search of birth mother. We leave tonight,

The City gassed off
 When they are sleeping. There will be no room for
 supplies or provisions of any kind — no rucksacks,
 coleman lanterns, stolen kisses, pup tents, touch
 stones, quantum entanglements. Not even your
 potholes or condom hollows or other vacant spaces.
 We must all walk out naked, lighter than hydrogen,
 or we will never get away... The parts shivered, shot
 furtive glances, nodded like cars backfiring, street-
 cleaners whisking cold curbs, hot grease singing in
 swollen dumpsters. No discussion was needed.
 When the sun went down, the boundaries blurred
 and

The City drifted to the ledge
 shepherding its soundless parts, obedient as a shorn
 herd of silicon chips or a flock of rebar encased in
 blind faith. Or maybe cheezwhiz. One by one each
 cannonballed into the chasm — chin tucked,
 shoulders hunched, knees clasped to sunken chest,
 rusty testicles plunging headlong, expelling last
 breath in a smudge of confusion, just a small
 parting gift to the occupying troops.

And The City was never seen again
 Although on sunny days, vague clusters of miasma
 leave fuzzy shadows on the footprint of the former
 site. Rumour has it

The City
 may have reformulated itself into white dwarfs and
 red giants in the winter skies, which astrophysicists
 now know are actually reflections of glistening fish
 guts wrapped tight as shrunken cowhide at the
 centre of the earth.

The Object of Worship
Claude Lalumière

The god settles on the table. Rose tears a piece from her toast, slathers a heap of cream cheese on the ear-sized morsel, and lays it next to the god. It consumes the tribute.

Rose smiles as the god's warmth permeates her body, enfolds her heart. She squeezes Sara's hand. "Your turn."

With an irritated sigh, Sara cuts a thin — too thin, Rose thinks — sliver from a slightly unripe banana. Sara's hand moves toward the god, but Rose grabs her wrist.

"That's not enough. At least put some peanut butter on it."

Rose recoils from Sara's glare.

"I don't need you to tell me how to worship." But Sara nevertheless dips her knife into the jar and smears a dollop of chunky peanut butter on her tribute before offering it to the god.

✦❖❖❖✦

Rose runs the six blocks from home to the video store. As assistant manager, it's her responsibility to open the shop in the morning. Rose usually gets to the store a half-hour early; she likes to attend to her morning tasks unhurriedly. But today the home god was too upset. It hates when she and Sara fight, or even when they exchange tense words. After breakfast, they had to cuddle silently on the couch with the god nestled between them until harmony was restored. When Rose and Sara finally kissed, the god rewarded them.

Rose looks at her watch as she reaches the storefront. She's made it with five minutes to spare. Two of the employees are waiting outside. And smoking. They know the staff rules. No smoking in front of the store. If they have to smoke, they should do it in the alley, or at least not so close to the door.

"We're not on the clock yet, so don't get on our case," says Vandana as she stubs out her cigarette under her black construction boots.

"Yeah," Maddie concurs, flicking away her own half-smoked cigarette with her long, crooked fingers. The green polish is flaking off her chipped, overlong nails.

Rose unlocks the front door, steps inside, then quickly punches in the security code on the pad next to the light switch. Ashley — cheerful and perfectly groomed, as always — arrives; Rose waves in all three clerks before locking the door again, so they can ready the store. But first things first.

The store god rests in its altar, which is carved into a column next to the counter. All four women kneel, cooing prayers at the god. The god glows, acknowledging their presence, but does not otherwise stir.

By the time the store opens, they're six minutes late; only one customer is waiting. Rose apologizes, but the woman — a tall redhead with a striking face, long luxurious hair, and big curious eyes — laughs it off. "I just got here." Her smile is playful; it's enough to wipe away the remains of Rose's tension.

Rose is grateful for this change in the day's course. She should thank the store god. There's a box of chocolates in her desk. She'll bring one out for the god. Maybe mint cream? Or almond crunch?

Suddenly, the god moans painfully.

The god darkens.

Vandana, Maddie, and Ashley are already trying to soothe it by singing to it. The store god loves song, but the clerks' efforts are having no effect.

The only customer — that beautiful redhead — is browsing through the new releases as if nothing untoward was happening.

Rose walks up to her. "Have you greeted the god?"

The woman frowns and tries to suppress a chuckle. "What?... No."

"The altar is by the counter. Perhaps a small prayer?"

"I don't think so."

Gods must always be greeted. It's the same everywhere. Showing proper respect to the gods is what holds society together.

Rose just stares blankly at the woman, who resumes browsing. She picks a shrinkwrapped DVD case off the rack. *Burning Sky*, Rose notices, remembering that Sara had asked her to bring a copy home.

The customer walks to the counter, holding the DVD. Rose follows her.

The three clerks are still trying to soothe the god, but it is more anxious than ever. Smoke spews from the altar.

The customer turns toward Rose. "Can I buy this?"

Rose snatches the DVD away. "Please leave. Right now."

"Because of that thing," she points at the god, "you won't take my money?"

"Get out."

After the woman leaves, Rose fetches the box of chocolates from her office and, piece by piece, feeds all of it to the god. Finally, the god appears to calm down.

Then the god leaves its perch, finds the DVD the woman had intended to buy, and destroys it.

→•[•[•[•←

Above the bed, in its niche in the wall, the altar lies empty. Rose stiffens and stops herself from reminding Sara that it needs to be cleaned. This has been such a stressful day; Rose wants it to end on a good note. But Sara's neglect nags at her.

Sara sighs. "I'll clean it tomorrow, okay? I can tell it's bugging you."

They hug, their breasts touching under the covers. Sara continues, "You shouldn't second-guess me so much. I know your family does things differently, but I've always taken good care of the god. We live in harmony."

The god's been in Sara's family for generations. Sara had been given to her mother by the god. And the god had given Sara's mother to Sara's grandmother... Sara grew up with the god, has spent her entire life with it. She and the god are ritually bonded; there are duties the god won't allow anyone else to perform. But Sara is not as fastidious as Rose would like.

"You're still thinking about it." Sara, grinning mischievously, tickles Rose.

"No, stop!"

Sara pins Rose down, holding her wrists tight against the mattress. She bends toward her and almost kisses her, almost lets their lips brush.

Rose snags Sara's lower lip between her teeth, and Sara lets herself slide down on top of her lover. They kiss. Sara jams her leg between Rose's thighs. They squirm against each other. They love each other.

>•I••I••I•<

Noise awakens Rose. It's still dark. She groans, knowing how hard it can be for her to get back to sleep when she's roused in the middle of the night. She looks up; the altar is still empty. The god usually watches over them at night.

Sara snores, lost to sleep.

Worried, Rose gets out of bed and grabs her robe. She follows the source of the sound.

Through the kitchen window she looks at the large inner courtyard shared by five neighbouring houses. The gods are gathered. The gods are singing.

A few other neighbours are sitting on their balconies, watching the gods.

All thirteen resident gods are there — one for every household with access to the courtyard. One of the gods lies in the middle of a circle formed by the other twelve. One by one, each god leaves the circle to rub itself against the god in the centre. They go around many times. With each round the singing intensifies, until it reaches a thunderous crescendo and all the gods swarm toward the centre.

Abruptly the singing stops, and the mass of congregated gods pulses with light.

Rose returns to bed, troubled and confused. Before moving in with Sara, Rose had never seen gods together, and she is still unfamiliar with their social habits. Unsettled by them, even. It's a city thing, with so many households close together. Rose is still a country girl at heart, despite having lived here for three years.

Eventually, just as dawn breaks, the god returns to its altar. Rose has not slept the whole time.

Rose whispers a prayer to the god as it settles in. The god glows. Then the god joins Rose in bed, slips under the covers. It rubs itself against Rose's toes, her soles, her legs, her stomach, her breasts... It shares its warmth with Rose. Rose's heart melts with love for the god. The god presses itself between her legs. She spreads her legs. The god accepts the tribute of her moistness. And then the god gives itself to Rose.

Rose gasps.

→•I•I•I•←

Rose makes pancakes for breakfast. Lots of pancakes. With blueberries in them. She lightly sautés sliced apples and bananas, to serve on the side.

Yawning, Sara emerges from the bedroom. "Babe, it smells so delicious!"

The table is already set. Plates. Cutlery. Juice. Pot of coffee. Mugs. Can of maple syrup.

"Do I have time to shower, or should I eat now and shower after?"

"The pancakes'll keep warm in the oven."

"Fuck it. That smell is too delicious. Let's eat now." Sara sits, and Rose brings the pancakes and the sautéed fruit.

Sara asks, "What's all that ruckus outside?"

"I think one of the neighbours is moving."

"Yeah... Didn't Jocelyn say she might be leaving? Something about a new job?"

"Maybe. I don't know. I don't really know her."

"Ah, who cares? Let's eat this great food before it gets cold. Thanks so much for making this, babe."

Sara stuffs herself like an enthusiastic child, grinning at Rose the whole time.

The god settles on the table. Together, the two women offer it an entire pancake, with banana and apple slices on top. The god consumes the tribute. The god hums.

Sara chokes.

Rose pats her on the back, and Sara coughs, clearing her throat.

"I've never heard the god sing like that after receiving tribute. Wow. It must love your pancakes."

"Maybe." Rose can't keep the hint of something more out of her voice.

Sara looks at Rose quizzically. "What aren't you telling me?"

Biting her lower lip and keeping her eyes focused on the god, Rose says, "I'm pregnant."

Sara skips a few beats. Then, "When...?"

Rose turns toward Sara. "This morning. At dawn. The god... it stayed out all night with the other neighbourhood gods. Singing. And something else. Dancing, maybe?"

Sara says, tersely, "They must've been saying goodbye to the god who's moving away. But whatever."

"Oh. That makes sense. Anyway, when it returned. It—"

"The god made you pregnant."

"Yes."

"You."

"Yes! I'm blessed! What will we call her?"

Sara looks away.

Rose gets up from her seat and hugs Sara. "I'm sorry, love. I'm sorry it wasn't you. I know I should've woken you, so you could be with me and pray to the god... but it was so sudden. So fast." She runs her fingers through Sara's hair. "Aren't you happy for me? For us?"

"Yeah... sure. It's just so... unexpected. I wasn't thinking about children at all. Not yet, at least. It's just kind of a shock. That's all."

Sara skips a few more beats, but in her silence she strokes Rose's arms.

Then, "Of course I'm happy, Rose. It's going to be great having a baby. Plus, with your looks, our daughter's gonna be cute as a button."

The god wedges itself between the two women, settling against Rose's belly, enveloping the family in a cocoon of divine warmth.

⊹⊱⊱⊰⊰⊹

The moon is nearly full, the starry sky cloudless. The night air is a bit chilly; Rose and Sara are cuddled under a thick red quilt, pressed against each other and holding hands. They're waiting for the gods to come out.

The new neighbour moved in earlier today, but neither Rose nor Sara has seen her. After dinner, Sara told Rose that, their first night, new gods are always welcomed by the resident gods. Sometimes, new gods will vie for dominance, especially rural gods, unused to the proximity of other gods. It never unfolds quite the same way, and it can be quite a spectacle.

So here they are on the back porch. Waiting. They wave at their neighbours. Everyone is out tonight, to witness the welcoming of the new god.

Time passes, and nothing happens.

Rose asks, "Does it usually take this long?"

"No. But let's wait for it. It's worth it." Sara kisses Rose, and they neck. Waiting for the gods.

Rose is woken by Sara's snoring. Dawn is breaking. "Shit. I missed it."

Tabitha, their upstairs neighbour, yells down: "You didn't miss anything. The gods didn't come out. I'm gonna need so much coffee today." Tabitha stomps back inside and slams her back door shut.

⊹⊱⊱⊰⊰⊹

Maddie called in sick at the last minute. Rose, unable to find a replacement, is stuck working the evening shift at the video shop. She calls home, to apologize. She's surprised that Sara doesn't pick up. She leaves a voicemail message.

It's a slow night. Petra and Ashley would have been able to handle it. The rules insist on a minimum staff of three, though, and Rose could lose her job if she left early and management found out. Ashley would probably rat her out; and she might get Rose's position if she did. It's not worth the risk, especially with a baby on the way.

At eight o'clock, while Petra and Ashley are taking a cigarette break out back, Sara walks into the store. Rose perks up. "Hey, you came by! Thanks."

Sara's carrying a little paper bag. "For you."

Rose opens it and finds an almond croissant. She leans over the counter and gives Sara a quick kiss on the lips.

Rose breaks off a tiny morsel of the croissant and hands it to Sara. "Would you...?"

"Uh... Sure." Irritation flashes on Sara's face, but she forces a grin. She places the tribute on the god's altar, hurriedly singing a line from a children's ditty. The god accepts the tribute.

"See, I even remembered to sing. Be right back."

Sara quickly scans the shelves and picks a DVD. Walking back toward Rose, she waves it in the air. "Weren't you supposed to bring one of these home?" It's a copy of *Burning Sky*.

"Shit. I forgot. Sorry. Take it, and I'll handle it."

"Alright, babe. I gotta go. I might be out late tonight. Don't wait up."

Sara gives Rose a quick peck on the cheek and is out the door before Rose even has time to utter, "What?"

Rose presses her face against the window. Already across the street, Sara walks away briskly, arms entwined with another woman's. A tall woman with long red hair.

⊷⊶⊷⊶⊷

The home altar is still filthy. The god is flaccid, discoloured. Sara has been neglecting it.

In Sara's absence, Rose offers tribute to the god, but it ignores her.

Rose worries about her baby.

✳⊹✳⊹✳

When Sara finally gets home in the middle of the night and slips into bed, Rose feigns sleep.

The god instantly latches itself onto Sara, glowing brightly. Through half-closed eyelids Rose sees it take tribute from Sara's mouth, drinking her saliva.

The god darkens, oozes stinking grey goo all over Sara, all over the bed. It rushes out of the bedroom.

"Oh, fuck!" Sara wipes her face on the clean underside of the pillowcase.

"You kissed her," Rose accuses. "That woman. That heathen."

"Not heathen. Atheist. Heathens worship invisible gods. Jane doesn't worship at all."

"How can anyone not worship the gods? They are with us."

"Whatever. Let's not argue." Sara gets up, walks to the bathroom, and cleans herself with a wet towel.

Rose follows her in. "I've met her before. At the store. She angered the god."

"Yeah, she told me. She was scoping out the neighbourhood. Jane's our new neighbour."

"An atheist? The resident gods won't accept her. It'll cause trouble for everyone. Look what you did to our god."

"Well, maybe we don't need the gods."

"The gods give us life, give us children."

"And why do you think the gods do that? Maybe because they need us to take care of them? Is that what you want our life to be about?"

Rose clenches her teeth. "We are the chosen of the gods. We are blessed. What can be more important?"

"Listen, babe, Jane has lots of ideas that I... that I agree with. Things that I've been thinking about but was too afraid to discuss with anyone, even you. Talking so freely, it made me giddy. It opened me up. We just kissed."

Rose makes an exasperated sound.

"Okay, well, maybe a little more. But it was just tonight. I was swept up by the evening. I still love you. And the baby."

"What about the god?"

"I didn't say I wanted to change our way of life... but things might not be how they seem, how we believe they are. Maybe society should change. It's worth thinking about, that's all."

"So... how does she live?"

"Well, she doesn't keep a god. Other than that, she's just like everyone else."

"But that's no life."

"Why not?"

"There's nothing to connect her to the harmony of the world. It's an empty existence. Meaningless. And it's irresponsible. Selfish."

"You don't understand. Maybe you should meet her. She's knowledgeable about the gods and their relationship to us. Talk to her."

"Never. Especially not while I'm pregnant. Promise me you'll stop seeing her. For the baby's sake."

"Rose... I can't do that. You can't dictate to me. Or blackmail me like that."

Both of them stay silent for a few minutes, while Sara gets fresh linen.

Rose helps Sara change the bed. "You saw how the god reacted tonight. If I can't stop you from seeing her — at least be careful. Please. But... I don't know what to do. About us. I don't know if I really believe that you still love me. Maybe I don't trust what you're becoming."

⁕⋅⫶⋅⫶⋅⫶⋅⁕

Sara didn't come home last night. She didn't even leave a message.

Rose is tired. It was a big day for new releases, with nonstop waves of customers. She unlocks the door to the apartment, wondering if Sara is gone for good.

Rose walks in to devastation. The couches are shredded. The television is on the floor, the screen shattered. Most of what was on the walls or on shelves is now on the floor, in pieces. The kitchen is a mess of broken china and splattered food. Everything is covered in dark, stinky slime.

The god.

Rose rushes to the bedroom. The bedroom is mostly intact, with only a trail of dark slime leading to the altar. The god rests in its niche, exuding dark smoke. The air is thick and odorous. Rose coughs.

"What the fuck... Rose...?"

Rose turns to see Sara enter the bedroom.

"What happened here?"

"What do you think? You're so selfish. You didn't come home last night. You can't just abandon the god like that. If you want to leave, fine. Leave. But there are rituals."

"I'm not leaving. We just talked late into the night yesterday. I didn't even sleep. It was simpler to go straight to work from Jane's."

"You think I'm stupid? The god knows what's really happening."

"Maybe the god doesn't know as much as you think it does."

They don't talk for the rest of the evening. Sara cleans up the apartment while Rose tries to comfort and placate the god.

In silent agreement, both women climb into bed at the same time, their backs turned. The god slips in between them. The women turn toward the god, toward each other. The god's warmth is so delicious. Rose is surprised when Sara kisses her, and she's surprised, too, that she lets her.

⟶•❦•❦•⟵

The god hasn't accepted tribute of any kind for days. It rarely leaves its altar, now, which Sara still hasn't cleaned. It reeks.

Sara is snoring, but Rose wakes her up. "We need to talk."

"Can't it wait, babe? I'm too tired."

"No. It can't go on like this."

"Fuck. What are you talking about?"

"Look at the god. You're ignoring it."

"So what? Why don't you take over? I'll even help with the transfer ritual. You care about the god a lot more than

I do. And clearly it cares about you more, too." Sara tips her chin toward Rose's belly.

"Is that what this is all about? You're jealous!"

"No... I'm sorry. I shouldn't have said that." Sara sits up and gently puts her hand on Rose's arm. "Look. I don't want to worship anymore. I started thinking about this stuff before the baby. And before I met Jane. I don't mind if you still worship, but it feels wrong for me."

"What does that mean? You can't live here if you don't worship. The god can't tolerate that. Look at it. Do you want to live like that woman? She can't even walk into a store without making trouble. Things are just going to get worse unless you stop being so selfish."

"I'm not being selfish. And neither is Jane."

Rose pushes Sara away. "Maybe you should just leave. Stop pretending."

"Have you ever thought that maybe the god is the problem, and not me?"

✦┅┅✦┅┅✦┅┅✦

Through the door, Rose hears voices inside the apartment. Isn't Sara supposed to be at work?

Rose walks in. Sara is sitting on the couch. With that woman, Jane.

The god is lying at their feet, collapsing on itself. Rose rushes to it, offers it her saliva, holds it against her breasts.

"What is she doing here? What were you doing to the god?"

Jane says, "Only what should be done to all of them." Sara interrupts her with a gesture.

"Rose, baby, this is for your own good. For the good of the baby. It's safer this way."

"You monsters. You were trying to kill it."

"Baby, you don't understand."

"Leave. Don't ever come back here. I'm having the locks changed. If you ever try to come near the god again, I'll call the police. I never want to see you again."

"It's my family's god, you know."

"Not anymore. The god blessed me."

Jane says, "Rose, the gods don't care about us."

"I don't want to hear your lies. Get out! Both of you!"

Sara and Jane exchange a glance, and the two of them get up to leave. Sara turns back, looks at Rose hugging the god, and opens her mouth to speak. But Rose glares at her, and she walks out and quietly closes the door behind her.

✥✥✥

Rose nurses the god back to health. She performs all the proper rituals. The god must let go of Sara, now. It must focus on Rose and the coming baby.

The god accepts tribute again. It lets Rose clean its altar. When Rose sleeps, it squeezes itself next to her.

Rose tries not to think of Sara anymore. That woman, Jane, has moved away. Good riddance.

✥✥✥

Rose is three and a half months pregnant. It's her birthday today. Twenty-five years old. She gives the god extra tribute at breakfast to celebrate the occasion.

✥✥✥

Despite the god, despite the baby growing in her body, Rose feels loneliness gnaw at her as she slips into bed.

The phone rings. "Hello?"

"Hi, babe. I just wanted to wish you happy birthday. I hope it's okay that I called. I miss you."

The god gets agitated, excited. It wraps itself around the phone, presses itself against the receiver, against Sara's voice. It glows and hums.

Rose yanks the phone cord from the wall. She's been faithful to the god. It must love her, not Sara. Not Sara.

In a flash, the god darkens. It fumes and crackles. It attacks the phone and shatters it. Dark smoke quickly spreads throughout the room. The god knocks Rose onto her back. It pushes Rose's legs open.

"No!" Rose stifles a scream.

The god squeezes itself into Rose's womb. Rose feels the god inside her, twisting and thumping. Taking back what it had given her. It pushes its way out of Rose's vagina. Blood oozes in the god's wake, flowing out of her womb and spreading onto the sheets.

Silently, Rose weeps, clutching at her belly.

The god accepts the tribute of Rose's tears and consumes them.

Tofino
Andrew Gray

Ahead of them people fall from the two towers support-
ing the bridge. They are visible as black dots from the
roadway as it leaves Stanley Park, resolve clearly into the
figures of men and women by the time the van is crossing Lion's Gate. They blur past the sides of the bridge and
out of sight. Bram catches a glimpse of streaming blonde
hair before he pulls his eyes back to the road ahead of them.
The sun is low across the Georgia Straight and long shadows flicker on the bridge deck as the jumpers flap past to
land back on the towers, ready to dive again.

"Night's coming," he says to Rachel. She's perched on
the back of the seat beside him, grooming her feathers. She
makes a murmuring squawk but doesn't look up. Sometimes she'll run her beak through his hair, sit on his shoulder and nestle herself in the crook of his neck. But it
distracts him when he drives, which is especially dangerous
with the state of the roads here.

"We'll need to find a place to sleep before we make the
crossing in the morning. There used to be that motel on
the way to Horseshoe Bay. Wouldn't it be nice to sleep in
a real bed, maybe have a shower too?"

Someone has planted sunflowers in the grass beside the
off-ramp onto Marine Drive. Two crows perch on a fallen
head, pecking at the seeds inside and Rachel watches them
intently. "I know, love," he says. "I know."

By some miracle the motel still operates. Bram holds
a sheaf of red and white bills hesitantly towards the clerk.

Rachel is in the van pecking at the leather covering on the steering wheel. He doesn't know if there's a policy about animals in the rooms, but he's not about to leave her out overnight.

The clerk is covered in silver scales. They glitter in the fluorescent light of the office. There's a TV on the desk, and Bram can see little moving images reflected in some of the scales. He can't tell the sex of the clerk at first glance, tentatively guessing male.

"We do take new dollars, sugar." The voice is that of a smoker in her fifties.

"They're lovely," he says somewhat awkwardly. "The scales are." It's so hard to tell how compliments will be received; he's had bad luck before.

The clerk shrugs. "Lovely don't buy dinner." She slides a key in exchange for more of the money in his hand than he thinks the room should be worth. "You'll be looking for the ferry in the morning, then."

He's startled for a moment and forgets to protest about the price. "The ferry?"

"People stop here for the ferry. Don't try and tell me you're going skiing."

He considers lying but can feel his face reddening; he's never been very good at it the best of times.

"Rumours are getting around." The clerk looks at the crisp bills in her hand, puts them in the till. "They won't take any of this for the ferry. No paper money."

"I heard maybe they would," Bram says.

"I'm sure you heard lots of things."

⊶⊶╬⊷⊷

The motel room is a motel-room. Lime-painted cinder-block walls remind him of a high-school gymnasium; the tub is stained and the faucet leaks. But there's a shower, and hot water, and he remains until the ache of driving fades from his shoulders and his neck, until his skin crinkles into a relief map of itself. When he leans his head against the tiles under the shower head, he sees the stain of mildew in the grout. Enough things have remained themselves that they sometimes throw the strangeness into focus, make him realize just how odd everything has become.

He and Rachel eat perched on the side of the bed. Their food is running low. The money belt under his shirt is getting thinner. He doesn't want to think about how far they've come on a journey sparked by rumours, by the word of someone so obviously askew, the desperation this suggests. He falls asleep with the image of falling bodies in his eyes, of their spreading wings skimming the water of the harbour past the rusting abandoned hulks of bulk haulers and container ships.

✦•❧•❧•❧•✦

They pick up a couple of hitchhikers on the road outside the motel in the morning; two children with a hand lettered sign reading 'ferry'. He is initially hesitant to stop, but from the way Rachel bobs up and down on the seat back and taps the glass he knows she wants the company. She's always liked children.

"I'm Hilda," the girl says as she hops in the side door. "And this is Dick." They look to be ten or eleven, but their names are the first clue to their real ages; names he associated with great aunts and friends of his grandmother. Another clue the knitting needles tucked into the side of her backpack. She looks around the interior of the van, at the clothes and water jugs, the half-empty flat of canned soup, a sack of birdseed. "No fish? You'll need fish for the ferry."

Bram notices they have a cooler with them. It sloshes as they haul it up and onto his floor. "I'd heard they take new dollars now."

Hilda looks at the boy. He shrugs. "Not that I know," she says, "But it's been a couple of months since we came over to the mainland. Maybe they've changed things." She looks at Rachel who has been following the conversation, her head tilted sideways, black eyes glinting. "Who's this?"

Rachel croaks, flashing her dark tongue. Her feathers have a violet shine in the morning light. "It's Rachel," Bram says. "You two buckle up, the roads have been rough." He can't help thinking of them as kids, though they're likely decades older than him.

The seatbelts fit awkwardly on their small bodies. The boy is looking out the window, uninterested. He has yet to speak. There's a pipe in his hand and he unscrews the stem, blows to clear it. The girl is still looking at Rachel. She holds her hand out and Rachel gives it a small peck. "Was she a person before or has she always been a raven?"

Bram starts the van and looks ahead. "Not really your business, is it?" Roots have pushed through the road in places and as he heads towards the Upper Levels highway he bumps over the cracked asphalt. He puts a disk in the van's stereo, a Latin folk album he'd swapped some classic rock for back in Mission, and the conversation is over.

At the ferry exit a school bus blocks the road. A man with long ragged blonde dreadlocks and a tie-died shirt gets out of the bus as they pull up. On the side of the bus are the rules of ferry passage written out on brown cardboard.

Bram asks about new dollars, one in his hand as if showing the money would make it less like the shaky promise it actually is. The man makes a complicated shrug-like motion. He might be miming the removal of an elaborate costume.

"Depends," he says. He looks at the kids in the back, at Rachel. "Dollars might buy passage for three, but not the van."

Hilda pipes up. "Don't worry about us son, we're paying our own way."

"We need the van," Bram says. "We've a ways to go yet."

Dreadlocks laughs. His hair moves like the coat of some wooly dog shaking out the water after a swim. "Well dollars won't do it then. Let's have a look at what else you've got."

In the end he wants half the food, a bottle of vodka, a pair of jeans, the cooler of salmon Hilda and Dick brought aboard and the remainder of the new dollars in Bram's wallet. At least the money belt still has something, but the food is a loss.

Bram had taken the ferry from Horseshoe Bay years before, remembered lining up in the sun on a hot summer day with RVs and minivans, kids and tourists running around on deck as seagulls flapped past, the wind smelling of ocean. This is a much smaller boat, big enough for only four or five vehicles, the rest of the deck filled with people standing, sitting, nursing babies, crammed in around boxes and bales of unidentified objects. They've painted flowers over the old ferry logo, a graceful portrait of a breaching Orca. Drummers drum in a grubby group; an improbably tall woman gracefully folds her legs to sit beside them, making room in a crowd of backpacks and sniffing dogs. Another woman stands by the ramp, folding her wings and unfolding them again absently as she talks with one of the passengers.

"You know," Hilda says, looking up from the knitting she's taken from her backpack. "It's really not so different than it was before. The Gulf islands always looked something like this, didn't they hon?" Dick snorts, the first sound he's made since Bram picked them up.

Voices buzz from the front of the boat, then Bram sees the shape of a fin cutting through the water. "Finally," Hilda says.

Dreadlock and a couple of his companions are dumping buckets of salmon into the water. More fins arrive; the water churns around the fish. Hilda claps her hands. "Come on Dick, let's go watch them get ready." With a little wave she and Dick slip through the crowd to the front of the boat.

The ferry isn't fast, but the passengers seem used to it. The pod of killer whales pulls steadily at their harnesses. Gulls rise and fall behind them, plucking salmon fragments from the water, fighting loudly. Someone's making bean tortillas over a small gas stove and Bram buys one with a new dollar. Rachel sniffs the salt air and flaps her wings with what he takes to be pleasure.

He's approached for rides by a dozen people offering jewelry, food, the laying on of hands as payment. One man even offers a fat bundle of old hundreds and Bram shakes his head at the worthless paper, amazed that the man would even try. When he tells them where he's heading some look at him with sympathy, but a few brighten, yes they say, we're going too. They ask him what he knows, but it's the same muddle of rumour and speculation they all have.

Before it all happened, he'd sneered at the horoscope readers, those who heard ghosts in the settling creaks of old houses, the hand of fate in every simple coincidence. Miracle cures and the like, the simple-minded believers in such bunk as naturopathy and energy fields to be pitied at best. Now he lives in a world that makes no sense at all. In the faces and voices of the people he's giving rides to — he and Rachel need the supplies, he's told himself — he sees a mirror of his own need and bewilderment.

"Is this foolish?" He's in the van with Rachel. She has tucked her head beneath her wing, the slow rocking of the ferry putting her to sleep. She looks up at him, inscrutable. Makes a quiet clicking sound. Perhaps she is being reassuring.

At some point in their past Rachel would have smiled at him indulgently, "Have faith," she would have said. At another point she would have been less indulgent. Far less. Now he could only imagine. Still, she always had some sort of faith — faith that things would work out, that some sort of benevolent force was keeping an eye on them. He wonders where her faith is now.

There is a dead giant in Departure Bay. He has fallen next to the ferry docks, splintering pilings and twisting the metal supports of the gangway. But the docks were built for larger boats, and the small ferry is able to come closer to shore where a space has been hacked into the remains of the old dock and a ramp rigged together from metal supports and plywood sheets.

Crows and turkey vultures wheel around the giant's head and chest. When he fell, he fell face-forward and his arms are splayed beside him, the remains of a trailer crumpled beneath one hand. His body is half submerged, and several sea lions rest in the hollow of his back. His head is turned away from the ferry dock and Bram is glad of it; from the cloud of birds he can imagine the ruin of the man's face.

One of the passengers is staring at the giant. Jerry, Bram thinks, or Jim or something like that. "You know how he died?" he says.

Hilda puts down her knitting needles, frowns. "He tripped?"

Jerry shakes his head. "Starved to death. Or at least to the point where he fainted and gravity did the rest of the damage. I think they all do, eventually. Can you imagine how much food a giant needs?"

Hilda looks sadly at the fallen body as they bump up the ramp and onto the roadway that leads out of the ferry terminal. "I bet he was heading to Tofino like the rest of you," she says. "I bet he swam from the mainland, but he just didn't have the energy to make it past the shore. Poor soul."

Bram is not interested in the giant. He has seen one before near Banff, also dead. It's just as stupid a thing to become as a billionaire in a world where suddenly every second person was a billionaire. Or a raven.

"God played a strange joke," Hilda says. It's a saying Bram's heard before. She's still looking back at the docks, though by now as they near the turnoff to the highway only the top of the giant's head is visible, along with the column of birds.

"People say that," Jerry replies. "Or that God is testing us. But there's so much we don't know about the world. Quantum mechanics, and string theory and the like. Maybe something happened in another dimension we can't even see. Isn't the world is supposed to make sense in eleven dimensions?"

Bram speaks then, surprising himself. "I think it was God," he says. "Nature doesn't care what happens to people, but you'd have to be cruel to think something like this up."

He supposes that the men and women flying from the Lion's Gate might disagree with him, but then they were the smart ones. Rachel is riding on the seat back behind him. She pecks his ear hard enough to hurt. He pretends not to notice.

Hilda and Dick get off at their house in Parksville. The place is a tidy bungalow overlooking the beach. Someone waves from the front door and Hilda smiles and waves back. The tide is out and a few figures wander across the long stretch of sand. A holiday postcard made surreal by the castle high above the water, perched atop an enormous floating boulder. Hilda stands beside the driver window for a moment looking up at Bram. Her voice floats up. "It's not all cruel," she says. "Just look at that castle. What a thing to wish for!" She hands him the result of her knitting, a single small sock.

Dick sits on his backpack on the front lawn, lights his pipe. He has the high voice of the child he appears to be. "Remember," he says. "It could always be worse."

❖❖❖❖❖

Road signs give them three hours to reach Tofino, but it takes more than a day. Trees have blown down across the highway, rocks have fallen in more than one spot, and it's slow going. There are other vehicles on the road, and people on horseback, hikers with backpacks and water bottles out for what could be a weekend jaunt save for their haggard expressions, for the direction they're heading.

Late in the afternoon Jerry speaks up. He and Bram have just finished siphoning gas from a car they found in the garage of an abandoned house. The other passengers are scouring the house and the garden for food. "Isn't it strange how few are coming the other way?"

Bram nods. He'd noticed too. "Almost all the traffic is going towards Tofino."

"And those coming the other way don't want to talk about it. Is that a good thing?" Jerry frowns, screws the gas cap back on the van. Bram realizes he doesn't know a thing about him other than his name. But then he doesn't know much about any of his passengers. They've only spoken to him of practical matters — food and water, map coordinates, finding gas. The reasons for their journey, for the people they see on the road carefully avoided, as if mentioning it would be dangerous somehow.

"It's a bit late to change our minds now," Bram says. Rachel sits on the roof rack, surveying the land around the house. "Quork," she says. She clicks forward across the roof of the van and launches herself into the air. She flies carefully up into a fir beside the road, flaps from branch to branch, pecking at pine cones.

"You don't ever worry she'll just fly away?"

Bram is watching Rachel intently. He shakes his head.

They overnight in another abandoned house and set out early. When the highway ends and they turn towards Tofino the road is lined with empty vehicles. They drive past cars and trucks, minivans, motorcycles, all empty. Finally, after they pass the national park and are nearing the town itself, they see signs of life. A wisp of smoke from the beach, someone rooting around in the trunk of one of the cars. There's a man on the road wearing an orange safety vest. He waves them to a stop.

Bram rolls down the window and the man, enormous, tattooed and bearded, hands him a ticket for each person in the car. The ticket says *Beer*. On the back there's a time and date stamped. The man notes their names on a log book then waves them through.

"What's this for?" Bram asks.

"You should know what it's for if you've come here," the man says. "Ask in town."

There are more people closer to town, but Tofino is still eerily quiet. Campers and RVs and tents speckle the woods and lawns, but most are empty. A woman in another orange vests directs them to a parking spot near Long Beach. "Take a tent or a camper," she says. "The empty ones have a blue tag on the door — just take it off when you decide which ones you want."

Jerry spends a few hours in town as Bram sets up camp on the edge of the beach with the others. There's a new-looking RV parked where the forest edges into the sand of the beach and some of his passengers take it over. He takes a large tent, removes the sleeping bags that are neatly laid out inside.

Jerry returns with a bag of apples. He hands everyone two. Bram hasn't tasted an apple for months. He feeds slivers to Rachel, perched on his shoulder. She plucks them carefully from his fingers, "Seems that this is the place, alright."

"So she's still here," Bram asks. "It's true what they say?"

Jerry nods. "Apparently. There's a few more folk in the orange vests in town. Sticking around to help out." He takes a bite of his apple. "I talked to a couple. Though nobody would tell me why all the empty cars. Say nobody *really* knows. Everyone gets their turn, eventually. Five minutes, stamped on your ticket."

"What will it cost?" Bram asks. "Did they tell you?" He's thinking of the dwindling supplies, the few new dollars he has remaining. The only thing of value left is the van.

"Couldn't quite get a straight answer on that either. Someone said it cost nothing. Someone said it was *everything*. But it must be worth it, don't you think? How often in life can you have a mistake erased, just like that?"

That night the sparks from a few scattered fires float into the air above the beach. They can hear singing from far away, just audible over the voice of the surf. The stars are the same as they always were, casting down their cold gleam. Bram sits on the ground by the tent with Rachel. She's almost invisible in the dim light. She makes a soft sound, *tock*, and he strokes her feathers. "It's almost over," he says. "You know I've forgiven you, don't you?"

The woman they've come to see lives in a house in the forest just off Chesterman Beach. There are more people in town than Bram had thought, or more had come in the night, as there's a small crowd in the front garden of the house. The way is blocked by orange vests, scrutinizing tickets.

Bram is only a little nervous. He waits on a low wall in the front garden, Rachel quiet on his shoulder. Someone by the front door periodically calls out ticket numbers. He's reminded of the lineup at a deli and almost laughs.

Now serving salvation. He considers saying this to one of the people who waits with him, but nobody will catch his eye: they're focused inwards, like patients in a doctor's waiting room awaiting their diagnoses. He wonders if they have doubt at this late moment, doubt about what their lives will be like afterwards. *At least*, he thinks, *I'm not in their shoes.*

When it's his turn he hands his ticket to the gatekeeper and walks into the house. A tree-trunk winds its way up through the foyer to the second floor. Skylights let in a wash of daylight. There's a kitchen ahead, opening up to a living room dominated by a stone fireplace, treelike posts and massive beams. On a stool by the kitchen island there's a young woman, maybe twenty, sitting with a mug, a magazine open in front of her. Another helper elf, he imagines, looking around the room. He's not sure what he expects to see — an altar? Some inner sanctum and a sage in a rocking chair? The woman pats the stool beside her, not looking up from the magazine. "I'm Marie," she says. "You've got your five minutes. Don't waste them."

He blinks. "You're her?"

She looks at him then. "Did you not read the rules?"

In the garden they'd handed him a photocopied sheet of paper, grubby from many hands. *The Rules*, it read.

Don't waste her time. Tell the truth about everything. She doesn't know why it happened any more than you do. Maybe they really were Angels, come to save us or test us with their promises. Maybe we failed. It doesn't matter. You only get one visit, so be sure this is what you want. And no, we don't know where people go afterwards. Please leave by the rear door and you will find out for yourself. Just walk towards the ocean.

He nods.

"So tell me the truth. What it is you want annulled."

He holds his hand out and Rachel steps onto his wrist from his shoulder. She looks around the room, tilts her head. "My wife," he says. "This, *transformation*, whatever you call it. It was a mistake; she needs to be a person again."

Marie touches Rachel's head. Rachel opens her mouth then closes it again with a gentle croak. "I can't annul someone else's wish for you."

Bram frowns. "It was a mistake," he says. "She never would have wanted this permanently. She was depressed. We had some problems, it's true, but they were getting better. It was just bad timing, that's all. If it had happened earlier, or later, on a different day—"

"Nevertheless, I can only change someone if they ask me. I'm simply not able, even if I wanted to. This is what I can do, nothing else."

"Fine," he says. "Rachel, ask her to annul your wish."

Marie looks at him with what he only later understands is an expression of deep sorrow. He feels something start to shift inside him. "You do realize," she says gently. "That this is a raven."

"Christ, of course I realize it. This is why they call you the wisest woman in the world?" There's an edge to his voice. He notices a movement from the corner of his eye and a burly someone steps out from the shadows behind one of the posts.

Marie shakes her head minutely. "It's fine Carl," she says. She holds out her finger to Rachel who pecks at it. "She is not in there as the person you knew, looking out and understanding what we say. This is a raven, not some raven-shaped person. She has become what she wanted."

"You're wrong," Bram says. "Look at her. She's standing right there. She listens to what I say, she follows me everywhere, she doesn't fly away. What normal raven would behave like that?"

Marie looks at the two of them for a moment. "What was your wish?"

"It's not relevant," he says. He's starting to feel sick. Prickles of sweat appear on his forehead and his face.

"You don't lie well." She gives him a look that he can't bear to see and he looks away. "This bird has a connection to you, but your wife is gone. You have to accept that. If you tell me your wish maybe I can help you both find some sort of release."

Rachel dips her beak in the mug on the counter and laps at the liquid inside. Bram smiles weakly. "She likes her coffee."

Marie touches his hand. "It's water," she says. "What was your wish?"

"I wished for money. Just like half the world did. You don't need to cure me of that, do you?"

She looks at him for a long moment. "No," she says finally. "That one took care of itself."

Rachel is looking outside the window at the beach, through the trees and Salal. Gulls glide over the water and Bram watches her follow them with a tilt of her head. "Perhaps it's time to consider letting her go," Marie says.

Bram looks back at her. He's not really sure what he feels. Through the windows by the front door, barely visible from his seat, there is movement outside, a suggestion of the crowd of people waiting in her front yard. The slats of her fence like the bars of some prison. "Can you do it to yourself?"

She's puzzled. "Do what?"

"Annul your own wish."

She touches Rachel's feathers lightly, leaves her hand there. She doesn't speak.

"Five minutes," Carl finally says from the shadows. "Time's up."

⇢•⫟•⫟•⇠

He drives away from Tofino. People on the road ask him about what they'll find. Is it true? they ask. Is she there? Will she make everything back the way it was before? Sometimes he shrugs and keeps on driving. Sometimes he lies to them. Lies seem to come much easier now.

When the moment had come to wish his one true wish he hadn't had to consider his choice for a moment.

Rachel sits on top of the passenger seat, watching the scenery go by. "Now you love me again," he says to her. She watches the trees. In the sky other birds fly around. "You do. What could possibly be wrong with that?"

Language of the Night
Elisabeth Vonarburg

(For Ursula K. Le Guin)

translated by Howard Scott

Jacob's hallucinations had begun two days earlier, shortly before he had descended down to the vegetation line. He wasn't too worried at first: ringing in his ears, tingling in his body, maybe just the after-effects of resuscitation, after his prolonged hibernation in the survival capsule. And then his eyes started playing tricks on him, making objects appear nearer or farther away than they actually were, blurring sections of the landscape, distorting perspective. He thought it was the altitude, the brutal light of the blue sun, the heat, the atmosphere, different from that of Earth — less dense, less oxygen. Perhaps even those millions of tiny, invisible spores, detected in the air by the sensors, a sign that the vegetation is in full reproductive profusion lower down on the plateaux and on the plains, but the analyzer is categorical: the spores are absolutely non-toxic, incapable of reproducing in a human body, in a word, harmless, just like the solar radiation, as long as you are adequately protected.

But the ringing became buzzing, which turned into a humming; Jacob stopped and looked around: nothing was moving in the already torrid heat. Finally, when he heard a series of inarticulate sounds that seemed almost like voices, he stopped in the shadow of a rock, and took out his *portable*; but the computer told him that his condition was normal — except for increased blood pressure due to anxiety, and fatigue from the walk. As for the environment, still nothing especially lethal in the solar radiation, no treacherous fumes from the ground or the rocks. Jacob's bizarre perceptions were due to stress. That was the only rational explanation. He couldn't deny it had been traumatic: he is alone, stranded millions of kilometres from home, for an uncertain period of time, on a planet where he is not yet quite sure he will be able to survive, It would be traumatic for anyone, even those with the very particular psychological profile they look for when selecting the Scouts, and even with the training they put them through.

Jacob accepted the verdict of the computer — it was indeed the only logical explanation — and he set out again, more slowly, checking where he put his feet and trying to forget the rest. In any case, he can only travel for a few hours after dawn and before dusk, when the savage winds that greet the sunrise have died down and the sunset winds have not yet risen, when the temperature is not too oppressive, and when the blue sun is still low enough in the sky. He spends the rest of the day in his little tent, under the rather limited shade of a boulder, trying not to pay any attention to what his mutinous senses are telling him. Under his closed eyelids behind his visor, in his tent, in the shade, he still sees the chaos of rocks as if it were etched on his retinas, their harsh outlines in the actinic light of the blue sun, the blinding gleam from those huge rock faces, which constantly seem to change in shape and dimension, as if in a kaleidoscope. He sees the light, he almost hears it, a huge subliminal crackling, and he feels like his brain is frying. When the sun goes down and he sets out again, for one or two hours before night fall — which is very sudden, like a slamming door — he can still hear it: the absence of light, the deepening cold of the night shattering the surface of the stones.

Then, when the cold becomes too intense, he stops. He doesn't want to use up his flashlight, even though it has almost the whole next day to recharge in the sun. He sets up his tent, and he places the proximity alarms — even though he still has seen nothing bigger than the animals that look like mongooses, or rather meerkats, in that vertical posture, watching, that they always adopt; he assembles the water condenser, which will draw the little moisture available in the air during the early hours of the night, replenishing his meagre reserves. Then, stuffed into his heated sleeping bag, he eats his concentrated rations as he gazes at the constellations that twinkle surreally in the overly pure atmosphere, distorted, almost unrecognizable; he could almost imagine he is back in space, in his space-craft, but no, the stars are too fixed, the sky too immobile, and he turns to lie down in his tent, he tries to quiet his unease and sleep. It's the fatigue, the light, the stress. He just has to get to a lower altitude, that's all.

The survival capsule came down at 2800 metres, not too high to make the descent dangerous, given the terrain, but high enough so that altitude sickness forces Jacob to climb down to a lower elevation and therefore to explore, which is his duty as a Scout anyway — it's crazy how much the Company trusts its employees: as if he were going to hibernate in the capsule for years while he waits for the recovery ship! He has no illusions, they would never respond that fast to his SOS: this planetary system is very ordinary, gas giants much too costly to mine, one or two ice balls, and in particular this terrestroid planet, or else why would they have sent a Scout? But it's more like a cross between Mars, the Andean plateau and the Himalayas. Thin atmosphere, barely breathable at high altitude, plus tiny amounts of surface water and very little atmospheric moisture under constant ultraviolet bombardment: not a cloud in the white sky, even above the barrier of the mountains.

For five days, Jacob has travelled, lugging his big back-pack. Obeying the directions transmitted to him by the capsule computer via the small communication satellite that it launched before setting down, he is following a stream that dried up millennia ago, and he feels confident: the uplands are made up of porous rocks, sandstone and limestone. Given the increasing abundance of vegetation as he gets closer to the plain — the old sea floor — there must be huge networks of aquifers, perhaps subterranean rivers; he'll have water anyway... Judging by the vegetation encountered so far, spindly shrubs and low bushes, it might be hard to find material to build himself a real cabin, but he could always move into a cave: the canyon walls are riddled with them, and there must be lots of them lower down too. He will have real shelter then, not just the translucent nylon of his tent... But he has to climb farther down, where the atmosphere is denser. He will breathe easier, he will sleep better. Lack of oxygen, that's all it is. That's why he has those hallucinations in the daytime, why he has those weird dreams at night, and he never dreamed before, or at least he never remembered his dreams.

In fact, for the last two days, it is as if he plunges into a world of dreams as soon as he closes his eyes. They are so slow though, the images — they take centuries to form, like gigantic bubbles, which then open to reveal unicorns, feathered snakes, owls with human eyes. After aeons, there is a coral castle under the sea, where sea horses are sacrificed with great ceremony on an altar of purple shells; then, for millennia, trees grow, as high as skyscrapers, in a livid light; a swarm of black umbrellas floats spinning by, open wide, sinister. Sometimes, there are no landscapes or animals, but just objects, a dance of metamorphosis, grotesque and terrifying in its incredible, its implacable sluggishness: boxes that swallow one another till they become buildings, rockets, coffins, snaking entrails of gleaming pipes, scarlet crucifixes with arms twisting like the serpents of Kali, the trunks of Ganesh, the horns of the Minotaur...

When he wakes up, today, he feels vertigo, it's as if the ground is pitching beneath him, and he doesn't dare open his eyes. It takes him several minutes before he can manage to turn over. He switches on the portable, connects the analyzer, sends his vitals to the computer in the capsule, which answers him, imperturbable, that he is very dehydrated, that he has to drink, and then everything will be better.

When he pokes his head out of the tent, one, two, no, a dozen small silhouettes suddenly stand up a few metres away, then remain perfectly still, in a row, turned towards him. The pseudo-meerkats. For two or three days, he has seem them running and jumping in large numbers around him among the rocks while he walked; they seem to be active during the same hours as he is, and they don't seem to be very shy. But this is the first time they have come so close. During the fraction of a second preceding the whistle of the proximity alarms, he has enough time to get a very good look at them: about forty centimetres high, short, sand-coloured hair, darker bellies, thin bodies, small round heads with long rodent teeth, vibrissae above the eyes, front paws held close to their chests as if they were praying, with long, very visible claws...

And the alarm goes off, but the animals don't even flinch. What? Is it possible they're actually deaf? Jacob sits stunned for an instant then, with very slow movements, clenching his teeth to stifle the nausea, he crawls out of the tent, deactivates the alarm... and he's too thirsty, to heck with the animals, drink first.

The water is still cold, and he lets it spill down his throat like a benediction, closing his eyes. When he opens them again, the nausea hasn't quite disappeared, and the pseudo-meerkats are still there. Have they come closer? Even though they're not very big, they have teeth, and claws. He takes his weapon from its holster, sets it to medium power — he's not one to kill for the sake of killing, though he will have to determine at some point whether these animals will become his main source of protein once his rations are exhausted. With the other hand, he turns on the portable, and points it towards the animals so the sensors can examine them thoroughly.

One of the animals breaks its stony stillness, drops down on all fours, moves closer with a curiously fluid movement and then stands up to sniff the device. Then, in a swift movement, it clamps its teeth down on the strap hanging from it, and pulls, almost jerking the portable out of Jacob's hand.

After hesitating a fraction of a second, he jumps back, and tears the strap out of the creature's teeth, shouting "Hey!" and the whole mob immediately scurries away, bounding among the rocks.

Then he has a good laugh about it, in spite of the slight vertigo that comes over him again. Really not very shy, these animals! Maybe he could tame some of them? He would have companionship, at least. Then he busies himself again with his daily needs: he eats, relieves himself, takes down the tent and dismantles the condenser, then he packs his backpack again and sets off again towards the last plateau. His early-morning worries finally dissipate: the vertigo is gone, and there is no sign of the hallucinations trying to come back. From time to time, out of a corner of his eye, he spots a movement, a sand-coloured patch, or he hears a high-pitched chirping: he has an escort of pseudo-meerkats. If it weren't for the rising heat and the intense light, painful even through his visor, he would almost feel good.

He stopped earlier than usual: the ancient mountain stream turned into a waterfall cascading onto the last plateau, and doing rock-climbing with this backpack on his back... Once at the bottom, though, it is not really fatigue that makes him decide not to go on: at the foot of the scree, he turned around and saw the cliff. Semicircular, white and taupe, it was at one time battered by tides, the marks are visible, and darker horizontal lines show the gradual drying up of the ocean. And all along it, at several levels, there are black holes of every size where the waves have eaten into the softer stone, where underground water, perhaps, has cut a path to the sea. Caves. Shade, real shade. Jacob straightens up under his backpack and walks towards the closest cave.

It turns out to be farther away, wider and deeper than he had thought — in this light, in this too pure atmosphere, the dimensions are hard to estimate. The least noise rouses cathedral echoes and Jacob feels tiny under the huge dome, the heights of which are lost in the darkness, but that extra hour of walking was worth it: the ground is covered with a thick layer of fine sand. In the shadows, it is almost cool. Jacob doesn't bother unfolding the tent. He just rolls out his sleeping bag and, after quickly eating, he lies down in it, his arms under his neck, delighted: a real roof over his head! He closes his eyes and for the first time he does not see the light through his closed eyelids. With a sigh of contentment, he lets himself drift off to sleep.

And in his dreams, right away, there are colours, slow but vibrant, surreal, colours he can hear sometimes, in arias, in fanfares, in the rumble of a thousand drums. And sharp, ecstatic, repugnant aromas; and on his tongue the taste of the storm, and the taste of love; and under his fingers silk, concrete, the exact texture of the rattan mat he slept on sometimes with his dog when he was little... And he laughs, and he cries, he trembles, he roars with rage, he opens child's eyes, terrified and filled with wonder, he meets his dead mother, his father he never knew, and all the women he left, he leaves them again, he asks them for forgiveness, he kills them, they kill him, wild bacchantes on the banks of a river with stone waters crossing the sky, and the slow vortex of images and sensations carries him yet elsewhere in his memory, and elsewhere, and yet...

A chorus of hooting and desolate whistles makes him jump up, and the sensation of air on his skin, almost cool air... He looks around wildly, his heart pounding, then his brain kicks in again, evaluates the low light, the time, the place: the sun is setting, he has been sleeping for a long time, it is the evening wind moaning in the cave, and perhaps in the underground passages that run through the whole cliff, transforming it into a gigantic flute. Smiling at his panic, he wipes a hand over his face, scratches his beard — if there's really water around here, the first thing he'll do is shave! — and he goes over to his backpack to open it and set up camp. Lulled by the cave and his illusion of being closed in on at least three sides, he forgot to set the proximity alarms, he realizes, feeling a little sheepish. But he permits himself another smile: it's not as if he was surrounded by vicious predators!

And then he realizes his portable has disappeared.

He put it down beside him before closing his eyes, and now it's not there, and Jacob does not wonder for long what happened: there's a clear imprint in the sand, surrounded by paw tracks.

Incredulous, furious, horrified — the portable is his only link to the capsule computer — Jacob follows the tracks of the pseudo-meerkats and their loot, which zigzag towards the back of the cave. He soon finds the entrance to the burrow: there is only one, just high enough and wide enough so that he can crawl through it on all fours, the strap of his flashlight around his neck — fortunately the Scouts are also chosen for their small stature and their light weight! His shoulders scrape against the walls, widening further what appears to be a freshly dug tunnel. After a bit, however, the tunnel meets another. It is not the work of the pseudo-meerkats, though: the rock walls have been worn smooth by the flow of long-vanished water. Jacob is spared having to choose which fork to take: the one on the left is completely blocked by tightly packed earth. He continues therefore towards the northwest, as indicated by his wrist compass.

This tunnel is considerably wider, and Jacob can put aside his fears of cave-ins, but he soon comes to another branch, which turns sharply downwards. Here again, earth and stones block one possible route. Strange. These animals are as industrious as ants! He has to stop thinking of them as Earth animals, in any case, even though they were perhaps attracted like magpies by the shiny metal case that protects the portable.

With a sigh of relief, Jacob notes that the walls of the tunnel are getting wider and higher ahead. Standing now, hunched over just a bit, the flashlight in one hand, the other following the striae of the stone, he continues on, stumbling from time to time on big stones that roll under his feet and disappear into the darkness in front of him, bouncing down the steeper and steeper slope. At irregular intervals there are fissures in the rock, though nothing that looks like another tunnel where the animals could have wormed their way through with the portable. The air is cooler, and less still, with a vaguely familiar smell. Wet patches begin to glisten on the walls, then more and more the stone is covered with large pinkish areas that are vaguely shimmering, with a bumpy texture, which Jacob examines for a moment, perplexed, before deciding they must be mushrooms. Soon the walls are completely covered with them, the floor too, with just a path of bare rock about twenty centimetres wide showing that the animals have frequently passed this way.

Then suddenly, the tunnel takes a sharp bend, the roof and walls disappear upwards, and a black void opens in front of Jacob, who is barely able to keep his balance. He hurriedly puts the strap of his flashlight around his neck again, then, his heart pounding, he sweeps the flashlight beam around him.

He is on a long pink shelf less than a metre wide, where the pseudo-meerkats' path snakes over... His eyes see, without at first understanding: red columns with irregular swellings, pinkish fangs hanging from the roof, others rising from the floor through a sea of sand in irregular mounds, and farther away an open area, dotted with sparkling lights. Crystal echoes are whispered between invisible walls in the blackness beyond his beam of light.

A cavern. Huge. Still alive, where the water rains down into a gigantic lake. Ancient stalactites and stalagmites. Covered with mushrooms. The words form slowly in his mind, at the same time as his eyes, then his feet, follow the animals' path along the shelf and over stacks of flat rocks that form a stairway. As he descends, in the jerky light from his flashlight, he begins to really become aware of the dimensions of the cavern. The stalagmites, and the stalactites, are as tall has he is, and the columns they are fused to are as wide as ancient sequoias; the red and pink mushrooms fan out from them in corollas that look bizarrely like crushed velvet and line folds big enough to swallow him up. Mounds of sand between the columns and stalagmites... They are pseudo-meerkats, lying motionless, hundreds of them, perhaps thousands, an unbroken carpet of sleeping animals. And that murmuring sound in the air, blending with the music of the water, is their mingled breathing.

Jacob tries to clear his head. The portable. Where is the portable? He sweeps his flashlight over the sleeping bodies, looking for a flash of metal that... There! Near the first stalagmite. He will have to cross the sea of animals. He pushes one with his foot. No reaction. Harder? Still no reaction. He squats down to examine the animal. The creature seems to be completely comatose. Jacob slides a foot between two small heaps of fur. Not a quiver. The other foot...

He is very close to the portable and reaches out to pick it up when something moves on the edge of his field of vision. He has time to turn, to see in the beam from his flashlight something swelling up between two velvety folds on the nearby stalagmite, then there is a dull explosion, a thin fog envelops him as a gush of air brushes across his face, damp, vaguely sticky...

Jacob stands unmoving for an instant, then, slowly, his hand turns off his flashlight. In the total darkness, he lies down, in slow motion, among the bodies of the animals, which have moved aside without waking up to leave him an invisible space. He stretches out, closes his eyes, he's cold, he sleeps.

He dreams.

But he knows that this is not a dream. He is there, he watches images that are shown to him, and at the same time it is him, it is from him that the images are being drawn, he is a soft, pliable substance, infinitely malleable, and all that remains of him is a minute kernel of terror, of rage, of refusal.

The cavern, with its reddish flesh clinging to the stone teeth. Bubbles constantly form and burst among the mushroom-filled folds. Billions of minute luminous particles spray out from them, forming an ectoplasmic fog that fills the whole cavern, rises through the tunnels, towards the daylight, outside now, on the plateau, on the mountain, moving backwards, the horizon becomes rounded, and everywhere floats the luminous fog of the spores.

Pseudo-meerkats in the sun: they run, they jump, they fight, they play. Their fur disappears, they seem to dissolve... no, they become transparent. A torrent of luminous particles pours into their lungs and comes out again almost immediately, in each quick breath, in each beat of their little hurried hearts.

Pseudo-meerkats sleeping. Their hearts beat slowly, their lungs swell and deflate languidly — and the luminous particles circulate synchronically, slowly following the network of alveoli and bronchi, lining the veins and arteries, concentrating in the weblike networks of the nerves, penetrating the convolutions of the brain where they twinkle as they carry out undefined, but transformative activities, then resume their steady course, fusing with the surface of the mucous membranes, spreading in sluggish layers through the nostrils and muzzles of the pseudo-meerkats, which have recovered their fur, stretching out in milky filaments along the tunnels, as far as the cavern with the stone teeth, as far as the fleshy, pulsating folds of a mushroom that is bigger than the others...

No, there is something in the heart of the mushroom. A pseudo-meerkat. Huge. The head is barely recognizable on the swollen body, undulating slowly, saturated with a luminous slurry. On the other side of the misshapen mass, there is like an intermittent teeming movement, which raises waves of the luminous fog. Baby meerkats, naked, whitish, gleaming, expelled from the Mother in groups of two or three, immediately engulfed by the spores.

Moving back at dizzying speed, a yellowish ball that floats in an empty void speckled with small points of light. Closer. It is entirely made up of entwined pseudo-meerkats. No, there are other animals in the living mosaic, something that resembles an ostrich, but with bigger wings, and a kind of hexapod horse covered in scales, and... but they are all penetrated by milky filaments. Closer still, through the layers of transparent animals, follow the filaments: they end in nodes spreading under the skin of the planet, the enormous Mothers buried in mushrooms.

A monstrous silhouette. It is standing like a pseudo-meerkat, but it only has hair on the top of its head, the front paws are too big and they are clawless, the torso too short and too wide, the neck too long, the hind legs too straight...

The silhouette is lying down now, sleeping, slowed down, bathed in the luminous fog. It becomes transparent, too, and finally, on the inside, it very much resembles a pseudo-meerkat and the shimmering particles find their paths, stick to the walls of the veins, to the sheaths of the nerves, moving up their crackling network to the brain, strange, alien but less and less so as the particles become integrated, are transformed with contact, go off again, return carrying new instructions...

Now there are two silhouettes face to face. One of them is the naked monster, linked by myriads of luminous filaments to the other silhouette, which looks a little like it, but turns out to be entirely made up of pseudo-meerkats and pinkish mushrooms.

Jacob wakes up screaming.

Jacob has made a fire again. He makes a fire every evening, now. In the daytime, he goes to gather dead wood. The sky is growing dark at the entrance to the cavern, the winds are starting to rise, night is not far off, another night. Glints of light dance faintly on the walls, the air shimmers carrying sparks towards the roof, which is lost in the shadows. There is enough wood to keep the fire burning all night long, at least Jacob hopes so.

When he woke up, there, below, he headed straight forward, perhaps crushing some pseudo-meerkats, he does not remember. He ran into the tunnel, then went on all fours through the tunnel with the earth and sand running over his shoulders, and he found himself back in the cave. In the dark. Without his flashlight. However, he had had a sense of seeing, all along, as he saw now, but there was no light to see, the entrance of the cave was barely visible against the sky, which was hardly any less dark before the dawn... And then he understood that he had not seen, but that he had *known*. Or at least that something, in him, knew, had steered him unerringly.

The mushroom spores. Not toxic, no, the analyzer was right. But the machine had simply not taken all the possibilities into account. On the surface of the spores, there are proteins that can be assimilated by the human body, since they are water-based and carbon-derived, like all life native to this planet. Artificial proteins, deliberately fabricated by the mushrooms to transfer information between the plant and its animal symbiots. And vice versa, because which is the symbiot of the other? The spores in every animal on the planet, the animals steeping in the emanations from the mushrooms — from the single pseudo-mushroom, in fact, the underground mycelium that carpets the entire planet, of which the Mothers form the modular brain, and all the animals the legs, the hands, the eyes — the wings.

A little ironic smile comes to Jacob's lips. All this calm scientific rationality, the fine logic of the whole system once you have the key. And the wonder of it, too: that a planetary consciousness could have developed this way... But he still hears himself screaming, he remembers the horror, the contorted terror that sent him racing blindly through the tunnels, which still makes him tremble when he thinks of the invasion, the contamination... Completed. Inevitable. He, too, is immersed in the invisible spores. His suit is not impermeable. And he will have to go back below to get the abandoned flashlight, and the portable that was stolen as bait.

He puts another branch on the fire. Glowing particles rise with a crackle. The invasion, the contamination. The contact, too. But not in the daytime, not in the light. The symbiotic consciousness cannot really communicate in the daytime: animal life moves too quickly, the spores are too slow. It requires sleep and the night. And when it speaks, it is not with words. The symbiotic consciousness knows nothing about proteins, neuron connections and chemical reprogramming. It found equivalents in Jacob's sleeping brain, or rather generated equivalents after scanning through his sensations, his perceptions; it sampled the human symbols in his dreams, reviewed his memories, groped its way to making correlations, a grammar, a common vocabulary. The Scout in Jacob admires this achievement, something he knew he would never be capable of.

But there is another Jacob. That Jacob is afraid of the dark.

He didn't know he was afraid of the dark. He loved the night when he was in his spacecraft. Limitless night, when he turned out the lights — but never really night. There were always around him the little coloured lights of the instruments and, farther away, the infinite sphere of space, on all sides, like a sparkling eye of which he was the omniscient pupil, an eye in constant movement, but which he could open and close at will by polarizing the perimeter windows. He thought he loved the night, but here in this cave, this is the night of the earth, a mouth half-closed on him, with bloody stone teeth waiting for him there, below, and a light that does not belong to him...

Jacob stands up. He walks up to the tunnel entrance and goes in. He crawls and then strides confidently between the invisible stone walls. At the end of the path, blinded by the darkness, but in the inner light of the symbiot, he contemplates the huge space, carpeted with sleeping life, waiting life. Tomorrow, or another day, he will take another step. But not right away. For the time being, he, too, is content with waiting. Motionless, in the breathing darkness. Standing on the edge of the lips of night.

With gratitude for the scientific assistance
of Norman Molhant

(Coping With)
Norm Deviation
Hugh A.D. Spencer

EXT. MORNING

LONG SHOT on an empty highway at the outskirts of town. Suddenly, an unmarked black van rolls past.

CUT TO:

INT. SHOT, VAN.

A SOCIAL CONTROL OFFICER sits in the back of the van, studying a glowing orange screen. The S.C.O. is dressed in black leather and riot helmet. He sees a blip on the screen.

                    S.C.O.
   I think we've got one.

CLOSE-UP

THE DRIVER nods and turns the steering wheel.

CUT TO:

EXT. BUS STOP. A FEW MINUTES LATER.
NORMAN, THE DEVIANT (aka D) stands at the roadside.
D looks deceptively like an ordinary teenager: jeans, army

jacket, T-shirt and running shoes. His hair is long and messy and he holds a stack of old paperbacks under one arm.

IN THE DISTANCE, the black van comes to a stop. D pays no attention.

ANOTHER ANGLE

The door of the van slides open and the S.C.O. steps out. A mirrored visor hides his face.

CLOSE SHOT

D turns and sees the S.C.O.

CLOSE-UP

The S.C.O. stops and removes an ELECTRONIC GUN from his holster.

EXTREME CLOSE-UP

A crackle of white-orange electricity leaps from the gun barrel.

CLOSE SHOT

D falls to the ground.

ANOTHER ANGLE

The S.C.O and the driver drag D towards the van.

PAN TO CLOSE-UP

D's books laying on the sidewalk. The CAMERA LINGERS on one of the book covers, The reads: "SIN IN SPACE!"

→•I•I•I•←

Here are some relevant facts:

1. Kodachrome is a kind of film; it gives you really great colours with a minimum of light. Does anyone remember film?

2. 1972 was the first summer after my parent's divorce and it was my first year with no vacation. So in late June, I found myself standing with my bicycle in my friend Leo's driveway. He had clipped a movie camera to the eyepiece of his uncle's reflector telescope and was filming the partial eclipse of the sun.

"Do you want make a film?" Leo asked as he adjusted the focus.

"Really? Like on our own?"

"Yeah, sure."

After a few minutes of not looking at the sun, I pedaled myself home, took the cover off my mom's electric typewriter and went to work. Just after midnight, I had finished the first (and only) draft of a script called **NORM DEVIATION**! Of course it was science fiction. I would star as the protagonist: Norman D. The casting decision was not based on vanity, it was just that I thought it be easier if I didn't have to explain all the motivations to someone else.

I soon learned that it was a lot easier to write the words than to put them on film.

→►I◄►I◄►I◄

INT. LABORATORY. CLOSE-UP

Norm D opens his eyes and lifts his head off a table top.

CLOSE SHOT, D'S POV

A bowl and spoon sit in front of him. Next to the bowl is a completely white carton with the words "MILK" stenciled on one side.

PAN TO CLOSE SHOT, STILL D'S POV

We see three cereal boxes. There are no words on any of the cartons. One is red, the other green and the last one yellow.

ANOTHER ANGLE

D reaches out and picks up the yellow cereal box. There is a brief burst of orange energy. The young man howls and falls to the floor.

CUT TO:

INT. OBSERVATION ROOM. A SECOND LATER.

BEHAVIORAL SCIENTIST #1 AND #2 watch D on a TV monitor.

CLOSE SHOT

We see cathode rays flickering on the lenses of the scientists' glasses as they make brief notes on their clipboards.

→∗⫶∗⫶∗⫶∗←

Next to the shots with the Deviant Detector Van, this was one of the most complicated scenes we filmed. Which kind of surprised me because when I wrote the scene I thought it was just going to be some people sitting, standing and falling down in two rooms.

It was Leo's fault. He convinced me that we had to do the scene right. Leo insisted that we had to see our poor hero on the TV screen. Video on film was pretty tricky to shoot back then because of the strobbing effect you'd get on the final film. But Leo said it would end up looking really weird and cool. He was right.

The hard part was getting the shots of me rolling around on the floor on videotape. Through the power of constant nagging, I got my dad to let Building Maintenance make a tape with the lab security cameras and even use one of their monitors.

So thank you Dad, Leo and Building Maintenance.

Dad also got us some labcoats for Margie and Rose to wear as the behavioral scientists. I suppose I could have just written them as "scientists" or "psychologists" but "behavioral scientists" sounded a lot more sinister.

It would have helped if the labcoats hadn't been four sizes too big but Leo shot Margie and Rose at angles that the bagginess didn't look too obvious. That was Leo, always solving problems.

The big post-production project for that scene was the big burst of energy when Norm D. touches the wrong cereal box. We decided halfway through shooting to make the behavioral scientists try and condition Norm against the colour yellow. We never got around to agreeing if the yellow-thing was just an arbitrary decision to test the power of their mind control techniques (in which case they could have decided to condition Mr. D. to fear umbrella stands) or if yellow was associated with some subversive future political movement (which could have been represented by umbrella stands if you think about it).

Again, it was mostly Leo pushing the envelope again. I didn't think we needed any visuals at all when D touched the wrong box. We were talking about electricity here and under most conditions you wouldn't see the current.

"It's more realistic without the effect," I said.

"Sometimes reality looks boring," Leo replied. "Besides, it's too *Star Trek* third season."

"Yeah." Yeah, he was right.

However, I was worried that when Leo was using a compass needle to scratch the emulsion, he would damage our only print.

"No worries," he said.

He was right. It was a great energy effect.

The cereal boxes and milk carton were the most difficult things in the scene. We wanted them to look like break-fast condiments from a depressing Orwellian future society so we wanted them to be uniform colours with just their contents stenciled on. No product placement here! Once again, when I wrote them into the script, I figured it would be no big deal to make them. Once again, I was mistaken.

I painted the boxes three times and Leo kept sending them back:

"Too streaky".

"The letters are on crooked."

"Now you're warping the boxes!"

Leo knew that the camera can be pretty forgiving so perfection in fabrication was not necessary. This should give you some idea of just how bad those babies were. My props were bad. *Mars Needs Women* bad.

After two days of messing about, Leo called in Allison who he knew from his art class last semester. Allison shows up at my house and looks at my latest set of pathetic boxes (they were sitting on the basement floor, sagging in on themselves).

"What kind of paints are you using?"

My sister's tempera paints — because they were left over from some fake stain glass windows she'd been making last December.

"Tempra's no good," Allison explained. "It's very uneven on opaque surfaces and you have to use too much water for cardboard surfaces."

She said she had some acrylics we could use. "Not as good as an airbrush but it should look okay on screen."

I resisted the impulse to ask her what acrylics were, or an airbrush for that matter.

"What kind of bond is the paper are you using to cover the boxes before you paint them?"

Bond? Paper? *Cover?*

"No wonder you were having so much trouble," Allison said. "If you don't cover the boxes with paper, you have to use tons of paint to hide the original illustrations on the box."

Oh.

In about 0.2 seconds, Allison undid the tabs on the boxes, folded them flat, and packed them in her knapsack.

"I'll bring them back tomorrow."

Click. Whiz. Allison disappeared down the street on her ten-speed.

Next day she was back with three perfect cereal boxes and a milk carton from a dystopian future.

Allison could be very focused about certain things. She then insisted on being there on the shoot when we were using her props. She was going to be sure that those boxes and the carton were photographed to their very best effect.

It was rather interesting that Leo didn't object when Allison told us that she was going to stick around and work on all the other props as well.

We had a third producer.

✦✦✦✦✦

INT. COMPLEX. TIME UNKNOWN. TRACKING SHOT, NORM D'S POV

TWO S.C.O.S drag D down an seemingly endless corridor. The concrete hall is lined with strange hydraulic gauges and dull-coloured pipes.

REVERSE ANGLE, CLOSE SHOT of D.

He is handcuffed and held between the beefy arms of the S.C.O.s. His expression is slack and stupid — most likely the result of drugs and electroshock.

CONTINUOUS PAN, SWING TO ANOTHER TRACKING SHOT

The three turn a corner, which changes the angle on D. Just beyond the profile of his face, we see many, many locked steel doors.

✦✦✦✦✦

Leo's pride and joy was a Bolex 233 Compact S Super 8 camera. It was a sweet little thing with a small but powerful zoom lens and a single-frame switch so you could do animation and superimposures. Leo had also rigged a

switch that linked the camera to a cassette tape recorder. This set up gave us:
· Limited synchronized sound.
· Colour!
· Mobility. The camera and tape recorder weighed less than five pounds all together, so we had the capacity to do some really cool camera movements.

The preceeding scene was also one of Leo's most sophisticated technical triumphs. In the original draft, I just wrote: "Two social control officers drag Norm D down a long hallway and throw him into a cell. D puts up no resistance suggesting that he has been drugged". To the point, but not what we ended up shooting.

Leo was probably the only 16-year-old in Saskatoon who knew all about Orson Welles' famous tracking shot at the beginning of *Touch of Evil* — which was why he was always looking for opportunities to "open up" our movie.

"Are we creating cinema, or are we just pointing a camera at a book?"

Statements like that make writers feel angry and guilty at the same time.

It was also my Dad's fault.

When I went to see him at his lab one day (no doubt to beg for an advance on my allowance to buy some new film) I brought Leo along with me to explain that I wasn't going to use the money to buy cigarettes, booze or dope. Somehow I knew that Leo would radiate the aura of "pure cinema" that would erase any of my Dad's doubts. I was right, two minutes into the conversation, Dad reached into his wallet and gave us 50 bucks. That was a lot of money in 1972. Then he took us out to lunch.

Maybe it was because we were such weird looking kids, or maybe Dad was getting into our SF mindset; but instead of taking us through the main lobby of the building, he took us down through the sub-basement and along the connector corridor between the labs and the university cafeteria.

Leo was completely gob-smacked by the industrial design of that hallway. "This is so cool!" he cried. "It's reality science fiction!"

A couple days later we returned to corridor with our
S.C.O.'s — Reg and Bob in their future-fascist gear. Leo
also brought a few things that I wasn't expecting:

 a) Allison - who was always welcome and;
 b) A circular wooden platform with four small
   wheels bolted onto the bottom.

The platform was about four inches off the ground and
Leo could sit cross-legged on it and point his camera in
any direction he liked. To me, he looked like a thin mobile
Buddha down there but that was how he got those great
tracking shots in the corridor.

While they were dragging me down the corridor, big
brother Bob was using his other hand to haul Leo along
on his rolling platform. The angle change, when we turned
the corner, was really an accident. Bob's grip loosened a
little and the platform rolled over to one side. Leo *very*
smoothly adjusted the angle of the camera to match the
speed of his drift and stay in focus.

Leo said that the shot worked because of exacting crafts-
manship governing the Bolex lens and the incredibly
forgiving properties of Kodachrome film. He was just being
modest. He was the one who pulled it off.

→•┼•┼•┼•←

INT. TESTING CHAMBER. LONG SHOT of D.

Strapped onto an examination table, wires and electrodes
have been pasted onto his head and chest.

CLOSE SHOT

The two behavioral scientists stand in the distance. They
make adjustments to a bank of electronic instruments.

EXTREME CLOSE-UP of an ECG monitor.

D's heartbeat bounces steadily along an illuminated check-
erboard.

BEHAVIORAL SCIENTIST #1
(OS)
His cardio-sino rhythms appear almost normal.

BEHAVIORAL SCIENTIST #2
(OS)
Almost deceptively so...

Her finger traces the pattern of the steady green curve.

BEHAVIORAL SCIENTIST #2
(OS)
It's *just* outside the range of true human parameters.

CLOSE SHOT

The behavioral scientists look at each other intently.

BEHAVIORAL SCIENTIST #1
Do you think this is more evidence of a genetically
engineered organism?

BEHAVIORAL SCIENTIST #2
We will need more tissue samples to tell.

CLOSE-UP

D, still groggy from medication, looks down in the direction
of his feet. His eyes widen in alarm.

ANOTHER CLOSE-UP, D'S POV

A thick articulated tube headed with an evil-looking
suction nozzle, gradually snakes its way up one of his legs.

❖❧❖❧❖

Okay, a lot of films have unintentionally funny moments
and *Norm Deviation!* was no exception. In fact, it was
remarkable that we had so few. But the tissue-sampling
scene was pretty hysterical.

It wasn't my fault. When I originally wrote the scene, the baddie scientists just used a needle to extract some blood. Fast, painful, plausible and good (I thought) on camera.

Not according to Leo.

"Too subtle. Besides, blood effects are hard to do."

Rose, who played Behavioral Scientist #2, suggested we go for a sperm sample instead. On reflection, I wonder how Rose even knew about sperm samples at that age.

Leo liked Sheila's idea. Doing the "jack-off machine", as he so delicately put it, immediately became a priority.

"It's edgy," he'd mutter. "Real edgy."

It was also a chance for him to experiment. He decided that he was going to use some clear fishing line to make it look as though the hose was floating towards my penis. If anybody watching this scene can stop laughing long enough to look, they will realize that we pulled off the effect rather well.

"Why don't you shoot it in stop motion animation?" Rose asked Leo.

That would have been pretty horrifying as it would have involved me laying there with my dork hanging out for two or three days.

Leo shook his head when he answered Rose: "Kodak would never develop films of a kid's wiener."

We shot most of that scene at the University's Phys-Ed Department. While the sets and props looked incredibly complicated and realistic, most of the shoot was pretty easy. Location, location, location is a principle that applies to more than real estate.

Some grad students there had gotten in to study the effects of cannabis consumption on the brain and physiological structure of teenagers. I'd heard my dad telling one of his colleagues that in reality the grad students were smoking up all-day and using the equipment to measure themselves. I can neither confirm nor deny this report, but I can say that when I called these guys up to ask if we could use their lab for a day, they said yes and giggled a lot.

The day we did that shoot was the same night that that *Night Gallery* was on TV. Leo and I went over to watch it at Allison's place because she was the only person we knew with a colour set.

Leo liked *Night Gallery* because he said it had great lighting. I liked *Night Gallery* because I was interested in anything weird or spooky and Rod Serling fascinated me. There was something mysterious and tragic about that little man with the deep rumbling voice.

Night Gallery was an uneven show at best, and you could tell that Serling was the host as well as the main writer — was really bothered about this. When the segment was dumb, he looked a sad and embarrassed. When it was a good show (usually something he'd written) his craggy, tight-skinned face looked pleased, even a little hopeful.

That night, there had been two stories. The first one was about a fisherman who used a magic potion to try and consummate his love for a mermaid with unfortunate results (dumb). The second segment was about a boy who has the ability to predict earthquakes and other future occurrences with *really* unfortunate results (good).

"Nice side lighting," Leo pronounced as he got out of his chair. "I gotta go."

Allison said that he should stay. The late movie was *When Worlds Collide* and she remembered that Leo said he wanted to see it.

"Can't," Leo replied. "We just got the first reels back from the developers."

"Hey!" Both Allison and I were pretty excited.

"I want to run them through the editor right away."

Of course we asked if we could come along.

"Not until the rough cut is ready."

Sometimes Leo was a team player. Other times he was such a bloody auteur.

Allison said there was no point in arguing with him. "You can stay for the movie," she said to me.

Since I didn't have anywhere else in particular to be I was happy to do so.

My main impression of *When Worlds Collide* was, like all the other Technicolor films of the 1940s and 1950s, that the brilliant and completely artificial colours made all that bad acting and terrible dialogue a lot more interesting. Not necessarily better, but different.

My memories of Allison that night were even more vivid but far more natural. About halfway through the movie, Allison was sitting very close to me on the couch and I became aware.

Aware of her.

Aware of me.

I kept noticing the lines of her bra underneath her T-shirt. I noticed the angled contour of her back; it looked strong and like it would be good to put your arms around.

Her hair was messy and a little oily, it hung in strands over her ears and the back of her slightly sunburned neck. Her real hair and skin were much more interesting than anything in Technicolor.

Kodachrome might suit her better.

I noticed the sides of her small breasts. Even though I was miles away from touching them, they seemed somehow warm. I wondered if it would be okay with Allison if I did touch her breasts.

I glanced over at the TV screen. More close ups of people talking and looking concerned about unfortunate astronomical events.

I looked back at Allison and noticed that she was watching me from the corner of her eye. At that point, I still wasn't sure about her breasts but it seemed definitely okay if I kissed her just then.

"Allison..."

Then something happened. One switch in my head clicked in and another one shut down. It wasn't that I was scared or even particularly nervous. I just suddenly knew that nothing was going to happen that night.

There wasn't anything wrong with me. There certainly wasn't anything wrong with Allison; she was absolutely perfect. She probably still is.

I just knew that this was not the time for her and me to be doing certain things.

So we went into the kitchen and found another bag of potato chips and watched the rest of movie. A little over an hour later we had killed a carton of colas while we watched the dawn on a new cartoon-ish planet and heard the voices of the Martian Tabernacle Choir swell as the end titles asked the profound question:

"The End?!"

"Or the Beginning?!"

Music swells. Fade to black.

End credits.

And there I was riding my bike home in the early morning darkness.

Wondering when it would be my time for such things.

→•I•••I••I•←

INT. CONTAINMENT CELL. NORM D'S POV

The door opens and three figures walk in: THE POLITICAL OFFICER, BEHAVIORAL SCIENTIST #1 and a SOCIAL CONTROL OFFICER.

ANOTHER ANGLE

D sits in the corner. His head has been shaved and there are red circles on his scalp.

CLOSE SHOT, D'S POV

The P.O. removes a computer punch card from his shirt pocket. He starts to read from the card.

POLITICAL OFFICER

I have been authorized to inform you — that after undergoing all legally mandated medical tests — you have been diagnosed as "Deviant Category No.1; according to all political and biological criteria.

CLOSE-UP of D.

He struggles to understand what the Political Officer is saying.

CLOSE-UP, REVERSE ANGLE of the P.O,

He smirks as he continues to read.

> POLITICAL OFFICER
> You have therefore been sentenced to vapour-
> ization without appeal. This action is necessary for
> the protection of the Greater Social Entity and will
> be executed within the next 24 hours.

ANOTHER ANGLE

The P.O. drops the card in front of D.

> POLITICAL OFFICER
> As a citizen it is, of course, your right to exam-
> ine the scientific data and text scores used to arrive
> at this determination.

The S.C.O. opens the door and the three leave.

CLOSE UP of D.

He picks up the computer card and looks at it carefully.
Then the he tosses the card aside and puts his head in his
hands.

SLOW FADE TO BLACK

We hear D's laboured breathing in the darkness.

→•I•I•I•←

The easy part was the computer punch card. It was just
one of our old electricity bills. Everything else that day was
pretty tough.

That morning Leo came up to me and announced:
"We're fucked."

Very helpful, I thought. "Uh, why?"

"No more money," Leo replied. "My mom says we should get jobs if we want to pay for the rest of the movie."

Jobs?!

We were indeed, fucked.

We still had some key scenes to shoot and no funds to buy more film.

Deliverance came from an unexpected source. I wanted to use the locker room at our school as the scene for D's confinement cell, so a few days earlier I had called up Mr. Pozzi, my visual communications teacher. I asked if he could help us get the necessary permissions to get into the building. I felt badly when I called him up again and told him that we were canceling.

Mr. Pozzi would have none of it: "I've got tons of film stock left over from last semester. It's past its expiratory date but it should be just fine."

Holy shit! I thought. "Thank you," was what I said

Mr. Pozzi also suggested that we cast Gordon Thomas, who was Student Council President, to make sure we could stay in the school building as long as we needed to. It was typecasting, but Gordon gave us a great performance as the Political Officer.

I was happy.

Leo still wasn't.

We had more than enough film now but the stock we got from Mr. Pozzi was Ectachrome.

Not Kodachrome.

→•I•I•I•←

INT. CONTAINMENT CELL. LATER THAT NIGHT.

THE CELL IS FLOODED WITH A STRANGE BLUE LIGHT AND WE HEAR AN EERIE ELECTRONIC BUZZING SOUND.

D stirs and sits up; he looks in the direction of the light.

CLOSE UP

D is astonished by what he sees.

NORM D'S POV

A TURQUOISE COLOURED ALIEN appears. The being is over six feet tall with incredibly thin limbs and body. It has a large oval head with two enormous jeweled compound eyes and a thin lipless mouth.

The buzzing rises and falls in pitch — as if the alien was trying to communicate to D.

CLOSE-UP

D nods his head.

D'S POV

The alien moves toward him. The being walks with an odd flowing motion as it were using some kind of force field to protect it from higher gravity.

CLOSE-UP

The alien points at the computer printout card that still lays on the floor. The thick paper starts to curl and smoke and finally burns away into a pile of ash.

CLOSE SHOT

The alien uses both of its hands to take hold of D's face. It gives D a long, lingering, kiss.

The blue light gets incredibly bright until the screen WHITES OUT.

CUT TO:

INT. CONTAINMENT CELL. SOMETIME LATER.

Norm D. stands there. He is alone.

D'S POV

The door to his cell is open.

→•‡•‡•‡•←

Okay, the summer of 1972 was the time of my great artistic and intellectual awakening. It was also the summer that I got kissed by a puppet. By the time we got to film that moment, I was happy and relieved to do so.

Leo kept on complaining about how hard the remaining scenes were going to be to shoot with Ecktachrome and that there was no way we had enough lights to shoot any interiors with that f-stop and colour balance. He announced that unless I could do a re-write with all exteriors we couldn't finish.

Leo could be really stubborn sometimes.

"How about we just kill D?" Leo said this over a plate of fries at our favourite fish and chips place. "The S.C.O.s march him out in front of a wall, shoot him with some electrical guns and them dump him in a mass grave with over a few hundred dead deviants."

"Very cheerful," I replied. I ate some of Leo's fries and thought about that narrative possibility for a moment.

"We could shoot the scene over by the concrete quarry," Leo continued.

This was getting risky, when Leo was doing logistics, he usually had pretty much made up his mind. So I swallowed and shook my head: "It's too much of a change in the tone of the film."

Leo grimaced. "As opposed to the feel-good-movie of the summer that you had originally conceived?"

"Besides," I continued. "Where are we going to get all those dead deviants? We don't have that many friends."

Leo was quiet for a moment. I had raised a legitimate technical problem. We ate his food and stop talking about the project for a while.

The next day we discovered that Mr. Pozzi had anticipated the photographic challenges of the new film format and lent us four banks of floodlights. Now we could shoot all the interiors we liked.

Leo still wasn't completely satisfied. "The film grain and the colour balance is going to be completely different," he complained.

"You'll make it work," I replied.

The look he gave me!

There were two other problems associated with that shooting that scene: Allison and the Alien.

Allison had vanished after the *When Worlds Collide* viewing. I was worried that she noticed that I had been staring at her breasts and had decided that I was a real-life deviant. Either Leo didn't know where she was, or didn't feel like telling me.

Never mind, I had an alien to worry about. Originally we were going to get Reg to play the creature. Leo had ordered a mutant monster mask from a *Famous Monsters* magazine that he thought we could use.

Easy, right?

Like many simple solutions, it turned out not to be a solution at all. When Reg put the mask on he looked like a big teenager with an old lady's ass stuck onto the back of his head.

Not quite the sense of awe and wonder we were hoping to invoke.

"How about something more conceptual?" I suggested.

"Conceptual?"

"Symbolic. Maybe the alien isn't something that we'd recognize as any sort of a life form at all. Like a huge prism or crystal or something."

Leo looked thoughtful.

I continued, sensing that I might have something here: "Or we could paint the door black and shoot it from a low angle, looking up, so that it looks like—"

"A monolith?"

I'm pretty sure I looked very embarrassed.

"You know," Leo said. "There's a difference between doing an homage and just being pathetic."

Allison reappeared later that day with a brilliant solution to our alien problem:

The puppet.

The absolutely beautiful alien puppet.

She had made this huge, fantastic marionette, taller than she was, from balsa wood. Allison had shellacked it with green varnish that came out turquoise on film. The eyes were made of mirrored beads, plastic "gem" stones and bits off old charm bracelets.

Allison must have locked herself in her basement all week, creating this amazing thing.

To hold it up we used the same fishing line we had used to operate the nozzle of the jack-off machine. Allison then lay on top of a row of lockers and pulled on the wires to make the puppet move its arms and legs.

Getting kissed by the alien was Allison's idea. After she'd put in all that work, what could I say?

Leo put a blue filter on the lens and turned on every one of our flood lights while we were shooting. The end result anticipated all those close encounter scenes that Speilberg and Cameron would be showing us for the next thirty years.

Homage, indeed.

⊹⊹⊹⊹

INT. COMPLEX, BASEMENT CORRIDOR.

D. steps out of his cell. He looks around.

LONG SHOT, D'S POV

D sees one of the S.C.O.s laying on the floor.

EXTREME LONG SHOT. PAN DOWN to reveal D running up the LABYRINTH OF STAIRS leading up from the sub-basement of the complex.

CUT TO:

NEXT LEVEL OF THE COMPLEX. LONG SHOT, D'S POV

The two behavioral scientists are on the floor. Their arms and legs are splayed wide open and they are surrounded by loose pages from their clipboards. Whatever hit them, did so very suddenly.

CUT TO:

GROUND FLOOR LOBBY

D pushes open a big set of double doors and stops to catch his breath for a moment. His eyes widen in surprise at what he sees.

CLOSE-UP, D'S POV

It is the Political Officer. He is also on the floor but his face is bruised and his head is twisted at an odd angle. A pool of dark arterial blood has pooled on the floor around his head.

CLOSE SHOT

D looks up.

TILT TO LONG SHOT, D'S POV of the top of the Complex's ATRIUM.

The P.O. must have been leaning on one of the upper rails when he lost consciousness.

CLOSE-UP

of D. He shakes his head.

CUT TO:

EXT. COMPLEX, MAIN ENTRANCE. DAY

D races down the stairs leading from the doorway.

CLOSE SHOT, D'S POV

He sees a ROW OF BICYCLES parked next to the building.

CLOSE-UP

D smiles.

CUT TO:

MONTAGE OF SHOTS:

D riding a bicycle at high speed. He leaves the COMPLEX CAMPUS, then rolls past the gray government buildings of the DOWNTOWN DISTRICT. There is no traffic, no pedestrians — the big sleep seems to have affected the entire city. Next D rides past wider SUBURBAN STREETS; finally he pedals down a seemingly endless ribbon of PRAIRIE HIGHWAY.

→·]•·]•·]·←

A couple of things of note at this stage:

1.   The Ectachrome stock did indeed look very different. But this worked to our advantage. It was a subtle thing — today we might call it "subtextual" — where it looked like the very nature of reality changed after the manifestation of the alien. I didn't write it that way and Leo certainly didn't direct it with that intent either but it was really quite powerful. Genius may be the willingness to exploit happy accidents.

2.   On the other hand, the tracking shots from
the bicycle montage was something that Leo had
planned to do and the final footage is marvelous.
He made a small L-clip out of metal and used it to
attach his Bolex to the front wheel of his ten-speed.
It is interesting to note that while I'm seen riding
the bike at the beginning and end of the scene —
it was Leo doing the driving during the montage
itself. It wasn't that I was an unreliable cyclist but
knowing Leo I think that he worried that if the camera did have an accident he didn't want to blame
anyone but himself.

⊷⊶⊷⊶⊷

EXT. PRAIRIE FIELD. MORNING

D brakes the bicycle to a stop. He looks to the sky.

LONG SHOT

D and his bike are dwarfed by the shining silver and
crimson hull of a huge SAUCER SHAPED SPACECRAFT.
There is a LOW RUMBLING SOUND as it descends and
a GANTRY WAY swings down.

CLOSE-UP

D is surprisingly calm.

LONG SHOT

D wheels his bike inside the saucer. The gantry way swings
shut.

ANOTHER ANGLE - GROUND LEVEL, LOOKING UP

There is another sound : A HIGH-PITCHED WHINE as
the saucer starts to spin and flies into the sky.

CUT TO:

SPACE. LONG SHOT.

The saucer, still spinning at high speed, coasts past the sun.

PAN

The camera follows the saucer as it recedes into the distance and disappears into the star-sprinkled void.

FADE

TO CREDITS

❖•⫶•⫶•⫶•❖

I was impressed with how Leo was able to manipulate the focus. It looked like I was walking into a gigantic spacecraft when in fact Leo was holding one of his little brother's toys very close to the lens while I was walking in the distance.

The rest of the film was essentially post-production work and that made Leo very happy because it gave him a chance to play around with the Bolex's stop-frame animation feature. He used one of the floodlights with a black construction paper background to re-create the sun and Allison sprinkled icing sugar on more black paper to create our starscape.

I never saw that set up. The project really didn't need me to be there all the time and my life was insisting on moving on.

My parents' breakup had entered an even uglier stage. Mom divided most of her time between brooding and trying to sell the house.

I couldn't just go and hang out at my Dad's lab any more either, because it looked like disloyalty to Mom. I only saw Dad on legally mandated weekends. Sometimes we'd take in a good movie but most of the time it wasn't very much fun. Dad was too distracted with all the wedding and new baby arrangements.

Every-fucking-thing felt awkward.

By early October that summer of creative magic was very definitely over. I had gone from making it about an oppressive future called *Norm Deviation!* to living the life of a norm deviation in an oppressive now.

There was a brief interlude around Hallowe'en. Leo had finished all the editing and post-production work and was ready to premiere the film.

The gala was staged in his family room and Leo had wired an ancient Bell and Howell projector to his Sony cassette player to play the soundtrack. In yet another display of technological prowess, he had connected the tape player to the amps and speakers of their eight-track stereo.

"Simulated Surround Sound," he explained.

It did sound great. Still, I'm glad I kept my dialogue to a minimum.

The audience consisted of cast members, bored siblings, proud (and bemused) parents (not mine) and Mr. Pozzi. Some of the kids were on their way to a costume party (not me) and were in costume (also not me, I was way too self-conscious). Allison was dressed up as a magical fairy. She wore a ballet costume with a frilly tutu and she had these amazing and beautiful delicate butterfly wings made from coat hangers and coloured Kleenex.

Reg and Bob were dressed up in their Social Control Officer (i.e. future leather boy outfits); there were also a few aliens and astronauts in the audience as well. In 1972 these were not cool themes so we should have felt honoured by the tribute.

The one thing that I haven't talked about yet was the musical score. In complete violation of international copyright laws, Leo had mixed in music by a band called Syrnx. They were pretty unconventional for the time, consisting of a percussionist, saxaphone player and — get this — a *synthesizer* artist! New age long before we even had the concept.

The music was perfect for our movie, particularly the ending with the bicycle escape and the ascent into space. While we were filming I imagined the music would be something a little more traditionally associated with science fiction/outer spacey stuff — like the theramine and orchestra composition that Bernard Hermann wrote for *The Day Stood Still*.

For the ending scene Leo used a piece called *December Angel*. Very haunting, gentle and ethereal music. Not only did it pull at your heartstrings as you watched poor lonely D disappear into the saucer, it was also a great accompaniment for looking at Allison and admiring how the light from the screen flickered on her face and those tissue-paper wings. I wished that I could have written her and those wings into the movie somehow.

I honestly don't remember the specifics of what people said or did after the show. Mr. Pozzi did corner me and said we should submit the film for course credit. I can't remember what grade we got.

Over the next weekend Leo and Allison and I got together and talked about making a sequel, where we see what happens when D reaches his destination somewhere on a distant planet. Leo envisioned it as a special effects extravaganza with lots of claymation.

"We could populate the planet with alien robot hybrids," suggested Allison. "I could do some model cities for them to live in."

"Some beings with wings, maybe," I added.

Somehow the sequel never happened.

About six months later, Mom sold the house and we moved to another city. This was essentially the end of our production team.

Leo and Allison went on to creative careers. He went into film (of course!). Allison did a lot of different things but ultimately ended up as an artist. She does good work.

We kept in touch, more or less, over the years and even used to visit each other in our various resident communities. I finally lost track of Allison by the early nineties. Perhaps she put on those fairy wings and flew off to be with more interesting people.

Leo never did become the next Stanley Kubrick. After *Eyes Wide Shut* and *A.I*, Leo probably doesn't feel too badly about that.

So what happened to me between 1972 and now? Well, things got better, things got worse, better, worse, you see the pattern, right? There's easily a dozen more stories there.

In the meantime, you could say that I'm coping.

Afterword
Holly Phillips

I had a humbling experience not too long ago. People who know me know that I'll launch into my favorite rant at the drop of a hat. If I had to pick a title for that rant, it would be something like "Speculative Literature, or why literary snobs should take me seriously even if I do write fantasy," and I'm quite sure a few of my friends have heard it often enough to get full marks if I ever gave a quiz. (The smart ones have also learned that you can usually stop me before I get started by offering me something to eat.)

Anyway, last summer I found myself with a brand new audience, an old friend I haven't seen since our crazy university days, and I was explaining to her with great enthusiasm that I was convinced it was possible to write speculative fiction that offered as great an insight into the human condition as capital-L Literature without losing the delights and wonders that are the mainstay of the SF/F/H genres — that in fact it was my highest aspiration to write that kind of fantasy (excuse me, fantastic literature) — and I was in full spate when I looked up and saw that my friend's partner, sitting on the floor with their two year old, was openly laughing at me.

Well, it's always good to get that ol' balloon-ego punctured now and then. I suppose it's possible I may even quit boring my friends one of these days. But I haven't given up my high-flying aspirations, and I must say, reading stories for Tesseracts 11 has only reinforced my convictions.

Yes, it is possible to write genre stories about real human beings. More, it is possible to write science fiction and fantasy that illuminates our lives in the here and now. In fact, what was so striking about the submissions for this anthology is that the vast majority of stories, fantasy, science fiction, and horror, were set in the here and now — or at least, in a world that is right next door. There were a few alien planets, it's true, and a few magical otherworlds, and we were lucky enough to capture a couple of them between the covers of this book. But most of our submissions were set in this world...even if it was this world a little bit changed.

Which leads me to ask: what ever happened to that whole SF-as-escapism thing? I remember reading what Ursula K. LeGuin once wrote about escapism (and I'm not going to dig around to find the actual quote, so bear with my paraphrasing). She actually had two things to say. One was something like, before you give people a hard time for reading escapist literature, consider first what they might be escaping from. If you're suffering, it's downright healthy to try and live a better, kinder, freer life, even if it's vicariously through literature. The other thing she said was sort of the flip side to that. Consider what readers are escaping *to*. Is reading about heroes striving against evil somehow supposed to be *bad* for people? Those kids burying their heads in Tolkien, wallowing in those shamelessly self-indulgent ideas about duty and self-sacrifice and love for one's companions on the road — tsk tsk! Shame on them! And, well, you get the point.

So what struck me in my reading, and I hope it's evident in the collection we finally put together, is that writers these days seem to be bringing those grand ideas, those, dare I say it, moral strivings, home. Is this a Canadian thing? I don't know. If I ever edit an American anthology I guess I'll get a chance to see the difference, if any. What I am fairly sure of is that it's a short-fiction thing. Cruise the SF section in your local bookstore or library (if you're lucky it's not still labeled "sci-fi") and there's no shortage of fantasy-world epics and Star Trek novelizations. That's what the market looks like right now, and it may even reflect what novel readers want. But in short fiction... ah, in short fiction.

Who ever makes a living writing short fiction these days? (Okay, okay, Ray Bradbury and Alice Munro. I mean besides them.) But we go on writing it all the same.

Why?

Well, okay. Break in, gain some pub creds, yadda yadda. The real truth is, short stories are addictive. Instant gratification, oh yeah, gimme that one cookie now. (Speaking as a writer. Speaking as a reader...don't you think reading a whole anthology in one sitting is a bit like working your way through a whole *bag* of cookies? A mixed bag where you never know if you're going to get chocolate or peanut butter or something weirdly healthy with birdseed and raisins. But I digress.) The point I really want to make is this: short stories are where writers sneak out to play. A novel is a serious undertaking. It takes forever to write, forever to market, forever to get into print. How many experimental novels — novels that play with genre, novels that play with form — get shoveled into the closet, the basement, the back of the garage? Sadly, we'll probably never know. But short stories are another matter. Short stories are where we Try Something New. And more and more, I believe, short stories are where we try bringing the weird stuff home to see what happens.

And I think that's what is happening in this anthology. We're the next generation of the speculative universe. We grew up with this stuff. We've seen science fiction turn into reality. (Yes, I am old enough to remember the first desktop Apple. World Wide Web? Man, I'd left university by then.) And I think we, you and I, the people who made this book and the people who are reading it, are the ones who are realizing, who know in our hearts, that this stuff, this wonderful, terrible stuff, isn't happening somewhere else — a somewhere else we can escape to, or from. It's happening right here, right now, in our living rooms. Heck, we don't even have to bring the weird stuff home. It's already here.

Copyright Notice

Biographies

D. W. Archambault has made competitive sport an important part of his life for many years. When he's not studying computer science at the University of British Columbia or writing, he can be found skating, playing ultimate, or running. Dan would also like to apologize for the language and actions of his characters in this one. They were kids who didn't know any better. "The Recorded Testimony of Eric and Julie Francis" is his third fiction sale. If you'd like to know what the author is up to, visit him at www.sff.net/people/danw-arch.

Madeline Ashby has lived on the outskirts of Los Angeles, Seattle, New York, and Toronto. She immigrated to Canada in 2006. She joined the Cecil Street Irregulars soon after, and in 2007 was a runner-up for the SF Idol competition at Ad Astra. (Her pal David Nickle won.) Madeline is a contributor to *Frames Per Second Magazine* and *Kokoro Media*, where she blogs about Japanese animation when not volunteering for the Sprockets division of the Toronto International Film Festival. This story is her first published in Canada.

Greg Bechtel's stories have appeared in *Prairie Fire*, *On Spec*, *Challenging Destiny* and *Qwerty* magazines. He has recently moved to Edmonton, where he is pursuing a PhD in English literature and attempting to resurrect his first novel, which saw its original incarnation as his MA thesis in creative writing at the University of New Brunswick.

At the moment of drafting this bio, "Blackbird Shuffle" has been nominated for the Journey Prize, a National Magazine Award, and a Western Magazine Award.

Nancy Bennett is an essayist, poet and fiction writer. Her work has appeared in such places as *Tales of the Unanticipated*, *Tesseracts*, *Flesh and Blood* and *Not One of Us*. She has made the recommended reading list for the Year's Best Fantasy and Horror three times. Her latest achievement, a cinquain poem, appeared in *In Fine Formî* alongside the works of P. K. Page, Robert Service and Margaret Atwood.

Lisa Carreiro is a writer and editor whose fiction has appeared in *Strange Horizons* and *On Spec*. She lives in Toronto with her partner and their small menagerie.

Peter Darbyshire is the author of the award-winning novel "Please" and numerous short stories. He is also the books editor of *The Province* newspaper. His fiction and columns have appeared in publications across North America and online. Visit www.peterdarbyshire.com.

Khria Deefholts was born in India to bi-racial parents. She grew up in Canada, and later lived in Japan, where she studied such arcane subjects as the tea ceremony and Japanese calligraphy. She has worked on a film in Germany, had close encounters with snakes and crocodiles in Australia and taught ballroom dancing. She speaks six languages with varied degrees of fluency and has published numerous shorter pieces of fiction and non-fiction. She lives in Ontario, with her husband and two cats.

Cory Doctorow is a science fiction novelist, blogger and technology activist. He is the co-editor of the popular weblog *Boing Boing* (boingboing.net), and a contributor to *Wired*, *Popular Science*, *Make*, the *New York Times*, and many other newspapers, magazines and websites. He was formerly Director of European Affairs for the Electronic Frontier Foundation (eff.org), a non-profit civil liberties group that defends freedom in technology law, policy, standards and treaties. Presently, he serves as the Fulbright Chair at the Annenberg Center for Public Diplomacy at the University of Southern California.

Candas Jane Dorsey's novel "Black Wine" won the Tiptree, Crawford and Aurora Awards. Her fiction includes *Vanilla and other stories*, *A Paradigm of Earth*, *Machine Sex and other stories* and *Dark Earth Dreams*. Her poetry includes: *Leaving Marks*, *This is for you*, *Orion rising*, and *Results of the Ring Toss*. She edited or co-edited four SF collections, served on boards/committees for several Canadian writers organisations, co-founded/edited *The Edmonton Bullet* arts newspaper 1983-1993, and in 1992 co-founded literary publisher *The Books Collective* and its imprint *River Books*. From 1994-2003 she was editor-in-chief and co-publisher, with Timothy J. Anderson, of *Tesseract Books*.

Susan Forest's first novel for young adults, "The Dragon Prince", (Gage Educational Publishers) was awarded the Children's Circle Book Choice Award, and was chosen by Gage as one of two young adult novels to represent the company at a book fair in Berlin. Her short stories, *Playing Games* (ONSPEC Magazine), *Angel of Death* (Tesseracts Ten) and *Immunity* (Asimov's Science Fiction), were published in 2006. This year, look to see *Tomorrow and Tomorrow* in Tesseracts Eleven and *Paid in Full* in Asimov's Science Fiction. Visit http://www.speculative-fiction.ca

Kim Goldberg was a political journalist for twenty years. She is the author of four nonfiction books. Her articles have appeared in *Macleans*, *Canadian Geographic*, *Columbia Journalism Review*, *The Progressive*, and many other magazines in North America and England. Her output has been poetry and short fiction, much of it speculative, appearing in *PRISM International*, *Dalhousie Review*, *On Spec*, *Filling Station*, *Chimera* and elsewhere. Her first full-length collection of poems, "Ride Backwards On Dragon", tracing her journey through an alien landscape of inner alchemy, will be released September 2007 by Leaf Press. She lives in Nanaimo where she periodically co-hosts an Urban Poetry Café on Radio CHLY. In 2006, she curated the Urban Eyes Art Exhibition featuring the work of 52 artists and architects on the theme of urban development after a vacant lot on her block was bulldozed for condos, exposing a homeless encampment. Little known fact: Under severe pressure, she will fake-out fellow birders on Big Day (when competition is cut-throat) with a white plastic bag tied to cattails in the middle of a marsh.

Andrew Gray's stories and poetry have appeared in numerous publications, including *On Spec*, *The Malahat Review*, *Prairie Fire*, *Event*, *Grain*, *Fiddlehead* and *Chatelaine*. He was awarded On Spec's Lydia Langstaff Memorial Prize in 1996, was nominated for the National Magazine Award for Fiction in 2000 and has been shortlisted several times for the CBC/Saturday Night Literary Award. He was a finalist for the 2000 Journey Prize for his short story "Heart of the Land". His first collection of short fiction, "Small Accidents", was published by Raincoast in the fall of 2001 and was shortlisted for the Ethel Wilson award in BC and an IPPY independent publisher's award in the US. He is now the coordinator of UBC's Optional Residency MFA program in Creative Writing and lives on Vancouver Island with his family.

Alyxandra Harvey-Fitzhenry's first novel "Waking" (Orca Books)is a Young Adult modern-day retelling of Sleeping Beauty, currently in bookstores. She has had poetry published in such magazines as *OnSpec*, *Room of One's Own* and *The Antigonish Review*. When not writing, she is a bellydancer and bellydance instructor. She lives in an old farmhouse with her husband, two dogs and hawk.

Stephen Kotowych won a first-place in the Writers of the Future competition in 2006 and recently was awarded the Writers of the Future Grand Prize. His stories have appeared in "Under Cover of Darkness" (DAW Books), and the forthcoming anthologies "Writers of the Future XXIII" (Galaxy Press, 2007), and "North of Infinity III" (Mosaic Press, 2008). He is a member of the Fledglings, a Toronto-area writer's group brought together by Robert J. Sawyer in 2003. Stephen lives in Toronto and enjoys guitar, tropical fish, and writing about himself in the third person. Check out his blog at http://kotowych.blogspot.com/.

Claude Lalumière's Lost Pages, a chapbook collection of six linked stories, will be published by GrendelSong in July 2008. Claude's fiction has appeared in *Year's Best SF 12*, *Year's Best Fantasy 6*, *SciFiction*, *Interzone*, *On Spec*, *Tesseracts 9*, *Electric Velocipede*, and others. He has edited six anthologies, including "Witpunk" (with Marty Halpern), "Island Dreams", "Open Space", and "Lust for Life" (with Elise Moser). His website is lostpages.net, and he blogs at lostpagesfoundpages.blogspot.com. Claude lives in Montreal.

John Mavin lives in Vancouver with his wife and two children, where he's enrolled in the University of British Columbia's MFA program. His fiction has appeared in *Spinning Whirl* and *Apex Online*. www.johnmavin.com.

Randy McCharles is an avid reader of epic fantasy and science fiction. He regularly writes short stories for public readings and has several novels in various stages of development. He also helps organize literary events and SF & F conventions in his home town, Calgary, Alberta. In 2005 he co-chaired the first Calgary Westercon, and is currently chairing the upcoming 2008 World Fantasy Convention. Randy is a long-time member of IFWA, the Imaginative Fiction Writers Association.

Steve Mills lives in Kelowna, BC, and would like you to read his novel, "Burning Stones", published by a small US press with terrible distribution and no publicity. Look for it online at your favourite bookseller. Currently he is getting over the death of one of his four cats and a non-fatal occlusion of the mid left anterior descending artery (his, not the cat's). Messages of sympathy (for him or the cat) can be sent via his website at www.stevenmills.com.

David Nickle is the author of numerous short stories and co-author of one novel, "The Claus Effect," with Karl Schroeder. His stories have appeared in several of the *Tesseracts* anthologies, and also in places like *Cemetery Dance*, *The Year's Best Fantasy and Horror*, the *Northern Frights* anthologies and the *Queer Fear* anthologies. He's a past winner of the Bram Stoker Award (for the 1997 short story "Rat Food," with Edo Van Belkom).

Holly Phillips was born on Christmas Day, 1969. She lived most of her early life in the West Kootenay region of southern British Columbia, Canada, and after a couple of stints at university, interrupted by jaunts to Ontario, England, and West Africa, she returned to the West Kootenay and enrolled in the creative writing program at the Kootenay School of the Arts. Holly currently resides in a crooked old house on a hillside above Trail, BC.

Kate Riedel was born and raised in Minnesota, but is now a card-carrying Canadian and lives in Etobicoke, Ontario. Publication credits include *Not One of Us* (including the recent anthology, "Bestof Not One of Us"), *On Spec*, *Realms of Fantasy*, and *Weird Tales* (story later included in Hartwell's anthology *Year's Best Fantasy 2*).

Hugh Spencer was born in Saskatoon, lives in Toronto and has worked as a cultural consultant in the United Kingdom, Hong Kong and Mainland China, Korea, Australia, Germany, the United States and Singapore. Hugh has published stories in magazines such as *On Spec*, *Interzone* and *Descant* and has twice been nominated for the Aurora award — the first time for his story "Why I Hunt Flying Saucers" the second for his work as co-curator for the National Library of Canada's exhibition on Canadian fantasy and science fiction. Hugh has also adapted many of his stories for the Satellite Network of National Public Radio as well as the original plays "21st Century Scientific Romance" and "Amazing Struggles, Astonishing Failures and Disappointing Success."

Jerome Stueart is a new landed immigrant, living in the Yukon Territory. His fiction has been published in *Strange Horizons*, *Redivider*, *On Spec*, and *Tesseracts Nine*. He earned honourable mentions for his story in Tesseracts Nine for both the Fountain Award and in the Year's Best Science Fiction (2006). This summer he was a student at Clarion.

Élisabeth Vonarburg was born in 1947 (France), and to science fiction in 1964. She teaches French literature and creative writing on and off at various Universities in Québec (since immigration, in 1973). A "Fulltime writer" since 1990, (despite Ph.D. in Creative Writing, 1987), i.e. translator, SF convention organiser, literary editor (Solaris magazine), and essayist.

This year, Elisabeth was awarded the Prix d'excellence pour la création en région, (5000 $), given by the Conseil des Arts et Lettres du Québec ; this rewards creation of any kind (all the arts, literature included) for quality, involvement in all things cultural and being well-known outside Canada. She was also awarded the French Prix Cyrano. Reine de Mémoire 3 & 4 received the Boréal Award for best novel(s).

Our titles are available at major book stores
and local independent resellers who support
Science Fiction and Fantasy readers like you.

EDGE Science Fiction
and Fantasy Publishing

Tesseract Books

Dragon Moon Press

www.edgewebsite.com
www.dragonmoonpress.com

Our titles are available at major book stores and local independent resellers who support Science Fiction and Fantasy readers like you.

Alien Deception by Tony Ruggiero -(tp) - ISBN-13: 978-1-896944-34-0
Alien Revelation by Tony Ruggiero (tp) - ISBN-13: 978-1-896944-34-8
Alphanauts by J. Brian Clarke (tp) - ISBN-13: 978-1-894063-14-2
Apparition Trail, The by Lisa Smedman (tp) - ISBN-13: 978-1-894063-22-7
As Fate Decrees by Denysé Bridger (tp) - ISBN-13: 978-1-894063-41-8

Billibub Baddings and The Case of the Singing Sword by Tee Morris (tp)
  - ISBN-13: 978-1-896944-18-0
Black Chalice, The by Marie Jakober (hb) - ISBN-13: 978-1-894063-00-5
Blue Apes by Phyllis Gotlieb (pb) - ISBN-13: 978-1-895836-13-4
Blue Apes by Phyllis Gotlieb (hb) - ISBN-13: 978-1-895836-14-1

Chalice of Life, The by Anne Webb (tp) - ISBN-13: 978-1-896944-33-3
Chasing The Bard by Philippa Ballantine (tp) - ISBN-13: 978-1-896944-08-1
Children of Atwar, The by Heather Spears (pb) - ISBN-13: 978-0-88878-335-6
Claus Effect by David Nickle & Karl Schroeder, The (pb) - ISBN-13: 978-1-895836-34-9
Claus Effect by David Nickle & Karl Schroeder, The (hb) - ISBN-13: 978-1-895836-35-6
Complete Guide to Writing Fantasy, The - Volume 1: Alchemy with Words
  - edited by Darin Park and Tom Dullemond (tp)
  - ISBN-13: 978-1-896944-09-8
Complete Guide to Writing Fantasy, The - Volume 2: Opus Magus
  - edited by Tee Morris and Valerie Griswold-Ford (tp)
  - ISBN-13: 978-1-896944-15-9
Complete Guide to Writing Fantasy, The - Volume 3: The Author's Grimoire
  - edited by Valerie Griswold-Ford & Lai Zhao (tp)
  - ISBN-13: 978-1-896944-38-8
Complete Guide to Writing Science Fiction, The - Volume 1: First Contact
  - edited by Dave A. Law & Darin Park (tp)
  - ISBN-13: 978-1-896944-39-5
Courtesan Prince, The by Lynda Williams (tp) - ISBN-13: 978-1-894063-28-9

Dark Earth Dreams by Candas Dorsey & Roger Deegan (comes with a CD)
  - ISBN-13: 978-1-895836-05-9
Darkling Band, The by Jason Henderson (tp) - ISBN-13: 978-1-896944-36-4
Darkness of the God by Amber Hayward (tp) - ISBN-13: 978-1-894063-44-9
Darwin's Paradox by Nina Munteanu (tp) - ISBN-13: 978-1-896944-68-5
Daughter of Dragons by Kathleen Nelson - (tp) - ISBN-13: 978-1-896944-00-5
Distant Signals by Andrew Weiner (tp) - ISBN-13: 978-0-88878-284-7
Dominion by J. Y. T. Kennedy (tp) - ISBN-13: 978-1-896944-28-9
Dragon Reborn, The by Kathleen H. Nelson - (tp) - ISBN-13: 978-1-896944-05-0
Dragon's Fire, Wizard's Flame by Michael R. Mennenga (tp)
  - ISBN-13: 978-1-896944-13-5
Dreams of an Unseen Planet by Teresa Plowright (tp) - ISBN-13: 978-0-88878-282-3
Dreams of the Sea by Élisabeth Vonarburg (tp) - ISBN-13: 978-1-895836-96-7
Dreams of the Sea by Élisabeth Vonarburg (hb) - ISBN-13: 978-1-895836-98-1

Eclipse by K. A. Bedford (tp) - ISBN-13: 978-1-894063-30-2
Even The Stones by Marie Jakober (tp) - ISBN-13: 978-1-894063-18-0

Fires of the Kindred by Robin Skelton (tp) - ISBN-13: 978-0-88878-271-7
Forbidden Cargo by Rebecca Rowe (tp) - ISBN-13: 978-1-894063-16-6

Game of Perfection, A by Élisabeth Vonarburg (tp)
   - ISBN-13: 978-1-894063-32-6
Green Music by Ursula Pflug (tp) - ISBN-13: 978-1-895836-75-2
Green Music by Ursula Pflug (hb) - ISBN-13: 978-1-895836-77-6
Gryphon Highlord, The by Connie Ward (tp) - ISBN-13: 978-1-896944-38-8

Healer, The by Amber Hayward (tp) - ISBN-13: 978-1-895836-89-9
Healer, The by Amber Hayward (hb) - ISBN-13: 978-1-895836-91-2
Human Thing, The by Kathleen H. Nelson - (hb) - ISBN-13: 978-1-896944-03-6
Hydrogen Steel by K. A. Bedford (tp) - ISBN-13: 978-1-894063-20-3

i-ROBOT Poetry by Jason Christie (tp) - ISBN-13: 978-1-894063-24-1

Jackal Bird by Michael Barley (pb) - ISBN-13: 978-1-895836-07-3
Jackal Bird by Michael Barley (hb) - ISBN-13: 978-1-895836-11-0

Keaen by Till Noever (tp) - ISBN-13: 978-1-894063-08-1
Keeper's Child by Leslie Davis (tp) - ISBN-13: 978-1-894063-01-2

Land/Space edited by Candas Jane Dorsey and Judy McCrosky (tp)
   - ISBN-13: 978-1-895836-90-5
Land/Space edited by Candas Jane Dorsey and Judy McCrosky (hb)
   - ISBN-13: 978-1-895836-92-9
Legacy of Morevi by Tee Morris (tp) - ISBN-13: 978-1-896944-29-6
Legends of the Serai by J.C. Hall - (tp) - ISBN-13: 978-1-896944-04-3
Longevity Thesis by Jennifer Tahn (tp) - ISBN-13: 978-1-896944-37-1
Lyskarion: The Song of the Wind by J.A. Cullum (tp)
   - ISBN-13: 978-1-894063-02-9

Machine Sex and other stories by Candas Jane Dorsey (tp)
   - ISBN-13: 978-0-88878-278-6
Maërlande Chronicles, The by Élisabeth Vonarburg (pb)
   - ISBN-13: 978-0-88878-294-6
Magister's Mask, The by Deby Fredericks (tp) - ISBN-13: 978-1-896944-16-6
Moonfall by Heather Spears (pb) - ISBN-13: 978-0-88878-306-6
Morevi: The Chronicles of Rafe and Askana by Lisa Lee & Tee Morris
   - (tp) - ISBN-13: 978-1-896944-07-4

Not Your Father's Horseman by Valorie Griswold-Ford (tp)
   - ISBN-13: 978-1-896944-27-2

On Spec: The First Five Years edited by On Spec (pb)
   - ISBN-13: 978-1-895836-08-0
On Spec: The First Five Years edited by On Spec (hb)
   - ISBN-13: 978-1-895836-12-7

Operation Immortal Servitude by Tony Ruggerio (tp)
   - ISBN-13: 978-1-896944-56-2
Orbital Burn by K. A. Bedford (tp) - ISBN-13: 978-1-894063-10-4
Orbital Burn by K. A. Bedford (hb) - ISBN-13: 978-1-894063-12-8

Pallahaxi Tide by Michael Coney (pb) - ISBN-13: 978-0-88878-293-9
Passion Play by Sean Stewart (pb) - ISBN-13: 978-0-88878-314-1
Plague Saint by Rita Donovan, The (tp) - ISBN-13: 978-1-895836-28-8
Plague Saint by Rita Donovan, The (hb) - ISBN-13: 978-1-895836-29-5

Reluctant Voyagers by Élisabeth Vonarburg (pb) - ISBN-13: 978-1-895836-09-7
Reluctant Voyagers by Élisabeth Vonarburg (hb) - ISBN-13: 978-1-895836-15-8
Resisting Adonis by Timothy J. Anderson (tp) - ISBN-13: 978-1-895836-84-4
Resisting Adonis by Timothy J. Anderson (hb) - ISBN-13: 978-1-895836-83-7
Righteous Anger by Lynda Williams (tp) - ISBN-13: 897-1-894063-38-8

Shadebinder's Oath by Jeanette Cottrell - (tp) - ISBN-13: 978-1-896944-31-9
Silent City, The by Élisabeth Vonarburg (tp) - ISBN-13: 978-1-894063-07-4
Slow Engines of Time, The by Élisabeth Vonarburg (tp) - ISBN-13: 978-1-895836-30-1
Slow Engines of Time, The by Élisabeth Vonarburg (hb) - ISBN-13: 978-1-895836-31-8
Small Magics by Erik Buchanan (tp) - ISBN-13: 978-1-896944-38-8
Sojourn by Jana Oliver - (pb) - ISBN-13: 978-1-896944-30-2
Stealing Magic by Tanya Huff (tp) - ISBN-13: 978-1-894063-34-0
Strange Attractors by Tom Henighan (pb) - ISBN-13: 978-0-88878-312-7

Taming, The by Heather Spears (pb) - ISBN-13: 978-1-895836-23-3
Taming, The by Heather Spears (hb) - ISBN-13: 978-1-895836-24-0
Teacher's Guide to Dragon's Fire, Wizard's Flame by Unwin & Mennenga - (pb)
   - ISBN-13: 978-1-896944-19-7
Ten Monkeys, Ten Minutes by Peter Watts (tp) - ISBN-13: 978-1-895836-74-5
Ten Monkeys, Ten Minutes by Peter Watts (hb) - ISBN-13: 978-1-895836-76-9
Tesseracts 1 edited by Judith Merril (pb) - ISBN-13: 978-0-88878-279-3
Tesseracts 2 edited by Phyllis Gotlieb & Douglas Barbour (pb)
   - ISBN-13: 978-0-88878-270-0
Tesseracts 3 edited by Candas Jane Dorsey & Gerry Truscott (pb)
   - ISBN-13: 978-0-88878-290-8
Tesseracts 4 edited by Lorna Toolis & Michael Skeet (pb)
   - ISBN-13: 978-0-88878-322-6
Tesseracts 5 edited by Robert Runté & Yves Maynard (pb)
   - ISBN-13: 978-1-895836-25-7
Tesseracts 5 edited by Robert Runté & Yves Maynard (hb)
   - ISBN-13: 978-1-895836-26-4
Tesseracts 6 edited by Robert J. Sawyer & Carolyn Clink (pb)
   - ISBN-13: 978-1-895836-32-5
Tesseracts 6 edited by Robert J. Sawyer & Carolyn Clink (hb)
   - ISBN-13: 978-1-895836-33-2
Tesseracts 7 edited by Paula Johanson & Jean-Louis Trudel (tp)
   - ISBN-13: 978-1-895836-58-5
Tesseracts 7 edited by Paula Johanson & Jean-Louis Trudel (hb)
   - ISBN-13: 978-1-895836-59-2
Tesseracts 8 edited by John Clute & Candas Jane Dorsey (tp)
   - ISBN-13: 978-1-895836-61-5

Tesseracts 8 edited by John Clute & Candas Jane Dorsey (hb)
   - ISBN-13: 978-1-895836-62-2
Tesseracts Nine edited by Nalo Hopkinson and Geoff Ryman (tp)
   - ISBN-13: 978-1-894063-26-5
Tesseracts Ten edited by Robert Charles Wilson and Edo van Belkom (tp)
   - ISBN-13: 978-1-894063-36-4
Tesseracts Eleven edited by Cory Doctorow and Holly Phillips (tp)
   - ISBN-13: 978-1-894063-03-6
Tesseracts Q edited by Élisabeth Vonarburg & Jane Brierley (pb)
   - ISBN-13: 978-1-895836-21-9
Tesseracts Q edited by Élisabeth Vonarburg & Jane Brierley (hb)
   - ISBN-13: 978-1-895836-22-6
Throne Price by Lynda Williams and Alison Sinclair (tp)
   - ISBN-13: 978-1-894063-06-7
Too Many Princes by Deby Fredricks (tp) - ISBN-13: 978-1-896944-36-4
Twilight of the Fifth Sun by David Sakmyster - (tp)
   - ISBN-13: 978-1-896944-01-02

Virtual Evil by Jana Oliver (tp) - ISBN-13: 978-1-896944-76-0